Whimsical Dreams, Book One:

Whimsical Haven

Tiffany E. Taylor

Whimsical Haven

Copyright © 2021 Tiffany E. Taylor

Published by Painted Hearts Publishing

About the Book You Have Purchased

All rights reserved. Without reserving the rights under copyright, reserved above, no part of this publication may be reproduced, stored in or introduced into a retrieval system, or transmitted in any form, or any other means (electronic, mechanical, photocopying, recording or otherwise) without the prior written permission of the copyright owner and the above publisher of this book. Distribution of this e-book, in whole or in part, is forbidden. Such action is illegal and in violation of the U.S. Copyright Law.

Unauthorized reproduction of distribution of this copyrighted work is illegal. Criminal copyright infringement, including infringement without monetary gain, is investigated by the FBI and is punishable by up to 5 years in federal prison and a fine of $250,000.

Whimsical Haven

Copyright © 2021 Tiffany E. Taylor

ISBN: 9798479924866

Publication Date: September 2021

Author: Tiffany E. Taylor

Editor: Kira Plotts

All cover art and logo copyright © 2021 by Painted Hearts Publishing

ALL RIGHTS RESERVED: This literary work may not be reproduced or transmitted in any form or by any means, including electronic or photographic reproduction, in whole or in part, without express written permission.

All characters and events in this book are fictitious. Any resemblance to actual persons living or dead is strictly coincidental.

Publisher's Content Guidance

This work of fiction contains a scene of disciplinary spanking and other instances of light BDSM that some readers may find triggering.

Acknowledgements:

To my amazing beta readers, Kim Byrem and Juliet Pishinsky, who were willing to take the first plunge into the intrigue and mystery of Whimsy, Florida with me. We have a lot more swimming to do, my friends, so brace yourselves.

Author's Note:

The fictional town of Whimsy, Florida is modeled on real-life Gulfport, Florida, located on the west-central coast of the state. Gulfport is a gorgeous little queer-friendly town of 13,000, where my spouse and I have made our home for the past 20+ years. (Our beautiful daughter, Katie, was born in neighboring St. Petersburg in 2004.)

Gulfport is a tiny blue dot in a very red state, and our eclectic Key West vibe—coupled with an approximate 30% LGBTQ+ population—makes it a truly breathtaking place. Visitors come from all over the world to soak up that Whimsy—umm, *Gulfport*—magick.

If you ever make it for a visit, it's entirely possible you just might glimpse an APS badass or two yourself as you stroll along our beautiful beach or through our funky little downtown. Stranger things have happened.

And...if you see a lady with curly hair and green eyes sitting in a wheelchair on the waterfront, diligently writing, come and say hi. I don't bite and I love to meet new people, so don't be shy. Any lover of lesfic is automatically a friend of mine.

For my beloved spouse, Donna—my best friend, my hero, my ride-or-die. You are everything a butch role model should be.

Chapter 1

Woodbridge, Virginia – November 17

"Rowan."

"*No*, Kel. No way. I. Am. Not. Fricking. *Going*."

"But, Ro…"

"*No!*"

Rowan Holland glared at her younger sister, Kelly, who shoved her hand through her dark red curls and sighed.

The Holland sisters were spending a quiet Sunday in their home in Woodbridge, Virginia.

Well. Maybe not so quiet.

Rowan and Kelly had lived in Woodbridge their entire lives. Their late father, Sgt. William Holland, had been a scout sniper, then a sniper instructor at Marine Corps Base (MCB) Quantico, which was only about ten miles from their home. Their late mother, Amanda, had worked for the military as a civilian cyber crime investigative analyst in a tiny, hidden satellite office.

The two girls were unfortunately on their own now since both of their parents were gone—Amanda, from a tragically unexpected burst aortic aneurysm five years ago, and Bill from a heart attack two years later.

"The Holland girls," as they were known, had struggled over the past three years with the loss of their beloved parents, trying to keep the mundane, colorless days from bleeding listlessly into one another.

To top it all off, Rowan had also picked up a stalker six months prior by the name of Dino Coravani, an ex-cop and private investigator who had developed a major obsession with her when he had interviewed her at the finance company where she worked.

Kelly, who had a vague-sounding job as an "information analyst" with the CIA, didn't like what she was finding out about Coravani. He was a pushy, nasty male who had only stepped up his game to pursue Rowan when she had politely tried to tell him she wasn't interested because she was gay.

"Oh. One of *those*," Kelly, who was also gay, had sneered when Rowan had told her about Coravani's redoubled efforts. "Asshole."

Because Coravani still had friends in the local police department, they hadn't been any help in protecting Rowan when she had filed a harassment police report at Kelly's urging.

"I bet if Dad was still alive, Coravani wouldn't be pulling his shit with you," Kelly had gritted out, her eyes narrowed. "Dad would have fucking kicked his sorry ass into the Potomac by now."

Coravani was getting bolder and Kelly wanted her big sister out of harm's way. She tried again to convince Rowan that she thought the best thing for her to do would be to leave the area for a while.

"You really don't have much of a choice, Rowan. Honey, I am not trying to be a bitch here, but you know I'm right."

Rowan met Kelly's serious green eyes with ill grace.

"That fucker is not going to let up on you, Ro. You know it and I know it. As much as you hate the thought, you need to leave for a little while. It's for your own safety, big sis."

The petite, hazel-eyed blonde growled in irritation and tapped her foot.

Kelly sighed and tried again.

"If there was any other way right now, we wouldn't be talking about this and you know it." Kelly was attempting to be reasonable.

"No, I don't know it, Kel. Dino Coravani is a boil on the butt of a sloth, but there is no evidence that says he is dangerous. He's just a pain in my rear." Rowan was stubborn.

"Sez you," Kelly muttered.

"Okay, smart butt." Rowan glowered. "Point-Counterpoint. And, *go*."

Kelly huffed in irritation, then growled in return.

"Fine."

When the girls were younger, Amanda Holland had introduced her daughters to a game she called, "Point-Counterpoint."

Whenever they had a disagreement about something, she would make them present their arguments in short, one-sentence sound bites, one taking the "Point" side and the other taking the "Counterpoint" side, arguing back and forth until either one of them ran out of arguments or Amanda had determined who had argued a stronger case.

Their mom wasn't around anymore to arbitrate, but the girls still occasionally played.

"Point." Since Rowan had called the game, she got to start. "Dino Coravani has not been seen in *this* neighborhood, so there is no evidence he is actually physically stalking me."

"Counterpoint." Kelly crossed her arms. "Dino Coravani still has friends in the police department, and he has stymied any attempts to have a patrol car come out to do drive-bys, when in fact, those are usually routine with a complaint such as this one."

"Point." Rowan thought for a moment. "Except for asking me to lunch a bunch of times and generally making himself a nuisance, he hasn't made an attempt to approach me."

"Counterpoint." Kelly looked Rowan right in the eyes. "Despite being dismissed for a 'lack of evidence,' there have been reports where several women involved in PI investigations run by Coravani have alluded to being sexually assaulted by him, even though these women are scared to death to come forward formally."

"*What?*" Rowan's mouth hung open, the game completely forgotten.

"Ahh, yeah, Ro." Kelly crossed the room and hugged her big sister. "I was trying not to scare you, big sis, but this dude is *bad news*. If he is doing what all reports are indicating he is doing, he is escalating, which means he is doing the same thing with you that he did with these other women and he won't stop until you get seriously hurt."

Rowan was silent for a long time, gnawing at the skin at the corner of one fingernail.

"I'm still not sure I believe it, but… What should I do, Kel?" she finally asked quietly, all her fight gone.

"I'm sorry I've kept this from you, honey, but I've been working on an escape plan for you since the minute I realized this joker was a threat." Rowan's eyes widened.

Kelly hugged her sister again. "Sit down, Ro. This is going to be a *long* conversation."

¥¥¥¥¥

Kelly drew a deep breath as she plopped down on the sofa next to Rowan.

"You know how Clem is from west-central Florida?" she asked.

Clementine Martin, Rowan's best friend, was from a small town outside of Tampa named Bartow. She and Rowan had met in their freshman year at MICA, the Maryland Institute College of Art in Baltimore, where Rowan had studied graphic design while Clementine had pursued a degree in animation.

Rowan nodded.

"I know you're aware she's wanted to move back home forever. Not necessarily back home to Bartow, but back to the greater Tampa Bay area."

Kelly's voice softened. "Clem's Gran is gone now and she said the rest of her family is nothing but a bunch of 'useless crack hoes,' as she called them, so there is nothing in her hometown for her to go back *to*. She won't leave us because she says we are each other's family now. You know that, that's no surprise to you either."

Rowan nodded again.

"But she misses the Tampa Bay area, especially the area around St. Petersburg. She misses Florida weather and living so close to the beach and the more relaxed way of living down there."

Kelly took another deep breath.

"I started doing some research, Ro. I found a little town called 'Whimsy,' right on the Gulf coast. It's maybe only thirty minutes southwest of the Tampa airport and is right next door to St. Petersburg."

"'Whimsy'? What the heck kind of name is that?" Rowan pursed her lips.

"Why not?" Kelly raised an eyebrow. "Florida also has a town named 'Christmas' and one called 'Frostproof,' plus a bunch of towns that have these funky Indian names I couldn't pronounce on a bet. Anyhow… Clem *loves* Whimsy, Ro. She said the locals call it 'little Key West' and it's about thirty-percent gay. It's a tiny little artists' town, with about 13,000 permanent residents. It only covers three square miles and is situated right on the Boca Ciega Bay, which feeds into the Gulf of Mexico."

"What do you mean, 'permanent' residents?" Rowan was mystified.

"Because this is Florida and local populations swell in what's called 'Season'—when the winter residents, or 'snowbirds,' make an appearance. Things get a lot busier and a lot more crowded then," Kelly said. "Snowbird season in Whimsy typically runs from the end of October to around mid-April. Populations diminish and everything is a lot calmer from mid-April through October. That's why there is a difference between a 'permanent resident' and a 'snowbird resident.'"

"Ah. I got it now."

"Clem says life is very diverse and open in Whimsy and the residents are completely live and let live. She told me about the time a little lesbian-owned yoga studio opened up in Whimsy. At their grand opening, the local bikers showed up. Their art community showed up. The residents from Sea Towers, their huge 55+ community complex, showed up." Kelly was charmed. "All of these diverse people showed up just to celebrate and wish them well. Clem says that's typical of Whimsy. Plus, she said, there is a very vibrant women's community there, so there will be ample opportunity for you to make friends."

"Kelly," Rowan growled out, suspicion taking root in her voice. "What do you mean, ample opportunity for *me* to make friends? What exactly are you trying to say?"

"So…" Kelly hesitated for a brief moment and then rushed on. "I bought us a house there."

"You. Did. What?" Rowan's voice was low.

"Rowan," Kelly said in exasperation, "this is the perfect solution. You will be far away from the reach of that dick, Coravani, where he can't get his filthy paws on you as easily as he can here in

Woodbridge. We now own a house in the perfect location in Florida for when we decide to retire, even though that is years off. Plus, it's the perfect vacation home as well."

Rowan forced herself to calm down and consider Kelly's argument for a minute.

"Okay. So let's say I'm open to going down there for a while until this mess with that idiot blows over. In the meantime, what about my job?"

"Ro-Ro, you fucking *hate* your job." Kelly gave her a look of disgust. "The only reason you even took that job is because Mary-Kate begged and pleaded for you to come and work for Grayson Financial, even though it isn't in your art field, because you are a fucking *legendary* data analyst and she said they desperately needed you."

Although Rowan's undergraduate degree was in graphic design, she had decided to go on to the University of Maryland and get her master's degree in data analytics, where she had graduated first in her class.

Rowan adored her art and had absolutely no intention of doing anything else permanently, but she had always had a thing for data manipulation, data mining, and predictive analytics because of her mother. Amanda Holland, no slouch herself in the predictive analytics field, had once reverently said there was no one in the entire universe who could mine, manipulate, and predict data outcomes like her oldest daughter.

Rowan could forecast and nail the likelihood of future outcomes in almost any sector with flawless accuracy, a talent coveted by virtually every industry. Because word of her ability had spread, she had more job offers than she knew what to do with, but she turned them all down. She wasn't the least bit interested; all Rowan had really ever wanted to do was get into the graphic design field full-time.

"You're right," Rowan conceded. "I hate it, and I really want to get back to my art. I guess moving to Florida would be a good reason to leave Grayson, even though I hate doing this to Mary-Kate."

"And see? That right there is your fucking problem," Kelly groused. "You can't say 'no' to *anybody* and these fuckers know that, so they always take advantage of you and your sweet nature. It's like you have this fucking savior complex or something, Ro. *Fuck* Mary-Kate and *fuck* Grayson."

"*No*," she cut Rowan off when she started to object. "You need to start doing what is best for *you*." Kelly dismissed the whole subject with a wave of her hand. "Okay, now. Next on the agenda."

Chapter 2

Rowan listened attentively, starting to get more into Kelly's plans.

"We have money, sis. A *fuckton* of money. I hate how we inherited that money because I would give both my arms and both my legs to have Mom and Dad back here with us instead."

Kelly's voice choked as Rowan's eyes instantly welled with tears.

"But since we have it, we are going to use it to make a new life for ourselves in Florida. At least for now. I found out that the daughter of Clem's old neighbor owns an ice cream shop in Whimsy. The daughter's husband has been transferred to another job out of state and the daughter now needs to sell. The realtor I contacted about the business has sent me a million pictures and I just love what I am seeing. The space is huge because it apparently used to be a restaurant. The owner has used part of the space for an ice cream shop and the other part of the space as like a little coffeehouse gathering place. That's fine, I guess, but there is already another coffeehouse in Whimsy, so it doesn't make a whole lot of sense." Kelly's eyes gleamed. "What I would like to do is keep the ice cream part of it, because apparently there is some ice cream-making wizard who works there and people come from all over for her ice cream.

But… I think we should turn the rest of the space into an art center of sorts."

Rowan's eyes rounded.

"First of all, there's a huge space that is unfinished on the second floor. We should finish it and turn it into an apartment for Clem and hire her to manage the art gallery." Rowan's eyes got huge. "In the art center, we can showcase the work of local artists. Hold art classes and workshops. Maybe eventually even have summer camps and meet-up groups."

"Holy crap, Kel. That sounds… that sounds amazing." Rowan was trying hard to assimilate everything. "Have you talked to Clementine about this yet?"

Just then, there was a sharp knock on the front door. Kelly grinned and got up to answer it. "Bet I know who that is." She smirked. "As usual, her timing is fucking impeccable."

A tornado burst through the door when Kelly unlocked it and slid to a stop in the middle of the room, revealing a cocked hip with one arm covered in silver bangles propped on it.

"I am going back to Florida, bitches!" the tornado, which proved to be Clem, exalted, both bangled arms now flying about excitedly. "No more fucking *snow*. No more fucking *potholes*. And, oh my blessed Goddess, no more fucking lame-ass people asking me what the fuck a manatee is."

Rowan squealed as Clem seized her and spun her around, laughing helplessly as Kelly looked on with a grin.

Clementine Martin was tiny in stature, only standing 5'1" tall, but her larger-than-life personality more than made up for her lack of inches. She had bleached blonde curly hair that reached just past her shoulders, brown eyes, and an eclectic way of dressing that definitely called attention to herself. For some reason, however, her outrageous style worked on Clem.

Clem stopped for a moment, uncharacteristically serious, as she hugged Rowan and then drew back to look into her eyes. "I know this is a lot to hit you with at one time, Ro-Ro," Clementine's tone was serious, "but I think Kelly is 100% accurate on what this fucktard is going to do. I want to move back to Florida in the worst way, you know I do, but you are my best friend and my priority will always be to make sure you are safe, whether it's here or there. Although frankly, I don't think it's here, at least not right now."

There was a pause.

"Another thing, too, Rowan," Clem added slowly. "I don't think it would be a bad idea for you and Kelly to sit down and talk about moving to Florida permanently."

Rowan gaped at her.

Clem ran her hand soothingly up and down Rowan's arm.

"Sell this house, baby. I know it belonged to your parents and you two grew up here, but you need to move out and go somewhere where you can make new memories. You haven't been happy here since your mom and then your dad passed."

Clementine gestured to Kelly with her other hand, then put her arm around Kel when she reached them.

"When Gran died," tears were streaming down Clem's face, "selling her house was probably the hardest thing I've ever had to do in my life. But it needed to be done and there was no way I was letting those crack-ho bitches in my family get their hands on *anything* that belonged to her, just so they could sell it for drugs. Not a problem you two have, thankfully. But my point is, when I let go of all Gran's stuff, I felt like her soul was free and I felt a lightness in my spirit that I really needed to feel." She squeezed them tighter. "You can't hold onto *stuff*, my sisters. Not when the memories are the real deal." Clem was practical. "Plus, you can always take the important things with you on your new adventure, the items that are truly sentimental."

The three of them stood quietly for a while, their arms around each other.

"So," Clem finally said, as she wiped her eyes, her equilibrium restored, "are we going to light this bitch up or what?"

"I already have a holding company set up for us to purchase the house and also the ice cream shop," Kelly informed them, ignoring Rowan's incredulous look. "Credit cards, utilities, vehicles, all that shit will be buried in it so anyone who is looking for Kelly or Rowan Holland, like good ol' Mr. Dickhead, won't be able to find us directly."

"I don't *ever* want to know why you can do this shit, Kel." Clementine rolled her eyes. "And *fuck* that guy," she added vehemently. "I hope his dick falls off."

Rowan raised her eyebrows and sighed. "I swear to the Goddess, the two of you have the worst language in the world."

"Yes, but you never swear, Ro, so Kelly and I need to fill in the imbalance that *you* cause by being such a goody two-shoes," Clem told her. "It's all about balance in the universe, my homegirls."

Rowan sighed again, this time with affectionate exasperation.

"We have a lot more to talk about," Kelly said, stretching and running a hand across her forehead. "But… I do believe we officially have the outline of a plan."

Chapter 3

Whimsy, FL – December 5

Bryn Armstrong sat at her desk at Armstrong Protection Services, better known as APS in the security community, looking down at the cell phone in her hand and contemplating the phone call she'd just received.

It had been a long time since she'd thought about Sgt. William Holland, the sniper instructor at MCB Quantico.

Good man. Fucking brilliant instructor.

Riley, Bryn's twin, had sworn her ass still bore boot marks for months after they were done with his instruction.

Now, Kelly Holland, Sgt. Holland's youngest daughter, had just called her.

Bryn had given Kelly her sincere condolences on behalf of her and Riley when Kelly told her that Sgt. Holland had passed away three years ago. The teensiest crack in that cool facade as Kelly had thanked her had told Bryn that Kelly was still deeply mourning her father a full three years later. Briskly, Kelly had come straight to the point of her phone call. She and her older sister, Rowan, were moving to Whimsy from Woodbridge, Virginia next week.

Rowan had apparently picked up a stalker about six months ago, a real nasty son of a bitch. He was suspected of several sexual assault cases in the Woodbridge area, although there was no proof and the complaints had been dismissed for "lack of evidence."

Kelly had convinced Rowan to leave Woodbridge, at least for a while, until this dick no longer had Rowan on radar.

Bryn had felt the hair on the back of her neck stand up on end.

When Bryn and Riley had left the Marine Corps and were planning how they could best settle into civilian life, they had spent time formalizing their long-held dream of what they wanted to do after college. Subsequently, the twins had started Armstrong Protection Services with their best friends upon graduation, using their military experience to offer security and protection services to women who might be more comfortable working with other females. It was a resounding success, since women in general often felt safer with other females instead of with males.

Bryn and Riley had meant no disrespect to the honorable males they knew, like their dad and their brothers. But it was true that other females were usually perceived as non-threatening when it came to relating to other females.

Now, ten years after they were formed, APS offered security consulting, investigation services, risk assessment, and bodyguard services for a primarily female clientele. The Armstrong twins and their friends had a reputation for being protective, swift, efficient, and, unbeknownst to the vast majority of their client base, positively deadly when the situation called for it.

Bryn brought her thoughts back to the current phone call with Kelly Holland.

"Ms. Holland," Bryn said cautiously, "we are absolutely glad to be of service. I could have a member of our senior management team contact you and—"

"No." Kelly cut her off with that short word. "I don't want to presume, Ms. Armstrong, but I would like you to take care of my sister personally."

"Please call me Bryn, Ms. Holland."

"Fine, thank you. And I'm Kelly."

Without pausing for acknowledgement, she went on, "I don't know if you are aware of this, Bryn, but my father often followed the careers of his former students."

Bryn heard the almost inaudible catch in her throat again.

"And more than a few times," Kelly continued, composure restored, "he made the comment that if he was ever going to trust anyone in the security and protection realm, it would be you and your twin."

Bryn was startled.

"I know you are probably extremely busy and again, I don't want to presume, but I am going to ask if you would please meet with my sister yourself when she first gets there. I would like you to look at our home and at our business and give us a general assessment. If you would like to pass the case on to anyone else in your organization after that, I completely understand. But I would really feel better if I could have your personal assessment of the situation first, Bryn. I would do this myself, but with my responsibilities at work, I am not in a position to leave Virginia right now. I can probably get down there in about six weeks, but it is impossible for me to leave at this time."

Bryn heard the virtually silent echo of frustration and uneasiness in Kelly's voice. Kelly Holland, Bryn decided, was exceptionally good at masking voice inflection and hiding any emotion in her words. 99.9% of the people talking to Kelly wouldn't hear the first thing amiss in their conversation.

Bryn, however, was a fucking *master* at hearing nuances the average person would miss and at reading between the lines.

Kelly Holland was scared. And for bigger reasons than she had shared with Bryn.

"Of course," she assured Kelly, deciding she was going to get to the bottom of this mystery. "I have a short business trip I need to take, but I'll be back next Thursday. I could meet with your sister that Friday. Will that be a problem?"

"No, no, that's fine. Actually, Rowan doesn't even fly in until that Wednesday afternoon anyway, so that will give her a full day to orient herself before meeting with you. She will be staying at the Gulf Breeze Inn in downtown Whimsy until the security on our house is complete, by the way." Kelly let a bit of amusement color her voice. "I'm aware that APS did the security at the Gulf Breeze, so that's a comfort."

WHIMSICAL HAVEN

After making an appointment for Rowan and Bryn at 11:30 on Friday morning, they hung up, Kelly once again expressing her gratitude.

Now, Bryn was staring at the cell phone in her hand and assessing the conversation she'd just had with Kelly Holland.

Bryn hit a speed dial number on her phone.

"Come to my apartment when you're done doing whatever it is you're doing, Riles," she said when her twin answered the phone. "It looks like a mystery has come to Whimsy."

¥¥¥¥¥

"And so here we are."

Bryn balanced her beer bottle on her lap, her long legs stretched out in front of her. Her twin, Riley, sat sideways on another overstuffed chair with her equally long legs thrown over the armrest. Because of their fitness commitments, neither twin typically drank much, but events today seemed to warrant a beer.

Bryn and Riley Armstrong were the oldest of five Armstrong kids. They were fraternal twins, age 35, with Bryn being the oldest twin by nine minutes—a fact she never, ever let Riley forget. Their mother, Rosario, had been born in Puerto Rico, while their father, Oliver, had been born and raised in London. They had two younger brothers, Noah, 33, and Keenan, 30. Their sister, Daniela, 27, was the baby.

WHIMSICAL HAVEN

Bryn and Riley were two of the owners of Armstrong Protection. Daniela worked in reception and took care of the purchasing. The two middle Armstrong kids were not involved with APS; Noah was a local police officer and Keenan was a neurologist. Noah, the family comedian, liked to screw with his brother and say that he, Bryn, and Riley fucked up people's heads when needed and Keenan was in charge of fixing them.

"What are you thinking?" Riley tilted up her beer bottle as she thought about the events of today that Bryn had shared with her.

"First, taking a cursory look at Kelly and Rowan's history, there's nothing much to see as far as Rowan is concerned. She graduated from MICA in Baltimore with a graphic design degree. She then went on to complete her master's in data analytics from the University of Maryland."

Riley frowned.

"I know, that sounds weird as fuck, right? Graphic design, then data analytics? Who does that? But her mother, Amanda, was a civilian cyber crimes investigator for the military, based in Quantico. So really, no mystery there if you really look at it. Rowan's best friend graduated from MICA with a degree in animation while Rowan pursued graphic design. From all accounts, and from her high school and college records, Rowan has always loved and been involved with art, but she probably also caught a data bug from her mom while she was growing up. It all fits, although I will get a better sense from her when I talk to her in person next Friday. Ms. Kelly, however... She's a generic 'information analyst' for the CIA, based in Langley. Cursory look…nothing to see here, folks. There are hundreds of employees at Langley with some kind of 'analyst' title. Even looking for her through our own systems, she checks out. Low-level employee, unremarkable security clearance, we can move on, right? Even the fact that she lives in Woodbridge, which is right outside Quantico and is a ways from Langley, isn't remarkable. The CIA has hundreds of small satellite offices everywhere and it would not be unreasonable to assume she has been assigned to one of those."

"Okay," Riley said. "So what's goosing your muse?"

"It doesn't add up." Bryn took a swallow of her beer, then gestured with the bottle. "First, she has a low-level title, but she was frustrated because the *earliest* she could get here was in maybe six weeks. You tell me what kind of a low-level 'information analyst,' especially one that works for the government, has to wait a minimum of *six weeks* to take some personal time off in peacetime when there's a potential family emergency?

"Second, I have never in my life met anyone who has control over their voice inflection and the reactions she displays the way this woman does. She is *scary* good, Riles. Again, what kind of a low-level information analyst can control her voice and her responses to that extent? Third, she mentioned she wasn't going to be able to do the security assessments on their house and their new business herself, which is why she was bringing us in. So, excuse me? What the fuck? A low-level information analyst is seriously worried about her sister's safety, but she was going to trust herself to do a proper security assessment on her? Yeah, yeah."

Bryn held up a hand, seeing Riley was about to speak. "I know she's Sgt. William Holland's daughter, which means she probably has more smarts in her little finger than 95% of the people out there have in their whole body. But...that's just it, Riles. She's Bill Holland's kid. He would have constantly drilled into her the absolute necessity of calling in the experts when you are facing a potentially threatening situation *where your own level of expertise isn't optimal.* Which means Kelly Holland was feeling 100% comfortable she could perform an adequate security threat assessment to gauge her beloved sister's safety. But she couldn't, simply because she's too far away and it will take way too long before she can get here herself. Hence, she called us in."

Riley blew out a deep breath. "Jesus Christ, Bryn. Who the hell are these women?"

"Frankly, I don't think it's Rowan, Riles. I think it's all Kelly. I think Rowan is a brilliant data analyst. She can manipulate data and hit the target on predictive analytics like no one's business, from what I've seen, but I think it's just a game to her. It's a puzzle she can keep putting together and taking apart for fun. Her art is where her real interest lies. Kelly, on the other hand? That's a whole different level of scary right there."

Bryn swallowed the last of her beer. She brooded on one more thing that was uppermost on her mind. "I said I thought there was something going on outside of what was happening with Rowan that has Kelly scared, that Rowan doesn't know about. I have no idea what the fuck it could be, but I think maybe we need to find out. I need to concentrate on Rowan, but why don't you start poking around Kelly to see if there is anything you can discover?"

Riley stretched and yawned. "Exactly my thought as well." She yawned again. "I'm beat, *mano*. I think I'm going to head over to my apartment and go to bed. Why don't we reconvene tomorrow and pick it up then?"

As Bryn walked her twin to the door, she said, "Sleep tight, Riles. We'll start chasing these women down tomorrow. Seems it's been a while since a challenge like this has come our way."

Chapter 4

Woodbridge, Virginia – December 12

Rowan and Kelly looked around at what remained of their home.

The moving company had just left with the remaining contents of their entire house, the things that hadn't been sold or given away or discarded over the past weeks. An auto transport company Kelly had hired had left several hours ago with Rowan's new car.

The house seemed so quiet and empty.

"We probably should get going," Kelly spoke gently. "It's at least a two-hour drive to Reagan National and I want to leave us plenty of time to get there so you don't miss your flight."

Silent, Rowan nodded.

"Clem is going to pick you up at Tampa International and drive you to Whimsy, Ro," Kelly continued. "She said that all the personal stuff we shipped for you made it there fine and she has it all at the inn. No worries."

"Are we doing the right thing, Kel?" Rowan said suddenly, her face ashen. "I can't... I can't wrap my head around the fact that I'm leaving my home of over *thirty years*. Maybe *forever*. I wish... I wish..." She choked, unable to continue.

"I know, honey. I know." Kelly's voice choked up, too. She wrapped her arms around Rowan's shoulders. The two sisters clung to each other for a long moment.

"But even though we grew up here in this house, this hasn't been home for us since Dad died. There is nothing left for us here but memories, Ro." Kelly wiped at the tears streaming down her face. "As much as all of this hurts right now, I have a feeling you and I will feel grateful and thankful to have a completely different place where we can make a fresh start. Nothing we do is going to bring Mom or Dad back," she hiccupped with emotion.

With effort, Kelly heaved a sigh and turned her mind to more practical matters.

"The guy with your new car should be in Whimsy by Friday morning. The Gulf Breeze Inn, where we will be staying until the security system is installed in our new house, is just two doors down from our new ice cream shop, according to Clem. When your car gets there, there is a designated spot for you at the Inn. You really shouldn't have to drive anywhere by yourself. Everything in Whimsy you should need is within walking distance, according to Clem."

Kelly tried to slow down her racing mind for a minute before moving on.

"Our new house is on Beach Key Drive, which runs parallel right next to the Boca Ciega Bay. It looks like it also runs perpendicular to the street where the shop is located, but Clem will show you how to get there. You have an appointment at 11:30 a.m.

on Friday with Bryn Armstrong. She's going to meet you at the ice cream shop. She'll look at the shop to make some assessments on what kind of security we'll need based on what I told her, and then she's going to go with you to look at our new house."

"Okay." Rowan slowly exhaled.

"Oh, and I forgot to tell you, Clem got the paint swatches we sent. She's going to help you hire someone to paint the inside of the shop—you know, the boring painting, not the artistic stuff."

"In the meantime," Rowan gulped in a determined breath of air, "I can get started making some plans tomorrow and Friday until Bryn Armstrong shows up for our appointment."

"Clem and I have already been emailing back and forth about the apartment space. We just need to find an architect and a contractor now, I think."

Rowan took a long look around the silent, empty house.

"Kelly, I don't want to drag this out anymore. If we need to leave, then I want to leave and do it now. We had such a wonderful life growing up here." Rowan did her best to slow down the tears that were falling. "But Clem was right, Kel. There's nothing here for us anymore. Not now that Mom and Dad are gone." Her voice quavered. "Depending on how we like Florida, I don't know if we're even going to *want* to come back to Woodbridge itself after all of this is over."

Straightening her shoulders in determination, Rowan took a deep breath.

WHIMSICAL HAVEN

"Whatever we end up doing, though, we have each other and we have Clem. And that will be more than enough."

The two sisters looked at each other for a long moment, then slowly walked to the front door.

"Goodbye, Mom. Goodbye, Dad," they whispered with their arms around each other as they walked out the door without a backward glance, leaving their old lives behind.

¥ ¥ ¥ ¥ ¥

Whimsy, FL – December 14

Rowan's cell phone rang as she was edging the trim on a painting she was restoring for the new ice cream shop and art center.

It had been a whirlwind two days. After a long drive to Reagan National Airport, an emotional "goodbye" with her sister, and an unscheduled fuel stop on her supposedly non-stop flight, Rowan's flight had finally gotten into Tampa late on Wednesday afternoon.

Clem had squealed when she saw her best friend and snatched Rowan's carry-on bag with energy, kissing Rowan on the cheek and all but dragging her out of the airport.

Rowan's mouth had dropped open as they hit the Howard Frankland Bridge heading south, the seven-mile span bisecting the shimmering waters of Tampa Bay, as the sunlight danced upon the waves.

WHIMSICAL HAVEN

"Oh my Goddess, it's absolutely beautiful here," Rowan breathed, watching the palm trees that swayed along the highway's edge when they had crossed the span. "And so *warm*. So different from Virginia. I can't wait to learn my way around."

By the time she and Clem had driven to Whimsy, checked into the Gulf Breeze Inn, unloaded Rowan's luggage, and grabbed something to eat, however, it was almost 9 p.m. and both Rowan and Clem were absolutely exhausted.

Clem yawned against her cheek. "Call me tomorrow when you wake up, Ro. They told me at the front desk there will be coffee, pastries, and bagels on the lanai in the morning, hon. G'night."

Lan-eye?

Rowan clearly had a whole new vocabulary to learn.

She'd spent Thursday making lists and trying to prioritize everything she wanted to get done.

She and Clem had also dropped by the ice cream shop to look around and get a feel for how they wanted to design the space. They checked out the upstairs and were satisfied their plans for Clem's apartment would work well there.

"I want to call the ice cream part of the shop, 'The Dream Creamery,' and the art center will be called the 'Whimsy Creative Arts Center,'" she told Clem, who gave her a thumbs-up in approval.

Kelly had no preference about what to do with either the ice cream shop or the arts center, so Rowan pretty much had free rein with all of her ideas.

"We need to find an architect we can hire, someone with experience in art galleries and art centers," she told Clem. "And a decent contractor. I'll make some calls, but it will have to wait until Monday, unfortunately. I have to deal with stupid security crap and that Bryn Armstrong person tomorrow."

Rowan hated dealing with anything "tech-y" and wished down to the bottom of her heart that Kelly was here to deal with it instead. Kel thrived on this baloney.

Even though Rowan was brilliant when it came to data mining and data manipulation, she had little interest in anything beyond the arts. Rowan had only learned how to shoot a gun because Bill had absolutely insisted on it. It was Kelly who was the one always walking up their dad's heels, learning this combat technique or that kind of mixed martial arts.

Unless it had to do with data when necessary, you would seldom find Rowan doing anything outside of art projects or yoga. Kelly had once teasingly snarked at Rowan that if she ever broke a fingernail trying to do any defensive maneuvers, she would faint dead away.

The phone rang and Rowan answered it with a sigh. "Hello?"

"Ms. Holland? This is Bryn Armstrong from Armstrong Protection Services. I was just checking to make sure we were still on for 11:30 today."

Now that, Rowan thought to herself, stunned, *was a voice that sounded like sex and sin.* She had a brief, unbidden fantasy of hearing that voice sliding over her in bed. *Where in the heck did that thought come from?* Rowan blinked in shocked surprise.

"Yes, of course," Rowan said faintly, shaking herself. "I'm already here so anytime that it's convenient for you to come over, Ms. Armstrong, is fine with me. I don't have any other plans today."

"Please. Call me Bryn. May I call you Rowan?"

"Of course." Rowan felt herself blush. "I'm so sorry, I never even thought to ask Kelly if I needed to have anything here for you to look at."

"Just your sweet self for today is fine, Rowan." Rowan blushed again. "I'll see you in a short while then. I'm very much looking forward to meeting you." They hung up the phone.

Rowan looked down at herself and promptly freaked out. Because she'd planned to paint all day and hadn't been worried about impressing anyone, she was wearing an old, paint-splattered T-shirt and faded jeans.

Rowan flew over to the old-looking glass that hung by the front door and looked into it. "Oh, *snap*," she whimpered.

She looked *terrible*. Her light blonde hair was pulled back into a messy ponytail with little blonde curly wisps that kept escaping, her skin was pale, and she didn't have a stitch of makeup on. In a panic, she fled into the bathroom to see if there was anything she could do to even slightly improve her appearance.

She splashed some cold water on her face and pulled her curls out of her scrunchie to try to subdue them. As she was tying her hair back up, she heard the bells over the front door ring, signaling someone's arrival.

WHIMSICAL HAVEN

Rowan stepped out of the bathroom and made her way back into the main part of the building.

She felt her heart flutter.

A handsome, extremely tall butch—probably close to 6'0"—with an impressive musculature and a badass presence, stood just inside the front door. She was wearing jeans, a dark blue T-shirt, boots, and a leather jacket. Thick, wavy black hair grew to just below her ears and she wore mirrored aviator sunglasses that rested on cheekbones you might find on a model.

Rowan knew without a doubt this was the fabled Bryn Armstrong. Rowan's breath froze and her lungs labored to take in enough air as she stared, unable to help herself.

Bryn pushed up her shades to reveal dark brown eyes with thick black lashes. They were focused on Rowan with laser-like intensity.

¥¥¥¥¥

Her voice, Bryn thought to herself, *is the sweetest, clearest, most innocent voice I've heard in years. She sounds...pure. Almost ethereal. If Kelly was the devil sitting on my shoulder, then Rowan was definitely the angel*, Bryn thought, intrigued.

For her part, Bryn was instantly and unusually captivated by Rowan. She had to be the prettiest woman Bryn had ever seen. Even the paint-splattered T-shirt and old jeans couldn't detract from Rowan's fresh, innocent, makeup-free beauty.

Rowan had light blonde, curly hair, a smattering of freckles across her nose, and beautiful hazel eyes that caught the light and seemed to throw a golden cast over everything they touched.

She was petite, standing a good seven or eight inches shorter than Bryn. She was also curvy, delicate, and had an innocent, otherworldly air that attracted the hell out of Bryn.

Bryn felt rage take hold of her unexpectedly. She was pissed at the thought that some asshole stalker was making this innocent woman's life miserable and had chased her from her home.

Something about Rowan was triggering all sorts of protective instincts in Bryn.

"Hi, Rowan." Bryn kept her voice deliberately gentle, sensing that Rowan was feeling a bit skittish. "I'm Bryn Armstrong. Thank you for seeing me this morning."

What the fuck? Thank you for seeing me?

Clients thanked APS for taking their case, *not* the other way around.

If Riley was here, she'd think Bryn had lost her fucking mind.

"No, thank *you*, Bryn," Rowan said sincerely in her lovely, ethereal voice. "You are doing us such a huge favor and I can't thank you enough for taking time out of what I'm sure is your enormously busy schedule for this."

She continued on in her sweet way. "I'm going to apologize in advance for what I'm sure will be my utter ineptitude in trying to understand everything. Unfortunately, Kelly is still up in Virginia right now, so you're stuck with me."

Rowan twisted her fingers nervously. "I promise I will do my very best not to be a nuisance and cause you extra work."

That was it. Bryn was fucking *done*.

This sweet, beautiful, innocent woman was being harassed, stalked, and had been chased out of her home—because some limp-dicked son of a bitch thought he had the right to take what didn't belong to him—and she was *apologizing* to Bryn and promising not to be a nuisance?

Oh, no. Oh, *fuck* no.

It was at that moment that Bryn Armstrong decided that Rowan Holland was *hers*.

Rowan may not know it yet, but she would never be alone, scared, or unprotected again.

And may the Goddess help any motherfucker who tried to get between Bryn and what was hers.

Chapter 5

"Rowan." Bryn stood right in front of Rowan and softly cupped her cheek. "You have nothing to apologize for, *dulzura. Nothing.* I don't need you to be a security systems expert or understand how this all works because that's *my* job."

Bryn gently caressed Rowan's cheek. "I'm going to look around and then ask you some general questions about your business. I know this is a new venture for you, so you might not have all the answers yet and that's perfectly okay. We will answer what we can today. After we're done here, we can go to your house so I can assess the situation there. Any questions we have past that, we'll deal with then."

Bryn wondered if it was too soon to insist that Rowan spend the night at her apartment. She was no longer comfortable letting Rowan out of her sight. Then again, there would be nothing in this world that would stop her from stripping Rowan bare and taking her the minute she so much as put one foot inside Bryn's front door.

Rowan looked at Bryn with huge eyes, feeling her heart beating triple time from Bryn's close proximity. "Okay," she whispered, her beautiful hazel eyes looking at Bryn with an innocent trust that blew Bryn away.

"Tonight," Bryn heard herself say, "we're going to dinner."

"D-d-dinner?" Rowan stammered.

"Dinner," Bryn repeated firmly. "When we're finished at your house, I'll drop you back at the Gulf Breeze Inn and I'll pick you back up again at 6:00 p.m. for dinner."

"I can walk back to the Gulf Breeze from the house, Bryn. It's not far and I don't want to inconvenience you. Besides …"

"*Dulzura*." Bryn's voice was implacable. "I said I will take you back to the Gulf Breeze when we're done."

There was a long, long minute of silence.

"Bossy," Bryn finally heard Rowan mutter under her breath.

The corner of Bryn's mouth quirked. It looked like her lovely Rowan might have a bit of bite to her under all that sweet after all.

Excellent.

¥¥¥¥¥

"With this kind of a security system, you'll be hooked to our central monitoring center. Our services will include alarm monitoring, service dispatching, technical assessment, and other support services. The system handles intrusion detection, and fire and access control."

Bryn leaned against a wall in the great room. All of Rowan and Kelly's household boxes had been delivered by the moving company and were now in storage, but the boxes they'd shipped directly themselves had been delivered to the Gulf Breeze Inn. Clem had brought them to the house earlier that day.

"You will be on camera 24/7. We have a surveillance room where we monitor all of our clients 24/7. In other words, my crews will have eyes on you at all times, both here and at your home."

"Why is all this necessary, Bryn? All this…this…this *overkill*." Rowan looked at Bryn in confusion for a minute, but then rolled her eyes. "Don't tell me. Kelly."

"Your sister said she doesn't want us to play and so we aren't. She also said you're single and you don't have anyone to keep an eye on you, so we're it."

"But—"

"But nothing, Rowan. This is for protection your sister feels you need and that *I* now feel you need. These cameras will always be on unless I'm with you or another APS associate is with you. I also have Trillian trying to run down some information on Coravani."

"Trillian?"

"She's our lead data and technical analyst at APS."

Rowan nodded, then couldn't help her curiosity. "That's an…uh…interesting name."

"Her mom is a total *Hitchhiker's Guide to the Galaxy* freak." Bryn smirked. "Her brother's name is Zaphod."

A smile tugged at Rowan's lips.

Bryn moved very close into Rowan's personal space until Rowan could feel the heat of Bryn's body just inches away from her.

Bryn reached around and cupped the nape of Rowan's neck with one strong hand to hold her in place, then used the thumb of the other to wipe a dust smudge off Rowan's cheek.

Rowan was paralyzed as desire swept through her unexpectedly.

"Let's go, *dulzura*," Bryn murmured in a low voice. "We can talk more at dinner tonight."

¥¥¥¥¥

"So, that's how I met Dino Coravani." Rowan took a sip of wine, then turned her attention to her shrimp salad. "He didn't make an impression on me one way or another, quite frankly. I certainly didn't think I'd made an impression on him either, outside of being someone he had to interview."

Bryn and Rowan were having a quiet dinner at the Pier House Grille in downtown Whimsy.

Bryn cut into a medium-rare ribeye. "How did you realize he had you on radar?"

"That's just it. I *didn't*. I'm still not feeling like he's a threat to me personally, really. He's just some dude who's asked me out and won't take 'no' for an answer... Which, okay, has made me anxious. But there are a million guys like him out there."

She hesitated.

"Kelly, however..." She hesitated again, then sighed. "My sister is a little on the overprotective side, Bryn. You'd think she was the oldest, not me. She sees ghouls around every corner, I swear." Rowan rolled her eyes. "Anyhow, she went digging into this guy's background and found some, uh, I guess you would call it disturbing stuff."

"Disturbing stuff?" Bryn's voice was neutral.

"Kelly said that some women have said 'off the record' that they were sexually assaulted by Coravani while he was conducting PI investigations. These women are too afraid to come forward, not that it would do any good anyway. He's a former police officer and they seem to protect their own, so…" Rowan shrugged, seeming to be upset but resigned.

"Hold on one second." Bryn kept her voice gentle, even though she was vibrating with rage.

She rapidly texted Riley and Teagan, another APS associate. "Pull everything you can find on a Dino Corovani or Coravani, PI and former cop in the Woodbridge, Virginia area. Stat."

She put her phone away. "Then why didn't you feel he was a threat to you, Rowan, if there were reports of potential sexual assault?"

"Well, *because*," Rowan burst out. "I haven't ever seen him around our house. He showed up at my job to ask me out to lunch a bunch of times, but he didn't seem mad or crazy when I told him 'no.' I explained to him that I was gay, but I think he's just one of those guys who doesn't like to believe there are women out there who aren't interested in men. I didn't think any of what he was doing would qualify as being stalker-ish, to be honest. I told Kelly he'd get tired of me turning him down and he would eventually go away, but…Kelly." An exasperated look crossed Rowan's face. "Kelly said he was 'escalating,' even though I don't know what that means, exactly. Escalating what? The only reason I even know this much is because I challenged Kelly to a game of Point-Counterpoint."

Bryn raised an eyebrow. "Point-Counterpoint?"

Rowan flushed. "It's a game my mom created when Kelly and I were young." She explained the rules to Bryn. "We'd only gotten a little ways into it before Kelly broke down and told me why she was worried about him."

Well, that was intriguing.

Because Kelly Holland was *not* the type of woman who broke down.

Not ever.

That meant she'd *wanted* her sister to know this information about Coravani, and had found a way to make Rowan think playing their old childhood game was her idea.

Devious. Very devious.

Kelly Holland was either going to end up being one of Bryn's best friends or her worst nightmare.

Chapter 6

Just then, Bryn's phone rang. She excused herself for one moment and left to walk outside so she could pick up the call. It was Riley.

"Listen, Bryn, I know you're at dinner with Rowan, but I needed to call you and let you know not to let her out of your fucking sight for one goddamn minute. The son of a bitch, Coravani, is a nasty piece of work. Not only that, he knows that Rowan has come down to the Whimsy area, so now he's headed down here himself."

"The *fuck?*" Bryn was incredulous.

"When Rowan turned in her notice at Grayson Financial, where she was working up there, she told her friend at work, Mary-Kate, where she was going," Riley said. "Looks like that piece of shit motherfucker beat the fuck out of Mary-Kate to get her to tell him where Rowan was heading. He also told her if she opened her mouth to anyone, he would come back and kill her."

Riley blew out an angry breath over the phone.

"Apparently, Kelly is currently unaware, which is a good thing. If she finds out, she'll land down here in a hot minute and the Holland girls will be in the wind so fast it will make your head spin."

"Who told you about Mary-Kate?" Bryn was livid.

"Kennedy." Kennedy was one of the APS management team leads, along with Teagan and Trillian. "Ironically, she's in Washington, DC right now for her little brother's graduation from Georgetown University."

Bryn could tell Riley was trying to keep her cool.

"Teagan had called her and filled her in on the situation. Apparently, it's only about a forty minute drive from Washington to Quantico and Woodbridge, so Kenn decided to see what she could find out about him. It took her all of two phone calls and one quick road trip for her to find out what that prick did to Mary-Kate. Kenn is fucking *seething*. I just got off the phone with her."

Fuck. And Bryn thought she had been feeling rage *before*?

"I'm taking Rowan to my house, Riley," said Bryn in a frigid tone. "I don't want to scare her, but I need to explain to her what's going on because she deserves to know. I'll get her to call her friend, Clem, tonight and Teagan can go over to help Clem pack up Rowan's shit. Clem is staying at the Gulf Breeze, too."

"Something else you should know, Riles." Bryn's voice went ice-cold. "Rowan doesn't know it yet, but I've claimed her. She's *mine*, and if that cocksucking bastard thinks he's going to touch one single hair on her head, I will cut his dick off and shove it up his ass so far, he'll be giving himself head."

Riley was silent for a moment.

"You chill, *mano*?" she asked her twin slowly. "I don't need to lock your ass down, do I? What's your temperature?"

"I've never been colder." Bryn's voice was even and ruthless. "I'm going to go finish dinner with my woman, then I'm bringing Rowan home to my place. We'll meet you back at my apartment." Bryn ran her hand through her hair. "As much as I don't want to, I'm going to have to give her a full explanation of everything that's going on. She's not stupid, Riley. Far, *far* from it, but she's naive as hell and she's exactly the kind of woman a piece of shit like Coravani likes to exploit. Women like Rowan don't like to believe scum like him exists."

"You know the entire crew will keep her safe, Bryn," Riley said. Bryn recognized the tone as one her twin used when trying to reassure worried clients. "Look, I was heading back from Tampa when the shit hit the fan and I'm still twenty minutes out. I'm going to my apartment first to take a shower, then I'll be over."

"Okay. Have Teagan get a hold of Clementine. Tell Teag to let Clem know what's up, and she can arrange to meet Clem at the Gulf Breeze to help pack Rowan's shit and bring it to my apartment. I'll see you in a while."

Rowan looked up at Bryn with a worried expression as Bryn rejoined her.

"Is everything okay?" she asked anxiously, looking at Bryn with uncertain eyes.

Bryn stretched her arm across the table and captured Rowan's small hand in her larger one.

"We're going to finish dinner, *dulzura*, then I am taking you somewhere we can talk privately, okay?"

Rowan nodded, still looking worried.

Bryn squeezed her hand. "The only thing you need to focus on right this second, baby, is understanding that you are as safe as you can possibly be whenever you're with me. And you always will be."

¥ ¥ ¥ ¥ ¥

Bryn's SUV passed through the silent door that swung open at their approach.

"Where are we?" Rowan asked. The door appeared to be set into the side of a dark, gigantic warehouse.

"My apartment," Bryn replied. "I live on top of the headquarters of APS." She pulled the SUV into one of three dimly illuminated parking spaces. "Riley lives here too, but her apartment is on the other side of the complex."

Rowan was confused. "But it seemed as though we were just downtown."

"That's because we were." Bryn opened Rowan's door for her and helped her out. "APS is actually just one block east of the main avenue on Whimsy, which is Cedar Key Boulevard. That's where your shop is. Cedar Key runs north-south and dead-ends into Beach Bay Drive, where your house is, which runs east-west along the bay. APS is on Biscayne Street South, which runs north-south one block east of Cedar Key."

Feeling like her head was about to explode, Rowan saw Bryn smile.

"I'll have to take you on a tour of Whimsy so you can connect the dots. It will be easier for you that way." She led Rowan to an elevator without a call button and inserted a key into it. "This is a private entrance and leads directly to my apartment. Riley has her own elevator and entrance as well."

The elevator door opened to a small vestibule with two doors. Bryn entered a code into the keypad mounted next to the huge steel door opposite the elevator and ushered Rowan in when the numbers on the keypad flashed green.

Rowan was awestruck by Bryn's apartment. The entire space was composed of steel, concrete, and black wrought iron with oversized furniture covered in cream, dark brown, and black fabrics. At the end of the large living room was a short flight of stairs banded with black wrought iron railings that led to a small open loft. A low, king-size platform bed draped in a thick black comforter was barely visible at the top. A kitchen with granite countertops and stainless steel appliances, separated by a granite-topped bar and high black leather bar stools, opened up on the right of the living room. A short hallway to the left of the space most likely led to the bathroom.

It was a powerful space that clearly suited its powerful owner.

Rowan felt two strong hands caress her shoulders before turning her around. She was mesmerized by the dark brown eyes that compelled her gaze, helpless to resist them.

Rowan's back hit the wall before she realized Bryn had been slowly backing her up and maneuvering her until she was caged against the wall by Bryn's powerful body.

Then Bryn's mouth descended and Rowan was lost.

Bryn kissed like she did everything else: explosive, dominant, controlling. Rowan held onto Bryn's muscular arms, shaking as she fell under Bryn's erotic spell.

Bryn's mouth trailed along Rowan's throat, holding her close and running her hands up and down Rowan's back. The feel of Bryn's body against her own was incredible.

"You're mine, Rowan Holland," Bryn said softly. "I'm claiming you as my own. I staked my claim on you from virtually the moment we met. You just didn't know it. I think I knew from hearing your sweet voice on the phone that you would belong to me."

"Bryn," Rowan gasped, feeling like her world was exploding. "How …?"

Bryn nuzzled the sensitive skin behind Rowan's ear. "Baby, I have walked this earth for thirty-five years. Never in all that time, have I ever felt even the slightest urge to claim a woman. I haven't been a saint by any means, *dulzura*. But I've never gotten involved with any woman beyond dating and superficial relationships. What I feel for you is so far beyond that already, Rowan." Bryn kissed her again. "I knew you were put on this earth for me the moment you apologized to me for Coravani's shit."

"I don't understand." Rowan felt as though her world had turned upside-down.

"Baby, look at it from my perspective. Here is this beautiful, sweet, innocent woman apologizing to me because she's afraid she'll be a nuisance." Bryn speared her with a stern look. "When, in fact, she was only here trying to make a new life for herself because some asshole had chased her out of her home with his bullshit. I felt rage, Rowan. Not at you, but at that pencil-dicked motherfucker. Because you were feeling like *you* needed to apologize to me for all the shit that was on *him* in the first place."

Rowan's mouth fell open. Bryn swept her up with her arms under Rowan's knees and carried her over to the couch, ignoring Rowan's gasp. She gently deposited Rowan onto the couch, then sat beside her and pulled Rowan into her lap. Bryn caressed Rowan's face with one hand as she wrapped her other around Rowan's back.

Rowan was reeling.

This handsome, sexy, dominant butch wanted her. Bryn Armstrong had taken one look at her and had decided in a flash that Rowan was hers.

Rowan didn't know what to do with that.

Bryn seemed to sense her uncertainty and stroked her gently.

"*Dulzura*, I wish we had the time to talk, really *talk*, about all of this right now. But there is another, more serious conversation we have to have tonight, so this other is going to have to wait."

"You keep calling me that, Bryn," Rowan said in confusion. "*Dulzura*. What does it mean?"

Bryn smiled. "It means, 'sweetness,' in Spanish, Rowan. *Mi dulzura*, my sweetness. Because that's what you are for me." She pulled a captivated Rowan closer to her body. "Now, just a few things before we need to focus on that fuckwit. Teagan, who is one of the 'Seven,' one of the management team leaders of APS, is meeting Clem at the Gulf Breeze tonight to get your shit and bring it here. I want you to consider this your home until yours is ready, Rowan."

Rowan's eyes were huge.

"I am not, under any circumstances, willing to have you unprotected any longer, and when we talk, I think you'll understand why. I need to know that you're safe and I can keep you safe, *dulzura*, but that means that you need to be where I can protect you at all times. If I can't be, one of the associates at APS will always be with you from now on, at least until we get certain situations taken care of. None of this will prevent you from doing anything you need to do to get your house or your business ready, but I'll feel much better if you have APS protection with you at all times. One last thing for now." Bryn captured Rowan's wrists so she couldn't move, leaned down, and spoke very slowly and very deliberately, her dark brown eyes never leaving Rowan's hazel ones. "If you *ever* apologize for something that wasn't your fault or was any of your doing in the first place again, I will turn you over my knee, little one, and give you a spanking you won't soon forget."

Rowan felt her jaw go kerplunk.

"S-spanking? Are you serious, Bryn? I'm not a child!" Rowan was outraged.

Bryn looked unperturbed.

"Baby, you have been claimed by an alpha butch with more than a few dominant tendencies. I spank when my woman puts herself into an unsafe situation, or when she physically or mentally or emotionally brings harm to herself. Or when," Bryn's smirk was wicked, "she acts like a brat and throws attitude."

"You... I... It's... You *have* to be kidding me," Rowan sputtered, indignant. "I am *not* a brat!" Deep down inside, however, Rowan found the thought of being spanked by Bryn surprisingly erotic. She already knew she wanted to belong to Bryn as much—if not more—as Bryn clearly wanted to possess her.

"Ah, but there I beg to differ, little one." Bryn nuzzled her neck, not relaxing her firm grip on Rowan's wrists. "Did you or did you not call your butch, 'bossy,' earlier today?"

Rowan's eyes rounded. Her mouth opened, but nothing came out. She closed her mouth with a huff and a snap.

"Good call, *dulzura*." Bryn swooped in and claimed her mouth for one more minute before letting her go. "However, we need to get down to some serious business."

Chapter 7

"He *beat* her?" Rowan, wrapped in Bryn's arms, was in tears.

Bryn had shared everything she knew about Dino Coravani with Rowan, including what Riley and Teagan had told Bryn tonight. Rowan had listened attentively to everything Bryn had said, until she'd lost it when Bryn told her about the beating Mary-Kate had taken at the hands of Coravani.

"Why would he do that to her?" Rowan kept her head buried in the crook of Bryn's neck, crying as if her heart was breaking.

Reason Number 58 for slicing Coravani's nuts off: He'd made Bryn's woman cry.

"Because he's a sick control freak, *dulzura*. You left Woodbridge, he couldn't find you since your sister knew how to bury your tracks like a pro, so he went straight to the only person he knew who might have information on your whereabouts."

"And because he's a fucking chicken-shit pussy," Bryn growled, "who will abuse a woman who is weaker than him, but doesn't have the balls to go up against someone stronger than him, Mary-Kate became his latest victim."

Bryn's phone gave off an odd chime, one that sounded different from a regular text message notification. She checked her phone, pressed her screen a few times, then kissed Rowan before moving her off her lap. Bryn got up and pulled Rowan to her feet, tucking Rowan into her side.

"Clementine and Teagan are here, and Riley should be here shortly. Teag also texted me a bit earlier to let me know she's filled Clem in on everything."

Bryn kissed her again, then let her go as the front door burst open. Clem came flying into Bryn's apartment, her face wrathful, and she grabbed Rowan from Bryn in the world's tightest hug.

"Ro, I swear to you, I am going to find this cock-sucking, pansy-assed, sorry excuse for a microdick and I'm going to pound his fucking ass into the ground."

"Clem. Jesus." Teagan Malloy, a handsome red-haired butch with startling green eyes, followed Clem into Bryn's apartment. "You need to calm down, sweet pea, before you get hurt."

"Before *I* get hurt?" Clem narrowed her eyes. "Dude, I am from fucking Bartow. You do *not* fuck with a Bartow bitch. Like, ever, because we will fuck your ass up before you even got time to put down the Cheetos."

Dismissing Teagan, Clem turned back to Rowan, who was again tucked into Bryn's side. "Ro? Who is this? Is there fucking maybe something you have forgotten to tell your *best friend*?" Clem narrowed her eyes at Bryn. "I know you haven't told your sister anything before all of this bullshit hit the fan, because I talked to Kelly this afternoon and she didn't say a word about you hooking up with some scrumptious butch."

"Clem," Rowan hissed. She pinched the bridge of her nose and took a deep breath, looking to Bryn as if she was trying unsuccessfully to calm down.

"This is Bryn Armstrong from Armstrong Protection Services, Clem. We... She and I... I'm... Umm..."

"She's now mine," Bryn informed Clem flatly. Teagan quirked an eyebrow slightly.

Clem arched her own brow at Rowan, surprise visible on her face. "Does Kelly know?"

"No, and we aren't telling her yet either." Bryn held up a hand, cutting Clem off as her eyebrows hit her hairline and she started to argue. "Riley, my twin, will be here in a minute and we'll make sure everyone is up to speed and on the same page."

She touched Rowan's face gently, aware that Clem was watching her like a hawk. "I need the keys to your car, *dulzura*. I'm going to have Teagan bring your car over and park it next to mine."

"Already done, chief." Teagan lounged against the wall, her sinewy arms crossed. She wasn't quite as tall as Bryn and Riley, but she had the same strong build.

Teagan continued, "Clem has a set of keys to Rowan's car, so she drove it over here and I followed her in my truck. We loaded Rowan's shit from the Gulf Breeze into her car." Bryn nodded in thanks and flashed Teagan a thumbs-up sign.

There was a knock at the front door. Riley Armstrong let herself in.

"Coravani hit town this evening and has already been sniffing around, looking for Rowan," she said by way of hello. "Looks like no one in Whimsy is telling him dick either. He's a high-handed jackass, and he's not exactly endearing himself to the locals."

Rowan paled while Clem's eyebrows dropped dangerously low.

"I swear to you…" Clem began, her voice crackling with fury.

"Hold up a second, Clem." Bryn's mild voice belied the anger in her own eyes. She gestured to her living room. "Let's all take a seat and compare notes. We have a lot to talk about, decisions to make, and agreements to reach."

¥¥¥¥¥

"What a motherfucking cluster fuck." Clem ruffled her bleached blonde curls and growled.

"You need to talk to Masterson, Bryn," said Riley. Captain Vince Masterson was the Whimsy police chief. "I called him to fill him in briefly and let him know to issue a BOLO, but I also told him you would be calling with more details the minute you could."

Riley dragged her hand through her hair.

Despite the tension, Rowan was struck by the similarities between the twins. Looks-wise, their differences were more pronounced—Bryn had black hair and dark brown eyes while Riley had medium-dark brown hair and amber eyes—but their mannerisms and way of speaking were eerily identical.

Bryn does that whole drag-her-hand-through-her-hair-when-she-is-aggravated thing too, Rowan thought.

Bryn interrupted her musings. "Baby, I'm going to assign Teagan as your bodyguard for now."

Teagan nodded solemnly.

"Riley and I need to do a bunch of shit to make sure this fucker doesn't slip our noose, which means I can't be with you constantly. So Teagan it is."

Rowan glanced worriedly at Teagan, sure she was disgruntled at being assigned to glorified babysitting duty, but Teagan didn't look unhappy.

"Rowan," Teagan said in a gentle voice, smiling warmly at her, "you're very important to Bryn, therefore, you're now very important to all of us. That's how it works at APS."

Teagan's green eyes twinkled. "Yes, that aggravating fucker is *technically* the boss," she ducked as Bryn threw a pillow at her head, "*but* she has also been one of my best friends for about a million years. Her and Riley both, Rowan. So I'm going to take a mighty dim view of anything or anyone who tries to fuck with you."

As she looked at Bryn, Teagan's green eyes and handsome face morphed unexpectedly into an expression so full of malice that Rowan and Clem gaped in astonishment at the transformation.

"I hope that sorry son of a bitch gives me a reason to blow him full of holes," she said in probably the iciest voice Rowan had ever heard. "I really hope he does."

Bryn and Riley and Teagan regarded each other, their cold faces reflecting perfect understanding and agreement.

Bryn squeezed Rowan gently, her face settling. "Teag will be here at nine o'clock tomorrow morning to pick you up. You'll both go and pick up Clem at the Gulf Breeze. Then you and Clem will focus on whatever the two of you need to do to get your business opened, *without* worrying about this assclown. Teag will pull whomever she needs to pull to make sure you have adequate protection, baby. I can promise you word has already flown around APS and associates are probably standing in line to sign up for bodyguard duty."

Clem spoke up, confused. "Just exactly how many damn people do you and Riley have working at APS, Armstrong?"

"Including support staff?" Bryn asked and smiled slightly. "Forty-five."

Clem and Rowan gawked. "Sweet baby Jesus, dude," Clem choked, slumping back and sharing a disbelieving look with a stunned Rowan.

Bryn caressed Rowan's arm. "Besides me and Riley, there are seven team leaders, of which Teagan is one. 'The Seven,' we call them. Each one of them is responsible for a specific area within APS, whereas Riles and I oversee the entire operation in general. The nine of us together make up the APS management team. Each TL has a crew of five associates under them. Trillian, our lead data and tech analyst, is one of our Seven, although her crew is more focused on cryptography, client monitoring systems, things like that, rather than field work. Trill, incidentally, is dying to meet you, baby."

Rowan was startled.

"For now, we'll have two other associates permanently on call for you, one of Teagan's and one of Kennedy's, since Kenn's already had a taste of this fucker's work and is familiar with what will be needed. She's the one who's up in Georgetown right now, but she'll be home tomorrow night."

"And she. Is. *Pissed*," Teagan added in a low voice.

"I'm going to call Vince, our police chief, tonight and bring him completely up to speed. Teagan will make sure our bodyguard crew for you and Clem is organized." Clem looked surprised, but didn't say anything. "And Riley," Bryn locked eyes with her twin, "will make sure our eyes and ears on the street are open."

"Whimsy is a very small town and everybody knows everybody, Ro." Riley leaned back and steepled her fingers. "There is absolutely no fucking way Coravani can hide for long, which is exactly what he's going to want to do when he realizes he's been made. He could probably lose himself in St. Pete, but he can't keep driving in and out of Whimsy without being spotted. There are only three roads directly into Whimsy from St. Pete, the rest of the Whimsy streets are cut off by a huge park. Whimsy is also surrounded on the other three sides by the Intracoastal, a 170-acre estuary and a 129-acre nature reserve. This little village is pretty inaccessible, Rowan."

Rowan felt better.

"I don't think I need to spell out all the reasons telling Kelly would be a seriously bad idea right now, *dulzura*." Bryn's gaze was steady as she looked first at Rowan, then over at Clem. "I am not, in any way, trying to deceitfully hide anything from her. Nor would I *ever* when it came to Rowan's safety. But…" Bryn hesitated for a moment.

"You've felt it, too?" Clem burst out unexpectedly. Bryn looked shocked as hell at the statement. "Felt what?" Rowan looked back and forth between Bryn and Clem, confused.

Clem sighed. "Ro-Ro," she began slowly, staring into Rowan's hazel eyes as Bryn watched her like a hawk. "You know how I make fun of Kelly all the time, saying she's a mini Daddy Holland who has a knack for fucking seeing ghosts around every damn corner?"

"Yesss." Rowan was guarded.

"I think Kelly is in the middle of something at work that might have her a bit…freaked out, babe. I dunno, just a feeling I get. She's been…weird…the past few months."

"Well, weird for Kelly, because my *chica* is a fucking nutjob anyway."

Clem held up her hand when Rowan tried to interrupt.

"All I'm saying is that maybe we shouldn't pour more on her plate right now, you know? Something with work clearly has her stressed the fuck out. Plus, she is separated from you, which you know she absolutely hates, while this numb fuck is playing whack-a-mole with his dick. Maybe we should just let Bryn and Riley and their crews handle what's going on down here without telling her so we don't fucking stress her out any more than she already is, okay?" Clem's look was beseeching. "Let her think everything here is hunky-dory for now."

"Maybe you're right," Rowan agreed ruefully. "I hate to hide anything from her, but we'll come clean about everything afterwards. At least then she can kick our butts when everything is back to normal and this cretin has been caught."

"Butts? Cretin?" Riley whispered to Clem, looking mystified. "Does Rowan ever swear?"

Clem snorted. "Who? St. Rowan? The patron saint of virtue?" She pursed her mouth sarcastically. "If she ever did, the world would tilt on its fucking axis and burst into flames."

"Clementine Martin …"

Bryn kissed Rowan, effectively cutting off her words. "Hold up, *dulzura*." Bryn quirked an amused eyebrow when she released Rowan's mouth. "You don't want to ruin that perfect track record."

Rowan's brows lowered dangerously as Clem smirked.

"How much shit does Rowan have to cart up?" Bryn asked Teagan, serious again.

"Either Riley or you, and I should make it in one trip, easy."

"Good. We'll bring Rowan's stuff up. You can take Clem to the Gulf Breeze while I'm talking to Vince. I'm assuming you already have an associate who'll be on guard duty for her overnight?"

Teagan inclined her head.

"Good. When we're done with all that, then we can meet downstairs at headquarters."

"You, go to bed," Bryn instructed Rowan gently as she took the tired woman in her arms. "You're exhausted and I promise I'll be back as soon as I can."

Bryn held Rowan to her and dropped a kiss on the top of her curly blonde head. "Never forget that you're safe here, baby. Always."

Chapter 8

December 15

Rowan woke up in the empty bed and stretched sleepily as she tried to orient herself.

She remembered brushing her teeth last night, then crawling into Bryn's massive bed, completely drained. Several hours later, she'd felt Bryn stripping off her nightgown and panties, then pulling her back, naked, into Bryn's muscled arms. Bryn had wrapped herself around Rowan and Rowan had fallen back asleep, feeling safe, protected, and warm.

Now, Rowan snagged her nightgown and panties from the end of the bed and put them on before making her way down the stairs.

As she reached the bottom, the front door opened and Bryn came in, looking hot and sweaty. She wore a T-shirt that was soaked with moisture and a pair of loose running shorts.

"Good morning, *dulzura*." Bryn blotted her hot face with a corner of her T-shirt that wasn't drenched and smiled at Rowan. "I'd kiss you 'good morning,' but I don't think you'd appreciate this kind of a bath," she teased, laughing as Rowan wrinkled her nose.

"Don't tell me," Rowan rolled her eyes, "you're one of those crazy 'running people.'"

"Ten to fifteen miles, six days a week. How far depends on if it's a day for me to lift weights, or do MMA, or another kind of gym work. I take it you're not a runner."

"Not even if I was being chased by hired assassins," she assured Bryn, who laughed again. "I'm a yoga girl, actually. Five days a week. Kelly is the runner."

"What do you need from me to make that happen for you, baby?"

"An Internet connection, a place where I can set up my iPad, and enough room to unroll my yoga mat. I don't need much."

"Such a demanding woman." Bryn's eyes crinkled at the corners. "How much time do you need for me to give you some peace and quiet this morning?"

"Is one hour okay?"

Rowan squealed as she leapt out of the way of Bryn's long reach. Bryn put her hands on her hips and stared at Rowan impassively.

"Bryn! I did not apologize! I am attempting to be a respectful guest while we are trying to fit our lives around each other." Rowan was indignant.

"Nice try, little one."

"I'm serious! Bryn, I would feel like crap if I got in the way of something you needed to do this morning. I asked if one hour this morning was okay because I didn't know what all you had planned yet. Not because I thought I didn't 'deserve' the time for my yoga or anything stupid like that, but simply because I didn't know if I should do it this evening instead." Rowan's voice softened tremulously. "It truly wasn't a big deal for me either way, Bryn. I just wanted to know in case there was something else going on this morning."

Bryn relented after a long moment of silence.

"Okay, *dulzura*. Acceptable answer. I thank you for your courtesy, then. Down this hall is the bathroom, which you probably remember from last night, and my office is the door beyond it. I'm going to take a shower, then go into the office. After you've done your yoga and taken your shower, come find me. We have a little bit of time before Teagan comes to pick you up, at least enough time to have some coffee and yogurt or fruit."

Rowan saw Bryn's dark brown eyes burn with desire as her intent gaze devoured Rowan.

"Last night, I wouldn't touch you because you were exhausted and overwhelmed, Rowan. You needed a good night's sleep more than you needed anything else. Right now, as much as I'd like to shut away the world and take you to bed, we can't do that either because we have too much going on today. Tonight, though? Tonight, you'll finally be mine in every way."

¥¥¥¥¥

Rowan looked around the reception area of Armstrong Protection Services with interest.

Warm earth tone colors and beautiful walnut wood furniture combined to create a space that was elegant, yet inviting. A sign that discreetly spelled out, "Armstrong Protection Services," was mounted behind the reception desk.

It was, Rowan decided, a place where a woman could come and feel an immediate sense of safety and comfort.

Behind the large walnut reception desk sat a young woman who looked so much like Bryn and Riley, it was not hard to figure out this was their little sister.

"Teagan!" the pretty young woman squealed and rushed from behind the reception desk.

"What's up, brat? Owww!" Teagan rubbed her arm where the exasperated young woman had smacked her, then gave her a lopsided grin and a big hug.

"Rowan, this charming young lady is Bryn and Riley's little sister, Daniela, AKA 'the Brat.'" Teagan dodged another smack.

"Daniela, this is Ms. Rowan Holland, artist extraordinaire and the fastest data analyst in the West." Both Rowan and Daniela looked at Teagan with arched brows at the same time.

"I'm very pleased to meet you, Daniela." Rowan turned away from Teagan, shaking her head, and smiled at Daniela in her sweet way.

"Annnnd, do you think any of you could have been bothered to tell me she was drop-dead gorgeous in addition to being brilliant?" Daniela huffed in mock outrage as Rowan flushed.

"Maybe it's because I didn't want you to embarrass my woman any more than you already are," a familiar voice spoke drily from behind Rowan's back.

Rowan turned around and stared at the handsome, dynamic butch leaning against the door jamb behind her.

Teagan had arrived this morning to pick her up before Bryn had had the opportunity to finish getting dressed. Now, Bryn was wearing jeans, an olive-green Henley, and an open button-down shirt with the sleeves rolled up. The shirt was in black with thin olive pinstripes and closely fit Bryn's lean and toned muscle structure, while showing off her sinewy arms.

Rowan felt breathless.

Bryn strolled to Rowan and kissed her, holding her gently as she looked into Rowan's hazel eyes.

Then Bryn stepped back, looking Rowan over head-to-toe, even though she'd already seen her that morning. Rowan had dressed simply that morning in black high heels with stockings, a pink-and-black striped skirt that came to just above the knee, and a pink cashmere sweater. Her blonde curls were twisted up into a messy, but artful bun, and her makeup was soft and understated. Rowan felt her cheeks flush under Bryn's heated gaze.

"You are so, so beautiful, *dulzura*. How was your day?" Bryn murmured quietly, sliding a blonde curl behind Rowan's ear. "Productive?"

"Incredibly productive." Rowan's eyes showed gratitude as she gripped Bryn's arms. "Clem and I are ecstatic at how much we got done with Teagan's help. Architect, commercial contractor, ice cream equipment suppliers…boom, boom, boom. She got them all on board so fast. She was awesome." She beamed with appreciation in Teagan's direction.

Teagan grinned at Rowan, then tossed a smirk Bryn's way. "They were all a wee bit more eager to cooperate when they heard that these ladies were part of the APS tribe now." She snickered. "Clem said she was totally using the *fuck* out of my name for everything from now on."

Bryn laughed.

"I know that Bryn and Teagan want to show you around, Rowan, but can I ask real quick if you're planning to have a grand opening party when you're ready to open the ice cream shop and the art center?" Daniela asked eagerly.

"Probably," Rowan sighed, "but I don't know exactly when yet because I don't know how long it will take for everything to be finished. As soon as I have completion dates from the contractor, Clem and I will sit down and make some plans."

"Teagan or I will get you some dates tomorrow, *dulzura*." Bryn's voice was implacable. Rowan stared at her in surprise.

"Come on, baby." Bryn slid her arm around Rowan's waist and hugged her close. "Let's take a tour."

After waving goodbye to Daniela, they went through the door Bryn had been standing in and walked down a short hallway. Bryn took Rowan into the first room on the left.

Rowan's eyes widened. It was a huge lounge, filled with tables and chairs and couches; there were also two big refrigerators, plus several microwaves on a big bar along the left-hand wall with a fully equipped coffee station. A big-screen TV was also mounted on the far side of the room.

There was also, in Rowan's estimation, about twenty people standing or lounging around, chatting, Riley among them. They all turned to look at Bryn and Rowan expectantly, and silence immediately fell when Bryn put her hand up.

"Everyone, this is Rowan Holland. She's the one who's currently being harassed and stalked by that piece of shit motherfucker who followed her down here from the Quantico, Virginia area." There were a few hisses as the assembled associates listened, instantly attentive.

"I also know there are more than a few of you here who were fortunate enough to have the late Sgt. William Holland as an instructor at MCB Quantico." Bryn caressed Rowan's shoulder. "Rowan is his oldest daughter."

A few surprised and respectful murmurs greeted Bryn's words.

"The world lost a great man when Sgt. Holland unfortunately passed on a few years ago. So I, for one, will be goddamned if his daughter will *ever* have to deal with an asshole scumbag like this prick if there's anything I can do about it."

Bryn pulled Rowan closer as a low rumble filled the room.

"Rowan is also mine now as well, which I know will come as a surprise to all of you, but that means I'm doubly vested in her safety and her welfare. Teagan and I are taking her around the complex today, but there will be ample opportunity to introduce yourselves and say hello later." Bryn smirked down at Rowan. "My woman is on the skittish side, so try not to give her a heart attack, will you?" Rowan rolled her eyes with a shy smile, prompting a laugh from the assembled associates.

As they went to leave, a voice rang out. "Rowan."

Rowan turned back around in surprise. Her eyes found the speaker and she waited.

"I'm Casey Christensen," the platinum blond, blue-eyed stunner said gently. She was maybe a trifle shorter than Teagan, but impressively muscled. "Sgt. Holland was one of the best instructors it was ever my privilege to have." Casey's tone was serious. "For everything he did for me and for my fellow Marines, I consider it my honor to now be of service to his daughter. I doubt there's anyone here who doesn't feel the exact same way as I do."

Rowan felt her eyes prickle with tears at the chorus of agreement in the room and bit her lip, touched, while ducking her head and swallowing in an effort to keep her composure. She was thankful when Bryn led her out of the room, one arm still wrapped protectively around her. Teagan followed silently in their wake as Riley joined the procession.

"Casey is also one of the Seven, *dulzura*." Bryn squeezed Rowan's shoulders in an effort to calm her. "She's another one who's ready to remove Coravani's balls with a dull butter knife." Teagan and Riley snorted.

The next door down was closed and locked. Another large room was revealed after Bryn unlocked the door by punching a code into the keypad mounted next to the door frame.

"This is our client monitoring room, or what we call the Recon Room. It's also Trillian's domain, where she and her crew do their thing. We stay as quiet as possible while we're in here unless we're in Trill's office," Bryn explained in a low voice as they entered.

The room was filled with equipment of all kinds. In the front of the room was another collection of APS associates, some of them keeping their eyes on large multiple viewing screens, some of them working busily on what looked like programs and graphs.

In the room's rear was a lone associate who was typing with blinding speed on a backlit keyboard with large print keys. On the monitor screen in front of her, which had to be a 34" LED ultrawide, code was scrolling rapidly.

"Trill?" Bryn called softly, not wanting to disturb the rest of the crew.

The fair-haired butch turned around, her eyes widening when she caught sight of Rowan.

She was a bit smaller than the rest of the APS associates Rowan had met so far, although it was clear she kept herself in the same great shape as the rest of them.

She jumped up from her chair and came excitedly over to them. She pursed her lips in a "shhh" motion, then gestured behind them to an office/conference room with a glass front wall.

As soon as they were all in the office with the door closed, the associate whom Bryn had called "Trill" blew out her breath.

"Rowan Holland, as I live and breathe."

Chapter 9

"I'm Trillian Dacanay, the lead data and tech analyst here at APS. I run the Geek Crew." She smiled with excitement, deep dimples peeping, as she and Rowan shook hands. "I think I've studied everything you've ever done in the field of predictive analytics, sweetheart."

Rowan's cheeks colored.

"I know you've bailed to pursue your first love of art, but I still hope and pray we get a chance to work together some day."

"What's this, *dulzura*?" Bryn, then Teagan and Riley, looked at Rowan with questions in their eyes.

Trillian gestured to a discomfited Rowan. "Apparently you're unaware, chief, but your woman there has a near-*mythical* reputation as a data analyst in the predictive analytics field. She's been scouted by *everyone*, from MIT to SAP to Oracle to Amazon to probably the fucking British royal family." Rowan fidgeted as Bryn's eyebrow elevated.

Riley looked at the floor, quietly contemplative at the news, as Teagan regarded Rowan with an intent look.

"I've always loved art, but my mom got me hooked on predictive analytics too." Rowan's voice was soft. "She was a civilian cyber crimes investigative analyst based out of Quantico, and was a tremendous predictive data analyst in the world of cyber crime." She shrugged, abashed, and fidgeted more. "Thanks to my mom, I turned out to be pretty good at it, too."

"Sweetheart." Trillian was incredulous. "Saying that you're 'pretty good' at predictive analytics is like saying Tom Brady can maybe kinda sorta throw a fucking football."

Rowan, taken aback, didn't quite know where to look.

"I think we might have to have a small chat later on about what your definition of 'good' means, *dulzura*." Bryn's eyebrow was still raised. Rowan flushed.

"When Mr. Dickhead is toast, I would love for us to have lunch one day if the chief here is cool with that." Trillian looked quizzically at Bryn.

"Sure, Trill." Bryn nodded. "I can see you two will have a ton to talk about together. Even though Rowan isn't working full-time in the predictive analytics field anymore, I'm sure she would love to have a conversation with someone who understands all that geeky shit, because that sure the fuck isn't me."

Rowan and Trill shared an amused grin while Teagan and Riley snickered.

"You also have the best marksman qualification scores of anyone in the fucking place, so I sure as hell don't have to worry about my woman's safety if you're with her."

With deepening interest, Rowan surveyed the fair-haired butch.

WHIMSICAL HAVEN

"Let me guess. USMC Pistol Qualification, or whatever equivalent you all have conjured up here at APS, and your scores are in the expert stratosphere?" Rowan asked drily.

Trill shrugged, her dimples peeking out again. She winked at Rowan. "Getting used to being at Badass Central yet, Ms. Holland?" she asked with a look of mischief in her light brown eyes.

"Umm, no. Not at all. Not on any freaking level." Rowan pressed her fingertips to her forehead as she tried to make sense of everything she'd been told and had seen so far.

She decided to start with the easy stuff.

"Everyone calls me Rowan or Ro, Trillian. I'm just a visitor, there is no need to be formal with me."

Trill smiled. "Oh, I think you are quite a bit more than just a visitor, or only Bryn's woman for that matter, Rowan. When Bryn mentioned your ice cream shop and art center venture to us, I was totally excited for you. I love art, I love ice cream even more, and I cannot wait to see it when it's done. But," Trill added, "I will admit I'm hoping we can leave the door open to contract you here for some one-off projects." She leaned against the table in the middle of the small space. "It wouldn't be anything frequent, Rowan. But I can think of at least two situations we've had in the past where it would have been glorious to have someone with your skill set."

Bryn, Riley, and Teagan all nodded in agreement.

"It would be entirely up to you, though," Bryn reassured Rowan. "No pressure, no expectations. You do what makes *you* happy, baby."

"Absolutely," Trill chimed in, bobbing her head in adamant agreement.

Rowan's face lit up. "That sounds amazing, actually. I'm an artist, first and foremost. But that doesn't mean I don't still love predictive analytics. I would definitely appreciate the opportunity to keep my toes dipped in the analysis pool every once in a while." She leaned against Bryn. "This sounds like the perfect opportunity for me to do that. And it will help me to feel closer to my mom." Rowan blinked away the moisture that had started forming in her eyes.

"Well then, baby, we'll have Gracie add you to the roster as an on-call consultant." Bryn kissed her forehead softly.

"Gracie?"

"She's one of our three back-office staff members. She handles payroll and employee records. Daniela takes care of reception, mail, and office purchasing. Effie handles accounts payable."

Bryn continued. "Trill actually handles accounts receivable because she's fast as fuck and she says she doesn't trust anyone else to do it. She also functions as our informal office manager. Not that anyone has ever asked her to do that function, but she says she doesn't mind and she feels better having her eyes on what's going on in the back office."

"Fucking right." Trill crossed her arms. "Daniela is family and Effie has been here since the day we opened the doors ten years ago, but Gracie has only been here for eight months, and she's not exactly my favorite person."

"Nor Daniela's," muttered Riley.

WHIMSICAL HAVEN

Bryn looked amused at Rowan's questioning look, but ignored Trill and Riley's comments about Gracie.

"Riley and I have known Trill since we were all three years old," Bryn said. "There are few people in this world we trust more than her. You'll find that Riley and I have a very close relationship with Trill and the rest of the Seven. All of them have been our best friends for literally years."

"That fucker still likes to rub it in because I didn't meet you all until we were five," Teagan groused and whipped an eraser from the whiteboard at Trill, who caught it and smirked.

"Weapons and other large purchases are done by committee between me, Riley, and the Seven," Bryn continued. "The rest of the office you haven't yet seen is the back office, my and Riley's offices, a huge-ass office for the rest of the Seven—which we call the Bunker—the Bullpen—which is open office space for the rest of our associates—a couple of conference rooms, a small bedroom-and-bath suite for any associate who might have to unexpectedly stay at headquarters for a few days, our gym—nicknamed 'Hades'—a shooting range, the 'Cage,' which is Kenn's armory, Blake's testing lab, Utopia—which we'll explain more about later—an infirmary, and the lockdown room."

"Holy crap." Rowan's head was reeling as she tried to make sense of it all. "What's a lockdown room?" she asked, puzzled at the unfamiliar label.

Bryn smiled slightly. "A male filled with testosterone has *nothing* on a hard butch whose woman has been threatened or is in danger. As a matter of fact, if you value your life, don't fucking threaten *anything* that belongs to them or is under their protection. We've had to lock down APS associates on occasion because they were unable to get their rage under control for various reasons and were downright dangerous."

Bryn stroked Rowan's back gently.

"We're all always armed because of what we do, baby." She pulled her unbuttoned shirt aside so Rowan could see the concealed carry shoulder holster under her arm. "Not just for what we do on the surface, but also for the things that go on under the hood that we haven't talked about yet. Needless to say, weapons and temper aren't a good combination."

"Oh." Rowan was quiet.

"I've never personally had to be locked down, *dulzura*. Although…" Bryn smiled without an ounce of humor and looked at her twin. "Riley did ask me about my temperature level the night she told me about Mary-Kate, and said Coravani was on his way to Whimsy to find you."

Chapter 10

Rowan gaped at Bryn, speechless.

Riley spoke up, regarding Rowan with a level gaze. "If she would have shown even a little less control than she did, Ro, I would have sent two of the APS Seven to extract her. Considering it was *you* and *your* safety that was triggering her rage, I know without a doubt I would have had to jump in to help them. Two of us wouldn't have been enough to lock her down."

Four unsmiling and very serious faces regarded Rowan as she stared stupidly at them.

"I don't even know what to do with that." Rowan's voice trembled.

Bryn swiftly gathered Rowan up in her arms. "This is nothing for you to ever worry about, *dulzura*. I keep telling you, we take care of our own. We've always looked out for each other, we have each other's backs, and we always will.

"*You* need to go about living your life and doing what it is you need to do to open your art center and get your house ready. You are to let *us* worry about things like safety and protection. Every single APS associate, especially the ones who met you today, will fucking annihilate anyone who comes within ten feet of you with ill intent."

Bryn rested Rowan's head on her chest. "This is new territory, baby, because none of us—at least me, Riley, or the Seven—has ever had a girlfriend who has meant as much to them as you mean to me. I suspect that we are going to learn *a lot* of new things along the way." She kissed Rowan's forehead.

Bryn and the others—Trill joining them—showed Rowan the conference rooms; the offices of Bryn, Riley, and the Seven; the Bullpen; the huge gym filled with workout equipment and mats for MMA and Krav Maga training; the shooting range and the door to the Cage; the small overnight suite; the infirmary; and the door to the lockdown room.

"Jaime, another one of our Seven, nicknamed the gym Hades and the name stuck." Bryn rolled her eyes with wry amusement. "That fucker."

Blake's testing lab, Utopia, was off-limits, Bryn told her, but when Rowan met her, she would be able to ask her a lot more questions and Blake would definitely arrange for her to take a tour then. Blake was also another one of the Seven, the one who was in charge of running combat simulations.

"Holy freaking cannoli. This place is *humongous*." Rowan felt besieged with information and visuals.

"Just one more stop, *dulzura*. Then I promise I'll let your brain rest for a little while. This is the back office."

Bryn unlocked the door via the keypad and escorted Rowan into the back office, followed closely by Riley, Teagan, and Trill.

It was a large, warm, open room, divided into three distinct work spaces. In one space sat Daniela, who was typing on her computer. She grinned at Rowan and winked, but continued typing rapidly, as she apparently had a deadline of some sort. The plaque on her cubicle identified her to anyone who came in as, "Daniela Armstrong."

In the second workspace sat a kind-looking woman who was probably in her late 40s. She had a headset on and was on the phone, but she gave Rowan a huge, friendly smile and waved, although she was clearly unable to interrupt her phone call. The plaque on the wall of her cubicle said, "Effie Jacobsen."

This must be the Armstrong associate who had been with Bryn and Riley since they had opened for business, Rowan thought.

Curiously, Rowan had a negative visceral reaction to the woman who occupied the third cubicle. She was beautiful—tall and thin, deeply tanned with long, straight dark brown hair, black eyes, and was clothed in a black designer suit with a short skirt that made the most of her long bare legs and small waist.

The plaque on her cubicle said, "Gracie Kavanaugh." This was the woman who handled the payroll and all of the employee records for APS, and the one both Daniela and Trill disliked.

"Hello, Bryn," Gracie purred with a provocative smile, then looked at Rowan with snobby distaste while crossing her legs so she could give Bryn a flash of lean, tanned thigh.

She looked down her nose at Rowan, clearly communicating that she was unimpressed and didn't feel Rowan was worth her time.

"Is this one of those temps or whatever she is that you need me to handle for you, Bryn darling?" she cooed, waving an indifferent hand at Rowan, then adjusting her blouse so the crew caught a glimpse of tanned cleavage.

One of those temps? Or whatever she was? Bryn, darling?
Oh. Heck. No.

Rowan was going to show this witch *exactly* what she was.

It had already been a super long day. She was tired, she was overwhelmed, and what she didn't need was some skank trying to stake a claim that wasn't hers to stake.

She gave Gracie the biggest, fakest smile in the world.

"Hi, Gracie," she purred back. "I'm Rowan. Oh no, I'm not a temp. They're going to hire me as an on-call data analyst for them. I have a master's degree in data analytics from the University of Maryland, and it turns out my experience in the predictive analytics field is something APS can seriously use on occasion."

She let her light laughter echo through the office as Gracie's brows lowered. Rowan turned and looked Bryn up and down.

"Bryn, *darling*, I'm afraid that any paperwork that Gracie might need is in one of my boxes at your apartment. Is it okay if I bring everything in by the end of the week? I should have everything unpacked by then, assuming that you will have had the time to make room for all my stuff." She batted her eyes innocuously at Bryn.

And, BOOM. The dislike on Gracie's face morphed into shock, then sheer hatred.

Daniela, who was sitting in such a way that Gracie couldn't see her, mouthed, "I love you," to Rowan with a huge grin on her face.

Trill suddenly had a coughing fit of epic proportions and grabbed for the bottle of water tucked into the side pocket of her cargo pants. Teagan didn't bother to hide her amusement while Riley gave Bryn a look that promised death.

The corner of Bryn's mouth twitched. "Of course, *dulzura*. We don't have any projects to contract you for yet anyway, so there is no rush." With wicked amusement in her eyes, she leaned over and kissed Rowan thoroughly right in front of Gracie.

Rowan wrapped her arms possessively around Bryn and kissed her back, feeling an almost primordial pulse of ownership that took her by surprise.

"We really just stopped by so that Rowan could see the back office," Bryn said, breaking the kiss and wrapping a muscled arm around Rowan. "We've given her a partial tour of the complex and I think she's about done for now. Are you hungry, baby?" Bryn caressed Rowan's face.

"I am, actually. I was so busy with doing things at the ice cream shop and the art center, I really didn't eat anything beyond a light snack. I'm starving."

Rowan leaned against Bryn for a moment, less interested in aggravating Gracie—who was clearly beyond pissed anyway—than she was in feeling Bryn's strong body against her.

"Let's go then." Bryn took her hand and helped her to the door.

"It was *so* nice to meet everyone." Rowan beamed at everybody, waved enthusiastically to Effie, who was still on the phone, and sailed out of the door, Bryn in tow.

Once safely outside of the room, Trill burst into raucous laughter.

"Jesus Christ, Rowan," she whooped, trying to catch her breath. "Remind me to never, ever piss you off. That was fucking *classic*." She swiped at the tears streaming down her face.

"What the heck was her deal anyway?" Rowan was mystified. "That was some serious shade she was throwing, at someone she knew for approximately ten seconds. What a witch."

"It's no secret. She wants Bryn or Riley or one of the Seven, and you moved in on one of her prime targets. Now, you are Public Enemy No. 1 in her opinion, because you skimmed the cream from the top of the royal reservoir right under her nose," said Trill sardonically. Rowan cast her eyes heavenward.

Riley, however, was not amused. She punched Bryn hard in the arm.

"Thanks, fucker," she grumped. "Now that she knows you're off the market, she's going to redouble her efforts to get me to go out with her."

"Yep. Royal cream. You're the only one left before she needs to dip deeper." Trill held up her hands in defense as Riley aimed an evil glare at her. "I'm just sayin', cuz."

"Why don't you all fire her if she causes such problems?" Rowan asked, leaning against Bryn again. It was rapidly becoming one of her favorite positions.

Bryn ran a hand through her own hair. "Because she doesn't cause problems, not really. Yes, we've both had to put up with her flirting and her innuendos and her clothing that's just on the verge of inappropriate, but to give credit where it's due, she *is* good at her job and doesn't make mistakes." She wrapped her arm around Rowan again. "She ignores Daniela and Effie because we made it clear during the hiring process that Riley and I expect adult behavior from our staff. We don't have time for drama."

"Well, she certainly doesn't bother me and I'm not going to be here enough for her and her witchiness to matter, at least as far as I'm concerned," Rowan remarked. "You all do what's best for the office and each other, and we'll call it a day."

"Baby, you know if she starts to be a problem, I'll get rid of her for you." Bryn stroked her curls.

"Pffft." Rowan snorted. "The day I can't handle a skank like her is the day I need to turn in my femme card." Bryn gave a low rumble of laughter.

Rowan turned worried eyes on Riley, who was grinning at her. "Are you mad at me, Riley? I did kind of start this whole Gracie thing and now you're in her cross-hairs."

"No, Rowan, no fucking way am I mad at you, sweetheart. Everything is fine, trust me. I can handle Gracie and I never turn down an excuse to punch my twin." Riley chuckled, now more relaxed than Rowan had ever seen her, her initial pique gone.

Bryn gave her the finger.

"Besides, I figure if I need any help, I'll get Clem to handle her." Riley smirked. "I might take the day off so I don't have to see the bloodshed, but it's all good."

Goddess have mercy, Rowan thought to herself as the APS crew burst into laughter.

Just what had she gotten herself into?

Chapter 11

Rowan waited quietly in the middle of Bryn's living room, her heart racing a million miles a minute.

When Bryn and Rowan had finally gotten home, daylight illumination had long left the sky, although the winter nighttime loss of light seemed to take longer to fall down here than it did up north. Rowan had set her purse down on the sideboard sitting by the front entrance. She hadn't bothered with a coat because December weather in Florida was so much warmer than December weather in Virginia. Any coats she had were too heavy for the subtropical climate anyway.

The dim space was barely lit by a few contemporary floor lamps, their settings turned down low, casting mysterious shadows around the room.

Rowan shuddered as she felt Bryn silently move up behind her to slide her strong hands along Rowan's arms, her mouth touching the soft skin behind Rowan's ear.

This was it.

"I've waited for you for a long, long time, *dulzura*," Bryn murmured in low tones as she caressed Rowan gently. "I've already told you, *dulzura* is the Spanish word for 'sweetness,' and you are every bit of the sweet I've waited for all my life, little one.

"I don't want to scare you, Rowan, but I plan to touch, taste, and ravish you tonight until there isn't a drop of doubt in your mind as to whom you now belong."

Bryn slid her hands up until they were cupping Rowan's full breasts. "I'm going to fuck you until you come *screaming* for me, baby."

Rowan shook in a combination of desire and nerves.

"Last night, when I stripped you bare and you slept naked in my arms, it was all I could do to let you sleep and not bury my tongue in your lusciousness."

Bryn ran one of her hands down the front of Rowan's body until her fingertips grazed Rowan's pussy through her skirt with a featherlight touch.

Rowan felt a flood of wetness soak her thong.

Bryn smiled into her hair. "We need to go upstairs. I want to be near my bed, so when it's finally time to take you, I'll have you right where I want you."

Rowan climbed the stairs to the bedroom loft, feeling Bryn's eyes on her as she followed Rowan into the loft.

"I've been imagining what's been under this pretty little skirt all day. I love stockings." Bryn slowly raised Rowan's skirt and slid a hand under the band of a sheer black stocking. "Women in Florida don't typically wear stockings, unless they're into certain lifestyles or want to please their lover. Or Master." Bryn's eyes were wicked. "Generally, it's too hot here. But," Bryn unsnapped her garters, "I'm all for laying down a few ground rules just so I can enjoy seeing these beautiful legs and this pale skin all wrapped up in black silk and lace on occasion."

She slowly rolled the black silk stockings down Rowan's legs. Bryn held her legs up firmly, one at a time, so she could slip the stockings off completely. Bryn unbuttoned Rowan's pretty pink cashmere sweater and slipped it off, leaving Rowan in a black lace bra. Bryn unhooked the back and let Rowan's bra fall from her, revealing full pale breasts with pink nipples that tightened in the coolness of the room.

Bryn's eyes kindled as she pulled Rowan roughly to her, claiming her mouth as she wrapped her strong arms against Rowan's petite form.

Rowan felt as though she was going to pass out. Bryn's mouth was commanding, dominant, taking control of Rowan and her will until Rowan slipped into a submission she had never felt before.

Bryn raised her head. "Have you ever given yourself to an alpha butch before, *dulzura*?" she whispered as she filled her hands with Rowan's breasts.

"No, Bryn. N-n-never," Rowan stammered, her legs quivering.

A slight smile lifted the corner of Bryn's mouth. "Then you are about to find out what it's like to be taken and dominated until you are begging for mercy, baby. Until your voice is hoarse from screaming, until you can't stop shaking from passion, until all you can do is submit to the will of your butch."

Rowan moaned as Bryn pinched her nipples and gently bit the curve of her throat, then suckled Rowan hard until her nipples were swollen and engorged. She hooked her fingers over the waistband of Rowan's skirt and slid it down over her hips, leaving Rowan standing in a garter belt and a thong.

"You're lucky I don't rip this from your body." Bryn blew out a deep breath and slipped the garter from Rowan. The thong followed suit until Rowan stood naked before Bryn, the moisture from her pussy trickling from between her thighs.

"On the bed, baby," Bryn commanded, waiting patiently for Rowan to obey.

Rowan pushed herself up on the bed, scooting her small body up until Bryn said, "That's far enough."

Bryn stood at the bottom of the bed and watched Rowan with a laser-focus as she took off her shirt, then pulled her Henley over her head.

Rowan's mouth went dry.

Bryn remained clad in a tight black sports bra that showed off every muscle she had. Her belly was flat, showcasing well-defined six-pack abs; her shoulders were broad, her biceps and forearms were heavily corded.

Bryn slipped off her jeans to reveal black boxer briefs that outlined a tight ass and a soft bulge in the crotch. Her legs were long and muscled, her skin tone a medium olive that reflected her half-Puerto Rican heritage.

She crawled up the mattress toward Rowan and came over her, caging her between her strong arms, and captured her mouth. When Bryn raised her head, she looked Rowan dead in the eyes.

"When an alpha butch claims her woman, there are certain things she expects, Rowan," Bryn said, her voice a little more stern, her face a little more demanding. "I'll protect you, honor you, and I give you my word that I'll do everything in my power to keep you safe, happy, and healthy." Bryn nuzzled behind her ear. "In return, Rowan, I expect both your submission *and* your obedience to me."

Rowan's eyes grew wide.

"Not submission or obedience that will make you miserable because you're being forced to live a life that makes you unhappy, little one. That's bullshit and I have zero desire to do that to you. But," Bryn lowered herself gently on Rowan, as if careful not to hurt her, "when I see you're tired and I tell you to go to bed, *you go to bed*. When you are upset and I expect you to tell me what's made you upset so I can fix it, then *you tell me what's wrong.* When something has you worried or scared, then I expect you to tell me what it is that has you worried or scared, *so I can massacre the fuck out of whatever is making your world feel unsafe or frightening.* When you aren't feeling good, for whatever reason, you do *exactly* what I tell you to do so *your health is always protected.*"

Bryn regarded Rowan seriously.

"I now own your physical, emotional, mental and, to some extent, your spiritual well-being, Rowan. You are a grown woman and I understand that you'll be happiest if you're allowed to look after yourself with my help and input. I wouldn't expect less from you, *dulzura*, and that's perfectly acceptable. But... I will *not* be happy if you jeopardize yourself in any way, Rowan. That goes for either putting yourself into any kind of an unsafe situation or talking about yourself disrespectfully."

Bryn stroked Rowan's belly and breasts.

"I spank, little one. We've had this conversation to some extent before. I can promise you that, unlike an erotic spanking, a punishment spanking does *not* feel good. They're supposed to hurt as a lesson and I'll make *sure* it hurts if we ever go down that path."

Bryn gently bit Rowan's throat again while she lightly teased Rowan's pussy with her fingers, releasing another gush of arousal.

Rowan whimpered with need even as she felt herself mentally and emotionally submitting to Bryn's words.

"For tonight, however… I want you to feel what it's like to be taken and sucked and fucked by the alpha butch who owns you until you can't even scream anymore because. You. Can't. Breathe. I've waited too long to have you and I'm not going to wait another minute to claim you."

Bryn slid down Rowan's body, separated her thighs with her strong hands and, with a long, savage look at Rowan, lowered her head.

Rowan cried out at the feel of Bryn's hot, wet mouth on her clit, and felt her body respond with another gush of liquid arousal. Bryn licked her labia with powerful strokes of her tongue, then sucked her clit into her mouth, gently holding it captive between her teeth and nibbling the sensitive flesh. Rowan cried out, her hands buried in Bryn's thick hair, her hips moving of their own volition as Bryn's wicked mouth devoured her.

"Nuh uh, *dulzura*." Bryn raised her head and spanked Rowan's pussy with her hand when Rowan tried to clamp her legs shut from the intensity. "Do that again and I'll tie your legs open, then keep sucking and biting until you pass out."

Unbidden, another surge of wetness slid down Rowan's thighs to soak the bed.

Bryn laughed, a low sinful sound. "My baby likes the thought of being restrained and sucked, it seems."

As she resumed licking Rowan's pussy, Bryn slid one long finger into Rowan's narrow channel, working her finger into Rowan's tightness and stroking her until Rowan clenched down on her finger. Bryn's finger slid in and out of Rowan until Bryn felt her clenching become more rhythmic. Bryn moved her finger around until she was stroking Rowan's g-spot, rubbing firmly as she sucked her clit until she felt Rowan about to go over.

Then she stopped.

Rowan screamed in frustration as her chest heaved, her body on fire. Her swollen pussy contracted around empty air as she cried out and tried in vain to find relief.

Bryn stroked her thighs. "Did you ask for my permission to come, baby?" she asked Rowan in an unbending tone, her fingers closer to Rowan's clit.

"What?" Rowan was half out of her mind with need and disbelief.

"Your orgasms, *dulzura*, are my gift to you." Bryn pulled herself up so she could kiss Rowan, letting Rowan taste her own juice on Bryn's lips. "When you're a good girl, when you do as you're told, when you show me your submission to me and your obedience…then you get to come. When you ask me to please make you come with your sweet voice, when you beg so pretty for my cock…you get to come. When you *aren't* a good girl," Bryn's mouth quirked in a diabolical half-smile, "you get restrained with your legs tied open, your hands tied down, and a vibrator buried in your pussy at a *very* slow speed. I can keep you on the edge without relief for *hours*, my love."

"Oh, no. No, please, Bryn." Rowan's eyes filled with tears. "I want to be a good girl. I don't ever want to disappoint you." Her voice shook and tears began to fall. "Please let me come, Bryn. *Please*. Please fuck me, I'm begging you. I want you. I need you to make me yours in all ways. I need… I need to feel like I'm yours."

Her voice choked as she started to cry harder. "I can't lie and promise you I won't ever disappoint you, Bryn. I wish I could, but I can't. That wouldn't be honest. But I *can* promise you you'll never find anyone who will try harder for you than I will," she whispered with her whole heart.

"My beautiful girl." Bryn kissed her tenderly, then kissed her tears away. "That was the most perfect answer in the world."

Bryn slid down Rowan's body again and very carefully inserted two fingers into Rowan's pussy, scissoring her open gently.

"It's time to make my baby come." Bryn let a tendril of her breath wash over Rowan as Rowan shuddered.

WHIMSICAL HAVEN

She lowered her mouth between Rowan's legs again, licking and sucking her while slowly beginning to fuck her pussy with her fingers. Rowan cried and shook, clenching down on Bryn's fingers greedily. Bryn fucked Rowan harder and faster while devouring her whole with her mouth. Rowan finally gasped, balanced on the precipice for one long, agonizing minute, until she screamed and kept screaming as she let go with a huge flood of hot, wet heat.

Rowan was barely conscious as she felt her body begin to relax with the release of the unbelievable sexual tension and need Bryn had created in her.

"Thank you," she whispered, barely able to speak from screaming, feeling the inadequacy of the words.

"You're welcome, little one." Rowan felt Bryn pull herself up once again, moving beside her and adjusting something between her own legs, even as one of Bryn's hands was slowly stroking her body, awakening her desire once more.

As Bryn rolled on top of her, Rowan felt the hardness of Bryn's cock poking into her thigh, causing Rowan's body to start to catch fire as she felt herself grow even wetter with desire.

Bryn kissed her fiercely. "I have never seen anything as beautiful as you were, Rowan, coming on my fingers and screaming your pleasure as you came in my mouth. But now… I'm going to fuck you with my cock until you scream yourself hoarse for me, my beautiful woman," Bryn growled. "I want you screaming, begging, pleading for me until you start shrieking for my mercy. These walls are soundproof, baby. I can make you scream so long and so loud that you lose your voice for days, and yet…no one would ever hear your screams as your butch showed you the ruthless side of her possession."

Rowan shuddered and whimpered.

"One day soon, I truly *am* going to tie your hands to the bedrails and then tie these beautiful legs open so I can do whatever I want with you." Bryn's voice was wicked. "Imagine me leaving you like that: naked, restrained with a plug in your ass, gushing pussy juice all over my bed as I talk to one of my Seven down below. You'd have to be so quiet, baby, so that you weren't caught."

Rowan moaned even as she shook her head 'no' in denial.

"Or… I could flip you onto your hands and knees, pull your legs open wide, and fuck you with my cock from behind. Imagine yourself working your pussy on my cock as I play with your clit, begging me to fuck you deeper and deeper…until I make you come so hard, you still feel my cock in you the next day. I could also make you get down on your knees and suck my cock until you make me come from the pressure and the friction, *dulzura*."

Rowan quaked and soaked the bed even more from all the erotic images that Bryn's words were conjuring.

"Tonight, though… Tonight, I just want to fuck my woman until she screams and passes out. Open your legs for me, baby."

Bryn inserted the tip of her cock into Rowan. As she firmly slid inside her, Rowan cried out and gasped as her pussy contracted around Bryn. 'I…oh, Bryn… I… I…"

Bryn massaged Rowan between her legs as she started to move. Rowan felt so full, so mastered, so *taken* by Bryn's skill and her dominance.

As Bryn moved faster and faster, harder and harder, Rowan felt her pussy start to flutter and clench in response. As she felt the first tremors of her orgasm deep in her pussy, Bryn commanded, "Come for me, Rowan. *Now*."

Rowan screamed as the most violent orgasm of her life hit her with the force of a tsunami. Bryn groaned as she came too, freezing with her cock buried in Rowan up to the hilt.

Rowan's world went black.

She woke up a short while later, curled in Bryn's strong arms, in fresh sheets.

While she was lost in a dazed and exhausted sleep, Bryn had bathed her, changed the bedding, braided her hair, and made sure she was warm and clean and safe.

Rowan was spellbound.

She was sore and drowsy, but she felt so cared for, so protected, so sheltered, that a few slow tears ran spontaneously down her face.

Bryn tightened her arms around Rowan.

"Go back to sleep, *dulzura*. Your very presence was a gift to me tonight." She kissed Rowan tenderly, then softly kissed Rowan's closed eyes.

The last thing Rowan remembered hearing as she slid into the most peaceful sleep of her life was Bryn's fierce whisper.

"You. Belong. To. Me, Rowan Holland. I've claimed you, I've possessed you, and now, I own you. And I will never, *ever* let you go."

Chapter 12

December 23

Rowan frowned at the unexpected knock at the locked front door of the Dream Creamery.

One week after Bryn had secured final completion dates from both the architect and the contractor, renovations on the Dream Creamery and the Whimsy Creative Arts Center were in full swing. Ember Renshaw, their architect, and Nia Rosenberg, their contractor, assured Rowan and Clem that six weeks was more than ample time to complete the downstairs where the Dream Creamery and the Arts Center would be.

"We already have brand-new plumbing and electricity run where we need it in this space since you were fine with leaving the existing footprint exactly as it is," Ember had said. "Plus, the air-conditioning was already completely upgraded, the lighting is all brand-new, and the bathroom was redone as well. As far as the Dream Creamery goes, what we have to do is largely cosmetic. The art center will take a bit more effort, but still nothing too time-consuming. Apparently, the last owner had already put a considerable amount of time and money into this place, thinking she was going to be here for a long time, so we have a lot less work to do."

Ember had been jubilant.

"The upstairs apartment, however, is a different story since it's really nothing more than empty space right now," she'd continued. "We have a ton more work to do since we are building from scratch and it is going to take us longer to collaborate on creating a design plan with you, then producing blueprints. But there is an outside entrance to the apartment in the back of the building, built in such a way that it will make the space easily accessible, even with bringing up cabinets and power tools and things like that. There are stairs, but it will be child's play to navigate them. We don't need to come in here at all to access the upstairs space. Since it is completely self-contained, it won't prevent you from having a grand opening here in six weeks."

Ember had smiled slightly. "Bryn Armstrong wanted to know what she needed to do to make sure you were our top priority, Rowan. We've negotiated that with her, so we are full speed ahead."

Given their conversation with Ember, Rowan, and Clem had decided on Saturday, February 6th for their grand opening.

Now, however, it was 7:00 p.m. in the evening and they weren't expecting anyone. Although there was nonstop activity all throughout the day, the workers were typically gone by now and the place was usually quiet until 7:00 a.m. the next morning.

Also, since Christmas was in two days, all work had completely stopped at 5:00 p.m. until the 26th. The entire building had been deserted for several hours as everyone had left to go home and be with their families for the Christmas holiday.

Rowan had given everyone a beautiful gift basket of wine and chocolate from her, Kelly, and Clementine, along with their thanks and best wishes for a happy holiday. Teagan had shaken her head and muttered, "classy," in a voice so low Rowan had almost missed it.

For Teagan, however, Rowan had surprised the hell out of her with a 3D-lighted stadium wall art piece, a replica of the "Swamp" of the Florida Gators, Teagan's alma mater…from her, Kelly, and Clem as well. Teagan had stared at it with her jaw dropped wide open, completely in shock, before she had grabbed Rowan and hugged the hell out of her, speechless.

"I can't think of anyone who deserves this more, Teag." Rowan hugged her back just as hard and kissed her cheek. "Clem and I will never be able to thank you enough for everything you've done for us. I know you haven't met Kelly yet, but I promise you she'll be just as appreciative as we are."

Now, everyone except Teagan was gone. Rowan and Clem had been about to shut down and go home themselves, when the knock at the door came.

Teagan reached for her gun in the concealed carry shoulder holster she wore on top of her fitted black T-shirt with "Armstrong Security" embroidered in white thread on the T-shirt's front pocket. She gestured with her head for Rowan and Clem to move away from the door and positioned herself to the side.

"Who is it?" she asked sharply when everyone was clear.

Rowan was never more reminded than at times like these that her sweet, happy-go-lucky APS friend was, in fact, a deadly predator.

"I'm sorry, I can come back another day if it's more convenient," breathy tones called out. "This is Nova MacLeod, the former ice cream maker here. I was on my way home and thought I would take a chance and stop by since I saw the lights on. Really, though, it's no big deal. I am more than happy to come back after Christmas."

"No, no." Rowan's face lit up. "Hang on a second, and we'll let you right in."

Teagan's face relaxed and she slipped her gun back in her holster.

"Nova?" Teagan shook her head, a huge grin on her face, as she reached for the front door lock.

There was a long moment of silence, then a happy, "Teag?!" came squealing through the front door.

Teagan opened the door and caught the tiny dynamo who rocketed into the Dream Creamery.

"Dude! What in the Mary Mother of God are you doing in an ice cream shop, of all places?" The dynamo threw her arms around Teagan in an enormous hug before she caught sight of Rowan and Clem. Disentangling herself, she beamed happily at the two before she turned her attention back to Teagan. "Aren't you supposed to be out causing mischief and mayhem with the rest of the APS badasses?" she snarked, smacking Teagan on the arm. "Aren't you going to introduce us?"

"Now, Nova. Mayhem? Me? I'm hurt." Teagan attempted to look innocent while Nova stared at her with an, "Are you kidding me?" expression on her face. "Girls, this is Nova MacLeod, hippy pacifist and legendary ice cream artisan."

Nova looked at Teagan with another, "Are you kidding me?" face for a moment before beaming at Rowan and Clem again.

"Nova, this is Rowan Holland and Clementine Martin. Rowan owns the joint and Clem is her best friend and right-hand woman." The three women shook hands with big smiles. "I've known Nova since she and her family moved to Whimsy when Nova was eleven. I used to date her older sister when we were in high school," Teagan shared casually.

"You used to date Nova's sister?" Rowan repeated in surprise.

"Teagan used to date *everyone's* sister, the horn dog," Nova shared drily.

Clem burst out laughing while Rowan's jaw went kerplunk.

"We'll have to go for cocktails while I tell you *all* my Teagan stories." Nova's face filled with glee as she stuck out her tongue at Teagan.

"I see how you three are already," Teagan said, scowling in mock offense.

"However, I will tell you my *favorite* Teagan story now," Nova continued with a smirk. "It actually involves her, and Bryn and Riley Armstrong."

Rowan's interest deepened, especially when Teagan actually flushed a little bit. "It's 5th grade. I am brand-new at Whimsy Elementary and I hated *everything* about Whimsy. I hadn't wanted to move here and leave all my friends in Jacksonville, but we moved because of my dad's job. So, there's this dick in my class named Brian Bonaire—he's *still* a dick, by the way—and he thought it was funny to bully the new girl."

Nova's eyes darkened.

"A week of dealing with this asshole and Teagan finds me one day, crying in the library. She asked me what was wrong and I told her. I didn't really mean to burden her with my woes, it just all came spilling out. She didn't say anything, but the next day at school, these rumors were flying all over that Teagan, Bryn Armstrong, and Riley Armstrong had put super glue on the toilet seat in Brian Bonaire's classroom, and somehow—I still to this day don't know *how*—made sure he was the first one to use the bathroom."

Rowan's jaw dropped to the floor while Clem howled, clutching her stomach and gasping for air.

Teagan shrugged, embarrassed. "We were protective of girls even back then. Although," a slow smile slid its way across her handsome face, "our techniques have been refined a bit."

"Did you get caught?" Rowan gaped.

Nova snorted. "Even back then, no one who valued their life would tattle on any classmate who was close to Bryn or Riley. Ironic that they've all ended up as APS associates, right?"

Teagan checked her phone suddenly, then sent a rapid text. "That was Bryn, she wants to know where her woman is. I told her Nova stopped by to meet Rowan, and we were getting ready to leave."

Teagan smirked at Nova after she checked her phone again. "She said to tell you Merry Christmas and to give her woman back...you two can play after Christmas."

"So, you are Bryn's girlfriend, huh?" Nova smiled. "Exciting news and we will definitely get together right after Christmas. Actually, the biggest reason I stopped by, Rowan, is that I would love to come back and work here, if you're open to talking about that."

"Are you *kidding* me? After all the amazing things I've heard about your artisan ice cream?" Rowan was excited. "I swear, I can't say yes fast enough!" She and Clem and Nova made plans to meet for lunch a couple of days after Christmas to talk.

"Lunch, ice cream plans for the new Dream Creamery, and stories about Teagan and the APS badasses. How could it be any more perfect?" Nova's smile was sly.

"Jesus Christ, let's go," Teagan groused. She heaved a big sigh. "Why do I have the feeling this new partnership is not going to end well for the APS badasses?"

Chapter 13

December 24

Rowan laid in bed with her head on Bryn's shoulder, basking in the afterglow of some very demanding and passionate sex.

They were going to Bryn's parents' house the next day for Christmas dinner and, although Rowan hadn't admitted anything, she was extremely nervous. However, Bryn—in her omnipotent way—drew her out.

"I know you're missing your parents tonight, *dulzura*," Bryn said softly as she ran her hands soothingly up and down Rowan. "Tell me about them. You already know your dad was one of my instructors when I was in the Marine Corps, me and Riley both. I don't really know anything about your mom, though, other than the fact she was apparently a kick-ass predictive analyst just like her daughter."

Rowan sighed. "I don't really know there's much to tell, other than they were the best mom and dad in the world and I miss them every single day. My mom died unexpectedly from a burst aortic aneurysm about five years ago." Bryn pulled her closer and tightened her arms around her as tears clogged Rowan's voice. "It was more horrible than anything you could imagine and it about killed my dad. He followed her two years later from having a heart attack. He loved Kelly and me more than anything in the world, but he sort of gave up after Mom died, Bryn. I really don't think he wanted to live without her." Rowan choked on the words, tears pouring down her face.

"Baby, I'm so sorry." Bryn caressed Rowan gently. "I didn't know your mom, but I knew your dad. He was a good man and he was a fucking brilliant sniper instructor. I was honored to know him."

Rowan was silent for a long moment as she struggled to bring herself under control.

"I didn't really know either of my grandparents. Mom's parents died when I was really young and Dad was estranged from his family. They were super Pentecostal holy-roller Christian, and Dad said he didn't want his own family anywhere near what he called, 'that brainwashing eff-ery.'"

Bryn permitted herself a smile. That sounded like something Bill Holland would say.

"Mom was an only child and her parents were in their late 40s when my grandma found out she was pregnant unexpectedly. They'd never planned on having kids and Mom was a big surprise to them, although from what I understand, they ended up being good parents and they truly loved my mom. Anyway," Rowan looked abashed, "my maternal grandparents were *extremely* wealthy people and when they died, Mom inherited it all. Which means that when *she* died, Kelly and I inherited all of it from her."

Rowan smiled a little bitterly.

"My grandmother had a half-sister and a half-brother, who were originally counting on inheriting all of grandma's millions themselves, because she didn't have kids and they'd never expected her to. Needless to say, Kelly and I don't have a relationship with that part of the family and never have. They didn't want anything to do with any of us because they perceived us as having 'stolen' their money from them." Rowan's tone grew more bitter. "They didn't even have the decency to send a card when Mom died."

Bryn kissed her forehead. "Fuck them, baby. I fucking hate people like that, greedy assholes who place more value on money than on family or love. Although I hate like hell that you've lost your parents, *dulzura*, I'm glad they were at least in a position to make sure you and Kelly were materially provided for when they were gone."

"The holidays are the hardest," Rowan whispered, burrowing further into Bryn. "I honestly don't know how well I'm going to do tomorrow with your parents, Bryn. It was beyond wonderful for your mom to worry about me and Clem, though."

Rosario Armstrong, Bryn and Riley's mother, had insisted that both girls spend Christmas day with the Armstrong family. Clem, however, had already accepted an invitation with some old friends of hers who lived in St. Petersburg, knowing that Rowan would be spending the day with Bryn. She had sent her thanks along to Bryn's mother, however, for thinking about her.

"Let me tell you something about Rosi Armstrong, *dulzura*." Bryn nuzzled her ear. "That is the only woman in the world whom every single APS associate is scared shitless of, including me and Riley."

Rowan's eyes widened.

"She is the kindest, sweetest, most loving person you'll ever meet in your life, and each one of the Seven are like her own." Bryn smiled faintly. "But do not piss her off. *Ever*. And don't threaten anyone or anything that belongs to her, because she'd just as soon take off your head than look at you if you do. I told her about you, Rowan. I told her you've lost your mom, you've lost your dad, and now you have some asshole stalker trying to find you. She. Is. *Livid*."

Suddenly, Bryn laughed low in amusement.

"My dad is 6'4", *dulzura*, and Mama is 5'2". Watching him try to calm her down when she's screaming like a banshee at the top of her lungs in Spanish because she wants a piece of this motherfucker *now*, is something that amuses the shit out of her kids, even when the reason itself doesn't."

"Oh, heck," Rowan said faintly, burying her face in Bryn's shoulder.

"Mama is Puerto Rican, baby, and Dad is English. He has the typical British stiff upper lip, which is a good thing when it comes to dealing with a hot-blooded Hispanic woman who doesn't suffer fools gladly."

Bryn kissed the top of Rowan's head.

"Another thing. I have *never* brought a woman home to meet my family before, *dulzura*," Bryn said quietly. Rowan gasped. "That alone makes you unbelievably special and they haven't even met you yet. I don't want you to worry about tomorrow, Rowan. My family is really looking forward to meeting you and I promise you they'll take care of you. You know Riley. Daniela, of course, you already know now as well. You are her hero for putting Gracie in her place the other day, by the way." Rowan felt Bryn smirk in the darkness. "I think Mama has already practically adopted you in her head, baby. And Dad is a former British Royal Marines sharpshooter, which means he would *love* to have a conversation with you about your father when you feel you can do that."

"Okay," Rowan whispered, touched.

"I have two brothers as well. Keenan is a neurologist and is the usual medical geek. Noah is a Whimsy police officer, and the biggest fucking pain in my ass ever, which is typical of a lot of little brothers."

"Are you and Riley the oldest?" Rowan asked.

"Technically, I'm the oldest of the family because I was born nine minutes before Riley was." Bryn smirked. "And if you want to totally piss my twin off, keep reminding her of that fact. Which I do, frequently."

Rowan laughed, her voice drowsy.

Bryn gave her a long, passionate kiss. "We have a big day tomorrow, so we need to get some sleep." Bryn lay awake, holding her woman until she heard Rowan's breathing even out and Bryn knew she was asleep.

"Merry Christmas, baby," Bryn whispered to the beautiful woman in her arms. "Let's see if from now on we can't make them all a little bit more merry for you than they have been."

¥¥¥¥¥

December 26

Rowan lay awake in bed, waiting for Bryn to get back from her run. Yesterday had been the most awesome Christmas she'd had since her mom died.

Kelly had seemed relieved when Rowan had called her Christmas morning and told her that she was spending Christmas day with the Armstrong family. She told Kelly that Bryn and Riley's mother, Rosi Armstrong, had found out Rowan was going to be alone and had insisted she come and spend the day with them.

Rowan was pissed her sister hadn't been given Christmas off, and couldn't understand why this assignment had gone on for so long or why it was so important that Kelly had to stay in Virginia during the holidays. But she had relaxed when Kelly cheerfully told her not to worry about it, to focus on getting their new life in Florida all set up so that Kelly could reap the benefits of all of Rowan's hard work when she got there.

Rowan had nervously given Bryn her present Christmas morning while the two of them were having coffee at the breakfast bar. They'd agreed that getting a tree this year was silly since Rowan had just moved in and Bryn didn't have room for a tree anyway.

"Next year, when your house is ready," Bryn had promised softly as she kissed Rowan's hair.

When it had been time to exchange gifts, Rowan had nervously decided to go first to get her part over with.

¥ ¥ ¥ ¥ ¥

Bryn looked at her anxious woman. In Rowan's hand was a large envelope that appeared filled with paperwork, which she handed to Bryn.

Then Rowan cleared her throat.

"Yes. Well." She looked at Bryn with all the enthusiasm of someone being led to the gallows. "I want you to know, I have *never* had this much of a problem picking out a present for anybody, Bryn." She huffed in exasperation as she counted the reasons Bryn was difficult on her fingers. "You already have everything you could ever want. You watch your diet like a hawk, so food isn't a good choice. You have a humongous, fully-outfitted gym at work, so anything that has to do with fitness is out. You don't really drink much, so that's a waste."

Then Rowan stopped counting and looked at Bryn thoughtfully.

"Something Riley said one day got me thinking, though. She mentioned the two of you liked to sip whiskey every once in a while. Like, the premium stuff, not necessarily the stuff you can get at the local liquor store. So…" Rowan blew out a deep breath, "I got you an annual membership to a whiskey club. You'll get a full bottle every three months of a whiskey of your choice and there are quite a few selections, plus a whole bunch of other stuff that comes included with the membership."

Rowan fidgeted.

"I know next to nothing about whiskey, but I called them and talked to this amazing guy there named John Crofton. He was extremely knowledgeable, very sweet, and extraordinarily patient with my questions. He told me to have you call him anytime about your membership and he'd be happy to share other resources with you as well. With your membership, you can choose from American or Scotch or Irish brands. John said they even have 'Japanese whisky,' which was weird to me, but what do I freaking know? I guess too sometimes, whiskey is spelled with an 'e' and sometimes it's not. John started to explain it, but my head exploded, so he took pity on me. So, there you have it. I thought it was kind of cool, so I hope you don't think it's too lame."

Bryn had stared at her for a long minute, completely at a loss for words, while Rowan waited with trepidation.

"*Dulzura*," Bryn had finally managed to make herself say, "this is probably the most phenomenal present I've ever received in my entire life."

She had pulled Rowan up into her arms and kissed her with a thoroughness and a desire that left Rowan gasping.

"Thank the Goddess. I'm so happy. I was so afraid it was completely lame, but I didn't know what else to do." Bryn cupped the back of Rowan's head with a strong hand as Rowan hid her face on Bryn's shoulder.

"Baby, it's so *not* lame. I cannot wait to tell Riley and rub it in her fucking face." Rowan giggled in sheer relief.

Goals for next year, thought Bryn: *Make Rowan giggle more.* It made Bryn want to bend her over the nearest hard surface and fuck her until she screamed.

"My turn." Bryn reached under the counter and pulled out a large, flat package that had clearly been professionally wrapped. "Merry Christmas, *dulzura*," Bryn said as she handed the package to Rowan, propping it on her lap. "I hope you like it."

Rowan slowly unwrapped the gift to find a 16x20 matted picture frame with a beautiful photo collage in it.

The collage included pictures of Rowan, Kelly, and their parents—pictures that ranged from when the girls were little to right before Amanda had passed away.

It was the Holland family, preserved in living color for all time.

And it was *beautiful*. Rowan didn't realize she was sobbing until she felt Bryn's strong arms move the collage safely onto the breakfast bar, then wrap her up as Bryn pulled Rowan onto her lap. Rowan couldn't stop crying, but neither could she stop staring at the beautiful collage of her family.

WHIMSICAL HAVEN

It was heartbreaking, but at the same time, it was joyous and loving and everything that Rowan wanted to remember about her family from when Amanda and Bill still walked this earth.

"My beautiful woman," Bryn said gently, stroking Rowan's hair. "You have mourned for so long. I don't ever want you to forget your parents and I will spend the rest of my days making sure they still live in your heart. But I want you to start healing too, baby. Clementine found the pictures in the personal items that had already been delivered to your new house, and she gave them to me. So, I had this collage made so you can start looking at your family every single day and feel peace and love when you look at the faces of your parents instead of sorrow and pain."

Bryn held her close. "It will take time, but I promise you won't ever have to do it alone."

Later, Rowan lay in Bryn's bed and admitted to herself that she was falling hard and fast for Bryn Armstrong.

It was the protective way Bryn kept Rowan's world safe.

It was the passionate way she took Rowan and fulfilled every fantasy she had ever had.

It was the gentle way she cared for Rowan and stood as a shield between her and her sorrows and fears.

It was the way she took Rowan with her dominance and her command, and then made sure Rowan was safe and cared for when she was exhausted and spent.

Rowan felt her heart flutter as she thought about the dark-haired, dark-eyed butch, who had become Rowan's world so unexpectedly.

WHIMSICAL HAVEN

Chapter 14

Meeting Bryn's family yesterday was also more than Rowan could have dreamed of.

When Bryn had brought her into the huge home located on the edge of Whimsy in the Marina Bay Club gated community, the first thing she'd seen was a very tall, fair-haired man standing in the foyer who smiled at her with kind blue eyes that crinkled at the corners.

"And this," he declared with a pronounced English accent, "must be the lovely Rowan. Merry Christmas, love. I'm Bryn's dad, Oliver."

Rowan blushed as he shook her hand and welcomed her to their home; then he hugged Bryn hard, kissed her cheek, and wished his eldest child a Merry Christmas.

Riley came into the foyer from further inside the house, hugged Rowan, and wished her a Merry Christmas, too. She punched her twin in the arm, then hugged her as well, as Oliver rolled his eyes.

"Rowan!" an excited Daniela squealed as she came skipping into the foyer to give her a hug.

"Oliver!" a pretty voice with a Hispanic accent called down the stairs. "Did you offer that child something to drink yet?"

"Maybe when she's finally gotten all the way in the door and your children stop assaulting her, love." Oliver grinned at Rowan conspiratorially as they all heard the exasperated huff coming from the stairs.

A small, beautiful woman with the same black hair and dark brown eyes as Bryn flew into the foyer.

"Oh. Oh, my," she said, looking at Rowan in her scarlet Christmas dress with her blonde curls pulled back into a proper bun. "Aren't you just *lovely*."

She kissed and hugged Bryn hard, wishing her child a very Merry Christmas, then looked around at Rowan.

Her face lit up as she went to the nervous blonde and regarded her steadily for a long moment before gently pulling Rowan into her arms.

"I'm Rosi, Rowan, Bryn's mama. I feel so blessed to meet you." Her dark eyes held warmth and the same kindness that her husband's had. "I know this is a hard time of year for you, *querida*, and I'm sorry we've had to meet for the first time like this. Whatever you need today, you ask for, even if it's just a few minutes alone."

She released Rowan and, just as she was about to say something else, a tremendous crash came from the back of the house and two raised male voices competed for volume.

"Noah! You fucking dingleberry! Mama is going to fucking kill you! On what planet is balancing that many plates a good idea?"

"Kiss my ass, Keenan! I have probably done that a million times and if your fucking assclown feet weren't in my way, I wouldn't have had a problem this time either!"

Rosi shook her head, pinched the bridge of her nose, looked heavenward, crossed herself, and then politely made her excuses as she sailed out of the room, motioning to Daniela to come with her.

Two smacks and a bunch of inflammatory Spanish was heard as Rowan ducked her head and tried to stifle her giggles. She looked at Bryn and Riley, who both wore wide grins, before she glanced at Oliver, who was laughing outright.

"I probably don't want to know what that means, do I?" she said, still trying to smother her giggles.

"No. No, you don't, *dulzura*, trust me." Bryn hugged her close and laughed.

Oliver grinned and gestured to her. "Let's go get you that drink, love, and flee the scene of this crime before a murder is committed."

Rowan laughed as she remembered how outrageously funny the entire Armstrong family was.

Bryn and Riley were much more relaxed than they were at APS headquarters, and Rowan felt welcomed by the entire family.

She had asked Rosi what the fabulous wrapped unidentifiable dish was that she couldn't stop eating, and Bryn laughed out loud as the rest of the Armstrong kids glared at Bryn in full force.

"Those, *dulzura*, are a traditional Puerto Rican Christmas dish, called *pasteles*, that takes two whole days to make and typically involves the whole family. They are labor-intensive and take a ton of time and work, and they are only something you make and eat at Christmas in Puerto Rican culture," she informed Rowan.

"As you already can tell, they are amazing and the last thing that any of us worry about on Christmas Day is our diet."

Bryn grinned. "My siblings are pissed, however, because I got out of helping with the *pasteles* this year since I was with you. But I am going to warn you, *dulzura*: We will both be on *pastele*-making detail next year."

Rowan had tried to talk Rosi into letting her help with the dishes after they'd finished eating their fabulous dinner, but was shooed away with a cheek kiss and orders to go and enjoy herself.

Since she had been banned from dish duty, she spent some time sitting with Bryn's dad and the twins in the living room, talking about her own father's career in the American Marine Corps as a scout sniper and sniper instructor.

"Do you carry yourself, sweetheart?" Oliver asked her casually, a glass of cognac in his hand. Bryn and Riley both, she noticed, were intensely focused on their conversation.

"I do. I have my Virginia concealed weapons permit, which is recognized in Florida, and I have a Beretta APX Carry, which is fairly new. Kelly talked me into getting it a few months ago," she said. "I'm not very big and my hands are small, so Dad liked compact guns for me. I keep it in my purse in a purse holster instead of actually on me, though, which my dad always *hated*. I have a leather IWB holster and an ankle holster as well, but I never use them because they aren't always comfortable."

Rowan flushed.

"As you can probably tell, I'm not a big fan of being armed all the time, even though Dad always insisted. My sister, Kelly, is the weapons aficionado in the family. Maybe you all can recommend a shooting range for practice for me, though, since Kelly won't be down for a while and I've only shot with my APX once. I promised her I would keep up while I was on my own."

"You can use the range at APS. I'll take care of it with Kenn, who's our Armory Master and is in charge of the shooting range." Bryn sat next to Rowan with her arm around her, stroking her arm. "And you aren't on your own, *dulzura*. Not anymore."

"Rowan, sweetheart," Oliver began, then hesitated. "Bryn has told both me and Rosi about that wanker who is stalking you." His blue eyes chilled. "I know this is probably presumptuous of me, love, but could I maybe persuade you to carry concealed in your IWB holster for a little while? Just until this wanker is caught? I have no doubt that you are as safe as you can possibly be with my Bryn at your back, but maybe you'll indulge an old man for a while?"

Rowan couldn't help it. She looked at Oliver Armstrong's 65-year-old, 6'4" lean, muscled frame and snorted. It wasn't hard to see where Bryn had inherited both her height and her body type from.

The twins burst out laughing as a huge grin spread across Oliver's face.

"I tried," he admitted with a chuckle. "But I'm being serious, love. It's too easy to be separated from your purse or even a backpack in chaotic circumstances, no matter how very, very unlikely they are."

"Okay," Rowan reluctantly agreed. "Although I don't buy this 'old man' business for even one second, you know." She raised an eyebrow at Oliver.

"Cheeky." Oliver looked at his oldest twin with a smirk. "Bet she's a handful just like your mother is."

"She is," Bryn agreed, smirking back and stroking Rowan's cheek. "She and Mama are going to get along just fine."

¥¥¥¥¥

Rowan's reverie about Christmas Day was interrupted when she heard Bryn's key in the front door.

"I'm being lazy and I'm still in bed, especially since *you* kept me up so late," she called out. "I figured I would let you take your shower after your run and then I'll take mine."

"Good, because we have a meeting with the Seven this morning, *dulzura*." Rowan heard Bryn laugh as she yelped in dismay, throwing back the covers and jumping stark naked out of the bed.

Rowan eyed Bryn with pique as they took the outside elevator from their apartment to the breezeway that led to the offices. She had flown around the apartment like a maniac getting ready, much to Bryn's amusement, and was still feeling completely discombobulated.

"I think," she announced carefully, "that we need to have a small discussion on timing issues if we have any more morning meetings, Bryn. You may be a butch and can get ready in ten minutes, but I am a femme and ten minutes is barely enough time to brush my teeth. So maybe we can renegotiate this whole getting-ready-in-the-morning thing?"

Bryn raised her eyebrow with a very slight smile. "So noted, *dulzura*. I'm sure, however, you appreciate that we usually start our morning meetings at six a.m. and I gave you a very generous break by starting at nine o'clock today."

Rowan's jaw dropped open in shock. "Six o'clock? In the *morning*? Who in the heck does that?" She paused for a moment. "Wait. And you still *run* before you get ready and go in at six a.m.?"

"Riley, I, and all of the Seven do." Bryn slid her arm around Rowan's waist. "Baby, you look like you're about to pass out."

"That's because I *am*. Holy cannoli, Bryn. *Crazy* people. My alarm doesn't even go off until seven!"

Bryn pulled her to the side and caged her, nibbling on her neck. "Bet I can think of a good way to get your motor running early in the morning, *dulzura*."

Rowan huffed, eliciting a low laugh from Bryn in response.

Rowan's heart rate was almost back to normal by the time they reached the smaller of the two conference rooms where the Seven held their meetings when they had visitors.

She stopped dead in her tracks right inside the entrance, feeling a wash of incredulity run over her and paused, paralyzed. Eight pairs of eyes fixed themselves unblinkingly on her pale face as Riley and the Seven carefully watched her startled expression.

Rowan decided she had never in her life seen a collection of more handsome, powerful, and deadly butches. She felt like a little tiny mouse trapped by a bunch of tomcats.

"Come on, *dulzura*." Bryn's gentle voice roused her from her paralysis as Bryn carefully wrapped her arms protectively around Rowan from behind. "They don't bite, baby. Not much, anyway, unless there's a reason for it."

"Rowan. Sweetheart." Teagan's soft voice broke through her torpor and she looked with relief at her friend. "Come on and have a seat, okay?" Teagan looked at her colorless face, concerned, and pulled out a chair at the conference room table for her. "No worries, my friend. Everyone has been seriously excited about meeting you, sweetheart. Did you have a good Christmas? Mama Armstrong is awesome, isn't she?"

Teagan kept her chatter light as she pantomimed a glass of water to Trillian, who caught a bottle of water Riley tossed to her and sat it down at Rowan's seat after she'd opened it.

Rowan sat down where Bryn guided her and sighed in relief as Riley, Trill, and Teagan's kind, worried faces came into view.

"I'm okay," she finally said quietly and smiled a bit.

"But...next time, warn a girl, okay? I don't think any of you has any idea of what an impact seeing you all collectively has, especially if someone is not prepared. A bad person would just stroke the freak out right on the spot. Annnd probably has."

There were a few chuckles as everyone in the room started to relax when Rowan grew more settled.

When everyone was finally in their seat, Bryn began.

"This, as you all know, is Rowan Holland." Bryn sat down next to her and moved her chair as close as she could so she could wrap her arm around Rowan's shoulders.

"We all knew your dad, *dulzura*." Bryn gave her a serious look.

Rowan let her surprised gaze drift around the room and saw the warm, gentle, respectful gazes directed back at her.

"Every single person in this room also had the highest regard for him, and there isn't one of us here who wouldn't kill to protect you as a result. Your dad gave each of us the absolute best of what he was during our time in the Marine Corps and now it's time for us to return the favor."

Bryn stroked her arm. "He may not be physically walking this earth anymore, *dulzura*, but he'll still know that each one of us has vowed to protect you always."

There were decisive nods from everyone in the room as Rowan smiled tremulously at them with thanks in her eyes.

Bryn squeezed her hand and gestured around the table. "First, I want everyone to introduce themselves and then we'll talk more about this fuckwit and where we want to go from here."

Volunteering first, Teagan raised her hand and Bryn nodded at her, which made Rowan feel a lot more comfortable as well.

"I feel like I'm the luckiest one here, Ro, because we've already gotten to know each other over the past ten days or so." Teag smiled at Rowan in her playful, warm way, then looked at the rest of the Seven. "Rowan is fucking *awesome*, so I can't wait until the rest of you get to know her too. *Total* little sister material. Well, unless you're Bryn." She smirked at her friend.

Rowan blushed and then actually laughed when Teagan added, "If any of you fuckers think you're stealing the Rowan bodyguard detail from me, think again."

Teagan grinned, then grew serious. "For the record, Rowan... I'm Teagan Malloy. I'm the APS Chief Communications Engineer. My team specializes in electrical systems and in telecommunications, which involves things like radio broadcast, computer networks, phone networks, and the Internet." She looked at Bryn. "I figured we would keep these short and sweet so Ro's head doesn't explode."

Bryn agreed.

"Good idea, Teag. I want Rowan to spend a day with each of you so she can get a deeper understanding of what each of you does, but this will be good for now."

Next up was Casey, whom Rowan remembered from her tour day. She smiled at Casey in recognition.

"I'm Casey Christiansen, Rowan," said the platinum blond with the bright blue eyes. "I'm the MMA expert and Krav Maga team lead. In case you're not aware, MMA stands for mixed martial arts. Mixed martial arts is a full-contact combat sport made up from various combat sports and martial arts from around the world. My team delivers that training to all the rest of the APS associates, which means we have a legit excuse to beat the shit out of our teammates." She nodded to the butch next to her and grinned as Rowan burst out laughing.

"I'm Kennedy Weston," said the brown-haired APS team lead with dark blue eyes who looked at Rowan intently. "Everyone usually calls me Kenn. I was the one who was up in DC when we heard about your friend, Mary-Kate, so I went to Woodbridge to do a little investigating." Her dark blue eyes iced. "She'll be fine, Rowan, but I was fucking *outraged*."

"Teagan said," Rowan muttered softly, looking at Kennedy in gratitude for her anger on behalf of her friend.

Kenn blew out her breath and continued. "I'm the Armory Master at APS, sweetheart. I maintain the Cage where our assault rifles, pistols, ammunition, parts, and accessories are stored."

Rowan's eyes widened.

"I'm also in charge of our shooting range. I've already told the chief there that I can set you all up with whatever you need: pistol drills, rapid reload practice, you just let me know." Rowan nodded shyly in thanks.

Trillian was next and Rowan smiled at her, happy to see another familiar face.

"It's so good to see you again, Rowan." Trill's eyes were soft and her dimples were on full display.

"I'm Trillian Dacanay and my team handles 'information security analysts,' which is just a fancy title for hackers, computer forensics, cryptographers—anything that falls under the data analysis and technology realms. I also handle the client monitoring teams."

She smiled smugly. "And you motherfuckers should know my team and I are going to get the opportunity to work with Rowan closely at some point, since she is about the best predictive data analyst on the fucking planet and APS can use her skill set on occasion."

The rest of the team just stared at Trill, who didn't lose her smug expression.

"I'm Jaime Quintero," said a black-haired butch with dark brown eyes and a slight Hispanic accent, whose coloring was almost identical to Bryn's. "I'm our physical security risk assessment expert. My team sneaks into buildings, picks locks, and works on conning people so they grant them access to restricted areas, etc. It can be great fun.

"We basically focus on testing actual *physical* security. We work closely with Trill and her team, who focus more on digital security, to try and outsmart each other."

I'm better, she mouthed at Rowan, making her laugh again, while Trill responded with her middle finger.

A calm, handsome butch with light brown hair and kind hazel eyes smiled gently at Rowan.

"I'm Drew Hollister," she said quietly. "I am our lead 'counterintelligence' expert. Basically, we mainly protect anyone or anything that falls under the APS umbrella from the opposition or anyone else that would like to infiltrate us. Our main skill set, however, is more on the 'darker' side of the organization here, which Bryn tells me she hasn't had an opportunity to explain to you yet."

"We are going to have that conversation very soon, the three of us." Bryn looked at Drew and she nodded, smiling reassuringly at Rowan, who was looking a bit confused.

"And last, but not least…drum roll, please." There were groans in the room as an auburn-haired butch—who had light green eyes with gold flecks—looked at her mischievously. "I'm Blake Seibert. I'm the gaming simulator expert."

Rowan frowned, mystified. "Gaming? As in, you play videogames all day?"

Blake smiled at her. "We do, sort of. We've designed and we sustain the most realistic combat simulators anywhere. My team has developed the absolute best first-person shooters anywhere, meaning we can simulate weapons-based combat in a first-person perspective with full-sized enemy combatants.

"After we create the sims, all of our associates are put through mock drills in our lab, testing their speed, reaction times, accuracy, things like that, against the sim models. Developing our sims was also how we figured out how to mimic marksmanship quals."

Rowan's jaw dropped.

Seeing they had come to the end of the introductions, Rowan regarded the Seven for a long, silent minute.

"Wow," she said softly. "Just…I don't know what to say. Every single one of you is so immensely talented, it leaves me speechless."

She looked at Blake and then at Kennedy. "You should both be prepared for my sister, Kelly, to come crashing down on top of you two the minute she gets here."

"She is an expert shot—seriously like a 392 on Marine Corps service pistol qualification simulations with my dad." 400 was a perfect score.

Rowan blushed scarlet. "Actually, what my dad always said was that Kelly could shoot the balls off an ant at thirty paces." The entire room cracked up.

"I will totally look forward to it, Ro," Blake said, then she paused. "I'm sorry, I didn't even ask. Is calling you Ro okay?"

"Everyone does," Rowan assured her. "It's perfectly fine."

"You can also call her sweetheart," said Teagan with a wicked grin. "Trill and I have already awarded her that nickname, too."

Rowan cast her eyes heavenward.

"However…" Teagan rapidly turned serious. "Now, we need to talk about the situation with this limp-dicked motherfucker and make a plan."

Chapter 15

"We do." Bryn caressed Rowan's arm soothingly.

"Why don't you tell us all about how you met him and what your interactions with him have been like to date?"

"All you have to do is talk, *dulzura*. We will ask questions if we need to, to clarify something or to ask for a little bit more information, but you don't need to worry about a thing. Just talk and let *us* worry about directing the conversation if necessary, okay?"

So Rowan talked. She told them about Dino Coravani coming to Grayson Financial, where she was working, to interview the staff because Mr. Grayson had suspected one of their clients was trying to defraud the company.

It was, Rowan told them, a pretty normal conversation. Coravani didn't ask her anything personal, she said. He wanted to know what her role was within the company, and asked about the interactions she had had with this particular client.

In other words, she didn't feel he asked her anything that was outside the scope of a normal investigation of this type. Things started to get weird, Rowan said, about a week after her interview. Coravani showed up, unannounced, and asked her to lunch.

When she found out the investigation was still ongoing, she told him that she didn't feel it was appropriate for her to go to lunch with the investigator in charge of the case. She figured that would be the end of it.

She figured wrong.

About one week later, Coravani popped up again and said that his participation in the case had ended. He asked her to lunch again.

She explained to him that she was gay and didn't have an interest in having lunch with a man, but wished him well. He smiled and left without a fuss.

After that conversation, he had seemed to redouble his efforts after she had told him she was gay.

He came the next week.

And the next.

She had asked the staff at the front desk to run interference for her, but it didn't seem to matter. He always found a way to come back to her office to ask her to lunch.

Rowan said she was getting a little bit paranoid, but she never saw him when she was walking to her car in the evening nor did she ever see him near her house.

Her sister, Kelly, who was an information analyst for the CIA, did some sleuthing and found out Coravani had sexual assault allegations against him, although no one had ever formally come forward to file a complaint.

Kelly had finally persuaded Rowan to leave Woodbridge and come to Florida because Rowan's best friend from college, Clementine, was from the greater Tampa Bay area.

They found Whimsy and Rowan had been here since the second week of December. Kelly, unfortunately, was unable to take a leave from her job until probably February.

Rowan had just found out from Bryn that Coravani had apparently gone to her old job and had beaten one of her female co-workers there to find out where Rowan had gone, since Kelly had covered her tracks so well, he couldn't get any information on her that way.

As Rowan looked up, with tears in her eyes, nine faces with the most unhappy expressions greeted her. "Sweetheart." Kenn's voice was extremely soft. Rowan looked at her with a despondent face. "How long did this go on, him harassing you like this?"

"I think about six months." You could have heard a pin drop and the air grew suffocating. "We filed a complaint with the police department, but because Coravani was a former cop and they apparently protect their own, nothing was ever done. They wouldn't even send out a patrol car to do occasional drive-bys even though we asked for one on two separate occasions." They could hear the frustration in her voice. "Kelly said that if Dad was still alive, he would have thrown his effing butt into the Potomac."

"That he would have," muttered Blake savagely. "And probably with long-range sniper rifle holes." Jaime, who was sitting next to her, snorted without humor.

Bryn tightened her arm around Rowan. "Is there anything else you can think of, baby? If not, you can always tell me at home if something occurs to you."

"Right now? No." Rowan shook her head.

"Okay then. In the meantime, I'm going to have Daniela come and get you and take you to the employee lounge with her. I'll have Gracie or Effie cover the phones so she can hang out with you for a little while.

"Teag will take you to the Dream Creamery when the team is done here, *dulzura*." Bryn leaned over and kissed her temple.

After Daniela had come and collected Rowan, and the two women had left following Rowan's sweet and sincere thanks to all of them for their time and attention, the atmosphere in the room had changed in a flash.

"Are. You. Fucking. *KIDDING*. Me right now?" Casey was so angry and her voice was so icy mean, Coravani would be a dead man from Casey's words alone.

"That sweet woman." Jaime's low voice was full of venom. She looked at Bryn with menace. "*Broki*, this piece of shit has to go."

"Rowan. Mary-Kate. Who knows how many other women this motherfucker has beaten or assaulted or stalked?" Kennedy was just as livid.

"It's even worse than you think." Trill looked at them with barely concealed rage, then looked at her laptop. "While we were finishing up talking with Rowan, some intel came back that I've been waiting on. Apparently, there were approximately eleven unconfirmed sexual assault reports over a five-year period from women who were directly or indirectly involved in cases where Coravani was the private investigator." Trill spoke through gritted teeth as a low growl rumbled through the room. "The worst part? Four of those women have since disappeared without a trace. Their friends, their families, their co-workers…no one has seen or heard from them since they were reported missing."

Bryn felt icy fingers trace down her spine as Riley and the Seven froze for a moment in utter disbelief.

Then Bryn snapped into action.

"Trill. Get a schedule together with double coverage on Rowan, 6 a.m. to 6 p.m. Four-hour shifts, one associate inside and one outside, only members of the Seven. She's with me at night, so we won't worry about anyone doing overnights, at least for now. Everyone will technically have two days off to use however they want, although I already know none of you will use them for personal time."

Trill was already typing rapidly on her laptop.

"Drew. Chase this motherfucker down into hell if you have to, but I want to know where the fuck he is and where the fuck he's been hiding." Drew was texting swiftly on her DarkMatter Katim phone.

"Casey," Bryn continued, "you're up to bat first as secondary coverage for Rowan until Trill can get the schedule done. I'm going to go out to the employee lounge with you and Teagan, and tell Rowan we decided as a team that we wanted two of you helping out for now. I don't ever lie to Rowan or hide things from her, but I want to wait to tell her everything we found out today until we have ourselves organized. Everyone else, keep on with your normal activities, but your eyes and ears should remain *wide* open."

Bryn's voice was icy. "Anything, and I mean *anything* that strikes you as out of place, no matter how fucking stupid you think it is, report it. Ear comms on 24/7 until this fucker is caught. I want open 2-way channels between all of us. Teag, we need to make sure we have disruptors set in case this fuck decides to get cute and tries to intercept our communications." Teagan nodded in acknowledgment. "Personally, I don't think he's that fucking intelligent, but I don't want to take any chances."

Bryn blew out a deep breath. "I also want an associate on Clem at all times now, not just at night, because we know the son of a bitch is good for using Rowan's friends to get to her."

"Already done." Teagan struggled for a brief minute with keeping her cool. "Remy has been with Clem this whole time and Kenn has Dakota on her now, too." Remy was Teagan's "second" and Dakota was Kennedy's. "Rem texted to say they've got Clem covered. She and Dakota are going to switch on 12-hour shifts until they can get a third."

"Teag, tell Remy that Campbell is going to text her; she'll be their third for now," Casey informed her. Campbell was on Casey's crew. "Okay." Bryn blew out another breath. "Clementine's covered. Rowan's covered. Drew is smoking the fucker out. Jaime, how do you feel about helping Trill out and digging into his background?"

"Hand me a shovel, *ese*." Jaime's smile was cold.

WHIMSICAL HAVEN

¥ ¥ ¥ ¥ ¥

That night, Rowan was quiet as she processed everything Bryn had just finished telling her.

She hadn't thought anything about it at first when Casey had come out with Bryn and Teagan when their meeting was over, and had announced she was joining their playdate at the Dream Creamery because, as Casey put it, "That fucker, Malloy, doesn't get to have all the fun."

But when they had reached the Dream Creamery, Casey had disappeared when Teagan and Rowan had gone inside.

Through the back door window, Rowan had seen Casey intently scanning the roof of the building, while Teagan had casually mentioned they were going to have the back door replaced with a steel door that had no glass.

Then Clementine, who had already been there for a while, had introduced Rowan to an APS associate named Remy—Teagan's "second," Clem had explained—whom she said would be rotating with a couple of other APS associates to "keep an eye on her," as Clem had put it.

Rowan's suspicions had *really* flared, however, when Teagan had kept texting with a grim face non-stop all day, all without ever moving more than five feet away from Rowan's side. And at the end of the day, to her shock, it wasn't Casey who met them outside, but Kenn.

Now, Rowan lay curled up on Bryn's shoulder as Bryn brought her up to speed on everything that had happened after Rowan had left the meeting that morning.

She understood Bryn's logic in not telling her until they had everything in place and figured out. She would have done the same thing.

At the end of the day, what good would it have done for them to tell her and then not have all the answers to what she really wanted to know: Where was that piece of crap and how could they stop him?

Bryn and her people had been busy over the past nine hours.

APS didn't keep their own plane, but they had resources from whom they could charter a private jet when needed. One of Jaime's associates and one of Trill's had subsequently flown up to Virginia this afternoon to dig into Coravani's background and find out more on his sexual assault and harassment activities.

Drew, Bryn told her, was fucking *seething* at the cold digital trail Coravani had left in Whimsy so far. When Rowan showed surprise that kind, quiet Drew was capable of such fury, Bryn laughed.

"You need to understand something, *dulzura*," Bryn said. "All *you* are mainly ever going to see from the Seven is kindness and gentleness. They all adore you already and the last thing any of them will *ever* want to do is scare you or let you see their tempers. A good woman in 'APS Badass World,' as Clem calls it, is to be protected and cherished and respected. Femmes can be some of the toughest creatures around—and we know it—but it still goes against every instinct in a hard butch to put one at risk. It's just how we're wired. So, Drew shows you her quiet and kind side, because that's the Drew she is with you. That's the Drew she *wants* to be with you. But I can tell you right now that Drew Hollister might well be the most dangerous one of the Seven."

Bryn stroked Rowan's bare breast.

"We call her our 'counterintelligence' expert, but that's not strictly true. Have you ever heard of the dark web or darknet, *dulzura*?"

"I've heard of it, but I couldn't tell you what it means." Rowan's words were cautious.

"Let's see." Bryn thought for a moment. "When you normally surf the Internet, the portion of what you see and access is what is called the clear web or, in other cases, the deep web. The clear web—which is sometimes also called the *bright web*—contains sites that are searchable by search engines like Google or Yahoo, and are publicly available. The deep web contains sites that can't be found just by Googling them, like some company sites that require a password, things like that. Okay?"

Rowan nodded. "Okay. That's easy enough."

"The *dark* web, however, is a very small sliver of the Internet that can make anyone and anything invisible. You need a special 'anonymity browser' to access it. There's no way to 'accidentally' stumble across the dark web, *dulzura*. There's a lot more to it, but the point is, you can keep yourself completely anonymous and completely untraceable on the dark web if you know what to do. Just because of its nature, there is a lot of chaotic and illegal activity that goes on there sometimes, baby. You can buy illegal drugs or weapons, purchase hacking services or cyber terrorism services, engage with a variety of cybercriminals. It's often not a very nice place and it can be dangerous as hell."

Bryn smiled slightly.

"Drew is at home there, *dulzura*, and actually has quite a reputation in certain circles."

Rowan's eyes rounded.

"The two of us want to have a private conversation with you about this more in-depth, probably within the next few days, because she is concerned you will be afraid of her if you find out what she actually does for us. Being afraid of Drew is something you don't ever need to be, though, baby." Bryn kissed her temple. "In other words, Drew is probably the most dangerous one of us all, but you personally are safer with her than almost anyone else in the world. She would utterly obliterate anyone who tried to harm one single hair on your head."

Bryn's phone rang. She dropped a kiss on Rowan's head and sat up before answering.

"Jaime. You have a status?" Bryn listened intently for a couple of minutes. Her face grew more and more forbidding as the conversation went on. "I'm switching to my comm so you can talk to the two of them at the same time. I want the rest of the Seven to hear this, too."

Bryn tossed her phone down, then touched her ear.

"Who's there from Trill's team? ...Darcy?" Darcy was Trill's second. "Ask Darce what the security on the laptop looks like... Child's play? ... She's in? Tell her I need her to copy all files and photos onto a flash drive, but to leave everything on the laptop completely undisturbed."

Bryn's face was dark and intent.

"Who from your team is there? ... Uh huh ... Can Morgan access that locker? ... Okay... Tell her I need film on EVERYTHING that's in it, Jaime, but she is to leave the contents exactly as she's found them... She's in? ... Okay... Okay."

Bryn paused for a long minute as she listened, her face so full of savagery that Rowan was actually frightened.

"They need to leave everything just as they found it, *broki*, and wipe any forensic trails. Given Rowan's experience with them, we need to explode this bomb so the dickheads in that department who are covering this pussy's ass are blown sky-high...uh huh...uh huh...call me back later on my cell."

Bryn touched her comm and sat for a minute, deep in thought, her face still savage. Rowan laid on the pillow next to her, scarcely daring to breathe.

"*Dulzura*." Bryn's voice was gentle even if the expression on her face was anything but. "We need to talk."

¥¥¥¥¥

Bryn lay back down next to Rowan and gathered her into her arms. "I told you there was no need to be afraid of anyone at APS—including me—and I meant it. I've never been as pissed in my life as I am right now, and you should still *never* be afraid, even when I can't control my mood right away sometimes."

She nuzzled Rowan's hair until she felt Rowan relax into her arms, and then spoke. "I told you earlier, *dulzura*, that four women who had said they were sexually assaulted by Coravani had gone missing?"

Rowan nodded.

"Two of our associates accessed his apartment tonight and found personal effects that appeared to belong to those women, stored in a locker."

Rowan gasped in shock.

"That's not the worst of it. Among others, they also found *hundreds* of photos of you, Rowan. Pictures of you walking to your car, coming out of the grocery store, arriving home from work…every day, every activity, every facet of your life."

Rowan's breathing stilled, tears welling up in her eyes.

"Most of them were digital and on his laptop, but several were printed out and…were hung up in his bedroom, *dulzura*." Rowan made a gagging sound.

Bryn wrapped her tightly in her arms as Rowan burrowed into them and started to cry. Bryn tried to swallow her rage, but was unsuccessful.

"Those women who are missing…their families…Bryn…Bryn…" Rowan shook with grief and anger as she sobbed harder. "I'm scared," she hiccupped with emotion, "and of course, I'm concerned about m-m-me, but I just can't get past what h-h-he must have done to those women."

Bryn held her and rubbed her back, letting her cry.

For the first time ever, she was helpless in her rage, knowing that her woman was hurting and scared, but that there was also nothing she could do to make it better at the moment.

"Even with all of this, I have *never* felt safer in my life, Bryn," Rowan said when her crying had finally slowed.

Bryn was completely unprepared for Rowan's words.

"I have you and Riley and the Seven to protect me, and I just dare him to find a way past any of you. *I. Dare. Him.*"

Bryn, astounded, held her woman tighter.

"But those women had *nothing*, Bryn. They were all alone, with no one but this lunatic at the end." Rowan hiccupped again. "I am so freaking *mad*. I *hate* him." Her chest heaved. She raised her head, her face tear-stained and blotchy, and suddenly, her eyes narrowed with wrath. "You and Riley and the Seven? You *get* this *motherfucker*, Bryn. You make it so that he can never hurt another woman again. *EVER*." Her voice wobbled in sorrow and outrage as she hiccupped a third time.

Bryn froze in shock.

Her woman *swore*?

Her. Rowan. Swore. Used a curse word she would normally never dream of using because her grief and her sorrow and her outrage were that goddamned deep over this prick and what he had done.

Bryn carefully wrapped Rowan up in her arms and held her until she calmed, rocking her and rubbing her back and kissing her until she knew she was asleep, feeling a savagery that she had never known before.

Bryn placed a final kiss on the top of Rowan's sleeping blonde head with steel in her soul.

"You want us to get this motherfucker, baby?" she whispered to her beautiful woman. "Then you got it. It's time for us to unleash hell, *dulzura*."

Chapter 16

"Rowan *swore?*" Bryn's words hit Teagan like a thunderbolt and her jaw dropped to the ground.

"My baby swore. She said, and I quote, *'You get this motherfucker, Bryn. You make it so that he can never hurt another woman again.*" Bryn, deceptively casual, leaned against a desk in the Bunker, the office of the Seven.

"Holy. Fucking. *Shit*. I don't even know what to do with that, cuz." Teagan dragged her hand through her hair and exhaled in a loud gust of air.

"I don't get it." Blake was mystified, looking between Bryn and Teagan. The rest of the Seven, except for Trillian, looked equally puzzled.

Trill crossed her arms. She had come up from the Recon Room for an impromptu meeting.

"Rowan doesn't swear, Blake. Not *ever*," Trill revealed. "I asked Clem about it one day and she said it was a quirk Rowan's always had. Kelly once told her she's been like that since they were younger. She doesn't care if anyone else around her swears, but she won't swear herself. No trauma, nothing ever happened that traumatized her about swearing, Clem said, it's just this little idiosyncrasy she's always had. Lord knows that Clem swears like a sailor and I guess Kelly isn't too far behind her, but Rowan doesn't and never did. It normally wouldn't be a big deal, but the fact that she actually said *'motherfucker'*..." Her eyes found Bryn.

Bryn looked at them all with a false sense of calm. "The fact that my woman swore, that she said the word *'motherfucker'* when she has never sworn in her whole entire life, that she was crying like her heart was broken, *mi corillo*, has me right on the fucking edge."

She switched her gaze to Riley, who was watching her closely. "I'm chill for right now, Riles, but you should know it won't take much to put me in lockdown. If Rowan wakes up calm, then I'll be good. But if she cries again like she did earlier, I will burn the fucking world down. Just so you know." Riley nodded in acknowledgment.

The rest of the team regarded them with dawning comprehension.

"Then I think we need to give our new little sister what she wants and drag this prick into hell where he belongs." Casey's smile was icy.

"Something else you should know." Bryn folded her arms. "During all this emotional upheaval I had with Rowan today, one thing she did say is that she has never felt safer in her life than she does with all of us." Bryn smiled slightly. "She said she has all nine of us to protect her and she dared Coravani with her next breath to find a way past us."

There was a long minute of silence.

"Jesus." Blake rubbed the back of her neck. "She's just... Fuck me." She looked at Bryn, focusing her attention back on Coravani. "So how are we going to explode the bomb that is finally going to put this fucking asshole on radar?"

"Darcy and Morgan should be back any time. We are going to assemble a 'care package' of some of the information we retrieved from Coravani's laptop and explode the package simultaneously across local news stations up there," Bryn informed them.

"Darcy changed all the administrator permissions and then locked the laptop so that only she can unlock it remotely," Trill shared. "That way, neither Mr. Dickhead nor any of his friends can go in and wipe the hard drive."

"To protect against physical threat, Morgan had Darcy install a laptop alarm that will *blare* and blow your fucking eardrums out if anyone unplugs the power cable, the mouse is moved or unplugged, or the laptop is shut down," added Jaime.

"Nothing the two of them did interfered with any of the data on the hard drive itself, so no one can make a case for evidence tampering, especially since they completely wiped their forensic trails," said Trill. "I think once Mr. Dickhead's friends realize they were protecting a sexual predator and probable murderer, they are going to run for the hills rather than risk personal exposure. They aren't going to put their cocks on the line for a former cop."

"Speaking of which, do we have any idea why he's a *former*?" asked Bryn.

"No, but I think it would be an excellent idea for us to find out," stated Riley.

"We'll wait until Darcy and Morgan check in, then they can work with the rest of Trill's team to get the package assembled," Bryn continued.

"I'd like to explode it at 6:00 a.m. It's shift change at the police station, so things will already be slightly chaotic there and they will be broadsided when reporters start calling for quotes and information. Morning local news broadcasts are typically at 7:00 a.m., so that will give the news stations time to run this down and to write a 'breaking news' broadcast lead. There will be reporters clamoring at Coravani's apartment. No one who initially tries to access the laptop will be able to get in and the alarm will blare if anyone tries to move it."

Bryn ran her hand through her hair.

"Darcy will unlock the laptop remotely once it is removed by the police digital forensics technicians and out of the reach of the officers. At that point, we won't need to maintain contact with the laptop anymore."

Suddenly, Bryn pulled out her cell phone and looked at it.

"Rowan's awake." Bryn's face was impassive, although everyone saw her shoulders relax the tiniest fraction.

She rapidly sent a return text and then addressed the crew. "It's midnight. Darcy and Morgan will be getting the package ready for delivery at 6:00 a.m. I don't know if there is much else we can do until the morning ourselves. Let's plan to meet back here at 6:00 a.m. and we will pick up where we left off."

"How does Rowan seem?" Riley watched her twin carefully.

Bryn shook her head. "She sounds like she's in decent shape, although I won't know for sure until I can see her myself." She showed the barest edge of a smile. "It is hard to remember sometimes how resilient femmes really are."

"I will see you all tomorrow morning at 6:00 a.m. It's time to take this motherfucker down."

¥¥¥¥¥

December 27

The next morning, Bryn was sitting with Rowan in her office when there was a knock at the door.

When Bryn had gotten back to her apartment the night before, she had found a calm, although still slightly shaky, Rowan. Rowan had thrown her arms around Bryn and thanked her fiercely for her support, saying that she was doing okay and she would be fine. Bryn had taken her woman to bed in response and had possessed Rowan with a passion and a ferocity that had startled the both of them.

In the very early morning hours, Bryn had unapologetically broken one of her cardinal rules and had skipped her run, instead staying wrapped around her woman until it was time to meet the rest of her team.

The package with the evidence of Coravani's activities had exploded at 6:00 a.m. with spectacular success.

Reporters were swarming, digging for information, smelling blood in the water as the story of the former police officer who was allegedly stalking and sexually assaulting women came to light. The families of the missing women were on every news channel that morning, demanding an investigation by the police. Under fire, the beleaguered police chief had made a statement, promising a full investigation.

Although there were rumors, according to the news channels, that some police officers had refused to give potential victims help when they had asked for it because Coravani was a former police officer, the chief had disavowed any knowledge and assured the public his department held the safety of the city's citizens as "their highest priority."

Darcy had remotely unlocked the laptop as it was taken by the forensics team, its contents safe and untouched.

Coravani had still not surfaced digitally, much to Drew's displeasure. She told Bryn she suspected he still had not left the area, but was making sure he couldn't be tracked by using any kind of an electronic device, including a cell phone.

Trillian agreed he probably had a burner phone.

Jaime had her crew doing physical reconnaissance in Whimsy, while Drew had descended into the dark web, putting out feelers for information there.

Bryn had decided that, while they were waiting for information to come back, this would be a good time for her and Drew and Rowan to talk.

"Come in," Bryn answered, caressing Rowan's shoulder with her hand.

Drew came in and smiled at Rowan, her kind hazel eyes crinkling at the corners. She took a seat in the chair across from the couch and eased back, her demeanor relaxed, but watchful.

At 5'10", she was only slightly shorter than Bryn and, as with the rest of the Seven, she had a highly developed physique. Her shoulder-length, thick, light brown hair was caught back at her nape with a thin band. She had hazel eyes like Rowan, but hers were a trifle greener and darker.

Like the rest of the APS Seven, she was absolutely gorgeous.

Seeing that Drew was about to speak, Rowan hastily jumped into conversation before Drew or Bryn could say anything. "I need to say something before we get started, you two, okay?"

Rowan looked first at Drew, then at Bryn. They glanced at each other and nodded.

"Drew." She took a deep breath and looked directly at the silent, handsome butch sitting across from her. "You are one of the quietest and kindest people I've met since I've moved to Whimsy."

Rowan focused tentatively on Drew's mild, but still-watchful eyes.

"I honestly can't see how what Bryn has told me about you so far and about what we are going to discuss meshes with the person I am starting to know." She paused. "It doesn't compute in my head. But something Bryn said to me yesterday kind of put everything into perspective for me and helped everything to make a little bit more sense. Bryn said you show me your quiet and kind side because that's the Drew you want me to know. I guess the rest of the Seven do the same thing. But, with you... Bryn also said you just might be the most dangerous one of them all."

Drew cut her eyes at Bryn, her face impassive.

Rowan paused again, seeming to search for the right words.

"I think…I think I actually understand how that contradiction can exist because of how Bryn explained it to me. More than that, Drew, I also think I'm really okay with it."

Rowan took another deep breath. "Bryn says I am safer with you than almost anyone else in the world, so I figure if you have scary stuff to tell me about what you do for APS, it's not anything I personally need to worry about."

Drew's face relaxed.

"I'm glad to hear you say that, Rowan." Her voice held equal measures of relief and comfort. "I don't ever want you to see 'Scary Drew' and I can't think of any reason why you should ever have to see her. The only reason I can think of is if you were being threatened. And I can promise you…I will exterminate whatever is causing that threat to you on the spot."

Rowan dipped her head in acknowledgment and relaxed against Bryn, at ease after Drew's words.

Drew continued. "Some of what I'm going to share with you, sweetheart, includes information that is a bit, shall we say, unsavory."

"I think that first, we need to more thoroughly explain that piece of our business to Rowan," Bryn said to Drew. Drew nodded in agreement.

Rowan frowned. "Your business is protection, risk assessment, and bodyguard services for women. Right?"

"You aren't wrong." Drew smiled slightly. "But that's the part of our business that's public and those services we provide are common knowledge. However, there are other parts that are a little more clandestine and not so well-known, and that's where me and my crew come to play."

Drew leaned forward and rested her elbows on her knees.

"Various organizations sometimes contract with us to apprehend individuals who are not the most upstanding citizens, Ro. They aren't formally on the books of any law enforcement agency as wanted because it isn't an official law enforcement agency who wants them. They are more along the lines of people who have defrauded or double-crossed or swindled others, individuals or organizations who take a very dim view of being fucked over."

Drew kept her eyes on Rowan.

"They have managed to evade apprehension for a variety of reasons and we are the ones these organizations call when other attempts to detain them have failed. We are very careful about the jobs we take, sweetheart." Drew was clear. "We will not get involved with actions against average citizens or people we term 'innocents.' In other words, we aren't interested in going after desperate human beings who maybe made some bad choices and got involved with the wrong people."

Drew stretched out her legs, still relaxed.

"We go after scumbags with criminal histories who scammed someone or took something that didn't belong to them from someone else, and now they're playing it cute and hiding. The individuals or organizations they've fucked over want them found and turned over so they can deal with them personally."

Rowan was still.

"My formal title at APS is 'Counterintelligence Expert,' Rowan. Officially, my team and I protect APS and its assets from our opposition or from anyone who might want to penetrate our organization. I do have one APS associate on my team who is in charge of that, but any threat is minimal and the work involved to contain that is minimal as well."

Drew's gaze was level.

"Unofficially, though, sweetheart? My title is 'Tracker' and my code name is 'The Shadow.'"

Chapter 17

"Code name?" Rowan said slowly. "I'm sorry, Drew. I don't quite understand."

"Don't be sorry, sweetheart," Drew replied. "There is no reason why you should understand." She regarded Rowan seriously. "You understand what the dark web is, yes?"

Rowan nodded. "Bryn explained it all."

Drew steepled her fingers. "Good. Then you'll understand why 'The Shadow' dwells there and accepts or rejects these kinds of contracts strictly on the dark web. I'm sure you want to know, 'Why do you do it?' Right?"

"Yes." Rowan was frank. "You are in the protection business, so why would you even care about people like these? They don't sound very nice."

Drew exchanged a smile with Bryn.

"About eight years ago, Dara, my second, happened to run into a guy she knew who was frustrated as hell because some asshole had ripped off a bunch of money from his organization and was in hiding. They knew he was still in the area, but no one could seem to find him. This acquaintance couldn't go to the police because the business they did was all under the radar and not exactly legal, so he didn't have any kind of recourse other than to smoke this guy out, then shake him down for the money. Dara called me about the conversation she'd had with her acquaintance, which had intrigued her. I talked to Bryn about it, and we decided to look into this missing asshole a little further."

"What we found," Drew shook her head, a grim look on her face, "was an asshole of absolutely epic proportions. He was about two years in arrears of child support payments. He had stolen from friends and family, including his 78-year-old mother, who was on a fixed income. In short, there was nothing good or salvageable about this prick. So, 'The Shadow' was born, Ro. Dara went back to this guy and told him she knew someone who could find the asshole for them for a price. They negotiated and, five days later, that prick's beaten, unconscious body was dumped on the front porch of Dara's acquaintance, courtesy of me and my crew."

Drew leaned back in her chair again.

"'The Shadow' now has a reputation of being able to find and deliver anyone in our seven-county area. We turn down more work than we accept because we have a very strict criteria for contracts we will take," she said. "Bottom line, the target has to be someone who, in addition to what we are being paid to track them for, has a pretty grievous history against a female or females, one that we can thoroughly verify. A total bottom feeder, for lack of a better term. In the beginning, we had a few dicks try to slide some potential targets at us who weren't the type of targets we'd made it clear we would accept." Drew smiled coldly. "Needless to say, it didn't end well for them. Some of the money we make is put into a special account. We track down the women who were harmed or abused by these fucks and give anonymous donations to those victims, especially the ones with children."

Rowan's jaw dropped.

"Drew! Why would this be scary stuff if you are taking aim at idiots who have done bad things to women and trying to give those ladies at least a little restitution?" Rowan demanded.

"Because, sweetheart," Drew said steadily. "The dark web can be a violent place. What we do often gets violent as well. The people we interact with are anything but honorable and our missions are dangerous. This felt like something we needed to do, but make no mistake, Ro. This is where 'Scary Drew' comes out to play."

Rowan was silent for a long time as she gnawed on the corner of one fingernail, thinking.

"Okay," she finally decided. "I can live with that. I'm going with that whole, 'The ends justify the means,' thing."

She peeped at Drew from under her lashes. "As long as I don't have to run into 'Scary Drew' in a dark alley myself," she teased shyly.

Drew actually laughed out loud. "No, sweetheart, I don't think that will be a problem." After glancing at Bryn, she stood up, preparing to go.

"One more thing. I know it's Bryn's intent to have you spend a day with each one of us, Rowan, but neither of us wants you anywhere near the dark web or the people I meet there, so we aren't going to have a playdate. We'll go have dinner one night—you, me and Bryn—and make that our playdate instead." Drew smiled at her. "If you ever have questions or want to know something more about that side of the business, you or Bryn can text me at any time, but I think keeping you in the light is the most sensible approach."

Bryn also stood and pulled Rowan to her feet. "Drew is being tactful because she's not your butch, so I'll say what she's really thinking, *dulzura*: Don't make me turn you over my knee for playing where you shouldn't."

Rowan's eyes rounded, her jaw dropped open, and she huffed in indignation.

Drew and Bryn looked at each other knowingly with a slight smile as Drew shook Rowan's hand, then leaned over to kiss her cheek.

"Alpha butches spank, Rowan," Drew reminded her as she went to the door. "Bryn's entire management team would be 100% on her side for this one."

As Drew closed the door behind her, they heard a low laugh.

Rowan slammed her hands on her hips and was about to say something, her face irked, when Bryn captured her mouth with her own, effectively shutting her up.

"No arguments, *dulzura*," Bryn said softly when she released Rowan's mouth. "Even though there are some sites and places there that are just fine, the dark web is too unorganized and hazardous of a place for me to ever feel comfortable letting you traipse all over. Besides, baby, you have an ice cream shop and an art center to get ready, a grand opening to plan, and far too much to do to have time to worry about this shit." Bryn kissed her again, long and deep.

Rowan melted into Bryn's body. "All right," she muttered when Bryn finally released her. "Although," she huffed again, "if you weren't such a daggone good kisser, you wouldn't have such an easy time getting your own way."

¥¥¥¥¥

December 28

"That's what I'm thinking right now, Rowan."

Rowan, Clementine, and Nova sat at a table in Seashells, a popular local restaurant located on the corner of Cedar Key Boulevard and Beach Bay Drive, discussing the opening ice cream menu for the Dream Creamery.

Teagan and Remy sat a couple of tables away, but had refused the girls' invitation to join them. The three women had snickered when Teagan muttered that the idea of joining a "girly girls' lunch" made her hair stand up on end.

Nova had suggested two standard flavors, which would remain constant, and two artisanal flavors, which would change every season. The fifth flavor would be a "flavor of the week" special.

Rowan and Clem loved the idea.

"I have another idea if you're up for hearing it," mused Nova, thinking out loud. Rowan and Clem waited.

"A former classmate of mine is moving back to Whimsy. Delaney Sedgwick. She hooked up with this, oh my Goddess, this super psycho bitch-from-hell named Tina when we were in high school, and moved to Michigan with her about ten years ago, which is where Tina was originally from." Nova sighed.

"We've kept in touch all these years. Delaney stayed with Tina because Tina's mother, who was apparently always very good to Del, was really sick and if Delaney would have left, she wouldn't have trusted Tina to take good care of her. Tina's mom died a couple of weeks ago, the funeral was last week, so Delaney said she is fucking *out* and coming home," Nova continued. "The thing is, Del trained to be a pastry chef after she went to college, and that's what she does. And believe me, if her professional desserts are *anything* like what she used to make for us when we were all in high school, the woman is a fucking superstar."

"I guess this means she wants to find a position locally as a pastry chef somewhere?" Clem asked.

"No," Nova pondered, "she said she's tired and she needs to do nothing but be Delaney for a while." Rowan and Clem nodded in total understanding. "But," Nova said, "I know Del. She will sit on her ass for about two weeks max and then will be going batshit crazy. I bet if I asked her about making a couple of ice cream-compatible small bite desserts for the Dream Creamery opening, she would totally be interested."

Clem arched her eyebrows, intrigued. "When is she going to be back in Whimsy?"

"Thursday. She has a flight out Thursday morning, she hasn't said dick to Tina the Twat, she's packing nothing but two suitcases of clothes and some toiletries when Tina is at work—because she said that bitch could have *every*-fucking-thing—and then our girl is *herstory*."

Nova smiled.

"Her parents still own the house she grew up in and she can stay there with them for as long as she needs. Anyhow, it's just a thought, something for us to keep on the back burner." Nova waved her hands. "In the meantime, ladies, we have a grand opening to plan."

"Ember says they are actually ahead of schedule," Rowan reported. "I think we can safely go ahead and put together a list of people whom we can offer a spot as a visual artist for the grand opening."

"I know exactly who to ask for input, too," bounced Nova excitedly. "Alyssa Riker and Brooke Marino. They are both Whimsy girls. Alyssa is a very popular art therapist in Whimsy and Brooke is an *amazing* graphic designer. You two would have a lot in common, Ro. Brooke specializes in craft breweries. St. Petersburg is one of the top 10 craft beer cities in the U.S. and Brooke does a *lot* of that kind of design work around here. She knows good art, that's for sure."

Rowan was amazed. "But aren't they busy? I'm sure they are *totally* busy. I couldn't ask them to do something like this with such short notice. Nova!" She was appalled.

Nova grinned. "Welcome to small town life, city girl. We've all been friends since grade school and we all still live in Whimsy. Text

Tall, Dark, and Handsome and see if she's up for going out for cocktails here tomorrow night so you can meet them. Delaney won't be home yet, but at least you can meet the other two."

And, just like that... Brooke and Alyssa confirmed with excitement, Bryn responded with humor that she expected a "reward" for taking her woman out, Teagan asked Bryn wryly—after overhearing the plans—if she needed some butch back-up, and Nova and Clem vowed to have the entire patron population of Seashells in an uproar of excitement by the end of the night.

"How about chocolate and vanilla for standard flavors since those are what kids like. A lot of adults like plain flavors, too." Nova's face was dreamy as she went off on another Nova tangent. "But...a Chardonnay caramel with fudge brownie bits and...a raspberry habanero for our first two artisanal flavors. Annnd...hmmm." Nova thought for a moment. "I've got it. A kaffir lime gelato for our first flavor of the week, in honor of our grand opening."

Rowan and Clem stared at her with their mouths hanging open.

"What?" Nova stared back at them. "It's my bitch, Delaney, who's behind the eight-ball. Now, she gets to design desserts around *my* ice cream, not the other way around," she finished smugly.

"Right, because finding desserts that will be compatible with Chardonnay, caramel, fudge, raspberry, habanero peppers, and limes will be a fucking walk in the park," Clem muttered.

Nova snorted. "Child's play for Del, trust me."

WHIMSICAL HAVEN

Teagan appeared at their table with Remy, informed them she'd paid the bill, and reminded Rowan and Clem they had a meeting with Ember Renshaw and Nia Rosenberg in a half hour.

"Oh, pooh." Nova stuck her tongue out at Teagan, who shook her head with a grin and folded her powerful arms across her chest.

"You'll all be together soon enough, creating daily havoc for the rest of us," said Teagan unsympathetically as Nova smirked.

The three women hugged and said their goodbyes, then Nova scampered off down Beach Bay Drive while Rowan, Clem, Teagan, and Remy headed back to the Dream Creamery.

"It's starting to come together, Ro-Ro." Clem high-fived her best friend. "Yasssir! We are definitely lighting this bitch the fuck *up*."

Chapter 18

December 30

Rowan knocked tentatively on the door of the Bunker and waited quietly as she heard the sound of footsteps on the other side of the door.

Kenn, who had evidently been heading out, smiled when she answered the hesitant knock and saw who it was.

"Hey, sweetheart!" Kenn kissed Rowan on the cheek and hugged her. "Guess you're here to see that ugly motherfucker over there, right?" She chuckled and winked at Rowan when Teagan flipped her off over her shoulder without turning around. "I need to get down to the Cage so I will see you all later. Don't beat her up too badly… 'Kay, Ro?"

Rowan laughed as Kennedy headed out and turned to see Teagan smiling at her.

"Are you ready?" Teagan indicated the chair next to her that she had pulled over for Rowan. She frowned for a minute. "Where is Bryn, sweetheart? I thought she wanted to sit in on all your playdates."

"She does and she will be in as soon as she can, she said. She got a phone call she had to take and told me to come on in. She's just down the hall," Rowan revealed.

Teagan nodded. "Okay, then. It's not like that fucker couldn't teach this shit in her sleep, so she's not going to miss anything."

Rowan giggled.

Teagan began. "I don't want to talk down to you, sweetheart, but I also want to make sure I cover all the basics because I don't know how much about telecommunications you know."

Rowan looked embarrassed. "I know how to surf the Internet, send and receive email, text on my phone, and that's about it, Teag. I'm sorry, I'm pretty hopeless," she admitted quietly with downcast eyes.

"You may be a lot of things, Ro, but 'hopeless' is not one of them. There's no need to be embarrassed or to apologize." Teagan looked at her consideringly for a moment, but decided to ignore what was on her mind and moved on. "There are a ton of different facets to telecommunications, but we are going to stick with the basic things that will be important to you: your email, the internet, and your phone, okay?"

Rowan nodded.

"Telecommunications also includes things like radio broadcast, computer networks or physical phone networks, but we aren't going to talk about those things today."

"Okay." Rowan assumed a serious listening demeanor that amused Teagan.

"Let's start with your mobile phone." Teagan leaned back in her chair and steepled her fingers. "Mobile devices in general aren't as secure as computers. The same security measures that companies use for workstations and servers usually aren't in place for mobile devices. A mobile phone can actually be the perfect spying device, Ro." Teagan smiled at the stunned look on Rowan's face. "Through a mobile device, you can listen to someone. You can look through the phone just as if it was a spy glass. You can track location. And you can view every phone call and every text a person makes."

Rowan's jaw dropped open.

"I don't know if you have ever heard of malware, sweetheart, but it's software created with malicious intent that can sneak onto your phone or your laptop or your tablet."

Rowan listened intently, her eyes never leaving Teagan's face.

"Malware is written with the deliberate intent to cause harm, Ro. Examples include viruses, which are software programs that find their way onto someone's mobile phone or computer with the specific intent to perform malicious actions. They can self-replicate, they can insert themselves into other programs or files, which will infect them as well, and they can capture the user's password and send it to an attacker. 'Ransomware' is another type of malware that can cause sufficient harm. It threatens to publicly publish the victim's personal data or, in contrast, it will block the victim's access to their own data permanently, unless a 'ransom' is paid."

Rowan blew out a huge breath. "My goodness," she said, her eyes huge. "I never realized there were so many different things that could negatively affect your day-to-day existence, let alone affect business and big companies."

"Unfortunately, that's just the tip of the iceberg, sweetheart." Teagan leaned forward. "Email hacking is also another serious problem. We've seen quite a lot of it in our business here."

Rowan slightly frowned at Teagan with a question in her eyes.

"Ex-husbands try to hire hackers to infiltrate their ex-wives' personal phones and email accounts all the time. Grown children will sometimes hire hackers because they want to see what kind of money Mommy has and if there is any way they can steal it."

Rowan's jaw dropped to the floor before her eyes narrowed.

"We protect our clients from that, and also from spyware, which is software that helps someone secretly obtain information about someone else's computer activities by transmitting data covertly from their hard drive."

Rowan looked indignant. As she opened her mouth to say something, there was a knock at the door, which opened to reveal Bryn.

"*Dulzura.* Teag. How's it going?" Bryn strode into the room and lifted Rowan up out of her chair so she could give her a kiss.

"It's going great, except I'm pretty sure Ro's head is about to explode." Teagan's eyes laughed before they turned grave. "Everything okay?"

"Drew caught the echo of a trail in Purgatory and she is in the process of following it up."

"Purgatory?" Rowan was confused.

"Our name for the area where Drew plays on the dark web, baby." Bryn stretched her long legs out in Rowan's vacated chair, then sat Rowan down onto her lap. "Don't let me interrupt. I got done with Drew as fast as I could, so I hope I didn't miss too much."

Teagan snorted. "Yeah, because you need the session so much, fucker."

Bryn smirked.

"Oh!" Rowan remembered what she was going to say when Bryn came in. "Bryn. Do you have *any* idea what these poor women are subjected to sometimes?" Rowan looked affronted. "These daggone fools are trying to steal these poor ladies' money and steal their information and generally trying to be nosy, trying to swipe all kinds of information from these ladies that isn't any of their business. It's *horrible*."

"Yes, *dulzura*, I kind of have a small idea." Amused, her eyes laughed with Teagan over Rowan's head, then she pulled Rowan closer.

"Teagan is very, very, *very* good at what she does, baby. When our clients come to us for protection, they are often paying us to prevent anyone from gaining access to their personal or financial information, as well as taking care of physical threats, and we make all of that happen. We did some of the same for you, too, *dulzura*."

Rowan gave Bryn a startled look.

Bryn nodded at Teagan, who continued her explanations.

"You don't have Internet service in your house yet, Ro, since work hasn't started in updating it, so the only thing at this point we've needed to worry about is your phone. Kelly told me it was a brand-new phone that you've only had since you left Virginia," interjected Bryn. Rowan nodded. "I had Teagan look at it and scan it when you were taking your tour. Since we don't permit visitors to have electronic devices beyond the reception area, you had left it with Daniela."

Rowan's eyes widened.

"It's also standard procedure for us to scan electronics that are brought into our office, as part of our risk assessment procedures," confirmed Teagan. "With you, however, I had your phone scanned deep, especially because of what is going on with this motherfucker."

Bryn stroked Rowan's arm. "Teagan said Kelly has your phone locked down so tight, it's doubtful that even she or Trill could get into it." Rowan's eyes rounded.

Bryn smiled. "I don't know what her plans are when she finally gets down here, *dulzura*, but I can tell you there will be a job for her here if she wants it. Your sister's skills are impressive."

"As far as surfing the Internet goes," Teagan continued on, "I'm sure you already know the common sense points, Ro. Even though you have some extremely impressive security on your phone, I know I don't need to tell you that it never takes the place of sensible discernment. Don't click on any links that you are unsure of, only stick to sites that are verified as safe. Don't download any extensions or applications or things like movies, music, eBooks, PDFs, or games unless they are from a trusted source." Teagan smiled at her. "I hope you find all this helpful for you, sweetheart."

"Thank you, Teag." Rowan's voice was grateful. "I guess maybe I kind of knew a lot of this stuff already, but I didn't know any of the mechanics behind it. This was an eye-opener and I have even more respect for what you all do now." Rowan sighed with relief. "Not as difficult to understand as I thought it might be."

"You are quite welcome, Rowan." Teagan smiled warmly at her again before becoming extremely serious. "You know, sweetheart, none of us should *ever* have to tell you there is no shame or embarrassment in not knowing something." Teagan's voice was kind, but extremely firm.

Bryn straightened to attention in her chair behind Rowan at Teagan's tone.

"You are an *extremely* intelligent woman and you pick up things quite quickly. But the entire realm of telecommunications isn't *your* job to know, Ro. Here at APS, it's *my* job to know. That's one of the reasons I have a bachelor's degree, a master's degree, and a bunch of certifications in this shit." Teagan arched an eyebrow at her.

"You only needed a little overview so you could understand how everything works together at APS and how it affects your day-to-day life. That's all. You are *not* incompetent because you don't understand the entire realm of telecommunications, especially when it is not something you do, Rowan."

Bryn gave Rowan a probing look, then turned to Teagan. "Was she putting herself down, Teag?"

Teagan folded her powerful arms across her chest and regarded Rowan with caring, but still unsmiling.

"She called herself 'pretty hopeless,' cuz. If I were you, I wouldn't be too happy about that. She's not even mine and *I'm* not happy about that."

Rowan's eyes had been getting bigger and bigger.

"Well. Hearing that definitely doesn't make me too happy either. Thank you, *broki*." Bryn lifted Rowan off her lap and stood up.

"I think maybe we need to go home and discuss that." She slid her arm around Rowan and kissed her before releasing her.

"Thanks again, Teag," Bryn said as they headed for the door, Teagan's green eyes resting on Rowan's disconcerted face. "Tell Riley I'll be in a bit later."

"Will do." With a final inscrutable look at Rowan, Teagan turned back to her desk and started shuffling through some papers.

"Did I do something wrong? Is Teagan or are you mad at me?" Rowan's voice was tentative as they made their way to the breezeway that would take them to Bryn's apartment elevator.

"Let's wait until we get home, *dulzura*," Bryn hugged Rowan to her side and kissed her temple. "We need to have a serious conversation and I would prefer not to do it in public, all right?"

¥¥¥¥¥

When Bryn and Rowan got back to Bryn's apartment, Bryn led Rowan directly upstairs to the bedroom loft.

"Sit, *dulzura*." Bryn gestured mildly to the bed. Rowan lowered herself on the edge in trepidation.

"At the very beginning of our relationship, *dulzura*, although it hasn't been very long, I told you there were a couple of things that would be an issue for me. One, I would have an issue if you ever put yourself into an unsafe situation." Bryn's voice was calm. "And two, I would have an issue if you physically or mentally or emotionally brought harm to yourself."

Rowan's heart was pounding.

"When Teagan said you told her today you are 'pretty hopeless,' I need you to understand I regard that as you mentally and emotionally bringing harm to yourself."

Bryn regarded her with steady dark eyes.

"That is a punishment spanking offense, Rowan, because I don't find you putting yourself down acceptable on any level. As Teagan pointed out to you, there's no shame in not knowing something. It's perfectly fine to say, 'Hey…that's something I didn't know,' and either leave it at that or ask for more information at that point. What you do not do, *ever*, is put yourself down and describe yourself as 'pretty hopeless,' simply because you don't know a thing." Bryn was stern.

Then her voice softened a fraction.

"I hope you understand, *dulzura*, that you brought harm to my woman today with your words, by saying, in essence, you believe you're inadequate or incompetent. I cannot and will not let that go unpunished, Rowan." Bryn gestured to her. "I need you to stand up and remove your panties. I'm going to sit on the edge of the bed and then you are going to lay face-down over my knees."

Rowan did as she was told, feeling anxious as she slid out of her panties. Bryn sat down on the bed, positioning her legs to form a stable "shelf" for Rowan to lay on and motioning for her to come down across her knees.

"I am not going to give you a set number of spanks because this punishment will be far more effective if you don't know how many are coming, Rowan. You will not be required to count them for me, although you will do so in the future if this ever becomes necessary again."

Rowan lay prone across Bryn's lap, scared and frozen with anxiety. She trembled as Bryn began to stroke the back of her thighs with a feather-light touch.

"Do you understand why you are being punished, *dulzura*?"

"Yes, Bryn." Rowan's voice was tremulous and full of tears.

With lightning speed, Bryn brought her hand down on Rowan's bare ass with a solid smack, causing Rowan to yelp as she jerked in shock.

This wasn't anything like an erotic spanking.

Bryn massaged the place she had struck for a few moments until she felt Rowan release the breath she was holding, then smacked her again. Rowan, stunned at how much it hurt, cried out and tried to put her hands over her rear end in protection.

"Move your hands, *dulzura*," Bryn commanded sharply, "or I will restrain them. I have allowed you the ability to move freely, but I will take that privilege away if you abuse it."

Rowan removed her hands and clenched them into fists, trying desperately to fight against the throbbing sting. Bryn gave Rowan a succession of hard smacks, pausing every few moments to massage her aching flesh. The pain intensified and spread as her white skin turned crimson under Bryn's firm hand.

Rowan fought back the huge tears pricking her eyelids and dug her fingernails into the palms of her hands. Nothing in her life had *ever* prepared her for this. She wanted to scream from the intensity of Bryn's punishment.

Through the haze of her punishment, Rowan remembered Bryn telling her punishment spankings were supposed to hurt and that Bryn would always make sure they hurt if one was ever necessary.

She held herself rigid, struggling to weather each smack as it came. After what seemed like hours to her, Rowan felt herself teeter on the edge of breaking down completely.

Bryn immediately sensed the change in her. "Unclench your fists, *dulzura*," she directed gently, her calm tone penetrating through the fog of Rowan's pain-filled mind. "You are holding onto the pain instead of allowing it to pass through you, little one. Let it go."

Rowan did as she was told and forced her hands open, relaxing her fingers.

As she did so, it was as if a dam burst inside of her. The tears she had tried so hard to hold back came pouring out of her in a giant flood. Rowan's body exploded into racking sobs, as if trying to purge itself of all its pent-up emotion.

As if sensing Rowan had reached the limits of her endurance, Bryn stopped, then pulled her up into her lap and wrapped her arms securely around her.

Despite the pain she felt from her burning, tender backside pressing into Bryn's jeans-clad legs, Rowan sagged against Bryn's body, still crying and holding onto her for dear life.

"I'm sorry, I'm so sorry," she sobbed, shaking, as she leaned into Bryn.

Bryn kissed her gently, running her fingers through Rowan's hair.

"Let it all go, *dulzura*," Bryn murmured softly as she rocked Rowan, rubbing her back and her arms, continuing to kiss her tear-stained cheeks. "It's okay, baby. Cry it out." Bryn continued to hold and caress her woman, soothing her with loving words, until the storm of tears was finally over and Rowan was calmer.

Bryn swept Rowan's damp curls back from her face, then gazed into her eyes with a tender look. She uncapped a bottle of water sitting on the nightstand and made Rowan drink some, then pulled a handkerchief out of her back pocket and wiped away the last of Rowan's tears.

When Bryn was done, she handed the handkerchief to Rowan so she could blow her nose and regain a measure of composure. After

Rowan had blown her nose and wiped her face, she buried her face in Bryn's shoulder and tried to articulate the thoughts that were going through her head.

"This world is new to me," Rowan started, her voice wobbly. "I've never... I've never been with an alpha butch before. I know w-we had this discussion, but I guess I didn't realize just how seriously you would t-take me saying anything negative about myself." Rowan's lip trembled. "What I said... I really didn't even think about it when I said it. And I'll be honest...n-now I'm scared that I'm going to have to monitor every single little thing I say so th-this doesn't happen again." She hiccupped with emotion. Bryn held her securely in her arms and kissed her.

"Then the way you avoid that, *dulzura*, is to make sure you never have a thought about yourself that is self-defeating or self-harming or negative again."

"How in the world do I do that, Bryn?" Frustration edged into Rowan's voice. "No one in this world knows *everything*. What I did is something *everybody* does."

"No, *dulzura*. You aren't listening to me. There is a *world* of difference between admitting you don't know something as opposed to calling yourself something derogatory because of it."

Bryn pulled Rowan back slightly and looked into her eyes.

"To be aggravated or frustrated or to even express anger because you don't know something is perfectly acceptable. We *all* do that. To call yourself an idiot or a dumbass or to say you're hopeless or incompetent because you don't know something, however, is *not*."

Rowan was quiet for a long time.

"Is Teagan mad at me?" she finally asked in a small voice.

Bryn continued to stroke her back. "She's not mad at you as much as she's upset with your perception of yourself, *dulzura*. She's an alpha butch like me, Rowan. Everyone on the APS management team is. And while you might perceive what she did as 'tattling,' she did what any alpha butch in her position would do. She saw or heard the woman of one of her *corillo*—her posse, her tribe—doing something that was harmful to herself. No alpha butch of *any* worth will stand for that, especially when it comes down to the woman of a member of her tribe. Casey, for example, would have done the exact same thing as Teagan did. Just like Jaime or Drew or any of the others would have as well."

Rowan was quiet again.

Bryn tilted Rowan's chin off and looked at her with a penetrating gaze.

"As unpleasant as it was for you to receive that spanking, *dulzura*, it was equally unpleasant for me to deliver it because I don't enjoy causing pain to my woman."

Bryn nuzzled her temple. "I hope for both our sakes that you'll be able to avoid putting yourself down in the future, Rowan."

After a while, Bryn slid off the bed after telling Rowan to stay put. She went down the stairs and Rowan heard water running. Bryn came back up the stairs with a warm washcloth and a tube of some kind in her hand.

"Turn on your stomach, *dulzura*," Bryn directed. "This is a cream that will soothe your bottom and lessen the pain." She washed Rowan's bottom gently, soothing her femme with her touch, and applied the cream. She leaned down and kissed Rowan for a long moment, before assisting her to get up, then helped her to put on her panties.

When Rowan was re-dressed and they had gone downstairs, Bryn sent a text. "I have asked Teagan to meet us here, *dulzura*, before you two go to the Dream Creamery. I think it's better if you two have a chance to see each other in private first."

When Teagan arrived, she didn't say a word, but went straight to Rowan and enfolded her in her strong arms. The two of them hugged each other silently for several minutes.

"We good, sweetheart?" Teagan asked when she felt Rowan fully relax.

When Rowan nodded, Teagan said, "Then it's done," kissed her cheek and released her back to Bryn.

"Time to get to work, *dulzura*." Bryn wrapped her arms around Rowan and kissed her. "As Teagan said, 'It's done,' and there's no need for any of us to ever mention it again."

"Now it's time for you two to get to the Dream Creamery and time for me to follow up with Drew to see if there was any more to this echo she found in Purgatory."

Chapter 19

Rowan was beyond happy at how everything was progressing at the Dream Creamery and the WCA Center, as they were calling it. "*Because*," she had told Clem, "saying the 'Whimsy Creative Arts Center' all the time is just too freaking *tiring*."

In the Dream Creamery, Nia's team was working on installing the Dream Creamery freezers, building the counters and installing the cabinets, finishing the painting, then laying the light wood floors. A few people from Nia's team were already working on building the counters, at the same time a couple more were prepping the space where the ice cream freezers would be installed.

When you walked in (through an antique door Ember had found that Rowan *loved*), the Dream Creamery ordering counter and freezers would be straight ahead against the rear wall and just to the left.

Ember came up with the suggestion of leaving all the walls completely white, especially since the art center would be off to the right and they didn't want any competing colors for the artwork that would be displayed.

The counters, and the tables and chairs in the Dream Creamery would provide accents of mint green and salmon. The walls would be constructed with decorative white PVC pipe panels, for both durability and design, which were currently being installed, too. However, the left side and back rear wall would be completely covered with a hand-painted mural that showcased ice cream-related art—cones, sundaes, sweet treats, gelato—all interspersed around the top with hearts and clouds.

Ember had designed a sign for the back wall above the ordering counter and the ice cream freezers that said, 'The Dream Creamery' in the same mint and salmon colors.

It was going to be *beautiful*. Roman couldn't wait to see it when it was all done.

The right side of the space was where the WCA Center was going to be. Immediately to the right of the front door was the art gallery itself, and Ember was busy working with Nia to get all the lighting installed.

They had installed a 3/4 wall with a door on the far right about halfway back through the space to separate the art gallery from the art classroom, but would still lend a feeling of openness to the space. In the classroom itself was a large craft table with comfortable, durable chairs where classes could be held. Solid wood floor-to-ceiling storage cabinets had been constructed against the back and right walls, providing ample storage.

In the midst of all the chaos going on, Rowan and Teagan hadn't had a chance to interact much, which made Rowan feel a little awkward. She kept peeping at Teagan from under her lashes, wanting to ask her a few questions about what had happened earlier that day, but not daring to try anyone's patience.

When Clem ran out with Remy to pick up something to eat for everyone at lunch time, Rowan heard Teagan sigh.

"Come on, sweetheart." Teagan gestured to Rowan toward the door in the rear hallway that opened onto the steps leading upstairs to Clem's apartment space. "You clearly need to talk and we clearly need to have this conversation somewhere where we can't be overheard."

Once upstairs, Rowan was startled at how much construction material had already been hauled into the huge space, but she turned around to look at Teagan, who was watching her impassively.

"I'm not asking you to hide anything from Bryn, I hope you know, it's just…well…" Rowan twisted her fingers nervously.

"Sometimes, it's easier to talk to a friend than it is to a lover," Teagan finished for her.

Rowan felt a wave of relief. "That's it, exactly. I mean, I know you're going to share everything about our conversation with Bryn, and I want you to, but it will be easier with you telling her anything she needs to know rather than me trying to figure it all out."

Teagan nodded with understanding.

"Bryn is the first alpha butch I've ever been with, Teag," Rowan said slowly. "She told me today that all of you are alpha butches just like she is, and that any of the Seven, and I guess Riley too, would have felt they needed to go to her just like you did."

Teagan nodded again. "That's true," she agreed.

Rowan took a minute to gather her thoughts. "I guess I'm just trying to understand how you're wired. You all…you're different.

Today, I told Bryn I was worried I would say something again that would make her...well, you know...do what she did today." Rowan flushed. "And the answer was so *easy* for her. She said to stop thinking about myself that way and I wouldn't have an issue. Boom, she was done. Problem solved. Like it's *that* easy." Rowan huffed and rolled her eyes.

"But it *is* that easy, Ro." The corner of Teagan's mouth lifted in a slight smile. "You want to know how the APS butches are wired, sweetheart? Then, I'll tell you. We're more or less 'classified,' I guess you could say, as 'hard butches.' We eat, we sleep, we fight, and we fuck. Virtually everything in our lives fits into one of those categories. We protect and cherish our women, Rowan. We massacre hell out of *anything* that's a threat in our world and we defend our tribe with our last breath. It's pretty simple, really." Teagan shrugged.

She smiled warmly at Rowan.

"You are part of our tribe now, sweetheart. That means any and all of us will defend you against the world, too—even if that means protecting you from yourself sometimes. That's exactly what I was doing when I told Bryn about your comment. I didn't like it, Ro." She looked intently at Rowan. "The fact that my *awesome* friend, who is kind and sweet and more fucking intelligent than virtually anyone I know...that this woman, this sister of mine, had the nerve to say she was 'pretty hopeless'?" Teagan quirked her eyebrow at Rowan. "If Bryn wasn't in the picture, sweetheart, I would have turned you over my goddamned knee for that myself."

Rowan was startled.

"Talk to Bryn, Rowan. You can go to her for *any*-fucking-thing." Teagan was serious. "She's your shield, she's your protection, she can make sense of our world for you. All she asks is you do the little bit she needs you to do for her so she can keep you safe."

"Okay, Teag," Rowan whispered.

Teagan leaned against a huge cardboard box. "To alpha butches, sometimes femmes *think* too goddamn much." She grinned at Rowan, making her laugh.

"We do not," Rowan defended herself and her sisters. "We just…don't like leaving anything to chance." Teagan threw her head back and cracked up.

"I hear lunch." They heard Clem downstairs, hollering for Rowan.

"We'll be right down," Teagan yelled back. "You good?" Teagan asked, smiling at her as they prepared to go back downstairs.

"Thanks, Teag. I feel a lot better." Rowan smiled gratefully at her friend as they started down the stairs.

Teagan paused as her phone rang. "Hold on one second, Ro. It's Bryn, calling instead of texting."

She frowned as she answered the call. "Yeah?" Teagan listened closely, her body on high alert. She cut her eyes at Rowan. "She's right here with me. Uh huh…uh huh…" Teagan slid in front of Rowan and listened for a couple of minutes. "Is she sure?" Teag nodded and kept nodding as Bryn continued her conversation from the other end. "Do I need to send the crews home and put us on lockdown?"

Rowan's eyes widened.

Teagan listened for another minute, then said, "Okay, then. We'll stay aware, we'll continue work as usual, and we'll see you when you get here." Teagan ended the call and raked a hand through her thick, red-gold hair before focusing on Rowan.

"Drew got a hit, sweetheart. Coravani's in Whimsy and he's been squatting in a vacant apartment in the Sea Towers."

¥¥¥¥¥

January 2

When Dino Coravani had realized he'd been discovered, he'd fled, sending Drew's bad mood into the stratosphere.

Jaime had physical trackers in pursuit once again, while Drew and her crew were "shaking the trees" in Purgatory. They were both working closely with Vince Masterson, engaging with the Whimsy Police Department now that there was an official warrant out for Coravani's arrest.

In the meantime, Kennedy was meeting Bryn and Rowan so she could give Rowan a bit of insight into her responsibilities with the Seven.

Bryn had stroked Rowan's cheek while they were waiting for Kennedy.

"I've known Kenn since first grade, *dulzura*. Actually, you'll find out that Riley and the Seven and I have all known each other since first or second grade, or even before. Kindergarten or preschool, like Trill and Teagan."

At that moment, Jaime had come in looking for Bryn, and the two of them had lapsed into an intense conversation in Spanish.

"Are you ready?" Fifteen minutes later, Kenn came into the Bunker. "Hey, Jaim."

"Yes, thank goodness, we're ready. At least I think we are. Goddess knows, *I* am." Rowan's tone was a wee bit disgruntled as she grumbled. "It's bad enough I don't understand anything about butches in the first place. Butches who speak Spanish? Pul-eez." Rowan glared at Bryn and Jaime until they both cracked up despite their serious demeanors.

"It's okay, *chula*," Jaime offered. "Femmes are as much a mystery to butches, too, no matter what the language."

"Now, see?" Rowan petitioned Kennedy, her hands on her hips. "I don't even know if what she called me is a good thing, or if it's just Spanish for 'crazy person.'"

Despite themselves, Jaime and Bryn burst out laughing.

"It means 'cutie,' *mi hermana*…which, before your head explodes, means 'my sister.'"

Rowan was slightly mollified, although she still huffed a bit.

"And on that note, since I have a dickhead motherfucker to help track down, I'm out." Jaime kissed Rowan on the cheek and high-fived both Kennedy and Bryn before making her way to the door.

Just as she was about to pull the door shut, she said one last thing in Spanish to Bryn, grinning, and left when Bryn threw her head back and laughed.

Rowan's eyes narrowed, then she looked at Kennedy. "Do you speak Spanish, Kenn?"

"Nope." Kenn raised her eyebrows. "If I want to know something bad enough, which I usually do *not* when it comes to these fuckers, I'll just ask later."

Her grin widened as Rowan huffed louder.

"*Dulzura.*" Bryn kissed her woman and continued, chuckling.

"Jaime said, '*Así se bate el cobre, broki*…which basically means, 'This is how it's done, bro,' and then she slid on out of here. In other words, she's a total pain in my ass who knows how to make an exit. But she was right—she needs to help find that cocksucker."

Rowan looked resigned, then sighed reluctantly in acceptance.

"I told Jaime we were keeping our playdate with Kenn, but we might have to interrupt it if things catch fire." Bryn kissed Rowan on the forehead.

"The range and the Cage aren't going anywhere, cuz, so if we have to postpone, it is what it is." Kenn spoke with the relaxed demeanor of someone who was used to abrupt interruptions. I figured I'd show Rowan the Cage first, then we'd head to the shooting range, yeah?"

The three of them set out toward the range.

Kennedy Weston was just as striking as the rest of the Seven. Her barely wavy, dark brown hair was cut into a fade and her eyes were a dark blue that appeared almost navy. Although a couple of inches shorter than Bryn, she was still a full six inches taller than Rowan. She was strong and athletic, unsurprising from someone who handled heavy weapons on a daily basis.

When they reached the shooting range, Kenn continued past its entrance to a vault door with a wheel vault lock and a digital keypad on the other side.

"This is what we refer to as the Cage, sweetheart. Bryn, Riley, and the Seven all have complete 24/7 access."

Kenn unlocked the Cage and ushered Bryn and Rowan into the large room behind the vault door. Rowan's jaw dropped open when she saw the contents of the room.

"The Cage was constructed with a solid moisture barrier and other dehumidifying options, sweetheart, because humidity is the enemy of firearms and weapons, and we live in Humidity Central," Kenn gestured as she explained. "The room's dehumidifiers and air conditioners are set to maintain a constant temperature, one that is optimal for long-term weapons storage. The walls, ceiling, and floor are also fireproof and constructed of 1/2" steel with a sheetrock facade. It's not readily apparent, but power has been run in here as well."

Kenn continued, "We have our own generator, plus a remote antennae, hard cable and a Wi-Fi booster, so we can access the internet and our security cameras. This way, we can have eyes on the entire property from inside the Cage. APS in general is an extremely secure facility, Rowan, and it's not like we live in a war zone exactly, so this was constructed less for an attack threat than it was for a hurricane or a tornado threat."

Understanding dawned on Rowan's face.

"There are tens of thousands of dollars' worth of weapons in here, so we have done everything we could to keep our collections secure."

Rowan's eyes were huge as she looked at the racks of weapons along the walls.

Kenn smiled slightly.

"We store weapons such as revolvers, semi-automatic handguns, 12-gauge pump shotguns and rifles—as well as long-range sniper rifles, Ro—plus ammunition and accessories like scopes, sights, and mounts. We also have self-defense weapons such as pepper sprays, knives, batons, and stun guns in here." She motioned at Bryn. "It looks like Bryn and Riley have me keep a lot, sweetheart, but there are nine of us in management, as well as all of our other APS associates—totaling almost fifty APS resources. That demands more equipment than you might think."

Bryn nodded in agreement.

Kenn regarded Rowan with a thoughtful look. "In the course of our work, Rowan—and by that I mean the complete scope of what we do at APS—all of these weapons have found a reason to be used at one time or another over our 10-year existence. The Seven trains often and makes sure their associates are up to speed with their weapons skills as well. We have a five-lane shooting range right here on premises, as well as a section of property some distance away that is very remote and can be used for things like long-range sniper rifle practice."

"Holy. Crap." Rowan was close to speechless.

Kenn laughed. "These are not things you ever have to personally worry about, sweetheart, but they're good to know at least from an education standpoint, yeah?"

"As good as Teagan is with communications, *dulzura*, Kenn is equally talented and a formidable armory and range master."

"My dad was a Special Forces Weapons Sergeant in the Army for almost 25 years, Rowan, before he retired." Kenn smiled with clear love for her father. "He was trained as a tactician, a paratrooper, and as a survival expert, plus the man knows a shitload of different forms of combat. I always wanted to be him when I was growing up. Now, the crusty old bastard's primary joy is giving me a rash of shit every time he sees me because I enlisted in the Marine Corps instead of going Army like him." Kenn grinned.

Rowan burst out laughing and Bryn shook her head with a chuckle.

"Kenn's dad is terrific," Bryn said. "We brought him in here once for him to look around and he was so proud of her, I thought he was going to combust on the spot."

Kenn smiled. "Let's go take a look at the shooting range then, sweetheart. There is a safety bay right near the entrance of the actual range if you need it for any reason."

They walked over to the shooting range after Kenn had secured the Cage.

"Like all range safety bays, the handling of ammunition is prohibited there. You can use the bay to repair, clean, and holster or unholster your firearm as needed."

Rowan nodded, comfortable with the familiar procedures.

"We use the standard range commands of 'ceasefire' and 'commence firing' here, Ro." Kenn looked at Rowan gravely. "You should know I am one of those Range Masters who believes that calling a 'ceasefire' for the simplest, most stupid reasons you can think of is far preferable than not calling one and wishing you had. You carrying right now, sweetheart?"

Rowan flipped up the bottom of her shirt a bit and showed Kenn the holster clipped to the waistband at her rear hip.

"I've always pretty much used a purse holster, but I promised Bryn's dad I would carry my gun on my body until that moron, Coravani, is caught."

"Good for Papa Armstrong." Kenn high-fived Bryn. "That man has powers of persuasion that are unbelievable. I swear, he could sell a fucking steak to a vegetarian." Rowan giggled in full agreement while Bryn smirked. "I see it's an IWB holster. Good. Leather?" IWB or Inside Waist Band holsters could get extremely uncomfortable and leather was typically the most comfortable option.

"Kelly said leather was probably the best option for me since I don't really ever unholster my gun unless it's night time. This holster is brand new and I still need to break it in a bit."

"I really need to meet Kelly," muttered Kenn.

"The whole fucking crew needs to meet Kelly," Bryn agreed.

After Rowan and Bryn were safely at their firing lines in their lanes with eye and ear protection and everything was ready, Kenn called out in a loud, clear voice, "This range is going hot. Commence firing."

To Rowan's relief, her new gun was comfortable for her to use and she quickly felt familiar with it.

After about an hour of practice, Kenn called a ceasefire so everyone could get ready to leave.

"Are we clear?" she asked after Rowan and Bryn had their weapons holstered, cleaned up their areas, and were ready to exit their shooting stalls.

"We're clear." Bryn slid her arm around her woman as they each left their stalls. "Rowan and I will clean our guns at home."

"Shooting will never, ever be my favorite thing," admitted Rowan as they left the range. "But you made that a whole lot less painful than I expected it to be, Kenn. Thank you so much." Rowan hugged Kenn and kissed her on the cheek.

"Well, you're welcome so much, sweetheart." Kenn hugged Rowan back. "We good, chief?" she asked Bryn.

"Thanks, Kenn. You know I wasn't fucking lying when I told Ro you were one of the best weapons masters around." Kenn acknowledged Bryn's words with a nod of thanks.

Rowan spontaneously hugged Bryn tight as well. "And thank you, too." She sighed. "Your Seven are awesome and I can't wait for the rest of my playdates."

"You are quite welcome, *dulzura*." Bryn kissed her for a long moment. "As far as coming to the shooting range, I know you don't like it, but you have a good eye and good aim, baby."

"That she does," Kenn agreed, then regarded Rowan with a contemplative gaze. "The biggest thing you need to remember, Ro—considering that fuckwit is still out there—is to never point the gun at anything you aren't ready to destroy. But when *you* are ready, then you shoot to kill, sweetheart. Never, ever hesitate…just remove that threat."

Chapter 20

January 3

The next night, Rowan, Clem, and Nova waited with Bryn, Teagan, and Dakota at Seashells for Alyssa and Brooke to arrive.

Suddenly, Nova gave a long squeal and jumped to her feet.

"S'up, bitches!" She threw her arms around two very pretty women who appeared at their table and hugged her back hard before they looked around at everyone.

"Bryn Armstrong. Jesus H. Christ, you still look like a fucking giraffe." The short redhead winked at Rowan, figuring out she was undoubtedly Bryn's girlfriend, and warmly shook her hand before hugging the hell out of Bryn.

Bryn laughed and kissed the irrepressible woman on the cheek before introducing her to Rowan. "*Dulzura,* this is Alyssa Riker, extraordinary art therapist and world-class troublemaker."

Alyssa huffed and rolled her eyes. "She still hasn't forgiven me for tying her shoelaces together when we were in third grade," she confided to Rowan.

Rowan's eyes rounded before she burst into peals of laughter. "How in the *world* did you manage to get away with that?" she asked between gasps.

"Easy. I hid behind Mama Armstrong, who wouldn't let Bryn touch me." Alyssa was smug as she stuck her tongue out at Bryn.

Rowan laughed until her stomach hurt and decided on the spot that she flat-out adored Alyssa Riker.

Rowan eyed Bryn, who narrowed her eyes playfully at her woman and let the heat of her eyes promise all sorts of delicious payback.

The cool blonde with Alyssa smirked and shook Rowan's hand in easy friendship as well. "Welcome to Looney Tunes Central, Rowan. Please keep your hands and feet inside the ride at all times."

Rowan giggled again.

The woman then caught sight of Teagan and laughed with joy.

"Casanova! How in the hell *are* you?" The pretty blonde, who was evidently Brooke, hugged Teagan tightly, then leaned over and kissed Dakota on the cheek. "Dakota! Holy shit, it's like fucking old school week in here."

She turned her attention back to Rowan and smiled at her happily. "I'm Brooke Marino, Rowan, and I do graphic design for a lot of the local craft breweries. Can I just say I am excited as hell about what you're doing? Seriously, we are both *so* glad we might be able to help you out and that the squirt there thought to call us."

Nova stuck her middle finger up at Brooke, who was about 5'6" tall compared to Nova's 5'1", then gave her a cheek kiss.

Rowan introduced Clem to the two women and everyone settled themselves with something to drink.

"When Nova called us, we were excited to find out your plans to open the Whimsy Creative Arts Center." Alyssa spoke seriously, putting her teasing on the back burner for a moment. "There are a lot of artists in Whimsy, Rowan, but we have never really had an organized central art center. I teach art therapy, which I know Nova's told you about, and I certainly don't lack for clients, but I usually meet with them at the Whimsy Rec Center. Some of my clients are managing addictions, some are coping with anxiety and depression, and some are simply tackling ways to control physical illness or disability." Alyssa's eyes were soft. "It will be so much more empowering for them to be able to do that from a true art center instead of from a multi-function recreation center." Alyssa Riker, Rowan was rapidly learning, was intelligent, committed, and completely focused on her calling behind her playful exterior.

Brooke added her own thoughts. "Every month, the city of Whimsy sponsors what's called ArtsMarket on the last Saturday of the month. It's fun and it attracts a lot of visitors to the city, but I wouldn't exactly say there are any kind of standards set for legitimate artists to show." The corner of Brooke's mouth lifted. "Frankly, there's nothing to prevent someone from buying a bunch of cheap glass at Walmart, painting it, and selling it as 'art' at a 500% markup."

Rowan and Clem looked at each other with raised eyebrows.

"Why doesn't the city put some kind of a jury process in place before they grant a display space to a vendor?" Rowan asked, talking about the process often used to determine if an artist was worthy of inclusion in various events by presenting their work to a panel of "jurors" or judges prior to an event.

"Because when you can charge $25 for a four-hour space rental and there are 200 available spaces, all of which are taken—*with* a waiting list of interested vendors—the city makes a cool $5,000 without having to lift a finger to do a fucking thing or spend a cent," Brooke said wryly.

Rowan unconsciously leaned against Bryn, who had wrapped her powerful arm around her.

Clem spoke. "Any artists we invite to show in the future at the WCA Center will have to be juried, although we'll have to relax our standards for the grand opening since we are so short on time."

Alyssa and Brooke glanced at each other. "Yeah, about that." Alyssa scrunched her nose. "There's already been buzz about the Dream Creamery and the WCA Center opening up next month. I mean, *good* stuff. People are so excited," Brooke assured Rowan and Clem. "From what I've heard, more than a few artists have expressed an interest already in being a grand opening artist."

"Yeah? Okay." Clem shrugged her shoulders. "We haven't even determined our selection process yet, though."

Nova's honey-brown eyes suddenly turned dark. "Why do I motherfucking know, just *know*, where you're going with this, Brooke."

She placed both her hands on the table and leaned forward in aggravation. "Do not fucking *tell* me…"

"We're telling you," Brooke and Alyssa chimed together as Nova positively hissed.

Rowan looked at the three women in confusion as Clem exclaimed, "Tell us *what*?"

Alyssa looked Bryn straight in her eyes.

"Apparently, Astrid Hallifax is expecting to be chosen as one of the grand opening artists."

A dead silence fell over the table for a minute.

"And who, pray fucking tell, is Astrid Hallifax?" demanded Clem finally, looking back and forth between Alyssa, Brooke, and Nova. "Does this miracle bitch shoot rainbows out of her ass in the shape of Michelangelo?" Clem raised her eyebrows and pursed her lips. "Does she think she's too good to go through the same selection process everyone else will and expects we're just going to plop a crown on her fucking head? What makes her so special?"

"Astrid is my ex-girlfriend," Bryn said calmly, but one look at her face made it clear to the entire table that she was pissed. "Because her mother is well-known and owns a Whimsy restaurant, which is one of the most popular restaurants in the Tampa Bay area, Astrid has a few issues with entitlement."

"Oookay," Rowan said slowly. "Operative part being 'ex,' from what I'm hearing." She turned to look at Bryn for a moment. "I'm assuming I don't have anything to worry about here, right?"

Bryn leveled a, "You have to be fucking kidding me" look at her. Rowan turned back to the girls. "And, as I expected, that would be a 'no.' So, why the freak-out?"

"Rowan." Nova spoke through clenched teeth. "Astrid is a major fucking cunt of *epic* proportions. I guarantee you she's heard about you, she now knows you're dating Bryn, so she's planning on galloping her big fucking horse feet in here to stake her claim."

"So?" Rowan shrugged. "Let her."

"What?!" Nova, Clem, Brooke, and Alyssa exclaimed together.

"I said, let her." Rowan sank comfortably into Bryn's side. "She won't win competing for someone who doesn't want her in the first place."

"Besides…" she looked at Bryn with mischief in her eyes as her mouth quirked up. "Gracie."

Bryn, despite being obviously pissed off, threw back her head and burst out laughing, while Teagan joined in, roaring.

Dakota smirked. "Yeah, the entire crew at APS headquarters heard about Gracie and the Rowan Smackdown the next day. Trill said it was fucking *legendary*."

"Gracie?" Clem and the other women were confused.

Teagan, laughing like crazy, recounted the whole Gracie episode to the girls, who were howling by the time Teag was done.

"So…" Rowan examined her nails while she gave them a slight smile, then kissed Bryn and leaned comfortably against her.

"I don't like to be a mean person," Rowan said. "Clem will tell you that's not my nature."

"Nope," Clem agreed. "Little Bo Peep here doesn't even swear." Rowan looked at Clem with exasperation.

"*But...*" Rowan continued, deciding to ignore Clem's comments, "if this Astrid person wants to start something, I suggest she bring her 'A' game. Bryn and I are together and she can either get over it and be nice, or find out what it means to look like an idiot in public."

"*Dulzura.*" Bryn kissed her temple. "Just ignore her. She's not worth you getting upset."

"Who's going to get upset? I know where we stand, Bryn." Rowan was matter of fact. "I'm only thinking I just might have to teach her where my lines are drawn and show her what happens when you cross those lines. But enough about her." Rowan waved her hand, done talking about Astrid, and moved on to the reason they were all there. "We need to figure out what kind of selection process we should have for this. It's kind of short notice to do anything major, unless we make it first-come, first-serve for individuals who fulfill a certain criteria," Rowan mused.

"Like, they have been invited to show previously in a professional setting," suggested Alyssa.

"And, they can provide three references from other individuals in the art field," added Brooke.

"Ooh, yes." Rowan gave them the thumbs up. "One more, since we don't have a lot of time before the grand opening."

Clem chimed in. "The art piece they plan to contribute is new and it's not something they have ever shown before."

"Perfect." Rowan was excited. "We'll publish a call-to-artists in this week's Whimsy Pioneer, list the criteria expected, and let everyone know that we will make our selections on a first-come, first-serve basis. As the manager of the WCA Center, Clem will be the point of contact. Nova and Delaney," Rowan continued, "are working on refining the grand opening menus for the Dream Creamery."

"Delaney?" Teagan was surprised. "You don't mean Delaney Sedgwick, do you? Didn't she move out of Whimsy years ago with her girlfriend?"

"She did, that twat girlfriend has finally been kicked to the curb, and Delaney is moving back to Whimsy on Thursday," Nova confirmed. Teagan looked intrigued.

"Anyhow," Rowan continued, "I can't thank you both enough for your input." She beamed at Alyssa and Brooke. "Your insight has been absolutely invaluable."

Brooke laughed. "Oh, girl. You ain't seen nothing yet." She winked at Rowan with a totally roguish look. "I think it's time to set Whimsy on fire."

Chapter 21

Rowan, on her knees, clutched at the headboard of Bryn's bed and cried out as Bryn used her wicked mouth and tongue between Rowan's legs. Bryn held her still, gripping Rowan's hips with her strong hands and wouldn't allow her woman to move as she licked and sucked her.

After getting home from their get-together, Bryn brought Rowan directly upstairs, stripped her bare, and buried her mouth in Rowan's pussy before she could even take a deep breath.

"Bryn! Please!" Rowan screamed in desperation. "I need to move! I need to…oh, please! Please make me come!"

Bryn slowed down her licks until she was barely making contact with Rowan's clit. Rowan cried and tried to wiggle, continuing to beg Bryn to let her come.

"Mmmmm. Did you not giggle tonight when Alyssa was telling her story about us as children, *dulzura*?" Bryn flicked her tongue teasingly over Rowan's entire pussy.

Rowan shrieked and fought unsuccessfully to move her hips. "I'm sorry!" she wailed, tears coursing down her cheeks. "She was funny! I couldn't help it! Oh, Bryn! Please!" Rowan cried harder. "I'll promise you *anything*. I don't know what you would want, but I'll give you anything if you'll only m-m-make me come."

"Anything, hmmmmm?" Bryn drew out the vibration right against Rowan's clit, making her scream again. "Will you let me give you an erotic spanking when your bottom is healed, *dulzura*? So I can reinforce the difference between a spanking given for erotic pleasure and one given for punishment to you?"

Rowan cried out, "Yes! Yes, you can! I ..." She stuttered to a stop, shaking like a leaf and unable to finish her sentence.

Bryn rose up on her knees behind Rowan, inserted her cock into her woman, and started to move. Rowan sobbed with relief as she moved with Bryn, arching her back and pushing back against Bryn's hard thrusts. Bryn wrapped one of her arms around her woman and anchored her down as she drove into her and supported the both of them with her other powerful arm.

Rowan arched back against Bryn, her legs shaking as Bryn penetrated her deeper. She moved her hips in rhythm to Bryn's forceful movements, gasping as Bryn sensed the first stirrings of her orgasm start to take hold. Bryn kept moving hard, nipping the side of Rowan's neck and flexing her hips to power into her woman.

"Come, Rowan," Bryn commanded her with authority. "Come now."

Rowan threw her head back and screamed as an explosive orgasm ripped through her. She kept screaming as Bryn fucked her through her orgasm, until Bryn planted herself deep and groaned as she came, too.

Rowan collapsed face-down on the comforter, her body still shaking. Bryn covered her with her own body, still deeply anchored within her. The two of them lay there until Bryn recovered her breath, then she cleaned up her woman and herself before pulling Rowan into her arms and holding her tight.

Rowan stirred drowsily. "I love what you can do to me," she sighed in a low, sleepy voice. "No one has ever made me feel this way before."

"*I* love what I can do to you, *dulzura*." Bryn caressed her woman. "You're beautiful and passionate and responsive. I love how you respond to my touch."

Rowan was quiet for a moment.

"Bryn." Rowan's voice, when it came, was hesitant. "You go down on me constantly, but I've never gone down on you yet. I guess I don't understand why you've never seemed to want that from me."

"You don't seem to object to me touching you with my hand between your legs, but anything else..." Rowan hesitated again. "Is that not something you want from me?"

"*Dulzura*." Bryn expelled a deep breath. "Believe it or not, I'm one of those butches that doesn't love that a whole lot. It's not that I hate it or that it freaks me out, but it's never really done much for me. My greatest pleasure, my joy, comes from making love to you, baby, not the other way around. I'm not a stone butch, refusing to let my woman touch my chest or between my legs at all. I clearly don't mind, and I'm completely comfortable when you touch me."

Bryn nuzzled her neck and gave a low laugh. "But I'm happiest when my face is buried in your pussy and I can make you scream while you gush all over my face, *dulzura*." Rowan's cheeks turned red as she buried her face in Bryn's neck.

They lay there for a few minutes as Bryn quietly stroked her back until Rowan finally admitted, her tone colored with hurt, "I've been called 'frigid' before, Bryn. It made me hesitant to trust anyone sexually."

Bryn actually reared up on her elbow. "Frigid? *You?*" she asked incredulously. "Baby, you are the fucking farthest thing from frigid I've ever seen."

"Well, I've now decided that, if I *was* frigid before, it wasn't my fault. It was operator error." Rowan sighed, her voice sleepy.

Bryn laughed outright, gathering Rowan in her arms again. They lay together once more, basking in each other's warmth, until Rowan broke the silence.

"I've only had a few lovers, Bryn." Rowan was pensive. "Relationships were always too messy. Too much drama and too many scenes and for what? It got to the point with my last girlfriend, that I would shut up and swallow my words rather than risk a three-hour fight. Because if she was happy, everything was fine. But if she wasn't?" Rowan gulped in remembrance. "Hoo boy. The mental stress just wasn't worth it."

"*Dulzura.*" Bryn looked at her in the dimly illuminated space and stroked her gently. "Am I hearing the reason why my beautiful, talented, amazing woman might be using words like, 'hopeless,' to describe herself?"

Rowan buried her face in Bryn's shoulder and nodded.

"I assume she wasn't a butch? Not that butches have a lock on healthy relationships, trust me." Rowan shook her head 'no,' but remained quiet.

"Needless to say, baby, your ex didn't know her ass from deep center field." Rowan broke into a startled giggle, then laughed outright.

"People like that?" Bryn continued to run her hands soothingly all over Rowan. "They are so insecure in themselves; they have to put others down in order to feel good. It's not a phenomenon limited to the gay community either. Unfortunately, sometimes others get caught in their trap and start to believe the bullshit they spew. Because there *are* good times in there. Times when everything is fun and happy and seems perfect, and it sucks you in."

Bryn kissed Rowan's temple.

"Then they start making you believe *you're* the one who's ruined the fun when the bad times come. They can't ever admit *they* were the ones who were wrong, so they do everything in their power to tear down your confidence and your self-esteem so you start to doubt yourself. You're left believing their words when they tell you you're stupid or hopeless or worthless, even if you know way deep down inside, *they* are the ones who are the problem."

"Are you psychic?" Rowan questioned in a small, astonished voice.

"Baby, I told you I wasn't a saint when we met. I've dated a lot of women and I saw this more times than I can remember." Bryn continued to caress her woman. "Psychological warfare, things like gaslighting, where you're manipulated until you question your own reality or perceptions, is common with narcissistic personalities." Bryn smoothed Rowan's curls back from her face and kissed her forehead.

"How do you know so much about this sort of thing?" Rowan was amazed at Bryn's insight.

"I've always been fascinated by psychology, *dulzura*. So much so, when I got out of the Marines and went to college, I decided to major in it. I knew I didn't want to be an actual psychologist, but I knew anything I would do would involve understanding the human psyche."

Bryn gave a low laugh. "Turns out, that was the perfect degree for my part in what we do at APS."

"Is that why you seem so omnipotent when it comes to figuring out the bad guys?" Rowan asked curiously.

Bryn expressed amusement again as she played with Rowan's hair.

"Probably. Although figuring out femmes took a lot more effort than figuring out the 'bad guys,'" she assured Rowan. "You all defy nature."

"Teagan says alpha butches eat, sleep, fight, and…uh…screw, although she didn't quite use that word, and everything in your lives fits into those categories. And she says femmes think too much."

"She's not wrong." Bryn's voice was amused. "Honestly, baby, you all make life a lot harder than it needs to be."

She wound one of Rowan's curls around her finger. "Teag and I talked for a bit on the phone when I was coming to meet you all at the Dream Creamery before we headed over to Seashells. She told me about the conversation you had with her this afternoon. You should know she'll want to put a hole into the fuckwit who dared to make you feel 'less than' about yourself because I'm going to tell her what we discussed about your ex tonight. That asshole hurt her little sister, so she's going to be fucking *irate*."

Rowan was speechless.

"While conversations I have with you are private and always will be, baby, she is worried enough about what happened today that I think she needs to know what prompted you to think about yourself as 'hopeless,' okay?"

Rowan whispered, "Okay," and buried her face in Bryn's shoulder again.

Bryn caressed her hair. "Teag is one of my best friends in this world, *dulzura*, and everything she told you today was spot on. You can come to me for *anything*. You're mine and part of my job as your butch is to make sure you're happy, and you always feel secure and protected."

"Teag says you alpha butches protect your women even if it means protecting us from ourselves sometimes." Rowan shyly touched Bryn in return.

"Jesus. Who's the one with the fucking psychology degree here, me or that fucker?" Rowan giggled as Bryn kissed her on the forehead again. "Another thing, baby. All of us at APS, at least the management team, we have all dated a lot. We are all highly sexual butches and sex is an integral part of our makeup. Sex, however, doesn't mean anything to us outside of the actual physical act. I can guarantee you each one of us has always made that perfectly clear to the women we date. Not one of us has ever gotten deeply involved with a woman before. Until now. Until I did with you, *dulzura*. I've told you already this was the first time in my 35 years of existence I felt even the slightest interest in claiming a woman as my own."

Bryn pulled Rowan deeper into her arms.

"When I claimed you, Rowan, I meant it. I meant it as a commitment for our entire life. I can't make that any more clear to you than I am right now. I have no intention of *ever* letting you go, *mi dulzura*."

They laid together again in silence, Rowan wrapped securely in Bryn's powerful arms, until Bryn heard Rowan's breathing get slower and slower.

Right as she fell asleep, Rowan sighed dreamily. "I think I'm falling in love with you, Bryn Armstrong."

Bryn kissed her woman's beautiful sleeping face.

"That's good, *dulzura*. Because I'm already in love with you."

Chapter 22

January 6

For Rowan's next "playdate," Bryn brought her to the Recon Room to meet with Trill.

As quiet as it was, the associates on duty nonetheless waved a warm welcome at them even as they never took their eyes from what they were doing.

Trill was waiting for them just outside the glass door to her office and the conference room. She ushered them inside, then she gave Rowan a hug and a kiss on the cheek and high-fived Bryn.

"Can I even begin to tell you how motherfucking excited I am?" Trill, at 5'7", was the shortest of the APS management team, but she was still a solid 4" taller than Rowan.

Just as good-looking as the rest of the Seven, she had dark blonde hair cut into a military fade, light brown eyes, deep dimples, and an impressive muscle structure that kept her from being called "cute." Despite the dimples, Trillian Dacanay, Rowan decided, was probably not someone she wanted to meet in a dark alley if she was on the wrong side of APS.

Now, however, Trill's dimples winked at her and she pulled out a comfortable-looking chair at the conference table. "Have a seat, Ro. Can I get you anything to drink?"

Rowan held up her water bottle and smiled. "I'm good, Trill. Thank you so much."

"Before we get started, though, can I ask you a personal question?" Rowan wrinkled her nose in embarrassment. "You know you can always tell me no if you don't want to talk about anything private, right?"

Trill's dimples popped out again and she took a seat in a chair across the conference table from Bryn and Rowan, coffee cup in hand.

"You want to ask me about my name, right?" Trill's eyes twinkled. "As in, why did Trill's mom *ever* think it was a good idea to name her kid from a quirky science fiction novel from the late 70s?"

Rowan laughed shyly. "I guess that's a question you get from most people, huh? You are probably sick of explaining it at this point."

"No, that's okay, sweetheart. I'm used to it and there really isn't much mystery behind it. When Mom first read the *Hitchhiker's Guide to the Galaxy* novel, she fell in love with the names in the book, especially the name Trillian. So, when I came along, Trillian I became. Totally simple." Then Trill cracked up. "The absolute mystery has always been why Mom named my younger brother Zaphod instead of one of the more normal names in the book, like

Arthur or Ford." She smirked. "I've given Zaph complete shit about his name since the day he was born."

Rowan giggled.

"Dacanay, incidentally, is northern Italian and is a pretty rare last name," she continued. "I think that, as of the last census, there were only about a thousand Dacanays in the United States. However," Trill smiled fondly at Rowan, "we aren't here to discuss genealogy, are we? We're here to talk about what my team and I do at APS and how your brilliant background in predictive analytics might be something we'd be grateful to leverage once in a while."

"Trill. Seriously? The Seven and Riley and Bryn have already given me so much," Rowan said passionately. "Your protection, your friendship, your understanding. All of you. I am the one who is so grateful to have you all in my life. The least I can do is run some analysis for you once in a while. Not because I feel obligated, but because…that's what family does for each other." Her face flushed as she looked at Trill and Bryn.

Trill's light brown eyes went soft. "You're so right, sweetheart."

Bryn leaned over and kissed her temple.

"There is a lot that goes on with my crew, Ro, so I think our best approach is to not worry about the tech and focus on security data instead, okay?"

Rowan nodded.

Trill leaned back and steepled her fingers. "The three biggest areas of security data we focus on here are information security analysis, computer forensics, and cryptography. An information security analyst is also known as an 'ethical hacker.' Whereas Teag's team focuses on creating secure networks that can't be accessed by outside parties, ISAs focus more on things like simulating, then defending against, data leaks or cyberattacks. Computer forensics involves launching digital investigations to obtain data related to computer crimes. Analysts recover information from computers and storage devices, and analyze that information to find digital forensics evidence."

Trill looked gently at Rowan. "I understand your mom was a civilian cyber crimes investigative analyst for the military, sweetheart."

"She was." Rowan's voice was quiet. "She actually worked with computer forensics a lot, Trill."

Trill looked at her kindly. "Then we'll step away from computer forensics, Ro, and concentrate on information security analysis and cryptography." She sipped her coffee. "An ISA, an information security analyst, primarily protects against and prevents cyberthreats to an organization. Cyberthreat elimination comprises the majority of an information security analyst's responsibilities. They focus on prevention, but they also conduct what's called 'penetration testing' to uncover a network's weaknesses. It's different from what your mom did, sweetheart, because she was investigating cyber crimes committed against a person or against an external organization. An ISA protects against and prevents internal threats and attacks."

Rowan nodded, absorbed in Trill's information.

"Ideally," Trill continued, "prevention is the optimal state to be in. We constantly play 'hacker' against our own systems, trying to find and exploit system vulnerabilities." She smirked. "Jaime's team and my team also go head-to-head with each other a lot. Jaime runs our physical security crew. Unlike us, they do *physical* penetration testing, so they are continually trying to test our physical vulnerabilities, by picking locks, sneaking into our buildings, and stealing physical property and data. Our locks are digital and so is our data, so APS headquarters is almost impossible to penetrate. However, Jaim is a fucking magician when it comes to breaching our physical security—which I will deny I *ever* said if asked—so our job is to keep her and her crew shut the fuck out."

Rowan giggled again as Bryn snorted.

Trill winked at her. "Next up to bat is cryptography. Cryptography, sweetheart, is simply the art of converting ordinary plain text into unintelligible text and vice-versa. It protects data from theft and it prevents data from being altered. Cryptographers are kind of like the edgy superheroes of the computer world, Ro. They must thoroughly understand how hackers go about invading computer systems in order to develop cryptography algorithms that will keep classified information safe. Also, cryptocurrency is a form of payment that can be exchanged online for goods and services." Trill smiled slightly. "Its appeal is because it is digital currency. It uses cryptography to render it anywhere from somewhat anonymous to completely anonymous. As you can imagine, it's used quite a lot on the dark web. We also set up some of our clients in the use of cryptocurrency so the nosy motherfuckers in their lives can't see their monetary transactions. There are almost 6,000 different cryptocurrencies currently available in the world, Ro."

Rowan's eyes widened.

"I really don't want your head to explode, sweetheart, and I know you have been absorbing one hell of a lot of information recently, so why don't we put this down for now and talk about predictive analytics, okay?"

Rowan turned and looked at Bryn with impressed eyes, then looked back at Trill.

"Yet another one of the Seven who absolutely blows my mind," she said, staring at Trill in awe.

"Yeah, well, now it's your turn to amaze, Ro." Trill leaned forward and smirked at Bryn. "Prepare to have *your* fucking mind blown, cuz."

Rowan took in a deep breath and fidgeted. "In a nutshell…predictive analytics are used to identify the likelihood of various future outcomes based on historical data, right?"

Trill and Bryn nodded.

"At its very simplest, we're using all these tools in the data analytics tool belt to predict the future. That's really the crux of it all." Rowan abruptly stopped, quiet. She gnawed at her lip in silence while she considered her next words. Her hesitancy struck both Trill and Bryn, who gave each other a sharp look.

"*Dulzura.*" Bryn leaned over and lifted Rowan easily onto her lap.

"You know you can tell me and Trill anything, right? What is troubling you, little one?" Bryn stroked Rowan's back, calming her woman, while Trill looked on, concerned.

Rowan looked down and blew out a breath.

"It's just…I know it isn't very scientific or analytical, but it's like I can 'feel' things sometimes," she burst out. "It's something I've always been able to do, as far back as I can remember. If my gut says something different than what the predictions on paper say," she admitted slowly, "my gut is going to be what wins. Every. Single. Time."

Rowan gave them both a grave look. "That's really why I'm offered so many jobs. I'm virtually never wrong. If I *am* wrong, it's because I ignored what I call my 'spidey-sense.'" Rowan fidgeted more. "That's why I can't ever teach anybody to do what I do. It's not like I haven't tried a million times before either. But I don't even know if there's a way to teach that kind of gut instinct. I have a tendency not to tell anyone about my 'ability,'" she made air quotes with her fingers, "because I made the mistake of doing that once and…and, it didn't end well for me." She swallowed and twisted her fingers nervously.

"Don't tell me." Bryn's voice was mild, although there was hellfire in her eyes. "It was that jackass motherfucker who always made it a habit of destroying my woman's self-confidence and her sense of self-worth."

Trill regarded Bryn with a raised eyebrow.

"And who was that?" Trill's voice was also mild, but the look in her eyes promised painful retribution.

Bryn kissed Rowan on her temple and ran her hands soothingly over her. "Some asshole she used to date in Virginia. Who should be thankful she's in Virginia right now and not anywhere near here."

"We seem to be making trips to Virginia lately for some very good reasons. It looks like I can think of another good reason now." Trill's eyes and smile were glacial and she shrugged at Bryn. "I'm just saying, chief."

Rowan smiled at her friend, who was clearly pissed on her behalf.

"I appreciate you more than you know, Trill," she said gently. "You can maybe help me out by thinking of a way I could do a viable knowledge transfer to others because I've never been able to figure it out myself."

Trill ran her hand over her short hair and calmed herself.

"Ro, sweetheart, I don't know if what you can do is something you can teach. If your ability works the way you describe, there is really no way to mimic that. However," Trill blew out her own breath, "you had better believe the associates in the Geek Crew are going to become your new favorite detectives, sweetheart."

Chapter 23

January 10

"You have to be fucking kidding me." Bryn was astounded as she stared at her twin.

Riley had stopped by Bryn's office to bring her up to date on her most recent investigation into Coravani to find out why he was no longer a police officer.

"Not kidding at all, *mano*. Get this." Riley stretched out her long legs while sitting on Bryn's office sofa. "The offense that *finally* got his sorry ass fired and his badge stripped was one where a 13-year-old boy was able to video excessive use of force by Coravani. He had been savagely beating an unarmed suspect, which the kid filmed while in hiding, and Coravani didn't know he was there."

Bryn's eyes narrowed. "That was a dangerous move by the kid."

"Apparently, the dickweed had been suspected of using unjustified force on more than one occasion for quite some time," Riley continued. "This, however, he and his fellow douchebags in the department weren't able to hide. When the boy's mother had threatened to go to the press with the video of Coravani, he was fired by the department chief in an effort to contain the damage to the department. Want to know the best part?" Riley speared Bryn with a look that promised hellish payback for someone. "Give me your best guess as to why Coravani has been able to get away with so much bullshit over the past few years. I'm surprised as fuck the newswires haven't lit up with this."

"Oh, fuck." Bryn didn't like what she saw coming. "Who does he know?"

"It's not who he knows, *mano*." Riley didn't suppress her look of disgust. "Try 'Who is he related to?' As in, the mayor is his mother's fucking brother."

"Son of a goddamn bitch." Bryn was livid. "You mean to tell me my woman has had to put up with this motherfucker and his bullshit just because Mommy has her brother making sure her baby is protected?"

"Looks like. However," Riley gave her twin a cold smile, "also looks like the last thing they were expecting was the package we exploded on them. There was no way for him to wiggle out of that one and they had no choice but to issue a warrant for his arrest. Since Mommy has a different last name, they've been able to suppress her relationship to Coravani up until now, which in turn protects the mayor. I have no fucking clue why the press up there hasn't been all over this like flies on shit, so there must be a bunch of money changing hands somewhere. Mommy's got some bucks."

Riley was direct. "I adore Rowan already and she is going to be my sister-in-law when you finally get your lazy ass in gear and marry her." She smirked, then turned serious again. "Therefore, I will destroy the fuck out of anything or anyone who dares to threaten or harm her, just like the Seven have also promised to do, *mano*."

Bryn was quiet for a long time. "You know I'm in love with her, right?" Bryn finally admitted to Riley slowly.

"Doesn't take a rocket scientist." Riley was equally serious. "She's everything you've ever needed and wanted your entire life, even if you didn't realize it. It's like she was made just for you."

Riley grinned briefly at her twin. "When all this bullshit is over with, Mama is going to lose her mind planning your wedding and Ro will probably lose her mind dealing with Mama." The twins cracked up for a moment.

"It drives me fucking crazy that she's not safe, Riles." Bryn quickly sobered and exerted a huge amount of control over the anger that immediately bubbled up. "It's become more than stalking now for him. It's become vengeance because she, in his mind, is the one responsible for his arrest warrant and for exposing him for what he truly is. He exhibits all the signs of a classic sociopath."

Bryn and Riley stared at each other until Bryn said what they were both thinking out loud.

"Which means he fully intends to find her, torture her, fuck her, and then kill her."

¥¥¥¥¥

There was an ominous feeling of danger in the conference room where Bryn and Riley were meeting with the Seven.

Right before the meeting, Bryn had told Teagan about Rowan and her past relationship with her asshole ex, and how her experience had colored her perceptions of herself. It was no surprise that Teagan went into the meeting seething.

Riley caught everybody up with her discoveries about Coravani's connections and his relationship to the mayor of Rowan's old hometown in Virginia, which caused more than a few thunderclouds to hit the faces of the Seven.

When Riley was done, Bryn shared her psychological evaluation of Coravani's mental state and what she believed his intentions concerning Rowan were.

Just like Rowan was never wrong when it came to predictive analytics, Bryn was never wrong when it came to psychological evaluations, and the Seven knew it.

When Bryn had finished, there was dead silence for a minute before Drew broke the murderous quiet. Her voice was so low and so full of ice, it was a wonder she didn't give the entire room frostbite.

"I know Rowan's yours, chief, and the right to dispose of this shitstain is also yours," she informed Bryn, "but I'll be honest with you. If I happen to come across him, I'm not going to be able to stop myself from taking his sorry ass the fuck out."

There was a general rumble of pissed-off agreement in the room.

"Any more echoes?" Bryn asked Drew after she nodded to her in acknowledgment, focusing everyone deliberately on their tracking information.

"Faint and barely detectable," Drew answered, still ice-cold. "Which makes me think he's found a contact of some kind here in Whimsy whom he's been able to start hiding behind. Given what we know now about his background, it's not inconceivable either Mommy or his fuckwit uncle have some local Florida connections, and he's started to leverage them, considering squatting didn't work out so well for him."

"I'm already digging into it." Trill's light brown eyes were dark with anger and her dimples were nowhere in sight. "The Geek Crew has made it their top priority. Just bear in mind we are talking about hundreds of connections here between the two of them. We'll dig as fast as we can, but be prepared for it to take a while. We can't risk missing anything. Once we narrow the data down some, I can ask Rowan to run some predictive analytics on it to pinpoint the most likely path Coravani would have taken."

Bryn nodded. "In the meantime, we are going to keep Rowan's life as normal as possible. She's working with her people to open the Dream Creamery and the WCA Center in the next few weeks, and I don't want her to be distracted if we can help it."

"Agreed," said Casey. "That sweet woman has gone through fucking enough. The least we can do is keep Coravani's bullshit away from her so she can enjoy this time with her friends and her new business. I'm up to bat next on the 'playdate' schedule," she continued. "Bryn and I are going to do a demo for her in the gym, but then we're going to teach her a few basic self-defense moves." She blew out a breath and ruffled her platinum blond hair. "The moves are good to know no matter what the circumstances, and fuck knows we are all on Rowan like white on rice these days, but Bryn and I feel she can't be too careful with this asshole on the loose right now."

The rumble that rolled through the conference room this time carried assent.

"I'm going to give Rowan a break for a couple of days," Bryn stated. "She's absorbed a fuck of a lot in a very short time and I'm exceptionally proud of her, but she needs some time to concentrate on her own responsibilities."

She looked around the room.

"I know it will make them absolutely crazy, but we need to assign an associate each to Nova, Alyssa, and Brooke, too. They'll understand the importance and they'll definitely do it for Rowan until this motherfucker is caught, but I already know they'll want to carve off Coravani's balls themselves."

"Love me some bloodthirsty femmes," Blake muttered under her breath.

"In the meantime, Drew will keep ghosting through Purgatory, and Jaime and her crew will keep running physical reconnaissance through Whimsy. Kenn, I'd like you and Riley to go ahead and make the armory adjustments we talked about earlier, okay?"

Kenn nodded her assent.

"Blake, I'm thinking some extra-intensive drills wouldn't be a bad idea for the associates who've been assigned bodyguard duty." Blake gave a thumbs-up. "Test their reaction times, accuracy and response times, especially against the newer sim models. We'll meet every day at both 6:00 a.m. and 4:00 p.m. to give status updates until this fuck has been neutralized once and for all."

Chapter 24

January 17

"Unbelievable, Ro." Clem watched the artisan who was painting the mural in the Dream Creamery as she worked on the show-stopping piece.

"I can't believe how much Ember and Nia's crews are accomplishing, frankly." Rowan scanned through her iPad. "This week's edition of the Pioneer is coming out today, the one with the call-to-artists, and we already have almost twenty responses, believe it or not. Delaney's plane gets in at two o'clock, and Nova is going to go and pick her up. They've already been going back and forth on what desserts to make for the grand opening."

Rowan shook her head.

"They are proposing miniature fudge brownies swirled with raspberry coulis for the raspberry-habanero ice cream, Chardonnay-white chocolate truffles with a caramel drizzle to go with the Cardonnay-caramel ice cream and jalapeno-lime cheesecake bites for the kaffir lime gelato."

"Those bitches are going to make my ass explode," Clementine moaned as Rowan giggled.

"Oh. And speaking of dessert," Clem burst out with total perplexity, "did you know Teag told me the badasses *never* eat dessert unless it's a holiday? Like, who fucking does that?" Clem was dumbfounded. "Are they crazy? Or just abnormal?"

Rowan snorted. "Yeah, well, ask me about the time Bryn explained to me they start their morning meetings at 6:00 a.m. *after* they've all run about ten miles."

Clem's jaw dropped and her eyes got huge.

"Fucking lunatics, every single one of them," Clem huffed in incredulity.

"Be glad it's us doing it and not you." They both turned around to find Teagan leaning against the door frame, smirking, her well-muscled arms folded over her chest.

When Rowan had seen Teagan for the first time after she knew Bryn had shared the story about Rowan's ex with her, Teag hadn't said a word. However, she had silently pulled Rowan into her arms and held her gently for a long couple of minutes, then kissed her cheek before letting her go just as silently.

Bryn told her later that Teagan had gone so ballistic at finding out everything Rowan's ex had put her through, she and Riley had seriously considered putting Teag into lockdown temporarily, which had made Rowan's jaw drop.

"You're family now, *dulzura*," Bryn had said, kissing Rowan with an authoritative passion. "We take family seriously at APS," she continued after she let Rowan come up for air. "We always have.

And, like it or not, you now have eight older 'siblings' who will rain hell down on anyone who thinks they can fuck with you."

Bryn had smiled slightly as she looped a blonde curl around Rowan's ear. "Not to mention, a very possessive, very protective butch lover who will kill anyone who even looks at you sideways."

Now, Teagan reminded Rowan she had a playdate with Casey.

"I'm going to take you back to Bryn's apartment so you can change. Bryn will meet you there and take you to Hades."

"Hades?" Clem asked in puzzlement.

"It's the name Jaime gave to their gym. And Clem…don't even ask." Rowan held up her hand as Clem started to speak.

¥¥¥¥¥

As Bryn and Rowan pulled open the mammoth glass doors and entered the area of the APS complex known as Hades, Rowan's huge eyes roamed over the enormous gym with awe.

There were a considerable number of APS associates in the gym, all of whom were engaged in some type of hard core activity: Rowan saw free weights, kettlebells, barbells, training benches, jump ropes, air bikes, plus a million other pieces of equipment that were totally unfamiliar to her.

On the far side of the gym were thick mats on the floor where Bryn said the martial arts and fighting practices were held.

"Hey, Rowan!" one of the APS associates yelled in welcome. A chorus of boisterous "Heys!" greeted her as she and Bryn started winding their way around the edge of the room. Rowan blushed, but waved back happily at everyone.

She clutched a long wrapped tube to herself, the contents of which she had refused to divulge to Bryn.

"You're sure Jaime is coming in today? I have a surprise for her." Rowan couldn't hide her mischievous grin.

Bryn raised an eyebrow. "She usually does about this time, baby, unless something has come up with her crew." She shook her head in bemused amusement and continued to lead her woman toward the back of the gym.

Rowan was dressed in a tight, long-sleeve shirt Bryn had given her the night before that she had called a "rash guard."

"A rash guard, *dulzura*, is a tight shirt typically made out of spandex or a lycra-like material that allows it to fit tightly to your body." Bryn's shirt was extremely similar to Rowan's except it had short sleeves. "They're lightweight and pull sweat away from your skin to help keep your body cool. They also minimize mat burn, which is important in contact sports since mat burns can hurt like a bitch."

Bryn stopped in the back and wrapped her arm around Rowan as they waited for Casey.

"The rash guard and those fight shorts you have on now are typical fightwear for MMA fighters, *dulzura*."

"*Broki. Chula.*" Suddenly, Jaime's Puerto Rican accent reached them as the black-haired, brown-eyed member of the Seven came into view.

Jaime hugged Rowan, mindful of the package she was carrying, and kissed her on the cheek. She high-fived Bryn, and then turned back to Rowan.

"To what do we owe this honor, *mi hermana*?" Jaime asked Rowan. She glanced at Bryn with a look of surprise on her face as Rowan handed her the package with an even bigger grin.

"We're here because it's time for my playdate with Casey. She and Bryn are going to do a martial arts demonstration for me and then Casey is going to teach me a few self-defense moves. But …" Bryn and Jaime looked at each other with raised eyebrows as a wicked look crossed Rowan's angelic face. "Bryn tells me the gym was named Hades because of you, Jaime, right?"

"Right." A twinkle appeared in Jaime's eye. "We work out extremely hard, *chula*, so I thought the name was perfect because it's hell getting through a lot of our workouts."

"That's what I thought." Rowan's grin grew bigger. "So, I thought this would make the perfect 'decoration' for the gym in your honor then, *mi broki*." Rowan looked proud with her Spanish attempt. "It's for one of the gym doors, Jaime. I hope you like it."

Jaime took the package from Rowan, bemused, as Casey joined the group just in time to hear Rowan's words.

"Well, come on, fucker." Casey kissed Rowan's cheek and hugged her, then crossed her staggeringly corded arms. "I want to see what little sis brought you."

"I'm scared," Jaime muttered. Rowan cracked up as Jaime made a 'scared' face, then watched in anticipation as Jaime tore the package open.

"What is it?" Jaime looked at the rolled tube.

Rowan sank into Bryn's side. "It's a window cling for one of the front doors," she said and started to giggle. "Unroll it."

Jaime unrolled the 24"x36" rectangle, then died laughing when she saw what it was.

The vinyl window cling had vicious-looking flames running around the outside of it. On the inside, in red and black Gothic lettering near the top, was the word, "Hades." Below it, in smaller black lettering, were the words, "Abandon hope all ye who enter here."

Bryn and Casey burst into laughter while Jaime bent over and tried to catch her breath between loud peals of hilarity.

"You know you don't actually have to put that on the gym door, right?" explained Rowan as she continued to giggle. "I just thought it was hysterical. There are a million other places we can put it, like in the Bunker."

"Oh, fuck no, *mi hermana*." Jaime looked appalled. "This is staying right here in Hades where it belongs." She smiled at Rowan with an uncharacteristically soft look in her dark eyes. "Thank you, *chula*. This is one of the best presents I've ever gotten."

She hugged Rowan tightly for a minute and kissed her cheek again before making her way toward the gym doors. After a few moments, there was a loud burst of laughter as other associates saw Jaime's present.

Bryn swept Rowan into her arms and kissed her.

"Do you see what I mean, *mi dulzura*?" she said softly as she rubbed her hands softly up and down Rowan's back. "You bring joy to everyone you meet just by being you."

Rowan buried her face in Bryn's shoulder.

"You ready to get this party started, chief?" Casey asked after a minute as she stripped off her loose T-shirt. Underneath, she was wearing a sleeveless rash guard in black which contrasted with her platinum blond hair and brilliant blue eyes, and had on black fighter shorts.

Like the others of the Seven, Casey was tall at 5'9" and was insanely muscled from her work as the APS martial arts and fight instructor. Her poker-straight hair was cut into a classic "skater cut," with the back and sides extremely short, but the front bangs long and swept sideways.

Once again, Rowan thought to herself she had never seen a group of butches as gorgeous as the APS management team.

"Sweetheart, I'm going to explain what my team does briefly, then Bryn and I are going to do a demo for you, okay?" Casey's vivid blue eyes were focused on Rowan.

Rowan nodded and leaned against Bryn, whose strong arm automatically went around her.

"First of all, MMA stands for 'Mixed Martial Arts.' It's what's called a full-contact combat sport, Rowan," Casey began. "It involves different martial arts and combat sports from all over the world, things like Brazilian Jiu-Jitsu, boxing, wrestling, and Muay Thai. My team and I train the APS associates in MMA and other fighting styles," Casey continued. "We also practice Krav Maga here at APS as well, although that falls outside the realm of MMA. Krav Maga was first developed for the Israeli Defense Forces as a military self-defense and fighting system. It can be a very dangerous form of combat. Like most martial arts, Krav Maga encourages the avoidance of physical confrontation, but if that's not possible or if you're in a situation where that's not safe, it encourages finishing a fight as rapidly and as ferociously as possible. You with me so far, sweetheart?"

Rowan nodded again, her eyes wide.

"When it comes to teaching you some self-defense moves, Krav Maga will actually be the most effective for you because it teaches you to leverage your natural instincts to make them more efficient and productive. Krav Maga, which translates to 'contact combat,' isn't about winning a fight, Ro. It's about doing enough to get away if you are attacked."

Casey paused for a moment to take off her running shoes before stepping onto the mat.

"We also do a lot of heavy bag training because the muscles in your arms, shoulders, chest, back, legs, and core are all engaged during a heavy bag conditioning session." Casey nodded toward a row of heavy boxing bags mounted from the ceiling at the far end of the gym.

Casey looked at Bryn who had also slipped off her own shoes. "You ready, chief?"

"Let's do this." Bryn kissed Rowan once more, then stepped onto the mat as well.

Rowan saw Teagan out of the corner of her eye as Teag moved towards her. She also noticed more than a few APS associates had gathered next to the mat, too.

"It's not every day they get to see one of the heads of APS grapple with the martial arts crew leader, Ro," Teagan informed her as she reached Rowan and kissed her cheek. "They are both so evenly matched, this could go either way."

Jaime slid up to Rowan's other side. "Do you want a chair, *chula*? I'm happy to go get you one."

Rowan smiled at her friend. "Thank you, Jaime, but I think I'm too nervous to sit." She looked at Casey and Bryn on the mat, positioning themselves in preparation. She noticed they were both relaxed and seemed almost casual in their stances.

"They'll only grapple since you're here, *mi hermana*. No striking." Jaime's voice was reassuring. "Martial arts can get extremely aggressive, but that's not why they're here today."

Before Rowan knew it, Casey and Bryn were in action.

"Grappling is used at close range to gain a physical advantage over an opponent, Ro," Teagan said, watching the two on the mat with intense concentration.

Rowan didn't think she had ever seen anything so spell-binding in her life.

WHIMSICAL HAVEN

Both Casey and Bryn were using pinning and holding techniques in an effort to wrest the other into a submission position. They were blindingly fast, exceedingly graceful, and their movements flowed from one position to another without a hitch.

They occasionally switched between dominant and submission positions, but more often than not, they were in "neutral" position, where Jaime whispered neither of them had the advantage.

Rowan's eyes were glued to the pair as they rolled, pinned, clinched, and gripped each other. She was absolutely mesmerized by their skill and couldn't take her eyes off either of them.

After ten minutes, an associate Rowan hadn't seen gave a short blast on a whistle, signaling a draw.

Casey and Bryn shook hands, then grinned and "bro-hugged" each other, both dripping wet with sweat, and made their way over to Rowan.

"A fucking draw. You asshole," Bryn needled her friend. Casey burst out laughing.

"I can't help it if you're losing your touch, cuz," Casey snarked with humor as she winked at Rowan, who giggled. "Sweetheart, we're going to go get cleaned up. Give us ten, okay?" The two made their way to the showers, stopping to accept congratulations from APS associates who'd seen the demo.

Ten minutes later, as promised, Casey and Bryn were back out with wet hair and fresh clothes.

"Ready, *dulzura*?" Bryn kissed Rowan, who snuggled into Bryn's arms.

"I have never seen anything as amazing as you and Casey today," Rowan said with awe after kissing Bryn back. She twisted in Bryn's arms so she could see her friend.

"I know nothing about self-defense moves, Casey, but I'm willing to work hard and learn. Just be patient with me, okay?" She backed out of Bryn's hold so she could slip off her sneakers and stepped onto the mat.

"That definitely goes without saying, sweetheart." Casey's eyes were soft. "The nice thing about these Krav Maga moves I'm going to show you is they're not hard to execute in and of themselves. They just take a lot of repetition to become efficient and effective."

"I practice yoga five days a week." Rowan gave Casey a considering look. "Are these moves I could practice in Bryn's apartment after my yoga or do I need to make arrangements to come down to the gym?"

"You can practice them in Bryn's apartment without a problem, Ro, especially if you move the bar stools at her breakfast bar. The moves don't take up a lot of room by themselves, although I'd like you to come down here to the gym maybe twice a week to practice them with a partner and in a more exaggerated fashion, okay?"

"Teag?" Rowan asked just as the handsome, red-haired butch said, "Consider it done."

Casey stood in front of Rowan holding a padded striking shield. "Okay, sweetheart. The first move I'd like to show you is named the 'Open Hand Strike.' Basically, you use the heel of your hand to 'punch' the face, the eyes, and both the front and back of the neck of an attacker." Casey slowly demonstrated the move.

"When you go to hit, don't draw your elbow back, Ro. You don't want to telegraph your intentions to your attacker. Keep your arms in front of your body, yeah? Now, I want you to practice hitting this shield and I want you to hit it *hard*, sweetheart. You can't hurt me, so give it everything you've got."

Rowan focused with extreme concentration, then "punched" the striking shield hard with the heels of her hands.

"Good! Good! Keep punching, sweetheart," Casey encouraged her. "You want to keep repeating the movement until you have incapacitated your attacker enough so you can run away."

"Beautiful, *dulzura*," Bryn praised her from where she was watching and Teagan gave her a thumbs-up in approval.

Rowan kept repeating the movement, with Casey making occasional small corrections, until she was satisfied Rowan could practice at home on her own.

"Great job, Ro! Okay, this is the next move. Believe it or not, this is the one self-defense move every woman has known practically her entire life and that's the 'kick to the groin' move.

"Kicking an attacker in the groin with the tips or top of your shoe when you are further away from your attacker or using your knee when you are closer in range is still one of the best self-defense moves there is, Rowan. It sounds simplistic, but it's a move you never want to forget about when you are under attack. Use all the force you can summon and, again, keep doing it until you incapacitate your attacker enough so you can run away."

Casey demonstrated the move in slow motion, then held the shield so Rowan could practice kicking or kneeing an attacker.

"You have amazing balance, *dulzura*, probably because of your yoga practice," observed Bryn. Casey and Teagan both agreed.

"Having great balance like you do definitely gives you an advantage with self-defense," Bryn encouraged her.

"Next is something named the 'Rear Bearhug,' which you can use when someone tries to grab you from behind." Casey smirked and beckoned to Bryn. "Chief, you want to restrain your woman as if you were trying to grab her from the rear?"

"With pleasure." Bryn's dark eyes rested on Rowan, then she slid her arms securely around the petite blonde from behind.

"The first thing you do is fold forward, Rowan. That will make you very heavy for an attacker to pick up, even as petite as you are. Then, while still bending, you slam your elbows back into your attacker from all angles, including their head and neck and ribs, twisting and wiggling until you loosen their hold. When they let you go—and they will—spin around and jam your knee *hard* into their groin. You can then escape to safety."

Casey's eyes twinkled. "We're going to do this one very slowly at a demonstration speed because I kind of like this fucker and I don't want to send her home crying to Mama Armstrong."

Bryn flipped her off as Rowan giggled and Teagan snorted.

Rowan practiced with Bryn and Casey over and over until Casey was finally satisfied Rowan understood how to execute the move exactly.

"One more for now, sweetheart. This is the 'attack from the ground' move. If your attacker throws you to the ground, it doesn't mean you're now completely vulnerable. You can judge your distance and then use your feet to defend yourself," Casey explained. "Kick your assailant, Ro, using both your feet at once. Thrust your hips off the floor for extra power if your assailant is directly above you. I'm going to hold my shield and you're going to kick me as hard as you can from the ground."

Again, Casey had Rowan keep repeating the move until she finally felt that Rowan had it down. Bryn extended her hand and helped Rowan up from the ground when they were done.

"That's good enough for now, sweetheart." Casey kissed Rowan on the cheek. "You did fucking awesome, kiddo."

"She's amazing, isn't she?" Teagan said with pride.

"If you practice these moves five days a week with your yoga, you will keep getting more efficient and more effective until practicing self-defense is totally second nature for you." Casey gave her a thumbs-up.

"Casey. Oh my gosh, *thank you*." Rowan hugged her friend tightly, then smuggled into Bryn's side. "You made this *so easy*. I was all nervous, thinking it was going to take me a while to keep up since I was starting from a place of knowing absolutely nothing, but you taught me all of this in one afternoon."

Rowan paused and mulled over a thought.

"Have you or your team ever considered offering something like this as a class, Casey? Maybe once a month or even once a quarter? I'm serious. It was so easy and I think the Whimsy ladies would love it because it was completely non-intimidating and didn't make me feel stupid. Even young girls could learn how to do this."

Casey, Bryn, and Teagan looked at each other.

"That's not a bad idea at all, chief. We could schedule a free class at the Whimsy Rec Center once a month as part of our community outreach," Casey mused. "I'll ask Jess if she'd be interested in teaching something like that." Jess was Casey's second. "She's such a good teacher already and she's a fucking beast when it comes to Krav Maga. Plus women, especially young girls, feel so safe with her. I can't see why she wouldn't be excited."

"Thank you, *dulzura*." Bryn kissed Rowan's temple. "That is a wonderful idea and I think it will be a great thing for the community."

"You fucking rock, little sis." Casey stepped off the mat and quickly put on her shoes. "I have a conference call in fifteen minutes, so I have to run. You or Bryn text me if you have any questions, okay? I'm just hoping you never need to use any of this shit yourself, sweetheart, because I'll have to kill someone if you do." A cold look crossed Casey's face before she made her way through the gym.

"I'll be back in five, Ro. I need to grab Jaime real quick before she leaves, all right? I'll be right back, sweetheart." Teagan headed off in the same direction.

When Rowan again expressed her amazement at the protection and support she had gotten so quickly from the Seven, Bryn looked at her seriously.

"Sometimes, I don't think you realize just how sweet you are, *dulzura*. You don't play games. You accept people for what they are. You open your heart and your arms immediately to anyone who needs you. You are so grateful for even the little things people do for you. You are fiercely protective of those you love. You think the Seven haven't noticed or responded to that?" Bryn nuzzled Rowan behind her ear. "I've told you before, we are highly sexual beings and that attracting women is not a problem for any of us, baby. Femmes especially like the cachet of being seen with an APS associate, especially someone on the management team. But finding women who simply cherish us for what we are and don't expect anything from us is a whole hell of a lot more rare."

Rowan felt as though she had been gifted the world when Bryn said, "You are that kind of rare, *dulzura*, and every single one of us loves you for it."

Chapter 25

January 20

Rowan stood in the middle of her house with Bryn as they talked about what needed to be done before Rowan could move in.

It had been a wonderful Sunday. First, Bryn and Rowan went to the Armstrongs for Sunday lunch with the family and Rowan had sworn she'd never laughed so hard in her life.

After lunch, with Rosi chasing her out of the kitchen yet again, Rowan had kicked off her shoes and curled up next to Bryn on the family room sofa, talking about her dad to Oliver. Bryn and Riley had loved hearing about the "family" side of Bill Holland and his commitment to his daughters. Although they were all extremely close, Rowan explained that Kelly was the daughter who was Bill's little shadow, whereas Rowan was the one who spent more time with Amanda, playing with data.

When Rowan had explained the "point-counterpoint" game that Amanda had created for her girls when they were younger, a gleam had entered Oliver's eyes.

"I think that would be bloody brilliant for Noah and Keenan, love. They constantly argue like kids and this might redirect some of their idiocy." Oliver rolled his eyes, but his love for his children was evident on his face.

Bryn and Rowan had left after a wonderful afternoon with the entire family. Bryn had come up with the suggestion to stop by Rowan and Kelly's house, so they could get a feel for what all needed to be done.

First, the two of them had taken a short walk along the sidewalk that banded the beach, Bryn explaining it was a little too cool that day to take off their shoes and walk in the sand.

Rowan had cast her eyes heavenward and stuck her hand on her hip, teasing, "Wimpy Floridians, I swear. This is like early summer in Virginia."

Bryn narrowed her eyes playfully at her woman. "I give you two years, *dulzura*, before I hear you whining that anything below 70° is positively arctic."

Rowan burst out laughing.

The view from her house, to Rowan's enchanted eyes, was nothing short of magical. Her house sat right on the waterfront of Boca Ciega Bay, one of the four aquatic preserves in the Tampa Bay area, which bordered St. Petersburg and other county municipalities.

From inside the house, they wandered to the huge French double glass doors at the rear of the house, which opened onto a beautiful lanai. Past the lanai, with its attached outdoor bathroom and shower, was a sparkling screened-in pool and an outdoor kitchen at one end.

Outside of the enclosed pool area was a private dock with a large boat lift right on the Boca Ciega Bay that made Bryn's eyes gleam.

"I need to buy us a boat, *dulzura*," she said casually. "My parents have one, but Riles and I have never bothered to buy our own because we really didn't have a place to keep it. So, we've always used theirs."

Bryn took Rowan into her arms and kissed her deeply.

"Even if it wasn't for this piece of shit motherfucker we're dealing with right now, baby, you've been busy getting the Dream Creamery and the WCA Center up and running—which is exactly what you should be doing right now—and we haven't really had any time for play."

Bryn cupped Rowan's cheek. "But I want you to prepare yourself, *dulzura*. You're a Floridian now and we all live on the water, so everything we do revolves around that. We swim. We fish. We sail. We kayak. We watch the wildlife constantly, herons and dolphins and sea turtles and manatees. What?" Bryn questioned when Rowan started to laugh.

"When we made the decision to move to Florida from Virginia," Rowan said, her eyes twinkling, "the first thing Clem said when she came over to our house was that she was going *home*, and she wouldn't have to deal with any more lame people asking her what the eff a manatee was."

Bryn threw back her head and laughed.

She slid her arms tightly around her woman. "The point is, my beautiful one, is that there is a *ton* of shit to do here, all year round. We work hard, but we play hard, too. Riley and I and the Seven love to be on the water, so we'll need to buy a boat that's a minimum of 35', *dulzura*."

"And apparently, stock in sunscreen, too." She smirked, stroking her woman's ivory-white skin with a deeply tanned hand, courtesy of her half-Puerto Rican heritage.

Bryn took Rowan's hand. "Let's scope out the inside and take a closer look at the house's footprint, baby."

The house was of newer construction, which was odd for Whimsy, but apparently the original owners had pulled down the old house to build this new one.

"I remember Kelly saying the old house sustained a lot of flood damage four years ago, from a big tropical storm, maybe?" Rowan said thoughtfully.

"Could be," Bryn replied. "This is Florida, we get a lot of severe storms, and the old houses often don't stand up to tropical storm-force winds. Sounds like they made the decision to rebuild after something like that happened."

"What I love is the fact that there is a huge master bedroom suite on one end of the house and then a big mother-in-law apartment on the other end of the house," Rowan enthused. "Kelly and I are close. I mean, we are *super* close, Bryn. We always have been. None of those sister fights or anything stupid like that, ever." Her eyes became slightly glassy. "When Mom and Dad died, we just became closer. I can't imagine not having her in my life or not being close to her, Bryn. It seems to me that this house was made for all of us; that is, if you want to stay here with me sometimes."

Bryn nuzzled Rowan behind her ear. "Riley and I are twins, *dulzura*. We are fraternal, but we might as well be identical with how we think and react and feel. We have been virtually inseparable for thirty-five years, so I get it. Unless Kelly has a major objection, which I can't see happening from everything I know about her," Bryn continued, "I'd like to split our time between this house and my apartment at the APS complex."

"It makes sense to me for us to take the apartment and leave the main house and the master bedroom suite for her. Not that we need to have a huge division of the house or anything, but that way we all have our own private space," Rowan agreed.

"And," Bryn held her woman to her securely, "once that dickhead motherfucker is no more and you can move around a bit more freely, it will be much easier for us to make plans to do things." Bryn smirked. "You should be aware, though, that I don't see that fucker Teagan completely giving up her bodyguard duties anytime soon, even when we finally get rid of Coravani."

Rowan shook her head with a small smile.

Bryn looked around the house. "Everything is new, down to the appliances. You, of course, are going to want to get a decorating plan together with Ember. When all that's done, APS can come in and install all the security. I'm warning you now, *dulzura*, you are going to have all eight badasses going over your new system with a fine-tooth comb." Bryn smirked again. "Teag is going to lose her motherfucking mind dealing with them all, but she'll get over it."

The late afternoon sun cast its golden haze over the waters of the Boca Ciega Bay, reflecting off the pool and throwing light over the inside walls of the empty house.

Bryn captured Rowan's mouth for a moment before she released it to make sure the house was secure before she steered Rowan toward the mudroom that led to the garage.

"I need my woman, *dulzura*." Bryn pulled Rowan to her as she wrapped her long, muscular arms around Rowan's torso from behind and gently bit the side of Rowan's neck.

"I'm going to take you home, and I'm going to strip you bare. I'm going to bury my face in your pussy and eat you until you've come so hard, you've almost blacked out. And I'll keep doing it until you are shrieking and begging me to stop. And then, *dulzura*," Bryn's voice was wicked, "I'm going to impale you on my cock and fuck you until you've lost your voice from screaming. Until your pussy is wet and swollen and has had so many orgasms, you're limp and completely submissive to my will."

Rowan was shaking from Bryn's passionate words.

"Let's go, baby." Bryn's voice was still wicked. "I can already taste you and I'm done waiting."

Chapter 26

January 27

Rowan surveyed the art classroom at the WCA Center with her hands on her hips.

The west wall floor-to-ceiling locking storage cabinets and storage drawers were all installed and ready to be filled with supplies. The craft table and chairs had been delivered and set up, fitting beautifully in the space. The east wall was covered with a neutral-colored tack board so future students had a place to display their work for discussion.

While everything needed in the Dream Creamery had been largely cosmetic, there had been more involved construction and electrical work needed in the WCA Center for the display lights in the art gallery and the electrical needs in the art room.

However, Nia was a magician who was making everything seem effortless while, at the same time, demonstrating her understanding of the electrical needs of art galleries and art classrooms.

Nia had installed the light switches, the fire alarms, and the thermostat in the narrow space between the corner of the room and the door so she didn't waste precious display wall space. She had also upgraded the electrical so there were more than enough outlets in the floor and in the ceiling for the appliances and equipment that would be used by the students.

Additionally, she had installed a light panel to control both direct lighting options and zoned lighting options that could be used whenever needed.

Behind the table on the north side of the room were drying racks for artwork and next to them was a big double sink for cleanup. Additional storage cabinets had been installed above the sink and drying racks as well.

It was perfect.

"Yo, bitch!" Alyssa's voice suddenly echoed loudly through the space from the front. "Where my homegirl at?"

"Jesus Christ, Alyssa." Rowan grinned as she heard Teagan snark. "Your homegirl is less than twenty-five feet away and now she's probably sticking earplugs in her fucking ears."

"Oh, pffft." She heard a loud kiss as it landed on Teagan's cheek. "It's all good, Casanova. Is it okay if I go back?"

"Come on back, Alyssa," Rowan yelled. "I'm just doing some last-minute thinking."

"Fucking save us all," Teagan mumbled, making Rowan's grin grow even more.

Alyssa skated into the classroom and stopped abruptly, her eyes rounding and her jaw dropping open.

"Isn't this *amazing*?" Rowan was jubilant. "Ember and Nia did such a freaking awesome job. I'm hoping *I* didn't forget anything, but Nia has done a lot of art gallery and art classroom construction, so I think we should be okay."

Alyssa wandered around the small classroom, peeking into cabinets and drawers, inspecting the drying racks, turning on the light system, and looking at the tack boards.

"Rowan." Alyssa's voice was incredulous as big tears ran down her face. "Fuck me sideways, sister. This is *incredible*. Art therapy will be so much more effective with all…all *this*." She sniffed as Rowan wrapped her arms around her and hugged her briefly. "I forgot to ask. How much are you renting the space for, Ro?" Alyssa wiped the tears from her face.

"Not a lot, just enough to cover electricity and supplies. I'm not looking to make a profit here, just cover my costs. It's an eight-person classroom, so I'm thinking $80 an hour, which includes all art supplies. That's like $10 per student for a one-hour session, which seems pretty reasonable to me."

"You have to be fucking kidding me, Ro." Alyssa's eyes were huge. "No fucking way! That's it? Holy shit, where do I sign up?"

"Clem will be managing the classroom schedule for the WCA, so just text her and she'll get you on. She's also going shopping to get the classroom art supplies, so let us know if you want to go with her so we make sure we'll have what you need." Rowan wrinkled her nose. "Bryn isn't crazy about me going shopping right now, even with the amazing Teagan as my bodyguard, so Clem and Remy are taking point on this one."

"I have my new pal, Blair, out there, so I'll have to introduce you two," Alyssa said. "She told me she's Blake's second, I think? Anyhow, she is extremely sweet, but I'm sure she's just like the rest of the APS badasses and can put a serious hurting on someone if she needs to."

Just then, Rowan heard Teagan's voice raise a bit and she frowned at Alyssa, wondering what was going on.

"I'll go. You stay here," Alyssa instructed. She was back not a minute later, her brows lowered dangerously, and her blue eyes spitting fire. "That fucking cunt-from-hell, Astrid Hallifax, is standing in the Dream Creamery, looking like the snobby, superior, asswipe bitch she is, and wanting to speak to 'that Rowan person,'" Alyssa seethed. "Teag looks like she's about to spit nails and just told that snobby fuck you were busy and didn't usually have time to talk to walk-ins without an appointment."

"No, she didn't." Rowan's eyes rounded.

"Yes, she motherfucking did." Alyssa's eyes still burned hellfire. "Rowan, no one can stand that bitch. She thinks she's all that because of who Mommy is, but she's not shit and you shouldn't have to deal with her."

"Relax, sister. I've got this."

Serenely, Rowan walked out of the art classroom, Alyssa hard on her heels.

"Can I help you?" Rowan inquired pleasantly, already feeling prickles of dislike running down her spine as she faced the woman coiled like a rattlesnake at the entrance of the Dream Creamery.

Teagan was standing by the front door with another APS associate whom Rowan didn't know, thunderclouds on both of their faces.

Astrid Hallifax was a tall, pretty brunette with light green eyes and pale skin. Rowan could definitely understand what had attracted Bryn to her in the first place.

However, Astrid would be prettier if her face wasn't twisted into a superior lemon-sucking expression, Rowan decided.

Astrid looked down her nose at Rowan and spoke to her as if she was the hired help.

"I'm Astrid Hallifax," she announced grandly. "I understand you are the one managing this little artist competition."

She heard Teagan snort.

"Actually, I'm the owner of the Dream Creamery and the Whimsy Creative Art Center." Rowan was already over this witch and her lofty attitude. "If you're interested in applying to be one of the grand opening artists, we issued a call-to-artists in this week's Pioneer. You can find all the criteria we require in there."

"I've already applied." Astrid was smug. "Actually, my good friend, Bryn Armstrong, is the one who has always encouraged my art." She looked at Rowan with a malicious smile.

"I see." Rowan smiled back serenely. "She can certainly be quite the encourager, that's for sure. As a matter of fact, she and I got into a rather…intense…*discussion* last night about her encouragement techniques when we both got home from work."

Rowan ignored Astrid's brows as they dropped low and she narrowed her eyes at Rowan.

"She and Riley and the Seven have already become such good friends to me. I've certainly seen how Bryn really encourages everyone around her to be the best they can be." Astrid's brows dropped lower.

"I'll be happy to let her know you stopped by when I see her tonight. She should get home at her usual time." Rowan looked at Astrid innocently. "At least, she hasn't texted me to say she'll be home late, but who knows?" She let out a light, rather breathless laugh. "They are all *so* intense and so focused, especially Bryn, but you know that, right?"

Astrid, Rowan thought with slightly catty glee, was *seething*.

"Now, unless there's anything else, I'm afraid I'm going to have to excuse myself," Rowan said sweetly. "I still have so much to do for the grand opening, although my new friend here, Alyssa, has been *such* a help. Teag? Would you mind showing Astrid out? I wish you the best of luck with the grand opening call-to-artists, Astrid. I have my gallery manager working on it and we are rather pressed for time, so I'm sure she should contact you with a decision within the next few days."

"Of course, sweetheart." Teagan's voice sounded slightly strangled. As Rowan walked away, she sensed Alyssa following closely behind, giggling quietly.

When they reached the classroom, Alyssa shut the door and burst out laughing.

"Sh-h-h!" Rowan shushed her. "These are only 3/4 walls, girl! Everyone can hear us!"

"She's gone. She left in a very fast, extremely pissed-off huff and she was *not* fucking happy, Ro, trust me."

Alyssa continued to laugh. "Girl, you are the *master* of the Catty Bitch annihilation, I swear."

Just then, Teagan exploded into the classroom, howling, with the dark-haired butch Rowan assumed was Blair on her heels, laughing, too.

Teagan hugged Rowan tightly and kissed her cheek, still cracking up, then pulled out her phone.

"Trill was right, little sis. Fucking *legendary*." Teagan sent a rapid text. "I'm texting Trill to let her know that the Rowan Smackdown 2.0 was initiated by Astrid Hallifax and that our little sis remains undefeated. Blair, cuz, from now on, we are making book anytime one of these stupid bitches thinks she's going to go up against Rowan and win." Teagan and Blair high-fived each other.

"Teag!" Rowan was appalled. "You're going to have everyone thinking I am the meanest person alive!"

"Sis. Seriously?" Teagan gave her another hug. "You are about the sweetest woman I know in existence, so I don't think you need to worry, sweetheart."

"Rowan, I'm Blair." The dark-haired butch introduced herself and shook Rowan's hand, gray-blue eyes twinkling. "I'm Blake's second. I'm afraid your reputation already precedes you. Everyone who has met you has nothing but the most wonderful things to say about you. I really wouldn't worry if I were you." Blair smiled kindly at her.

"See?" Alyssa poked Teagan in the ribs. "Next time there is a Rowan Smackdown imminent and you're making book, I want in. You'd better ask Clem, Nova, and Brooke if they want in, too." Rowan rolled her eyes.

Just then, Rowan's text notification chimed.

"*Dulzura*," the text read, "what's this I hear about my woman being at the center of the largest betting pool in APS history?"

Rowan groaned and pinched the bridge of her nose for a long moment before responding.

"It's not my fault! Your friends are lunatics and I'll explain tonight," she texted back and sighed.

Rowan glared at some of those lunatics, who had taken up residence in the art classroom.

"Clem should be here with Remy any minute. Maybe Alyssa and Blair can go art supply shopping with them so we can keep the chaos to a minimum for the rest of the day?"

"One can only hope," said Teagan, grinning. "But I've got to tell you, sweetheart, I don't think the Rowan Smackdown show is going to end anytime soon."

¥¥¥¥¥

"Why do you all call Teagan, 'Casanova'?" Rowan—along with Clementine, Brooke, Alyssa and Nova—was in the art classroom of the WCA Center, unpacking the huge haul of supplies and equipment Alyssa and Clem had brought back from their shopping expedition.

Teagan, Remy, Blair, and two other APS associates—Devon and TJ—were in the main part of the center, but would be unable to hear their conversation if they kept their voices low.

Nova sighed. "Let me make one thing perfectly clear," she said. "I adore Teagan. We *all* adore Teagan and always have. Like all the other badasses at APS, she is as loyal, trustworthy, protective, and as ethical as they come. But Teagan, more than the rest of the Seven, truly is a real Casanova." She looked at Rowan seriously. "She'll date, and she dates *a lot*, but the minute things start looking like they might even remotely become serious, she's out. Honestly?" Nova mused with a faraway look. "She's been hung up on Delaney Sedgwick for years. Teagan wanted to start dating Delaney back when Del was in the ninth grade, but Del was already being sucked in by that fuckwit, Tina the Twat."

"What do you think Delaney saw in Tina?" Rowan unpacked sketchbooks and drawing paper pads.

"None of us could *ever* understand what Del saw in Tina in the beginning. But Delaney was very quiet, very shy, and Tina played her like a motherfucking fiddle because Tina's mom was already sick and Tina pulled the 'poor, pitiful me' card. When Delaney graduated from college, Tina talked Del into going to Michigan with her and her mother because her mom wanted to go back there—

that's where she's from—and Tina was not about to get stuck taking care of her mother by herself."

Nova sighed again.

"Believe me, Delaney knew from the minute her foot hit Michigan soil that she had made a huge mistake. But Tina's mother had always treated Delaney like gold and Del knew if she left, Tina would neglect—possibly even abuse—her mother and Del wasn't going to risk it."

"Wow. I never fucking knew." Brooke was pissed. "I remember that bitch, Tina, from high school. She thought because she was good-looking, she could get away with all sorts of shit." Brooke made a sound of disgust.

"Speaking of high school…Remember how Delaney used to bake for all of us?" Alyssa exclaimed quietly.

"Oh my Goddess, Rowan, she was absolutely amazing. I swear, she could take a stick of butter, a handful of flour, and a handful of sugar and make a fucking Michelin three-star dessert out of it. Her parents paid for her to go to culinary school and become a pastry chef while she was in Michigan because that's what she's always wanted to do, and Christ knew she didn't have any money because all she ever did was take care of Tina's mother."

"Del's parents fucking hated the situation, but they understood why Delaney was staying," Nova revealed. "Del told me her going to pastry school was the one huge blowout fight she and Tina had." Nova smirked. "Tina was whining and basically being an asshole about Delaney taking time for herself to go to school. In essence, she told Del she couldn't go. But Delaney told her she was going to school and if Tina didn't like it, then Delaney was coming back home to Florida and Tina could suck it."

"What a motherfucking asshole," muttered Clem, who had been quiet up until this point.

"I think Delaney shocked the shit out of Tina. She's so quiet and so passive, I guarantee you it was the only time in her life she ever fought back against Tina. Anyhow," Nova blew out a big breath, "she's back home with her parents now. Tina's mother died, they had the funeral last week, and the last time I messaged Del, she told me she was fucking *out* of there. She hired a Lyft on Thursday while Tina was at work, took just two suitcases worth of shit with her, went to the airport, bought a one-way ticket to Tampa, changed her phone number, and said, '*Sayonara*, bitch.' She is *so* excited to see you two again."

Nova smiled at Alyssa and Brooke.

"She can't wait to meet Rowan and Clem either, and thank them for giving her the opportunity to be a part of the Dream Creamery. In a lot of ways, she is still the same sweet, shy Delaney we all knew and loved in high school. But," Nova was pensive, "she's...damaged. I don't know any other way to put it. She's always been quiet and extremely shy. However, now she's skittish as fuck. Loud noises, people yelling...it's like she folds in on herself so she isn't noticed and makes herself a target. She's so fucking guarded now."

Alyssa, Brooke, and Clem growled with anger.

"If Teagan is still hung up on her, that's going to make Teag go absolutely ballistic," Rowan said quietly. "Heck, even if Teagan *isn't* still hung up on her, she isn't going to react well. None of them from APS will."

"In a way, I guess you could say I was kind of like Delaney's lifeline because we stayed in touch all those years," Nova said sadly. "She wasn't allowed to have any other friends and honestly, I'm not sure fucking Tina even knew how much Delaney and I really talked. I think Delaney hid it from her. Also…" Nova hesitated. "I'm not meaning to dig deep into Delaney's personal shit. But I know things were already pretty much over between Delaney and Tina even when they first moved to Michigan. I doubt Del has had any kind of sexual contact with *anyone* since she was 21 years old. Probably even younger. And Teagan?" Nova rolled her eyes. "Well. Teagan."

"Fuck." Alyssa ran her hand through her red hair.

"I need to tell Bryn or Riley that Delaney is back, and let them know some of what she's gone through since she's been away." Nova looked at Rowan. "That way, they can tell the rest of the Seven, or at least Teagan. She's fragile, she hasn't felt safe in years, and the only thing she needs right now is to rest and recover and focus on the career she loves without some motherfucking maniac up her ass 24/7."

"I can tell Bryn when I go home tonight, although I'm sure she'll have a bunch of questions I won't be able to answer." Rowan's voice was still quiet. "But at least she'll have the gist of it and she can call you for the details. In the meantime …"

She gave Nova a huge hug. "You are *such* a good friend. I shudder to think how much worse it would have been for that poor woman if she didn't have you. Now she's back among friends and family, she already has a little bit of the work she loves here at the Dream Creamery, and we will all do everything we can to give her her life back."

"Ro?" They heard Teagan's voice calling. "Everything okay? You all are mighty quiet."

"Yeah, we're good," Alyssa improvised loudly, setting a big whiteboard near the front of the room where it could be mounted. "We're just busy sorting and counting and getting the cabinets organized. Everything good out there?"

"Getting a bit lonely without all of the girl chatter we're used to hearing," Teagan teased. "I'm feeling a bit neglected."

"Jesus Christ, Malloy," Nova snarked. "The day you feel neglected is the day I take out an ad in the Pioneer to announce it." They heard Teagan laugh.

"Delaney doesn't plan to make any public appearances until the grand opening," Nova whispered as she sorted another pile of different paints and inks. "That gives her almost two weeks to sleep and bake and let Mrs. Sedgwick spoil the shit out of her without having to field a bunch of questions. I told Del we'd keep it amongst ourselves until then."

The girls all nodded.

"Nova." Rowan stacked some palettes with a considering look on her face. "Why don't we use the grand opening to announce formally that Delaney's back? Make pretty signs for the dessert area, 'Crafted by Delaney Sedgwick,' or whatever. Have Del come up with a signature dessert for the Dream Creamery grand opening in addition to what you've already planned, a real showstopper? Maybe make sure she gets some local press. Anyhow, we'll talk later and we definitely need to ask her how she feels about it, but see where I'm going with this?"

The faces of the others positively glowed with excitement.

"Yes!" Nova pumped her fist in the air, forgetting to keep her voice down. "That's fucking brilliant!"

"What's fucking brilliant?" Teagan opened the door and stuck her head around it.

"Getting you or one of the other badasses to hang this whiteboard and help us out putting supplies away on the upper shelves." Nova didn't miss a beat. "Since you've felt neglected so much, now you get to work."

Teagan groaned good-naturedly.

The four women shared a conspiratorial look as Teagan went to call the others.

"Looks like Operation Delaney has now commenced."

Chapter 27

January 30

Dressed in her fightwear, Rowan walked through the halls of the APS complex, hand-in-hand with Bryn, to meet with Blake at Utopia.

Several days ago, Rowan had shared the conversation she'd had with Nova and the rest of her friends about Delaney Sedgwick. She also told Bryn of Delaney's desire to keep her return a secret from everyone until the night of the grand opening, knowing she was putting Bryn in a bad position with one of her best friends.

Bryn reassured her. "Breaking someone's confidence is a deadly sin at APS, *dulzura*. Teag might be pissed I knew Del was back before she did, but she won't be pissed at me for honoring Delaney's wishes." Bryn's brows lowered dangerously. "I hope that motherfucking piece of shit doesn't get any bright ideas about coming back to Whimsy, because I know a management team who will draw straws for the privilege of throwing that fuck a beating."

They stopped at a large steel door and Bryn touched the comm in her ear. "Are we clear, *ese*?" A minute later, Rowan heard a click and Bryn pulled the door open.

Rowan didn't know what she had been expecting, but the large, exceedingly plain room with dark walls wasn't it.

A very sophisticated lighting system was visible on the walls and ceiling, although only the regular room lights were on. Other than that, the room was bare. A booth at one end of the room that stretched from wall-to-wall was dark and unilluminated. Blake came out of a doorway at the very end and grinned when she saw them.

"Hey, sweetheart! Cuz, how goes it?" Blake hugged Rowan with one arm and kissed her cheek, then gave Bryn a high-five.

Blake Seibert was 5'9" with extremely short auburn hair, and light green eyes with gold flecks in them that seemed to carry sunlight. Although still incredibly muscular, she wasn't quite as heavily muscled as the rest of the Seven, which made sense: Blake Seibert was built for speed instead of bulk, given her role as the combat simulation crew chief.

Her extremely handsome face was often filled with fun and laughter, although those light green eyes could darken with malignancy when the situation called for it, and she was known far and wide as a gaming genius with uncanny instincts.

A small metal locker was tucked under Blake's arm and she was extremely careful not to bump Rowan with it.

"Ready to have some fun, Ro?" Blake's eyes twinkled. "I'm going to explain a few things while we're gearing up, okay?"

Rowan nodded.

"First of all, this is the only place within the entire APS complex where our associates are ever completely unarmed. The only weapons that are permitted in here are simulation weapons. What we do in Utopia is use combat simulations to test and measure our speed, our timing, our accuracy, and our offensive and defensive knowledge."

Blake knelt down to open the metal locker.

"We use weapons that look identical to their real-life counterparts, except the sim weapons have a large blue marking on either side of the grip. Instead of bullets, they shoot laser-light with pinpoint accuracy. What we don't want is to have holes shot into my lab walls or, God forbid, into each other because we've forgotten we are fighting within a simulation and not in real life. It can be easy to forget where you really are in the heat of the moment."

Blake smiled up at her gently. "The sims in Utopia are incredibly life-like, sweetheart, so I don't want you to be afraid when I turn the system on."

Blake stood up and nodded toward an almost-invisible corner.

"There's a safety bay there used specifically for the purpose of arming and disarming yourself with your real weapon, sweetheart. Only one person is permitted in the bay at one time. Enter the bay, clear your weapon, and put it in one of the pistol cases provided before you exit."

When both Rowan and Bryn were cleared and disarmed, Blake showed them an almost-invisible wall locker where they could store their pistol cases. When they were done, Blake took out eye and ear protection for each of them from the small metal locker, then she extracted life-like weaponry she handled as if it *was* real.

"Just because there is a blue mark on the grip doesn't mean you should assume it's a simulation weapon, Ro. You clear it as if you expect it to fire live if you don't."

Rowan nodded.

"Press that small button on the outside of your ear protection." When Rowan did, she heard a faint whirring sound as a speaker came to life.

Blake stood directly in front of Rowan and looked at her seriously.

"Sweetheart, this whole room is about to come to life, or 'go hot.' You are going to feel surrounded by enemy combatants and, no matter how prepared you think you are, your first time in the sim is scary as fuck."

Rowan blew out a breath with trepidation.

"The sim is on 'freeze,' so nothing will be moving, but I want you to stand right next to Bryn until you feel oriented, okay? When we are ready to go, we'll be on super slow-mo speed so you don't have to worry about rapid attacks.

"Are you ready?"

Rowan gulped in a deep breath of air and nodded as Bryn soothingly rubbed her arm and wrapped her other arm around Rowan's waist. Blake disappeared into the control booth.

Her voice echoed clearly through the speaker in Rowan's ear protection. "Combatants, this sim is going hot."

The whirring sound in her ear grew a bit louder as the regular lights dimmed, the sim lights came on, and the room suddenly seemed filled with life-like, menacing figures in camouflage who held a variety of weapons in their hands.

Rowan squealed and buried her head against Bryn's chest, completely unprepared despite Blake's warnings.

"Relax, sweetheart." Blake's calm voice fed through her ear protection. "Like I said, your first time is always scary as fuck no matter how much you think you're prepared. Bryn isn't going to let the first goddamned thing happen to her woman, so you relax and take your time, okay? We'll start whenever you feel ready."

When Rowan felt her breathing start to return to normal, she raised her head and stared at the sim figures surrounding her.

"Remember, the sim is on 'freeze,' *dulzura*." Bryn slid one hand up and down Rowan's back. "How about we take a walk around so you can see the sim from different angles, then maybe we can try super slow-mo speed when you are feeling a bit more comfortable?"

Feeling braver, Rowan walked slowly around the sim with Bryn, pausing to peer at the incredibly realistic combatants and their weapons.

"My dad would have lost his mind," she said softly, feeling a pang of sorrow that he wasn't here to see this, but thankful she wasn't feeling the heavy grief she had felt over the past several years just by thinking about him. "And Blake?" Rowan felt her mouth kick up into a slight smile. "My sister will challenge you like nobody's business once she gets a load of your 'toy.'"

"Then you tell her we have a scrimmage challenge date on the schedule, little sis." Blake's voice was filled with humor. "I can always use a new playmate. Now, are you ready to try some actual simulations? Remember, we will be in super slow-mode, so it will be very easy to outmaneuver and out-gun these fools."

Rowan laughed.

The sim shimmered for a brief moment as Blake prepared to take it out of freeze mode.

"Bryn is going to be standing right next to you the whole time, but this will be all you, Rowan. It is not uncommon to feel a little disoriented because this will be different than shooting at a flat target like you do at a shooting range. Bryn will talk you through the simulation the whole way. Because this is a 360° combat simulation, you also need to remember to 'check your six' at all times, Ro. It's conceivable that one of the sim attackers will sneak behind you and try to take you out that way."

"Fabulous," Rowan muttered, making Blake and Bryn grin.

"Accelerating from level 0 to level 1 now," Blake announced over her ear comm, and the sim started to creep.

"Because you are in the middle of the room, *dulzura*, it will be easy for one of these fuckers to get behind you and attack that way," Bryn coached. "Keep checking your six and maneuver into a position where you still leave yourself room to move, but you make it very difficult for someone to slip behind you. Right now, you have no cover so remember to crouch and roll for your protection if you have to until you are in a more defensible position."

Suddenly, Rowan crouched down and fired back at a sim attacker who was aiming at her, hitting him.

She checked her six, then rolled to the right, extending her weapon while laying it on the ground for control. She came up, brought up her sim weapon, and aimed at another attacker, shooting and firing until she "killed" him.

"Ooh, it worked!" she cheered animatedly, crouching back down.

"Whoa, whoa, *whoa, dulzura*," Bryn said in shock, putting up a hand signal so that Blake would freeze the sim again, then immediately asked if they were clear when all motion had stopped.

Bryn put her hands on her hips as soon as Blake confirmed they were clear.

"Hold on just a goddamn minute here, baby. How in the mother *fuck* did you know how to do that?" Bryn speared her with dark brown eyes that were half proud, half questioning.

Rowan looked proud of herself as she stood up from her crouching position.

"I knew I was coming today, so Teagan and Remy taught me how to do that as a surprise," she reported excitedly. "I have those stupid foam pistols that Clem gave me as a gag gift a couple of weeks ago, and a ton of room in the art gallery since it's still empty and the floors aren't finished yet, so we decided to put it to practical use."

Blake, who had just come out of the control booth, started to laugh as Bryn ran her hand through her hair, shook her head and smirked, unable to help herself.

"Those fuckers," Blake whooped. "I am going to kick their asses into next week for this, although I have to tell you, Ro…that was a damn fine job you did there."

"That she did." Bryn looked at her woman with heat in her eyes as she went over to Rowan and pulled her into a possessive hug.

"Can I ask you two a favor?" Rowan looked up at Bryn and kissed her, then looked to the side at Blake. "I'd really love to stand in the control booth and observe you two demonstrate the sim the way it was meant to be used, not just in slow-mo. Can we do that?"

Bryn gave Blake a slight smile. "I'm up for it if you are, *broki*," she said with a gleam in her eyes.

"Always, cuz." Blake grinned back, looping a small controller around her neck and under her rash guard, which she told Rowan controlled the sim from outside the control booth, and geared up.

"Do you want us both on the same team or do you want us to face off against each other, *dulzura*?" Bryn holstered her sim weapon. "I'm also going to suggest we do this with sim knives, not guns, *ese*. I think she'll be able to see fighting techniques better that way."

"Same team, please," Rowan said. "I want to see firsthand how the APS management works together as a unit." Rowan was intent.

They both smiled at her, then at each other. "Sim knives work for me." Blake shrugged, clearly not caring, and unlocked another almost invisible door to get the sim knives.

When they were ready and they'd made sure Rowan was safely inside the control booth, where she could hear either of them if they spoke through their ear protection, Blake announced clearly, "Combatants, this sim is going hot."

The sim blazed to life with a vengeance as Blake and Bryn fell into back-to-back knife fighting stances, and Rowan gasped.

This wasn't the measured no-motion/slow-motion sim Blake had set up for her.

This was a deadly playground with three sim attackers on each side of the APS duo, so both Bryn and Blake had to fight off three attackers simultaneously each.

Rowan felt her heart clench in fear even though she knew this was only a simulation.

The two APS partners stayed back-to-back, barely touching, as they used underhand strikes, overhead strikes, and slashes against their attackers to both defend and mount an offense. It was almost uncanny, the way they moved together. Somehow, Bryn always knew if Blake was going to make an offensive move and Blake could always sense when Bryn needed a shift in their position.

If the last few weeks had taught her anything, it was that Bryn and Riley and the Seven were the most vicious, deadly, efficient fighters in the world.

Rowan knew that even the crew chiefs who hadn't demonstrated their fighting skills firsthand, like Teagan or Trill, were just as lethal as the others.

There had to be a deeper explanation for what they did, Rowan thought suddenly. She didn't doubt they did all the things Bryn had already explained to her.

But.

Why would an organization of almost fifty "badasses," as Clem called them, have to train so daggone hard and be so well-versed in weaponry?

Why did they all have a skill set that was far, far beyond what you would expect a "normal" bodyguard or risk assessment service company to have?

Granted, Drew's work with her crew in Purgatory was a lot deeper and darker than anything "official" APS did. But what Drew's crew did wasn't nearly enough work to consume 40+ resources full-time.

Was it?

Rowan forced her attention back to the fight. Both Blake and Bryn only had one attacker apiece left active in the sim. As Blake defeated her remaining attacker with an overhand stab, Bryn used her considerable height to mount a circular attack from above.

The sim grew quiet after all of the attackers disappeared, only the low hum of the speaker remaining.

"This sim is clear." Blake shut the sim down in its entirety.

As the door to the control booth clicked open, Rowan slowly opened the door and made her way out onto the sim "stage." Bryn and Blake were there, sweaty and talking quietly about their demonstration.

"I think I'm overwhelmed," Rowan admitted, her voice barely audible, standing before both of them and twisting her small fingers.

"As of now, I've had a playdate with everybody but Jaime. And it's all...just...it's just so *much*," Rowan burst out.

Bryn and Blake looked at her, concerned, but waited patiently for her to finish her thoughts.

"You two did what you did and you made it look so easy. And I know it's not easy because even the tiny bit I managed to do today was completely exhausting." Rowan paused. "I'm not saying I expect to be able to do these things, let alone at your level, because they aren't what I do, they aren't what I'll *ever* do, and I'm okay with that. But..." Rowan hesitated. "I'm having a very hard time reconciling what I know about APS as an organization against the...the near-*mythic* abilities I've seen from its management team." She fidgeted.

Bryn and Blake glanced at each other.

"My head is exploding because I'm trying to figure out why you all can do what you do when it seems to be head and shoulders above the abilities a company like this actually needs." Rowan looked down at the ground and refused to meet their eyes. "That's all." Rowan's voice was a near whisper.

"*Dulzura.*" Bryn's voice was calm and very, very reassuring. "We have covered so much about what goes on at APS and, in a lot of ways, we have still only scratched the surface of everything we do. I promise you, no one has been seeking to deceive you or to be anything less than honest." Bryn tilted Rowan's chin up and looked deeply in her eyes.

"Oh, no!" Rowan was appalled. "I didn't mean that! Every single one of you has more integrity than anyone else I've ever met in my life! I'm just having such a hard time making sense of everything." Her eyes filled with tears as Bryn cupped her cheek.

"Sweetheart." Blake's gentle voice was extremely kind. "If you had *any* idea how much you've absorbed and learned and understood in the last two weeks, you would demand a fucking medal because you totally deserve one."

Blake leaned against the wall and crossed her powerful arms.

"Bryn's been one of my best friends since first grade, Ro. I knew if there would ever come a time when she chose to share her life with a woman, she'd find someone beautiful and loving and so fucking smart, she'd scare the shit out of the rest of us. Someone just like you."

Blake was candid. "But this organization has been *ten years* in the making, sweetheart. There is no way in hell you're going to understand everything about it in a few short weeks, so don't put so much pressure on yourself. Please." She grinned. "Let this fucker do what she's good at—well, besides driving us all out of our motherfucking minds—and trust she'll teach it all to you in due time. Because she will."

"Okay, Blake." Rowan felt a lot better. She laughed as Bryn flipped Blake off and she felt a lightness settle over the sim.

"Seriously, Rowan, you and Bryn just need to let me know anytime you want to come in here and use the sim." Blake gave her a thumbs-up. "There are a ton of variables to using this and you don't have to be some crazy badass in order to get a benefit from it."

"Blake, thank you." Rowan gave her a kiss on the cheek. "This was so informative for me and the sim is absolutely breathtaking. I want you to promise me I'll have a front row seat from the control booth when you and Kelly go head-to-head. And I'll have to owe you that hug until after you've had a shower, okay?"

Blake threw back her head and laughed.

"You got it, sweetheart," she said. "Your butch and I definitely need to hit the showers before we kill anyone with our stench or offend any more girls."

"Thank you, *broki*," Bryn said and caught Rowan by the hand. "As usual, you are the ultimate sim master. I think, however, it's time my woman and I had a long-overdue discussion."

Chapter 28

Rowan curled up next to Bryn on the comfortable oversized sofa in Bryn's living room after Bryn had emerged from the shower.

"The bedroom would be a bad idea, *dulzura*, because we need to have a serious discussion and distractions are not what we need right now," Bryn said, the corner of her mouth lifting slightly and the heat in her eyes unmistakable.

Rowan waited with trepidation.

"I've hesitated to hit you with too much at one time, baby, because your head is absolutely, positively going to explode." Bryn caressed Rowan's cheek. "But I think at this point, the 'not making sense' is causing you more anguish than if I just go ahead and throw it all out there.

"Whatever you do, *dulzura*, don't try to memorize or remember everything because you just can't." Bryn nuzzled her behind her ear. "You will drive yourself insane if you try."

"Like Blake said, this is an organization that has been ten years in the making, baby. You can't process ten years' worth of data in thirty minutes, not even an analyst who is as miraculous as you are. I am going to suggest you just take it all in, absorb it and let it wash over you. We'll figure out the rest of it later."

Rowan nodded.

"Everything you know about us so far is absolutely true, *dulzura*," Bryn began. "I have never lied to you and I never will. If I'm guilty of anything, it's 'sin by omission,' which I fucking hate, but I couldn't bring myself to dump 5,000 pounds of data on your head at one time. That was my decision and the consequences are my responsibility alone."

"Bryn." Rowan reached up and kissed her. "I understand why you did what you did. It was kind. You worried about how I would react, having to absorb so much information at one time. Frankly, I feel better equipped to handle everything now because you forced a slowdown in the beginning."

Bryn hugged her and dropped a kiss on the top of her head. "Thank you for that, baby." Bryn settled Rowan more firmly against her. "Let's talk about all the things we do that we *haven't* talked about. I have a lot to say, *dulzura*, and I will try to be as clear as I possibly can.

"In a nutshell, what you know about us is that we do security consulting, investigation services, risk assessment, and bodyguard services, right?"

Rowan nodded again.

Bryn's voice was calm. "Our other interests include domestic violence, threat assessments, threat intelligence, stalking," Bryn speared Rowan with a look, "physical security intelligence, covert surveillance needs, surveillance and hostile surveillance operations, security patrols, sometimes search-and-rescue missions, bounty hunting, and various other clandestine services."

Rowan's eyes kept getting bigger and bigger.

"These are things that go on under the hood, *dulzura*. No one knows about them unless we want them to know. We have a roster of clients who pay us very, very well for some of these services, either contracting us for a one-off situation or retaining us so they remain an ongoing client."

Bryn's gaze was level.

"Some are not services, per se, but internal processes that allow us to fully execute our responsibilities. We do not operate outside of the law. We do not get involved with individuals or organizations that expect us to operate outside of the law."

Bryn stroked Rowan's back.

"Many of our clients are severely at-risk females who originally had difficulty procuring some of these services because of their gender, which is utter bullshit when you think about how at risk a woman is in general. But it appeared that male-owned companies were often reluctant to enter into a contract with a lone female for any kind of significant protection which, again, was total bullshit."

Bryn touched Rowan's face.

"When APS was first started, we had all gotten out of the military and were on our way to college. We're all roughly the same age, you know, so we were starting at ground zero after we left the Marine Corps. We had all served four years active duty and, as per our enlistment commitment, we were serving four years inactive reserves, but in peacetime, it is extremely unlikely that you will ever be called, so we went ahead and enrolled in college. We all knew we wanted to do something to protect women, had talked about it together as far back as grade school, but we weren't sure exactly what we needed to do. We spent our college years figuring it out."

Bryn smiled. "The nine of us have been inseparable since we were anywhere from three to six years old, *dulzura*. Riley is my biological sibling, but I am just as close to the Seven as I am to her in almost every way."

Bryn blew out a deep breath.

"We knew we wanted to help and protect women, and the more I looked at some of the services we provide now that were also available at that time, there was no one out there directly targeting women and their unique needs in a significant way. The more I dug, the more I realized there was a definite lack of protection services, risk assessment, everything I've outlined, *for females by females*. So, APS was born and it eventually morphed into what it is today. It may seem like overkill, but this is a dangerous world if you are a female—especially a female alone—and it's our mission to make that world a little bit safer for them."

Bryn paused for a moment.

"That's why we work out so much, focus so hard on martial arts, and keep ourselves in peak condition, *dulzura*." Bryn looked calmly into Rowan's eyes. "That's why we train with weapons the way we do. *All* of us at APS. The work we do and the services we render are often dangerous and there is a big risk inherent in simply keeping women safe. You wouldn't believe some of the stories I could tell you about things that have happened over the past ten years that just keep proving over and over that women are a target, and how often violence has cost them their lives. I would like to say that most of these women are at risk because of a stranger, but that's simply not the case."

Bryn's eyes darkened. "Husbands, boyfriends, fathers, sons…so many males in these women's lives are a bigger threat to them than any stranger on the street. Over seventy-five percent of the harm and death inflicted on women today is done at the hands of someone they know. Some of our clients are extremely wealthy, so a portion of the money they pay us is earmarked to help women of limited means. We never wanted our services to be out of the reach of a woman who desperately needed us, but lacked the ability to pay, *dulzura*."

Bryn wrapped her arms around Rowan. "I just threw a fuckton at you, Rowan, so I think I'm going to stop here for now. I hope you understand what we do a little better and I hope now you get why everything wasn't making sense to you. One of my new goals is to give you the life I also want these women to have, Rowan." Bryn looked deeply into Rowan's eyes. "To do everything in my power to make sure you are safe, happy, and healthy. To keep your world secure and without fear."

"I love you, Bryn." The words were simple and came straight from Rowan's heart as she looked at Bryn with love. Bryn jerked in shock.

"When my mom and dad died, my world shattered." Big tears began to roll down Rowan's face. "I didn't think I would ever find joy or peace or happiness again. I had Kelly and Clem, but it wasn't the same.

"And then along came you." Rowan was sobbing now and slid her hands up around Bryn's face. "When I first saw you standing at the entrance of the Dream Creamery, my heart fluttered. I was absolutely mesmerized by you.

"This right here, everything we've talked about, everything you've told me about you and what you do, just proves to me you are what I've been looking for all my life."

Rowan drew in a deep, shuddering breath. "If I can give you even one-tenth of what you have already given to me, what you have already given to the *world*, I will feel like I'm a success."

"My Rowan." Bryn swept Rowan up into her powerful arms and kissed her passionately. "I am so in love with you, I never even believed it was possible for me to feel this way about a woman.

"You are the kindest person I've ever met, *dulzura*. You're sweet and you're passionate and you're caring, and everyone who meets you falls in love with you just because of the woman you are.

"And you're all mine."

Bryn looked at the petite blonde in her arms. "This isn't exactly the way I'd planned on doing this, *dulzura*, but I think the Universe has had other plans." She kissed her gently.

"Rowan." Bryn took a deep breath and looked at Rowan with an uncharacteristic softness, her heart in her eyes. "Will you marry me?"

WHIMSICAL HAVEN

¥ ¥ ¥ ¥ ¥

"Do you think Delaney can incorporate some type of crepes or waffles into our dessert menu? Not for the grand opening, but as part of the regular menu going forward?"

Rowan was extraordinarily sleepy, but she was also the happiest she had ever been in her entire life.

After Rowan had cried, "Yes!" to Bryn's proposal with big tears, hugs, and kisses, overcome with joy, Bryn had kept her up until almost five in the morning, making love with her until Rowan was spent.

She fell asleep in Bryn's arms, tears sliding down her face again as she heard Bryn's whispers of love and protection, burying her face in Bryn's neck and vowing to always love, honor, and obey her for the rest of their lives. They had both agreed to keep their engagement a secret for now. Bryn wanted to get Rowan a ring before they told anyone—plus, they were both a little too unsettled with Coravani still roaming free to make an announcement yet.

Drew was 100% convinced the motherfucker was still in the Whimsy area, even though all of his digital trails had gone cold. His disappearance off the radar had Drew enraged and she was working furiously with her crew and others to dig him out.

"He knows somebody—or Mommy and his fuckwit uncle know somebody who is hiding him so he can stay off the grid," Drew predicted when she met with Bryn and Riley. "But Jaime has some physical echoes she's having her team follow now and she's closing in."

Her smile was cold. "Good luck to that asshole if he thinks he's going to hide from Jaime for too long. He might think he's some big-shot private investigator and knows all the tricks, but there isn't a person in this world she can't find."

Now, Nova smirked as Rowan ended her question with a big, jaw-cracking yawn.

"Does this mean Tall, Dark, and Handsome kept you up past your bedtime again, sister?" Nova was flippant as she raised an eyebrow. Rowan blushed as Nova laughed playfully and winked.

Despite the supplies and equipment currently occupying the space, they were all sitting in a makeshift "office" on the top floor where Clem's apartment was going to be, so the last finishing touches could be put on both the Dream Creamery and the WCA Center.

The artist they had hired to paint the mural in the Dream Creamery was done and the finished mural was absolutely breathtaking. The counters, storage cabinets, freezers, and dipping cabinets had all been installed, and the Dream Creamery was just waiting for flooring.

Ember and Nia had both told Rowan they expected the floors to be started in the next couple of days. Then they could arrange for the WCA Center gallery system displays to be installed, the Dream Creamery furniture to be delivered and set up, and the final touches to be completed.

The gallery opening artists who had been selected would be able to bring their art to have it installed several days before the grand opening.

Teagan and Devon were sitting a little ways away from Rowan and Nova, covering the entrances to the apartment—one coming from the downstairs and one coming from the outside.

"To answer your question, Ro…we'll add it to the 'Things to Ask Delaney' list. I am so happy, especially because she was blown away by your offer to announce her return during the grand opening."

"After hearing her story, can you think of anyone who deserves it more? Because I can't," Rowan asked in a low voice. "Well," she said louder, "she's this super-amazing artisan just like you are, and I am *so* blessed to have you both.

"I wish Kelly was here," Rowan suddenly fretted. "I miss her so much. The last time we were separated this long was when I went to college. She's three years younger than me, so she was still in high school when I started college. I went to MICA—the Maryland Institute College of Art—which is only a little over an hour's drive from Woodbridge, but Mom and Dad didn't want me to commute. They said it would make for way too long of a day, especially with all the studying and art projects I would have to do. So we sucked it up and stuck it out, although Dad had to put the brakes on Kelly because she wanted me to come home every weekend or for them to visit Baltimore all the time."

Nova smiled. "You two sound super close," she observed.

"We are." Rowan sighed and then laughed out loud. "Art is *not* Kel's thing and she's never been interested in it. She originally wanted to go into the military like my father." Rowan continued to grin. "I love her to pieces and there are so many things she is exceptionally good at. However, she can't even draw a straight line to save her soul."

Nova giggled.

"But she decided she was going to apply to MICA anyway so we would be able to see each other every day." Rowan shook her head. "Mom had to sit her down and very gently explain to her there are a lot of things she didn't have that she needed in order to apply to an art school, and that she probably wouldn't be accepted. Kelly was *so* mad. She ended up going to the University of Maryland College Park, which worked out because that's where I went to graduate school."

"Didn't she end up being a Marine like your dad?" Nova was interested.

"Uh…n-no," Rowan stuttered, uncomfortable, seeing Teagan and Devon's interest. "Sh-she, umm, had decided to go to college first, and then she was offered a position she said she couldn't turn down with the CIA. She's been with them ever since. Speaking of art, I have to start working on the designs for the table signs for Delaney's display at the grand opening." Rowan changed the subject, aware that Teagan and Devon were still looking at her with sharp eyes. She pulled out a sketchbook and started to sketch, avoiding their gazes.

"When will Kelly be able to move here?" Nova asked, oblivious to Rowan's discomfort.

"At first, I thought it was Christmas, and then it was New Year's, and now we are hoping she will be here by the grand opening. Right now, we aren't sure. Her job makes me so freaking mad sometimes. This latest project she's been assigned to is taking a lot longer than they expected," Rowan replied, clearly relieved they had moved away from the subject of Kelly joining the military. She sighed as she continued to sketch. "It's not like this hasn't happened before, her being assigned to a project that ran over the expected end date, but this is the longest delay I've ever seen her have."

"What does she do for the CIA?" Nova asked, then her eyes widened. "Is that something I can even ask?"

"You can definitely ask," Rowan said with a laugh. "She is an information analyst, nothing super-secret spy-like. She gets to travel overseas every once in a while and occasionally, she has a project that gets delayed, like this one, but she says it's nothing too exciting."

Rowan missed Teagan casually pulling out her phone and rapidly sending a text.

"There. What do you think?" Rowan turned her sketchbook around so Nova could see what she had drawn.

"Ooh, Rowan." Nova clapped her hands. "Talk about talent."

The sign Rowan had drawn was a pretty oblong shape banded by curlicues with a simple, "Crafted by Delaney Sedgwick," in a fancy script in the middle.

"I'll get my sign gal to add this to her list of signs to make," said Rowan. "She already said it wouldn't be a problem."

"When is Delaney due in?" Teagan asked casually, putting her phone away.

"She had a few things to do before she came down, but she'll definitely be in Whimsy baking a few days before the grand opening," Nova said, equally casual. "She and I have been communicating via email, which has worked out great, and we've already rented some commercial kitchen space for her. Unfortunately, she won't be able to bring any of her baking equipment down with her and will be starting over from scratch, so I told her to let me know what she'll need for the grand opening baking and I'll make sure she has it."

Rowan admired Nova's ability to spin the truth in such a way that no one would suspect that Delaney was already in Whimsy.

She knew Nova absolutely adored Teagan and the rest of the APS crew, and would never lie to them, but she was also fiercely protective of her friend's wish to keep her return a secret until the grand opening.

"Once Delaney is down here and has time to think about what she wants to do—become a pastry chef in a restaurant or open her own place—we can all help her figure it out then." Rowan was nonchalant. "In the meantime, I found this professional pastry chef school that had a great article on the top twelve items a professional pastry chef would not be caught dead without. I think I should order those items and we should all give them to Delaney as a 'Welcome Back to Whimsy' present," Rowan said, beaming.

"You order it, and the Seven and the twins will pay for it, Ro," instructed Teagan. "Add anything else you think Del will need to get started, have Bryn give you one of our credit cards, and pay for overnight shipping so we're sure it will be here for her in time."

"Teag, what the hell is wrong with you?" Nova snarked, but her eyes were soft and suspiciously shiny. "Who hands a femme a credit card and tells her to go shopping without giving her a limit?"

"What I'm saying," Devon muttered, but there was a smirk at the corner of her mouth.

"Bitches!" Clem yelled as they heard her feet pounding up the outside stairs.

"*Jesus*, Clem," Teagan groused as she and Devon put away the guns they had automatically started to withdraw when they heard the commotion.

Clem came sailing through the front door, Remy right behind her.

"Dudes." Clem put her hand on her hip. "I *yelled* so you would know it was me. Fuckin' A. You're worse than the fucking Secret Service with this stupid shit."

Remy's brows dropped dangerously low. "I swear to you all, as God is my witness, Clem is going to end up over my knee before this fucking bullshit is done." Clem huffed and rolled her eyes.

At her limit, Remy took Clem firmly by her upper arms and looked at her with a serious, menacing expression, causing Clem's eyes to widen.

"This isn't a *game*, Clementine," Remy gritted out as Clem's face paled. "What if you assumed, just like you did, that these guys were the ones who were up here, but they weren't? What if that jackass motherfucker Coravani was the one up here, waiting for one of Rowan's friends so he could use them as leverage against her?"

Clem's eyes grew wider.

"But you were right there," Clem stuttered, shaking a bit from the threat in Remy's voice.

"Right there, *potentially taking a bullet*, Clementine, because you didn't leave me in a position to clear the room and make sure it was safe *before* you went in. After I went down, Coravani could then snatch you and use you to lay a trap for Rowan. And wouldn't it be fun for Rowan to watch her best friend take a bullet to the head because you outlived your usefulness and he didn't need witnesses?"

Clem was growing paler and paler, and big tears started spilling down her cheeks with Remy's last words. Everyone else in the room was deathly quiet.

Remy gently hugged Clem as she buried her face in Remy's neck and started to cry.

"Honey, no one is trying to make you feel bad or guilty," Remy soothed, stroking Clem's back. "But I need you to understand why it is that we do what we do, and also understand there is a very good reason why we ask you to do some of the 'stupid shit' we do."

"I'm sorry. I'm so sorry, Rem," Clem whispered into Remy's neck. "Maybe I haven't taken it seriously because I never feel any sense of danger, and maybe that's because you all are just that goddamn good at what you do."

Remy hugged her harder. "We all adore you, crazy girl, plus you're Rowan's best friend, so we will do everything in our power to keep you away from that maniac. We can keep you safe, we just need you to meet us halfway, yeah?"

"Yeah." Clem took the handkerchief Remy handed her and blew her nose.

Teagan came over and rubbed Clem's shoulders. "All good, honey?"

Clem nodded and sniffed, visibly calming.

"Incidentally, you should know Remy was serious about turning you over her knee. APS butches spank when the occasion calls for it, Clementine, especially when a woman under our care puts herself in danger." Clem's eyes widened again. "If I were you, I would consider this your one free pass."

"Yeah, APS punishment spankings are no fun," Rowan, who had been quiet up until now, muttered under her breath. Nova looked at her sideways, startled.

"So, we're good and we're done, and it's time to move on." Teagan looked at Clem. "Now, you flew in here all excited, crazy girl. Any particular reason?"

"Oh. Oh, yeah," Clem remembered and took a deep breath. "Rowan, Ember, and Nia said the finish work has gone so well, they are going to start installing the floors *today*."

A huge smile broke out across Clem's face.

"Two days for the floors and then they can install all of the art gallery hanging systems and display stands. They can move all of the tables and chairs into the Dream Creamery at the same time, and then they are *done*."

"Oh my gosh." Rowan felt faint.

Chapter 29

February 1

Rowan had never seen Jaime Quintero as stressed out as she did right now.

When Rowan and Bryn walked into the Bunker to meet Jaime for Rowan's final playdate, they found Jaime already there, finishing up a text.

She looked at the two of them and smiled, but the smile didn't quite reach her eyes and Rowan got the sense of banked violence simmering just beneath that handsome surface.

Rowan didn't care.

She went over to Jaime, gestured to her to stand up and, when Jaime did, Rowan wrapped her arms around her friend and wordlessly squeezed Jaime in a tight hug. After a moment of astonishment, Jaime hugged Rowan back and rested her cheek on Rowan's curly blonde head. Rowan was gratified to feel Jaime's muscles relax a bit.

After a good long minute, Jaime straightened up, kissed Rowan on the cheek, and softly said, "Thank you, *mi hermana*."

Jaime Quintero was Puerto Rican—*Boricua*, Bryn and Riley called her, meaning she was native Puerto Rican-born. Her mother had moved from Puerto Rico to Whimsy, where she had a sister living, when Jaime was six years old, right after Jaime's father had sadly passed away.

Jaime had moved to Florida not knowing how to speak a word of English, but she and Bryn and Riley immediately became extremely close because of their shared heritage. Jaime found her acclimation to life as a mainland American kid much easier because of the Armstrong twins, and she found herself naturally and easily a part of the future Seven.

She was 5'8", with the same black hair, dark brown eyes, and deeply tanned skin that Bryn had, and extremely heavily muscled because of her work as the APS physical security crew chief.

"Riley and I are of Puerto Rican descent, *dulzura*, but we are not *'Boricua'* like Mama or Jaime because we were born in America, not in Puerto Rico—which is actually an archipelago instead of a single island," Bryn had explained, smirking a bit as she saw Rowan's eyes begin to glaze over. "Your head will explode if I get any deeper into it, baby, so we'll leave it at that, at least for now."

As with the rest of the Seven, Jaime was exceptionally handsome, although her lighthearted and fun-loving exterior covered an interior that was passionate and often deadly, given her particular responsibilities.

"Jaime." Rowan looked at her seriously. "You're going to catch that piece of crap. I *know* you are. Bryn told me Coravani apparently has contacts down here who are hiding him, which is making finding him a little bit harder, but he isn't *nearly* as smart as you are. You'll figure it out."

Jaime blew out a huge breath. "I know we will, *chula*. What makes me crazy is that *you* are at risk the longer this dickhead motherfucker is on the loose. I just want to start burning shit down."

"Well, you can't, because my butch here will throw you into lockdown. Then, who am I supposed to play with to learn how to pick locks and escape from bonds and all kinds of cool, fun stuff like that?" Rowan teased her.

Jaime threw back her head and laughed, evidently feeling better. "True, *chula*, true."

"Although," Rowan got serious for a minute, "I totally understand if we need to not do this now and wait for a better time."

"No, *mi hermana*, no. My crew has it under control for now and they will call or text me if they need me. Frankly, I have been looking forward to spending some time with you and *mi broki* here, and I think the break will do me good." Jaime smiled at her, clearly more relaxed.

Bryn, who had been silent up until now, spoke up. "*Mi dulzura* is absolutely right, *broki*. That piece of shit's days are numbered and I have no doubt you and your crew will chase his ass down soon. Just so you know," Bryn said, "Rowan and I had a long conversation a couple of days ago and she is a lot more well-versed in what we do, Jaim. No need to sanitize anything anymore."

"Good." Rowan felt Jaime's relief. "That will make things much easier. Have a seat anywhere then, *chula*, and we'll get started.

"My crew and I run physical security, Ro," Jaime began when everyone was comfortable. "In a nutshell, physical security describes the processes put into place to prevent unauthorized access to things like a building or hardware or other resources. It protects equipment, people, and property from malicious access or harm because of things like theft or espionage or even terrorist attack. Many of our clients are at high risk for physical harm, *hermana*, which we closely monitor because of the nature of our work." Jaime's eyes darkened. "We do risk assessments on their homes or their workplaces or their physical property to keep them and their assets protected, using covert or hostile surveillance, even counter or anti-surveillance. We have a few clients who are extremely high risk, Ro, where there are indications that foul play is enough of a concern that we relocate them to a safe house."

Rowan gasped, appalled.

"In those cases, we actually teach the client how to escape from being tied up with rope or zip ties, or even how to pick handcuffs, all of which I've already told you we're going to do today." Then Jaime smirked. "When this shit with that motherfucker, Coravani, is over with, I'm taking you on a facility-breaching tour, *chula*. In physical security, we conduct something called 'penetration testing' or a 'pentest,' where we try to compromise a facility's physical barriers to gain access. It's a way to identify weaknesses in a facility's physical security systems." Jaime smiled wickedly. "We'll do one here for fun and I'll teach you how to pick a door lock. It'll make

Trill lose her motherfucking mind if we breach and sneak past her systems."

Rowan squealed excitedly, making Bryn shake her head in amusement.

"You ready, *ese*?" Jaime asked Bryn, who nodded.

"I've been meaning to ask you what that means," Rowan said as they all stood up. "*Ese*. I meant to ask you the other day and I forgot."

"It's just like saying 'dude,'" Jaime explained. "I still have a habit of peppering my American speech with Spanish terms, and especially Puerto Rican slang. Even after almost thirty years on the U.S. mainland, my mother's English still isn't very good, so we exclusively speak Spanish with her and old habits die hard."

"You haven't seen anything until you've seen Mama and Señora Quintero get on a Spanish-speaking tear together, *dulzura*."

Bryn grinned at Jaime, who snickered, before she started her instruction with Rowan.

"Okay, *chula*. First of all, we're going to start by making sure you can move your arms in front of you if someone binds or handcuffs your hands behind your back."

Rowan nodded solemnly.

"Bryn tells me you do a lot of yoga." Rowan nodded again. "Good, then your flexibility is going to make this maneuver a lot easier for you. Plus, you're small, which is going to be another advantage. I'm going to have Bryn restrain your arms behind your back with a set of handcuffs, *hermana*, so we're mimicking true restraint conditions as closely as possible."

When Bryn had Rowan's hands cuffed behind her back, Jaime continued.

"First, you need to sit on the floor, *chula*. As you lower yourself to your knees, move your hands under your bottom. When you're seated, lean forward and fold your legs so you can slide your hands past your feet and in front of you." Rowan listened intently and watched as Jaime used arm gestures to demonstrate the movement. "Since you're small and very flexible, Ro, this shouldn't be difficult, okay?"

After a few false starts, Rowan was wide-eyed with astonishment when she was able to slip the cuffs under her feet so her hands were cuffed in front of her.

"Beautiful, *dulzura*." Bryn's voice was full of pride.

"Now, when your hands are in front of you, it will be much easier to maneuver out of cuffs or zip ties or rope bindings, *chula*. Zip ties are the easiest things in the world to remove if you have a bobby pin or long fingernails or anything you can use to lift the lock bar on the zip tie, which will make it slide right off."

Jaime showed her what she meant as she "zipped" a tie and then used a bobby pin to easily undo it. She had Rowan do it herself a few times so she could get used to the feel of the release of the lock bar.

"With handcuffs, if you're lucky, the cuffs will only be what we call 'single lock' cuffs, which are the most common, although police departments issue cuffs—and there are some higher-end professional ones—which are called 'double lock' cuffs. They are a lot harder to get out of. This isn't going to be easy, Ro, so I want you to take your time and think your way through this slowly, okay?"

Rowan blew out a deep breath and nodded.

"With double lock cuffs, you actually have two locking mechanisms to open instead of one. The first thing you do is form a 'pick' with a bent tip from a bobby pin that looks like this." Jaime took a bobby pin and formed a "pick" for Rowan that looked a little bit like a hockey stick, then had Rowan imitate her.

Jaime continued. "Then we proceed to disengage the double lock."

"Insert your 'pick' into the handcuff key lock, then rotate and apply tension in a left, counter-clockwise direction to mimic the motion of a key. Do that until you feel your pick 'give,' and then stop."

Jamie's voice was calm and kind. "Don't be surprised if you can't get this right away because it's something that typically takes a good bit of practice, Ro. Relax, focus, and concentrate on what you're feeling within the lock without beating yourself up."

"You've got this, *dulzura*." Bryn's voice was equally calm and encouraging.

After about fifteen minutes, when Rowan was completely aggravated and ready to give up, she was all of a sudden ecstatic to feel the "give and stop" of the pick that Jamie had told her she was looking for.

"Fucking fantastic, *hermana*!" Jaime shouted as she and Bryn high-fived. "Now, you're going to disengage the single lock by doing the exact same thing, but in a right, clockwise direction. Most handcuffs only have a single lock, so they are much easier to get out of than double lock cuffs because you only have to do this step."

After another five minutes, the cuffs fell from Rowan's hands.

"I did it! I did it!" Rowan shrieked as Bryn grabbed her and spun her around. Jaime beamed with pride at Rowan's accomplishment and kissed her cheek.

"I know you're tired, *chula*, but we're going to briefly talk about rope restraints, okay?" Rowan beamed and nodded, still flushed with her success.

"Rope is a pretty common restraint, but the good news is that most people *suck* at tying knots in rope, so they can be easy to get out of."

Jaime looked at Bryn. "*Broki*, would you bind Rowan's wrists together in front of her?"

When Bryn was done, Jaime started her instruction by saying, "Begin by pushing or twisting the rope to see if you can release the tension, then grab the cords on each side of the knot and keep pushing them together to loosen the knot." She waited until Rowan had tried to loosen the rope for a bit, then she said, "Wiggle your hands and wrists, Rowan, and keep wiggling them to loosen the knot more. With a bit of perseverance, you can get the knot to unravel."

After about ten minutes, Rowan was able to slide the rope from her wrists.

"Oh my gosh, I am *so* tired, but that was awesome." Rowan hugged and kissed her friend, then leaned against Bryn. "I need a nap."

"*Chula*, you did absolutely amazing," Jaime praised warmly, hugging Rowan again. Then her dark brown eyes got even darker as a glint of danger entered them.

"You shouldn't *ever* need to do this personally, Rowan, because Bryn, plus Riley and the Seven, will burn the fucking world down if there is even the *hint* of a threat to you. But it is still something good to know."

Just then, her phone chimed and Jaime checked her text messages.

"It's Desi." Desi was Jaime's number two. "She's picked up another echo, *broki*, and it might be a fairly substantial one," Jaime informed Bryn. "I'll check it out and keep you posted. *Chula*, duty calls and I have to run," she said as she made her way to the Bunker door. "Again, that was a beautiful job you did." Jaime smirked. "Don't forget, we'll be scheduling a 'Drive Trill Out of Her Fucking Mind' playdate when all of this bullshit with Coravani is over with." And she was gone.

Rowan turned around to see Bryn looking at her consideringly.

"What?" Rowan was taken aback.

"I'm starting to wonder if encouraging you to play with the Seven is a good idea, *dulzura*." Bryn nuzzled her behind her ear. "It seems to leave a lot of room for mischief and mayhem to make an appearance when you do."

"Bryn! It's not my fault!" Rowan gasped even as she felt the electricity from Bryn's touch. "How is it my fault?"

"Oh, I don't know." Bryn bit the side of her throat. "They see their sweet new sister learning new things and being playful and expressing all sorts of curiosity, and they just dive headfirst into trouble with her."

"That is so not fair," Rowan moaned as Bryn ran her hands over Rowan's body.

Bryn's eyes gleamed. "Let's go back to our apartment, *dulzura*, and you can tell me just how not fair it is."

Chapter 30

February 4

"Two days. I cannot fucking *believe* the grand opening is in two days, Ro!" Clem exclaimed excitedly.

After six weeks of planning and scheduling and making decisions and supervising, the Dream Creamery and the WCA Center were complete. Rowan and Clem, along with Brooke, Alyssa, and Nova, were basking in the finished space.

The Dream Creamery, Rowan decided, was a million times more beautiful than Rowan ever hoped it could be.

The ice cream and sweet treat mural, hand-painted by local artist Masara Williams, was absolutely breathtaking and the focal point of the ice cream side of the house. The light mint green and salmon colors of the tables, chairs, and counters were muted and blended seamlessly into the space.

A large, beautiful sign in mint green and salmon that said, "The Dream Creamery"—which was designed by Rowan and Ember—hung over the ordering counter next to the freezers and the dipping cabinet. A stand-alone counter on the other side of the freezers was designated as Delaney's display counter, and would be where Delaney's amazing artisan baking would be displayed.

The girls were just finishing up stocking the storage cabinets to make sure everything they needed for the grand opening night was there.

On the WCA Center side, the local artists who had been chosen by Clem as a grand opening exhibitor had brought in their work, and it had all been installed and displayed.

For the most part, Rowan loved the artwork that had been chosen: paintings, sculptures, carvings, photographs, drawings, and prints. To her eyes, the art gallery was stunning and the lighting installed by Nia was perfect.

In the back of the art gallery, the art classroom was open for public inspection. Clem had already "staged" the classroom so it appeared that a class was in progress, with drawings on the tack boards, paintings "drying" on the drying racks, and various pieces of equipment and works-in-progress on the table.

Unfortunately, because Astrid Hallifax had met all of the submission guidelines, she had been chosen as an exhibitor. Last night, when she had brought in her artwork, Rowan was once again subjected to her meanness and snobbery.

"I so admire the way you've taken what little art talent you have and used it for the good of the community, Rowan," Astrid said, her tone acerbic. "Well, you know what they say...those who can't do, volunteer. So wonderful of you to provide real artists a place to showcase their work."

Just then, however, Bryn had come in, making a rare and unscheduled stop into the WCA Center. Her eyes had immediately found her fiancée and rested on her, glowing with heat, as she observed Rowan in her natural element.

But when Astrid had seen Bryn, she had cut Rowan off and swiftly inserted herself into Bryn's personal space instead. "Bryn, darling," Astrid had purred, clutching at Bryn's strong biceps and fluttering her eyelashes. "Have you come to see some real artwork by some real artists? I knew I could count on you to be here." Astrid cast a poisonous sideways look at Rowan.

Bryn's face turned impassive. "Hello, Astrid," she said flatly, disengaging Astrid's clinging hands, then immediately moved to Rowan's side. "Hello, *mi dulzura*," Bryn whispered softly, lowering her mouth over Rowan's in a passionate kiss.

A slam of the front door told everyone that Astrid had left in a rage. Bryn released Rowan's mouth and smiled at her with a wicked look in her eyes.

"Thank the Goddess." Clem rolled her eyes after Astrid's viperish exit and heaved a huge sigh. "All I kept hearing from that useless bitch was how she was exhibiting an 'important' painting called 'Ostara,' celebrating the goddess of Spring."

Clem sniffed. "I don't fucking think so—her shit looks like SpongeBob meets the Powerpuff Girls. I wouldn't hit a dog in the ass with it."

Bryn's lips twitched in amusement as Teagan, Remy, and the rest of the APS badasses on bodyguard duty howled.

Bryn nuzzled behind Rowan's ear and quietly whispered, "Is it just me or does Remy seem extremely attentive to Clem all of a sudden, *dulzura*?"

"She hasn't been able to take her eyes off Clem since the day everything came to a head over Clem and her protection," Rowan whispered back. "I think Clem is oblivious because she is distracted with the WCA Center and Dream Creamery opening, but I do know that Clem is attracted to Remy."

"Clementine needs a strong butch like Remy who can handle her, baby," was Bryn's opinion. "Anyhow, I stopped by to see if my woman would let me take her out to dinner tonight. With everything that has been going on with that fuckwit, Coravani, and you trying to finish the Rowan Complex, we haven't been able to go out and have a quiet dinner by ourselves since the night I decided you were mine."

"The Rowan Complex?" Rowan giggled and leaned comfortably against Bryn. "It's not just mine, you know. It belongs to Kelly, too."

"Well, we can't call it the 'Holland Complex' because you're going to be an Armstrong soon." Bryn raised an eyebrow. "Never mind, baby, we'll figure it out. In the meantime, Teag can bring you back to our apartment in a few while I finish taking care of one more thing. You can get ready and we can go out. I want to go outside of Whimsy tonight. There is an amazing Latin/Caribbean restaurant over in St. Pete that has the best fucking ceviche in the world."

When Rowan wrinkled her nose, Bryn smirked and softly smacked her ass when no one was looking.

"Remember, you're a Floridian now, *dulzura*. You need to start getting used to Hispanic, Caribbean, and Latin cultures and cuisines outside of the homogenized shit you find in Washington."

Rowan rolled her eyes.

Bryn kissed her one more time and then headed for the door. "I'll see you shortly, *dulzura*." She glanced over her shoulder with a small quirk to her lips, and then she was gone.

Rowan stared after her fiancé, lost in a haze of all that was Bryn.

"Earth to Rowan. Yo, my bitch, you got shit to do," Alyssa interrupted Rowan's reverie. "You can think about jumping your luscious butch later, homegirl."

Rowan flushed.

"I think everything is ready for our big reveal, Ro."

¥¥¥¥¥

Rowan and Bryn left the restaurant after dinner, with Rowan grudgingly admitting that ceviche might be her new favorite thing.

"Let's take a walk by the beach, *dulzura*." Bryn caught her hand. "It's a beautiful night and the moon is illuminating everything."

"Do you have any idea how weird it feels to me to be walking near a beach at night, in early February, with nothing on but a light sweater and be feeling perfectly comfortable?" Rowan asked, enjoying the beauty of the night.

"No, because this is perfectly normal for me, baby. Even when I was in the Marines, the farthest north I ever had to go was Quantico, and that was in the summer. I was stationed in South Carolina, which was a lot colder in the winter than it is here, but it doesn't really snow in Beaufort and the temps weren't anything I couldn't handle. I grew up in Whimsy, so I have no idea what it's like to have to deal with massive snow or sleet or any of that bullshit that goes on up north."

Bryn guided Rowan a bit deeper into the beautiful waterfront park until she stopped under a massive tree with exposed roots, which she told Rowan was called a banyan tree.

"These trees are native to India and usually aren't found this far north in Florida because it gets too cold. However, because this particular county in west-central Florida is, in essence, its own tiny peninsula on the coast and is surrounded by so much warm water, we actually have a subtropical climate here," she told Rowan.

Then, silently, Bryn faced Rowan and took her small hands into one of her own. In her other hand, she held a ring box she had pulled out of her pocket.

"In Hindu mythology, the banyan tree is the tree that provides the fulfillment of wishes, *mi dulzura*, my Rowan. And *you* are the fulfillment of every wish I have ever had in my entire life."

Tears streamed down Rowan's face as Bryn flicked open the ring box to reveal a gorgeous diamond engagement ring.

Bryn went down onto her knees and looked at her beautiful woman. "I know I have already asked you this, and I know you have already said 'yes,' but Rowan Holland…will you marry me?"

Rowan nodded, totally unable to speak, and cried great tears of joy as Bryn slid the beautiful ring onto her finger.

Bryn stood up and took her future wife in her arms, kissing her with passion and heart and soul, both of their tears mingling together.

"How did I get so lucky?" Rowan whispered when she could talk, leaning against Bryn's strong body.

Bryn nuzzled behind her ear. "I ask myself that very same question every single day, baby."

She continued to hold Rowan in her arms, but pulled back so she could look Rowan in the eyes.

"The girls are going to finish up anything that needs to be done tomorrow, *dulzura*, and they've assured me there's really nothing left to do. You have the day off."

"Everyone—and that includes Riley, my parents and siblings, the Seven, anyone that has been on bodyguard duty for any of you, and your girls—are meeting us at the APS complex tomorrow at three o'clock."

"That's our tribe, beautiful one, and we are going to tell them all we are engaged." Bryn caressed her face and kissed her again. "We are going to have a real engagement party somewhere other than APS headquarters when the grand opening is over and that asshole motherfucker, Coravani, is finally behind bars. But I didn't want us to celebrate all of the hard work you have done for the Dream Creamery and the WCA Center on Saturday and still be hiding our engagement."

Rowan nodded and hiccupped with emotion.

"I am way beyond pissed that Kelly can't be here for this, and you can fucking believe I am going to try my damnedest to convince her to come work for APS and tell the CIA to fuck right off when she finally gets her ass down here."

"I love you, Rowan Holland, soon to be Armstrong." Bryn wrapped her powerful arms protectively around her woman. "Let's go home, love of my life, because I have an even better idea of how I would like to celebrate with you."

Chapter 31

February 6

Rowan stood right beyond the entrance to the Dream Creamery and the WCA Center, greeting and saying goodbye to guests as they flowed in and out of what Rowan was now thinking of as the Whimsy Arts Complex.

It had been non-stop craziness for the past two days. When Bryn and Rowan had met with their tribe the day before, and Bryn had announced their engagement, the entire place had exploded.

Rowan had been picked up, spun around, hugged and kissed on the cheek by so many badasses, including Bryn's dad and her two brothers, she had privately confided to Bryn that it was going to take her at least a day before she could walk without dizziness.

The girls, including Bryn's mother and sister, had screamed and cried and hugged Rowan excitedly. Rowan wished her sister could have been there to share in the joy and excitement, but she consoled herself with the thought that Kelly would at least be there for the formal engagement announcement and party.

Nova had whispered to her that Delaney sent her heartfelt congratulations, couldn't *wait* to meet Rowan, and wanted them to do lunch as soon as possible after the grand opening so they could start getting to know each other.

Nova also said Delaney had cried upon receiving the "Welcome Back to Whimsy" present from everyone, and had vowed to use the fabulous equipment she had been given to make Bryn and Rowan the most amazing engagement cake on the planet for their engagement party.

After the initial excitement of their engagement had died down, however, Bryn had held up her hand and asked for everyone's attention.

Dino Coravani, she said, was still on the loose and, although they were confident APS was closing in and would have him cornered in the next day or two, they still needed to keep everything quiet until he was finally behind bars.

They didn't, Bryn explained, want to have the grand opening of the Whimsy Arts Complex without those closest to them knowing about their engagement, but any formal announcements or plans for an engagement party would have to wait until he was in custody.

Everyone totally agreed, although Rosi had muttered she would slit the bastard's throat herself if it meant she could go wedding gown shopping with her new daughter sooner.

When Rowan had looked at Oliver with wide eyes, he'd kissed her on the cheek and grinned.

"Welcome to Rosi World, love," her future father-in-law had said, smirking. "She gets a bit cheesed off when any of hers are threatened and now you're one of hers."

WHIMSICAL HAVEN

A huge crush of visitors had come for the grand opening. There had been so many people in attendance that night, there was scarcely any room to move around inside and a significant number of guests had spilled out into the street, chatting and laughing and comparing notes on the new center.

Nova and a temporary assistant they'd hired for the evening could barely keep up with the orders and demands for Nova's sublime ice creams and gelato. Nova was in her element, chatting and laughing with patrons as she dispensed her magic from behind the counter.

Delaney Sedgwick turned out to be a pretty black-haired woman with deep blue eyes and skin as pale as Rowan's own. She was a couple of inches taller than Rowan was, but still petite and shapely.

The excited squeals coming continually from the direction of the artisan dessert counter as Whimsy residents saw Delaney and learned she had moved back home for good were heartwarming.

Delaney's dessert counter was nothing short of miraculous. As she and Nova had decided, there were miniature fudge brownies swirled with raspberry coulis to go with the raspberry-habanero ice cream, Chardonnay-white chocolate truffles accented with a caramel drizzle for the Chardonnay-caramel ice cream, and jalapeno-lime cheesecake bites for the kaffir lime gelato.

Exclusively for the grand opening itself, however, Delaney had constructed a dramatic small-bite display that included two different sweet and savory small bites: the first, a savory goat cheese, honey, and rye crust mini-tartlet, and the second, a dark chocolate, pistachio, and tahini truffle.

Bryn, who *never* ate dessert, had told Rowan the truffles conjured up images of ravishing her woman in a desert tent while licking chocolate off her body.

She had looked consideringly at Rowan's outfit of a black, beaded tank top, silky honey-colored harem pants, and black stiletto heels. Her blonde curls were pinned up in an artfully messy loose low bun and her makeup was a bit more dramatic than she usually wore it.

"Then again, there seems to be a lot of things that lead to thoughts of ravishment lately, *dulzura*," Bryn murmured in a low voice with heat in her eyes as Rowan blushed.

Delaney had been chatting with some old friends when she'd caught sight of Teagan for the first time. Her pale skin grew paler, then she flushed, dropping her eyes before she brought them up to look into Teagan's face.

"Hi, Teag," Delaney had said softly, her deep blue eyes looking shyly into Teagan's striking green ones.

Teagan hadn't said a word, but she'd lifted one of Delaney's hands and kissed the knuckles softly, her green eyes never leaving Delaney as she took in every nuance of the woman she hadn't seen in over ten years.

Rowan would have loved to observe the interplay between Delaney and Teagan even more, but Astrid Hallifax chose that moment to make a dramatic entrance, looking down her nose at the others in the Whimsy Arts Complex.

Rowan caught Astrid looking at her speculatively with a smirk and an evil glint in her eye. Mentally rolling her eyes, Rowan ignored Astrid and continued to talk to others who were stopping by to wish her congratulations on their way out.

"*Dulzura.*" Rowan turned around to see her handsome fiancé—looking incredible in dark jeans, boots, a deep red button-down shirt, and a leather jacket—with Riley and several members of the Seven.

"Congratulations, sweetheart!" Kenn kissed her on the cheek and hugged her. "Holy shit, Ro, this place is absolutely amazing. It looks beautiful in here."

Blake was up next, followed by Drew. "We are all so, so proud of you, sweetheart," Blake said, hugging Rowan while Drew added, "The rest of the Seven who couldn't be here tonight send their love and their congratulations, too, Ro." She leaned over to hug and kiss Rowan like the others.

Riley kissed her future sister-in-law on the cheek and hugged her as well.

"*Felicidades, mi hermana*, congratulations. You have done a simply incredible job in here." She arched a brow at her twin, her eyes twinkling. "And even though I think you're crazy for taking on the job of keeping this fucker in line, I wish you both the very best of everything always, Ro. I can't think of anyone who deserves it more."

"Asshole." Bryn's voice was low, but it was clearly evident by the emotion in her eyes she was touched by her twin's congratulations, both for Rowan and for herself.

Suddenly, Drew raised her head and narrowed her eyes at someone. Rowan looked around to see Astrid Hallifax, who was now coming from the back, staring at all of them.

Noticing she had attracted their attention, Astrid abruptly turned her back on the APS crew and walked outside.

"Isn't that fucking Astrid Hallifax?" Drew bit out, an acerbic cast to her tone. "What the hell is she doing here?"

"She's one of the exhibiting grand opening artists," Rowan told her. "Unfortunately, she met all of the selection criteria for inclusion, so Clem and I had no choice but to include her on the grand opening roster."

"Where is Clem anyway?" asked Kennedy, her gaze rapidly scanning the crowd, which was briskly starting to dwindle as people took their departure.

"Even though the party is just about over, Nova is freaking out because she's convinced she's going to run out of napkins, she's served so many people. Clem and Remy volunteered to run to the store for her to get more. They'll be back any second."

Drew pulled Bryn to the side and whispered something in her ear. Bryn looked dispassionately at her friend, nodded, then came over and took Rowan in her arms.

"I'm going to kidnap my *corillo, dulzura*—my posse—and we're going to go outside where we can hear ourselves think and talk for a bit. It looks like the crowd is finally thinning out fast, so hopefully everyone will be gone in the next half hour. In the meantime, you stay in here with Teagan until I come and get you, okay?"

"*Sí, el capitan*," Rowan replied, saluting smartly, making Riley, Blake, Kenn, and Drew dissolve into laughter. Bryn raised her eyebrow at her woman, although a glimmer of amusement shone in her dark brown eyes.

Rowan grinned impishly and wrapped her arms around her fiancé.

"Teagan checked the back door *again* to make sure it was locked not fifteen minutes ago, Bryn. I saw her myself. Blair, TJ, and Devon have also been here all night, helping Remy to keep watch. I've told you before, I'd like to see that idiot get past any of you. Now, since the party is pretty much over, I think I am going to slide into more comfortable shoes. My feet are killing me and I am *not* about to help Nova, Delaney, and the girls clean up in stiletto heels." Rowan kissed Bryn, hugged the rest of the APS crew, and excused herself.

They all watched her go.

"You know you're in for it, right, cuz?" Blake asked Bryn with a smirk.

"I know." Bryn watched her fiancée as she left, stopping to chat and laugh in her sweet way with the few people remaining as she made her way to the back so she could hit the bathroom and change her shoes. "I wouldn't have it any other way."

Once outside through the front entrance, Bryn asked Drew to repeat what she had told Bryn inside as they continued to watch people depart.

"Cuz, my gut is firing on all eight cylinders tonight." Drew blew out a big breath. "Casey and Jaime and their crews are quietly scoping out the terrain within a six-block radius.

"Trill's back at headquarters, running more analysis to try and track this fucker. She is so fucking frustrated, I think she's going to start throwing her computers out the window. We haven't seen the first goddamned thing, but I am as sure as I can be that asshole motherfucker is extremely close and planning something tonight."

Bryn touched her ear comm. "Jaime. Casey. Status." Her voice was hard.

Their earpieces hummed. "We don't see any evidence of breach anywhere." Jaime's frustrated voice came clearly over the comm. "Casey and I and our crews have been all over every goddamn inch of terrain within a six-block radius."

"We could expand the grid area, but that just doesn't make any goddamn sense. Everything is fucking clear, *ese*. What in the *motherfuck* are we missing, *mi corillo*?" Jaime was in a rage.

Casey's voice chimed in. "Trill's scouring the connections between Mommy and that piece of shit mayor, and Whimsy resources," she said, her voice just as hard and angry as the others. "She did pick up an echo and is following the thread now, although it's still too soon to tell if it will pan out."

Teagan's voice came over the comm. "The center has really emptied out. Rowan said goodbye to the last few attendees about ten minutes ago. She was running to the bathroom to change her shoes, then she was going to help collect the trash that couldn't wait until tomorrow. The girls all agreed they were going to meet the cleaning crew here then and would make sure everything was back in its place, so Clem, Alyssa, Brooke, and Nova are going to take off with their bodyguards. Delaney just got here, so she hasn't needed a bodyguard up until now, but Campbell has volunteered to take point so Del isn't alone. Cuz, you're right outside so you can take your woman home, right?" Teagan asked Bryn.

"I'll be in to get her just as soon as the girls leave, Teag." Bryn couldn't prevent the crashing and snarling of her gut.

What the *fuck* were they missing?

Ten minutes later, the girls and their APS bodyguards came out of the WAC complex, chatting and laughing, and rehashing the night. Blair re-locked the front door behind them.

"Rowan said she was going to the bathroom, then doing one last walkthrough to make sure any perishable garbage wasn't left lying around," Clem reported. "Teag was trying to secure and close up the classroom. The door was giving her a fuckton of trouble for some reason. When she got done with that, she was going to double-check the back door for like the five thousandth time tonight. Didn't Rowan say she was going to the bathroom to change her shoes and do a final walk-through about fifteen or twenty minutes ago?"

The demon in Bryn's gut roared.

Just then, everyone's earpiece flared to life.

"*Breach! Breach!*" Teagan screamed, appearing at the front door as she unlocked it. In a flash, all six of them had guns in their hands.

Bryn, Riley, and Blake rapidly moved into the entrance to the building as Drew and Kenn ran between the buildings to access the back alley.

"*Who touched the motherfucking back door?*" Teagan roared, her gun in her hand. "I checked it maybe twenty minutes ago and it was *fucking locked*. Now, it's goddamn *wide open*. Rowan would have *never* touched that fucking door herself!" Teagan was almost apoplectic.

Bryn's heart was in her mouth as she approached the bathroom door, which was closed. She tested the door that led to the upstairs, which was still locked, then stood to the side of the bathroom door.

"Rowan? Rowan?" she yelled sharply, but there was no answer.

She placed her boot next to the door lock and popped the bathroom door open with a sharp rap. Behind her, Teagan, Riley, and Blake waited uneasily while Drew and Kenn hovered right inside the back door.

Inside, Rowan's stilettos were lying on their sides, discarded. One of her thick gold hoop earrings was lying next to her heels, her phone was on the floor, and there were blood spatters on the sink.

But Rowan was gone.

¥¥¥¥

Bryn felt her lungs freeze and thought her world was ending.

Riley, knowing her twin needed a moment to pull herself together, stepped up to the plate.

She touched her comm. "Code 12. I repeat, *Code 12*," she said sharply." Code 12 was the highest-priority breach code at APS. "Rowan is missing and presumed abducted. Launch your teams and await further instruction."

"Thank you, *mano*." Bryn detached and turned off her emotions, knowing Rowan's best chance of survival was for Bryn to function as an ice-cold, unemotional robot.

She touched the comm in her ear. "Trill. Status."

"I am so motherfucking close, I can taste it." Trill's voice was hard, angry and verging on vengeful. "Blanche Pierson, Coravani's mother, has lit up my board with Whimsy indicators, but I don't have a goddamn name yet. My systems are fucking burning through data examinations, and I am just waiting for that one motherfucking hit."

Bryn's voice was glacial. "I want to know how in the fuck he managed to get her away in fifteen minutes. And Teag?"

"Yes." Teagan was impassive.

"Stop fucking beating yourself up about the back door. I already know there is no fucking way you left that door open. What I want to know is, who in the fuck unlocked it because it's clear to me that piece of shit motherfucker paid, bribed, or persuaded someone from Whimsy, whom they knew would be at the grand opening, to unlock it. He can't get Rowan out of Whimsy because we have the town completely locked down. There are police cars stationed at every entrance and exit. The assumption should be that she was unconscious because of the blood spatters and the fact she never called or cried out."

Bryn was stony-eyed and detached.

"The question becomes, was someone waiting to help him with her in that fifteen minutes? Someone with a vehicle who parked behind the WAC, a vehicle so familiar in Whimsy, no one would have really noticed it because it belongs here? She's small, so we could conceivably be looking for a familiar vehicle in which he was able to load her and get away fast. Get your associates out on the street," Bryn directed, her tone still frigid. "They are to ask everyone they see if they saw anything at all around the WAC right before and after the grand opening ended. *Anything*, no matter how small."

She didn't say what she knew they were all thinking.

Coravani was aware there would be no way for him to smuggle Rowan out of Whimsy.

So, he planned to kill her when he was done raping and torturing her, escape out of Whimsy himself, and leave her dead body behind.

Chapter 32

Rowan slowly came to, feeling dazed and disoriented. Her head hurt, her left shoulder felt inflamed, and a gag had been tied over her mouth, making her incredibly thirsty.

Some instinct told her not to move or open her eyes, so she lay there in the huddle she'd woken up in, pretending to still be unconscious. She could already tell she'd been restrained with her hands behind her back, although she couldn't tell yet what had been used to restrain her.

The last thing she had remembered was going to the WAC bathroom at the end of the grand opening party to take off her stilettos and change into a pair of sneakers. She was washing her hands when a small sound made her look up, and she was terrified to see Dino Coravani staring at her in the bathroom mirror. He had clapped his hand over her mouth roughly, causing her nose to bleed, then he grabbed her skin at the junction of her neck and her upper shoulder and squeezed hard.

The next thing she remembered, she was waking up here.

The toe of a steel-toed boot nudged her in her back, making her want to flinch, but she forced herself to remain still.

"You useless cunt." A low voice she identified as belonging to Dino Coravani reached her ears. "You and your fuck buddies thought you were so clever. You all thought you were going to be able to hide from me, and those pieces of shit thought they were going to be able to outsmart me and keep you hidden."

Rowan could hear the contempt in his voice.

"Like all women, the only thing you're good for is what's between your legs. You're all stupid, shallow, and not worth shit." He laughed, a mean sound. "And you bitches are all so spiteful, you'll sell each other out in a heartbeat, just like your bitch friend, Astrid, did to you."

Rowan felt her breath freeze in her lungs, but she was still extremely careful not to move.

"All it took was me spinning a sob story about how you and I had a huge fight, about how we really did love each other, but you were so mad, you threw yourself at Armstrong just to get back at me." Rowan could hear the smirk in Coravani's voice. "Because that stupid cunt wanted Armstrong for herself, she went along with anything I said, just so she could get rid of you and get you out of the picture. Dumb bitches," Coravani muttered.

All of a sudden, Coravani started laughing like a maniac.

"The best fucking part, cunt? You're stashed here on the top floor of your worthless little art gallery. Those stupid sons of bitches are out running around like the fools they are, running like assholes all over this city trying to find you, and here you are—right under their noses. Ha!"

He nudged her with his boot once again.

"I need you to wake the fuck up so I can do to you what I've wanted to do to you for months, which is to fuck you and use you like the whore you are."

He sighed. "But since you're still taking a nap, I think I'm going to take this opportunity to sneak out and see what's going on out there tonight. I already have my very own hiding place in the Hallifax home, cunt, so I have a place to go to ground from your fuck buddies if I need it. When I get back, be prepared to spread those legs and take my dick just like the whore you are."

He laughed cruelly and Rowan heard him prepare to leave.

"Don't go anywhere, cunt," he sneered as he left through the outside door and Rowan found herself alone once more.

¥¥¥¥¥

"Bingo!" Trill shouted, as her application gave one long, loud beep, signifying she had a hit. "We have a hit!"

She rapidly read the results and then cursed. "You have to be goddamned motherfucking *kidding* me," she snarled maliciously.

"Tell us, Trill." Bryn was calm.

The APS management had spent the past several hours following up on every single lead their associates had generated. It was tedious, anxious work made all the more anxiety-producing knowing Rowan was in the hands of a maniac, and that the clock was ticking.

Trill's hit was the first indication of any potentially positive news.

"Apparently, Blanche Pierson and fucking *Doris Hallifax* are friends," Trill was reading her screen at a fast pace. "They both collect vintage antique jewelry and they met at an antique jewelry auction about eight years ago."

Doris Hallifax, Astrid Hallifax's mother, was the owner of Café Provence, a very popular French restaurant located in Whimsy. Café Provence was consistently ranked as one of the top 10 restaurants in the greater Tampa Bay area. Doris was a fairly decent woman, but her daughter was spoiled rotten and Astrid had always had serious entitlement and attitude problems because of it.

"I'm going to go out on a limb here and speculate that Coravani spun some kind of bullshit sob story about him and Rowan to Doris and she fell for it hook, line, and sinker." Trill made a sound of disgust.

Casey's icy voice filled the comm.

"I'm going to speculate further that little Ms. Astrid, whom we all know has been hung up on Bryn since as far back as high school, saw this as the perfect opportunity to get rid of Rowan and try to win Bryn back."

"So she threw Rowan to the wolves." Kenn was in a rage. "She may not have known Coravani was a sexual predator or a suspected murderer, but she isn't fucking stupid. You can't tell me she didn't know something was off about that fucking son of a bitch and she threw Rowan to him anyway."

"Well…" Bryn's voice was matter of fact. "I think it's time we paid Doris and Astrid a visit then."

The entire APS management team knew only the tightest control was keeping Bryn focused and on track. They also knew that if she let herself go even the tiniest bit, it would take almost all of them to lock her down.

With wordless agreement, they moved forward, concentrating on making sure Bryn had no distractions so she could do what she needed to do to bring her woman home.

¥¥¥¥¥

The minute Rowan felt the door slam and heard Coravani's feet disappearing down the outside stairs, her eyes flew open and she assessed her current situation.

Okay. The first thing Rowan knew she needed to do was to get her hands, which had been bound behind her back, in front of her. Because she was lying on her side on the floor, she knew this would be more challenging than it had been when she was standing and she had been practicing with Jaime.

Another challenge was that she had been in this position so long, her arms and legs had started to go numb.

"Suck it up, buttercup," she chastised herself, refocusing. "We don't have time to act like a baby here. Let's get it going, girlfriend."

Rowan managed to pull herself up into a sitting position, using her stomach muscles, until she was sitting on the floor with her arms bound behind her.

Carefully, she forced herself to remember Jaime's instruction. She got her bound feet underneath her, stood up a bit to balance herself, and managed to jump over her hands until they were in front of her without falling over.

"Yes!" She took a deep breath, resting for just a moment, and then spent a minute inspecting her binds in the non-existent light.

Zip ties. Hallelujah, glory be to the Goddess.

Rowan lifted her bound hands to her hair and pulled a bobby pin out of her curls.

It took her a little while in the dark, but she managed to release the locking bar on the zip ties on her hands and pulled her wrists free.

Rowan cried out when massive pins and needles hit her hands as her circulation started to work again. She spent just a little time massaging her hands and wrists until the pins and needles sensation went away. She pulled off her gag and then she turned her attention to releasing her feet. Once her feet were free, she again spent some time massaging them until the pins and needles sensation in her feet went away and she knew she could stand.

She stood up and then blew out an enormous sigh of relief when she realized her gun was still in the holster strapped to her inner thigh.

When Rowan had originally realized her ankle holster didn't fit well because she was so small, she had followed Oliver Armstrong's suggestion and decided to order a less-common inner thigh holster.

Because the harem pants she had wanted to wear tonight had a tight cuff at the ankle, plus her IWB holster would show with the low-riding harem pants, Rowan knew her thigh holster would be the best choice. The Goddess must have been looking out for her, Rowan realized, because Coravani would have discovered her gun had she used either of the other two holsters tonight.

She managed to rip both legs of the harem pants off from the thighs down so she could reach her gun more easily in case she needed both hands free at any point.

Rowan was somewhat familiar with where everything on the second floor was being kept, but she wasn't familiar with how everything was specifically arranged, especially in the dark.

However, now that she was free and she had her gun, she decided this was where she felt the safest because she wasn't willing to get caught by Coravani a second time if she tried to leave as he returned.

Rowan shrank down on the far side of the room beside a huge box where she couldn't be seen, and waited.

Chapter 33

"Doris. May we come in?"

Doris Hallifax's eyes widened when she saw Bryn and Riley Armstrong, Drew Hollister, Trillian Dacanay, and Blake Seibert standing on her front porch.

"It's…umm… It's a little late, don't you think?" Doris blustered, discomfited. "I'd really prefer if you all came back tomorrow." She started to close her front door.

Bryn stuck one of her boots in the door jamb. "Well, here's the thing, Doris," she said mildly. "I'm quite sure Vince Masterson would be *extremely* interested to know Whimsy's most famous restaurant owner has been harboring a wanted man."

"*What?*" Doris exclaimed, shocked and bewildered. "What wanted man? Wanted for what?"

"Dino Coravani? Your old pal, Blanche's boy? The one who currently has a warrant out for his arrest for being a sexual predator and suspicion of murder?" Bryn smiled, not a nice smile, her voice still mild.

Doris' eyes got huge and she looked as though she was ready to pass out.

"So, no, Doris... I don't think it's too late and if you don't want me to start throwing around words like 'aiding' and 'abetting,' you'll go ahead and invite us in."

Doris slowly stood back and waited until the APS crew filed in, her face pale and her hands trembling.

Just then, Astrid came around the corner and looked shocked to see all of them standing in her mother's living room.

"What do you all want? And why are you bothering my mother?" Astrid looked more than a little nervous and tried to cover up her nervousness with aggression.

"You wouldn't happen to know anything about the back door at the WAC being mysteriously unlocked tonight, would you?" Blake hit her hard and fast.

Astrid's face paled in shock and guilt hit her face like a tsunami, but she tried to bluff her way out of it.

"I have no idea what you're talking about," she tried to insist in her arrogant way, but it was clear she was lying through her teeth.

"Here's what I know in a nutshell, ladies." Bryn came right to the point. "You've been hiding Dino Coravani for, oh, I'd say approximately four or five weeks now. The same Dino Coravani, incidentally, who has a warrant out for his arrest as a sexual predator and is also wanted on suspicion of murder. How am I doing, Drew?"

"Stellar, chief." Drew folded her muscular arms across her chest and looked at Astrid and Doris with arctic eyes.

"Well, good. Because Dino Coravani came down here to Whimsy *specifically* to look for Rowan Holland—because he's a fucking sexual predator and he became obsessed with her when he went to her workplace in Virginia to interview the staff about a client. Rowan was able to disappear then, since her sister is a fucking *champion* at helping people to disappear, but… because Coravani is a ruthless, conniving dirtbag, he beat the fuck out of one of Rowan's female co-workers until she told him where Rowan had gone."

"Trill? Blake? We still good?" Her glacial eyes carried the light of hell in them.

"You're golden, cuz," Blake answered with the same malice while Trill then took up the tale.

"Honestly, Doris, none of us thinks you're guilty of anything other than extreme gullibility." Trill tapped her fingers consideringly against her mouth with a dark look in her eyes. "Little Astrid here has always been a blind spot for you, however, and—unfortunately for you, Doris—little Astrid has been guilty of a whole hell of a lot more than gullibility. Jealousy, spite, hate—these are just a few of the things Astrid feels for Rowan Holland, and why she has been complicit in Dino Coravani's plans to abduct her." Trill was remorseless as Doris grew even paler. "She didn't care what happened to Rowan afterward, just as long as she went away so Astrid could have Bryn here all to herself."

Drew tsk'd with a venomous smile. "Unfortunately, however, Astrid was too self-centered to realize Bryn would never be seriously interested in a shallow bitch whose sole focus was on herself and what she could get out of people."

"You can't prove *any* of this," Astrid spit out, angry and afraid.

"Ah, but I don't have to." Bryn's smile was as venomous as Drew's. "Actually, it's Doris who controls what happens to the Hallifax women from here on in."

Bryn looked directly at Doris, the weight of her words falling into the deafening silence.

"You have two choices, Doris. The first is to send Astrid to live somewhere other than Whimsy, with the full understanding she is *never* allowed in this town again, not even for visits. If you do that, your restaurant will continue to grow and thrive, with broad public exposure in the greater Tampa area as a business APS supports and promotes. If you do *not*, however... APS will completely destroy you and your business. We will make it known you were complicit in the abduction of Rowan Holland and that you harbored her kidnapper, who is currently wanted by the law for both sexual assault and suspected murder."

The horror on Doris' face kept growing and growing.

Bryn's face was impassive and without sympathy. "We will tell the community that your daughter actively made it possible for Dino Coravani to abduct Rowan, knowing she was engaged to someone else and knowing her actions would cause significant harm to APS and to the community."

"You can't do that!" Astrid screamed her fury, her face red and mottled with anger.

Bryn smiled—the coldest, most malevolent smile anyone had ever seen on her face.

"Oh, but I can and I will, Astrid," Bryn said viciously. "Not only will you be the most hated woman in Whimsy, your mother will lose the business she's spent almost twenty years building."

Then Bryn's face flashed with a rage that froze both Astrid and Doris in total fear.

"If anything happens to Rowan," Bryn said softly, "I will burn your lives to the ground."

Bryn turned to go.

"You have twenty-four hours to get Astrid out of Whimsy forever, Doris, or I promise you that you will not like what happens next."

Just then, Casey's voice came over the comm.

"Shots fired at the WAC," Casey reported tersely.

¥¥¥¥¥

Rowan heard the stomping of boots up the outside staircase and held her breath.

Her eyes had adjusted to the darkness and she could now faintly make out the outlines of the tools, supplies, and equipment stored in preparation for the construction to begin on Clem's apartment.

Coravani came through the door and swept the beam of a small flashlight around the space. When he discovered that Rowan was missing, he bellowed in anger.

"You goddamned cunt!" he screamed, throwing the flashlight against the wall in a fit of rage. Rowan heard it shatter and break, leaving them once again in darkness.

"Where are you, you useless bitch? I know you're still fucking up here." Coravani was frothing at the mouth. "When I find you, cunt, I'm going to break every goddamned bone in your body. You don't need intact bones in order for me to fuck that pussy."

Rowan noiselessly slid her gun back into her thigh holster as she heard Coravani draw closer to her hiding place. Still squatting, she braced her feet to anchor herself and held up her hands, palms out and relaxing her body.

She had no time for fear.

When Coravani appeared around the box and loomed over her, Rowan struck.

Aiming for Coravani's nose, throat and eyes, she viciously hammered him with savage open hand strikes until he screamed. She heard his nose break as he gagged from her blows to his nose and throat.

As he started to bend over in automatic self-defense, Rowan lifted her knee and jammed it between Coravani's legs for all she was worth.

He fell to the ground, screaming and writhing in pain as he curled up in a defensive little ball. While he was incapacitated, Rowan fled to the other side of the room behind another large stack of boxes.

She pulled out her gun and aimed it through one of the upper floor windows, hoping and praying the noise would bring someone. The glass shattered as she shot, and a cacophony of barking dogs immediately filled the night.

"You are DEAD, you fucking piece of shit whore!" he roared. Rowan saw the glint of a muzzle on the other side of the room as Coravani painfully struggled to get to his feet.

Rowan went down and rolled to the right, then came up on one knee, raised her gun, and fired right above where she had seen the glimmer just moments before.

She heard a grunt and then a large, heavy object hit the ground with a huge crash before there was complete and utter silence.

"Rowan! Rowan!" she heard Teagan scream a long moment later, as the thumping sound of several pairs of boots reached her ears.

"Teag," she said faintly, her hands frozen around her gun as her adrenaline rush started to wear off. "I think I shot him, Teag. I think…" Tears streamed down her face as she tried to get her limbs to move and white spots appeared in front of her eyes.

"Sweetheart." Out of nowhere, Kennedy appeared on her right side, gently taking Rowan's gun from her, as a muted light came on and illuminated the space.

Kenn rapidly cleared the gun, shoved it in her jacket, then pulled Rowan to her feet, wrapping her arms protectively around her.

In seconds, they were joined by Casey, Teagan, and Jaime, who formed a protective barrier around her next to Kennedy, all of them securely holding her, as Teagan hit her comm.

"We've got her," Teagan said, her voice trembling slightly with emotion. "She's safe and unharmed, although I don't think the same can be said for Coravani. Apparently, the miserable son of a bitch had her stashed on the second floor of the WAC where Clem's new apartment is going to be." Teagan's voice filled with wrath. "We're going to need some blankets to keep her warm."

Rowan began to shake as the enormity of what she had done hit her and the last of her adrenaline wore off, her tears still falling and a fog falling over her mind.

"Water," she croaked, her mouth parched. Someone held a water bottle up to her lips and she drank, thinking she had never tasted anything so delicious in her life.

"Slowly, sweetheart, slowly," Jaime cautioned as she took the water bottle away long before Rowan was done. "You're dehydrated and we don't want you to throw up. We'll give you more in just a little bit, okay?"

More boots pounded on the staircase. Rowan felt everyone let her go before a strong, powerful pair of arms came around her and wrapped her up so tightly, she felt enfolded in love, warmth, and security.

"*Dulzura.*" A firm hand held her head gently into Bryn's neck and Rowan felt the last of her control disintegrate as Bryn kissed her forehead.

"Bryn," she whispered almost soundlessly and choked on a sob before she began to cry in earnest. "I d-d-don't... I c-can't..."

"Shh, shh, *mi cielo*, don't talk," Bryn soothed her, stroking her back. "You're in a bit of shock and nothing is functioning the way it should be right now. You've been dumping adrenaline and your body is trying to compensate, *dulzura*. We need to keep you quiet and warm."

Bryn wrapped a thick, warm blanket around Rowan before she sat on a low, sturdy box with Rowan in her arms.

"Don't turn around, *mi dulzura*," she instructed, cradling Rowan's body protectively to her. "I'd love nothing more than to take you home right now, but we need to wait for Vince, our police chief.

"You'll have to answer some questions and tell Vince what happened, but because this was clearly a case of self-defense and Coravani was a sexual predator who stalked and abducted you—and who was also wanted in connection with several murders—it will just be a formality. Vince is good people and I know he will try to make this as painless as possible for you." Bryn kissed Rowan's temple and held her even closer.

Despite her fatigue, Rowan smiled when Trill, Blake, and Drew knelt down next to them.

"You gave us quite a scare, sweetheart," Trill said softly, rubbing Rowan's arm. "I don't mind admitting I don't think I've ever been that scared in my life."

The rest of the Seven, along with Riley, knelt around them as well.

Rowan caught Kennedy's eyes.

"You taught me that if I was ever going to aim my gun at something in the first place, Kenn, to always make sure I was prepared to shoot to kill." Rowan looked at her friend with tired, emotion-filled eyes. "So I went into this ready to destroy."

Kennedy struggled for a brief moment, trying to contain herself.

"That you did, sweetheart," she finally said in an extremely gentle voice. "We are all so incredibly proud of you, Ro."

Just then, an older man with a short, graying military fade and kind, light blue-gray eyes came over to them.

"Hi, Rowan," he said quietly and squatted down next to her and Bryn. "I'm Chief Vince Masterson from the Whimsy Police Department, but you can just call me Vince. Okay?"

Rowan nodded.

"Most importantly, before we get started talking about what happened tonight, do you feel as though you need any type of medical attention?"

"No, no... I'm fine except for feeling thirsty and my wrists and ankles are sore from being bound." Rowan ignored the lowered brows around her.

"That's good to hear." Vince looked at Bryn. "My forensics team needs to process the scene, so will there be any objection to us taking this downstairs?"

"I want them all to come with us," Rowan said abruptly. "I think they all need to hear about what happened because they all indirectly had a hand in my rescue tonight."

Vince smiled at her kindly. "Rowan, I've known all of them for most of their lives. I work very closely with APS and I know exactly what they are capable of doing. If you want them there, then there is no reason they can't be there."

"I can walk," she informed Bryn, who still held Rowan on her lap. "At least down the stairs, okay? We can use the inside stairs to get down to the Dream Creamery, and there are plenty of seats down there for everyone."

"Fucking resilient femmes," Blake muttered as Bryn firmly held Rowan while she slowly stood up.

"Right?" Jaime rumbled back, keeping eagle eyes on Rowan in case her legs started to give out.

Once everyone was downstairs and seated, Vince addressed Rowan, who was sitting across from him, curled up in Bryn's lap.

"Rowan, the first thing you should know is that Dino Coravani is dead from a gunshot wound to the head." Vince's voice was even and professional. "My people are upstairs processing the scene and making some forensic determinations on what transpired there tonight."

"Am I going to be arrested?" Rowan's voice trembled with fear as Bryn tightened her arms around her.

"From what I can see so far about what actually transpired, Rowan, you were acting in self-defense. Coravani stalked you, kidnapped you, bound you, and gave every indication he intended to inflict bodily harm against you. In Florida, we have something known as the Stand-Your-Ground law, Rowan," Vince explained in a calm, matter of fact voice. "I'm not versed in Virginia law, so I don't know what the equivalent would be there. In Florida, however, if you are attacked when you are somewhere you have the right to be—you're not trespassing or anything like that—you also have the right to stand your ground and meet 'force with force,' including deadly force, if you honestly believe that's what you have to do to escape being killed or gravely injured yourself." He looked at Rowan kindly. "I think the last thing you are going to need to worry about is anyone bringing charges against you for defending your own life in this particular case."

"Okay," Rowan whispered, blowing out a deep breath.

"I want you to tell me in your own words exactly what happened tonight, Rowan. I'm going to let you talk and I'll go back and ask questions later. I don't want to influence your recollections in any way, so you start from the time you were in the WAC for your grand opening and tell us how things progressed from there."

"Okay." Rowan took a swallow of water from her water bottle before she began.

She told them she had been in the bathroom taking off her heels and putting on her sneakers, and was washing her hands when she looked up and saw Coravani's reflection in the bathroom mirror.

"He put his hand over my mouth, which made my nose bleed, and then he did something to my shoulder, which hurt. I don't remember anything after that until I woke up on the floor upstairs. Something told me not to move and keep very still, as if I was still unconscious. Then I felt Coravani poking me in the back with his boot. He started talking to me as if I was awake." Rowan swallowed. "He called me a useless c-c-c…"

"I think she's trying to say 'cunt,' Vince." Bryn kissed the top of Rowan's head. "She never, ever swears, so she has a bit of difficulty saying curse words." Rowan looked at Bryn gratefully.

"Understood. Thanks, Bryn." He nodded to them. "Continue, Rowan, please."

"He said that I and the APS management team thought we were so clever, keeping me hidden. That the only thing women are good for is for what's between our legs, that we're stupid and shallow. And then he said we're so spiteful, we'll sell each other out in a heartbeat. That's how I found out Astrid Hallifax was involved."

Vince looked at Bryn just as Bryn said, "Taken care of, Vince," in a mild tone.

"He made fun of the APS team because I was just right upstairs from the art gallery and he said they were all running around the city like a bunch of fools trying to find me. He was gloating because he had a safe haven in the Hallifax home, because he'd spun some kind of sob story for Doris Hallifax that she fell for and agreed to hide him. But he told me Astrid just wanted to get rid of me so she could have Bryn back." Rowan felt Bryn's arms tighten again.

"You should know Rowan and I are engaged, Vince. Those of us here, Rowan's friends, a few other APS associates, and family members are the only ones who know at this point. We were holding off on making a formal announcement until Coravani was caught." Bryn kissed the top of Rowan's head again. "Continue, *mi dulzura.*"

"He said because I wasn't awake yet, he was going to go and scope things out, but that I should prepare to spread my legs for him when he got back." Rowan's voice was quiet. "He sneered and told me not to go anywhere, then he called me that 'c' word again and left."

There was a very dangerous vibe in the room that Rowan had been able to ignore up until now. She finally permitted herself to look at Riley and the Seven, however, and saw some murderously pissed-off faces.

She forced her eyes away from them and continued. "When I heard the door slam, my eyes opened and I knew the first thing I needed to do was figure out where I was and what kind of shape I was in."

Rowan looked directly at Vince and then she closed her eyes. "I've spent time over the past several weeks with each one of the Seven, learning what it is they do and taking lessons, Vince."

Her eyes opened, glassy with tears, and her voice trembled. "You need to know they saved my life because of it."

Chapter 34

"I was restrained and my hands were bound behind my back. My feet were tied too, and I had a gag in my mouth. I couldn't tell what had been used to restrain me at that point, though. Luckily, I do yoga and I'm pretty flexible, so I was able to get my hands in front of my body because of a trick Jaime taught me."

Jaime closed her eyes, listening intently.

"When I got that done, I explored the binds and realized they were zip ties, which I had just discovered were easy to remove if you knew what to do. My hair had been pinned up for the grand opening, so I took out a bobby pin and used that to release the locking bar mechanism on the zip ties, so they fell right off."

Jaime blew out a huge breath and slowly shook her head.

"I had promised Bryn's dad, Oliver, that I would stay armed until Coravani was caught. So, tonight, I was wearing these harem-style pants that were loose and flowing but tight at the ankle, and were a little low-riding, so my inner thigh holster was the only one that would work.

"I feel I was extremely lucky because I think if I would have used either my ankle holster or my IWB holster, Coravani would have discovered my gun. But he didn't, so I was still armed. I ripped off my pants legs from the thighs down for better access to my holster."

Rowan paused to drink some more water, aware that every single person in the room was intently absorbed in her story.

"I crouched down next to a huge box and I waited. I didn't want to try and leave, because I didn't want to risk him capturing me a second time. After a while, I heard him stomping back up the stairs. When he discovered I was gone, he started screaming and cursing. He was so mad, he threw his flashlight against the wall, which put the room back into darkness. I knew he was going to search the room, so I got prepared. When he looked around the box I was hiding behind, I attacked him." Rowan trembled a bit at the memory.

"Casey had spent some time teaching me some Krav Maga self-defense moves, so I broke his nose and made him gag with some open hand strikes, then when he leaned forward in automatic reaction, I nailed him right between the legs with my knee."

Casey pumped her fist in a "Yes!" response. Her own eyes grew a bit glassy and she shook her head just as Jaime had.

Rowan looked intently at Vince. "Every single one of them, no matter if they had taught me something I used directly or not tonight, all I heard were their voices in my head, coaching me and cheering me on. Because of them, I didn't feel alone and they gave me the strength to do what I knew needed to be done."

A few tears fell, and then she refocused back on her story.

"I ran to the other side of the room, then I shot out a window, praying someone would hear the noise and send the police. He roared, calling me an effing piece of crap whore, and he told me I was dead. Then I remembered a conversation Kenn and I had had one day while I was waiting for Bryn. She mentioned something about going down on one knee when you were in a situation where you needed to get low and you didn't want to lose your balance.

"She also said paying attention to reflections in low-light conditions was important and that if you happened to see the glint of a muzzle or the barrel of a gun, you wanted to aim a little bit higher than that glint to make sure you hit the target. So that's what I did. I saw the glint, I dropped to the floor and rolled to the right just like Teagan had once taught me to do to get out of the line of fire, I came up on one knee, and I shot about six inches higher than where I'd seen that glimmer. I heard a grunt, then a huge crash and then I didn't hear anything else until I heard Teagan screaming for me a minute later." Rowan stopped, exhausted, as both Kennedy and Teagan quietly dropped their heads and closed their eyes. "I remember Kenn coming and disarming me. I remember Riley and some others of the Seven being there, too. And then Bryn was there, and I knew I was finally safe."

Rowan wrapped her arms tightly around Bryn and looked at the rest of the APS crew, her tears falling harder and faster.

"Thank you," she whispered. "I love you all so much, my precious family. You saved my life today with your teaching, with the tools you gave me to escape that maniac, and your caring, cheering voices in my head that let me know I could do it. Because of you all, I never faltered." She buried her face in Bryn's throat.

Vince gave Rowan and a very emotional APS management team a few moments to get themselves together before he gently directed everyone's attention back to the situation at hand.

"Rowan," Vince said in a straightforward manner, "I need to share some information with you that will be disturbing for you to hear, given everything you've been through this evening."

"Okay." Rowan sniffled as she tried to calm herself. Bryn dropped a kiss on her disheveled curly blonde hair and handed her a handkerchief so she could blow her nose.

"I haven't had the time nor the opportunity to examine the area where Coravani's death took place in any amount of detail. I *can* tell you that, with what you have told me, the scene and your recollection of events match very, very closely."

Rowan nodded.

"A lot of new information has come to light about Coravani over the past week," Vince continued. "The suspicion of murder investigation has morphed into full-blown homicide investigations.

"Dino Coravani left a substantial amount of evidence in his apartment that points to him being involved in the murder of at least eleven women that we know of as of now, and that number is expected to climb."

Rowan felt as though someone dumped a bucket of ice water right over her head.

Vince looked at Rowan with a direct, extremely serious stare.

"Had you not been able to escape, Rowan, you would most likely be dead right now."

WHIMSICAL HAVEN

¥¥¥¥¥

Rowan lay in her and Bryn's bed, waiting for Bryn to finish up a phone call.

After Vince had finished with Rowan for the night, he left, promising to keep everyone posted and congratulating Bryn and Rowan on their engagement. He thanked Rowan for her cooperation, told her she was in good hands with the folks at APS, and said he would be in touch.

Riley and each one of the Seven took turns spending a precious few minutes with Rowan, hugging her closely, reassuring themselves she was physically okay and asking her what they could do to help her process through the trauma.

At the end, Rowan addressed everyone collectively.

"I know this will probably sound weird, and things might look different to me by tomorrow morning, but I'm not feeling much in the way of regrets for what I did tonight."

Rowan's eyes flashed.

"He's killed, only the Goddess knows, *how* many women and I was next on his agenda. He was a sick, evil man and I don't think he deserved the life he had been given. I think if I end up having any challenges processing this, it will be the fact that I had to take a life at all." Rowan spoke slowly, trying to convey exactly what she meant. "But, I wasn't the one who made that decision. He did. I feel that I actually honored life by avenging the women he killed."

Bryn hugged her woman closely. "*Dulzura*, that's exactly the way you should be looking at it. Sometimes we are all called on to do extremely unpleasant things for the greater good of the whole."

Rowan continued, snuggling into Bryn's embrace. "It was also greatly empowering to realize I could take care of myself if I had to. *Not*," she said to Bryn wryly, "that you are *ever* getting out of guarding me for the rest of your days." Bryn smirked and caressed Rowan's face.

"I never again in my lifetime want to do what I had to do today." Rowan blew out a deep breath. "But I don't see any reason why I would ever have to, to be honest. And I don't think that means I have to give up my playdates with the Seven, right?"

"No fucking way, sweetheart," Jaime declared. "Besides, you and I still have one more playdate, right?" She winked slyly at Rowan, silently reminding her of their planned Trill breach.

"Oh *helllll* no, fucker," Blake declared emphatically just as Casey crossed her heavily muscled arms and said, "You so cheat, asshole."

Rowan laughed, but then Bryn looked at her with serious eyes. "All kidding aside, *dulzura*, each one of us has taken life. Each one of us knows how it feels to be exactly where you're sitting right now."

Rowan's eyes widened.

"So, you come to me or to one of the others if things start to feel too heavy, okay? You don't ever have to process this alone. I know you feel okay and I believe you *are* okay, but you're still going to have those moments where it all hits you, which is perfectly normal. Every one of us is here to help you through it when it does."

Bryn smiled and caressed Rowan's face. "You said it yourself tonight, beautiful. This is your family now and we will all be here for you until the end of time."

Now, Bryn took the loft steps two at a time and slid into bed next to her woman. It was five in the morning and they were both almost ill with exhaustion, but Rowan basked in the safety and security she found in Bryn's arms.

"That was my dad on the phone," Bryn said. "I need to call him tomorrow about this whole Coravani bullshit. He has things to tell me. In the meantime, he and Mama send their love and said to get some sleep."

"Why would your dad need to talk to you about Coravani?" Rowan asked sleepily

Bryn nuzzled her behind her ear. "Before he retired, my dad was one of Florida's district state attorneys, Rowan. He still knows a fuckton of people in the justice system, and he's still called on all the time for advice. Not that we expect any problems whatsoever, but Dad is going to make sure no one from the state attorney's office gets any stupid ideas because they're looking to make a name for themselves." Bryn held her tight. "We are going to sleep for as long as we want tomorrow, *dulzura*, and then we'll have coffee and chat some more. I think we are both way too tired to even *think* about saying one more thing."

She kissed Rowan on the forehead. "I love you with my whole heart and soul, *mi cielo*, my sky. You are my everything and I will always come for you, no matter what.

"Always."

¥¥¥¥¥

The next day, Rowan woke in the late afternoon to find that Bryn was already up.

She snagged her nightgown from the bottom of the bed and slipped it on, then went downstairs to find her fiancé.

She found Bryn sitting at her breakfast bar, talking intensely on the phone, a coffee cup in front of her. Rowan went down the hallway to the bathroom, did her business, brushed her teeth, and took a quick shower, then returned to the living room to hear Bryn finishing up her call.

"I'll definitely keep you posted," Bryn said. "She slept really well last night, so I'm a bit more relaxed, but the next week will tell us more about where she is mentally."

"Uh huh…uh huh…okay, then. We'll touch base soon." Bryn ended the call.

Rowan cleared her throat and smiled at Bryn when she turned around.

"How long have you been awake?" Rowan went to Bryn when she held out an arm, and climbed into Bryn's lap.

"Since about nine o'clock, *dulzura*." Rowan's eyes widened. "Four hours of sleep seemed to be all I could manage since I had so much on my mind still. Luckily, I've had more than my fair share of nights with abbreviated sleep hours, so this isn't anything I haven't done a million times before."

Bryn kissed Rowan deeply and Rowan felt herself melt into Bryn's heat.

"How did you sleep?" Bryn nuzzled Rowan's neck.

"I thought I would have nightmares, to be honest." Rowan leaned against Bryn. "But I was comfortable and I slept so hard. Everything seems a little surreal. I'm glad he's dead, Bryn. I'm glad that now I get to explore my new home without worrying about what he'll do."

Rowan paused for a moment, collecting her thoughts. "It's like I was scared to death at first, but as soon as he left and I remembered all those fabulous tricks the Seven had taught me, then boom! No more fear. I just knew I was going to be okay, one way or another."

Bryn wrapped her arms even more tightly around Rowan, then used one hand to hold Rowan's head to her chest.

"Your strength is an inspiration to every one of us, *dulzura*. Riley and each of the Seven have already called today to check on you and to share how in awe of you they are. Jaime and Blake in particular keep muttering about how resilient femmes are."

Bryn drew back and looked into Rowan's eyes. "I am so enormously proud of you, my love."

They kissed each other for a long moment, then Bryn looked at Rowan once more.

"I've been burning up the phone lines today, *dulzura*. We have a lot to talk about."

When Rowan declined a cup of coffee, Bryn settled her more comfortably on her lap and started to bring Rowan up to speed on events.

"First, I talked to all your girls and other APS personnel, like Remy, to let them all know you are doing just fine and you'll see them tomorrow. They are all relieved as fuck and can't wait to see you, especially Clem. Second, Blanche Pierson was notified early this morning of her son's death and subsequently spent several hours being questioned about her knowledge of his criminal activities, as well as his suspected homicides, over the past few years. The news wires in and around Woodbridge have exploded with the news. Coravani's uncle, the mayor, is in deep shit politically from those revelations and has focused all of his attention on stemming the bleeding. He has disavowed all knowledge of his nephew's activities, but the police department and the chief of police have come under intense scrutiny as a result. The mayor's chief political rival has called for investigations into their culpability in using their positions to mask Coravani's actions."

Bryn caressed Rowan's cheek. "It's a total shit storm, *dulzura*. I don't think you need to worry about any of them ever again. Third, Astrid Hallifax has left Whimsy permanently. She will no longer be an issue for anyone here, least of all you. She and her mother were…persuaded…that it would be in their best interest for Astrid to find another residence outside of Whimsy. Fourth," Bryn stroked Rowan's back, "I had a long conversation with your sister. I didn't go into great detail, because I didn't want to make her worry more than I knew she already would, but I told her Coravani was dead and that you were safe.

"Because of all the press attention in Woodbridge, she now knows what kind of a predator he was and she is extremely relieved you no longer have to deal with him and his threats. I told her you had been kidnapped and were taken, but had managed to escape. What I did *not* tell her was that you were the one who pulled the trigger that ended his life. I have a feeling that would make her freak more than anything else, so we will have that full conversation face-to-face when she is down here."

Rowan nodded.

Bryn observed her steadily. "The last time you talked to your sister, *dulzura*, did she give you any indication she was worried about anything outside of this Coravani bullshit?"

"Not really," Rowan said slowly. "She was incredibly stressed and I knew she was worried about me, but she didn't lead me to believe it was because of anything outside of Coravani."

Bryn didn't tell her she'd asked Riley to do some digging to try and figure out what was worrying Kelly in addition to the situation with Coravani.

"Okay." Bryn kissed her temple. "Kelly still doesn't have an end date for her project, unfortunately, but I have a feeling she is going to tell her bosses to fuck off so she can come see you with her own eyes."

"And she will, too," Rowan muttered.

"As of right now, you and your girls are bodyguard-free, although Teagan kicked a little bit and insisted on escorting you to work and home, unless you're with me, for a while longer. I think it's a good idea to let her, *dulzura*. She and the Seven, not to mention me and Riley, had the biggest scare of our lives when you were taken, and I think they need this for a while until they feel more secure."

"Done." Rowan laid her head against Bryn's shoulder. "Maybe I should also make an appearance at headquarters soon and hang out in the lounge for a while. I know there were a lot of people worried about me and I need to give hugs to anyone who wants one." Her eyes twinkled. "Even freaking Gracie, although I won't hold my breath that she'll ask for one." Bryn threw back her head and laughed.

"You are a good woman, *dulzura*." Bryn gave her a long passionate kiss. "I would take you out to dinner tonight, but I know we won't get a minute's peace out in public if we do. Mama and Dad are dying to see you, so Mama is going to bring us dinner and we're going to eat here. Tonight is ours, Rowan." Bryn's dark brown eyes grew even darker. "I know you were unconscious when Coravani carted you upstairs, but the thought of that fucking piece of shit bastard having his hands on you in any way has had me on the point of violence. I'm going to mark you so thoroughly, I'm going to destroy every last remnant of his essence on you."

Bryn tightened her arms around Rowan.

"I'm going to fuck you until you can't breathe, until it is clear to the Universe that you are *mine* and I will obliterate anything and anyone who dares to try to take you from me again."

"Good." Rowan nuzzled Bryn's jaw. "I hope the Universe takes the hint."

Epilogue

The next morning, Rowan was finishing up cleaning the WAC with her girls when Clem came in with the mail.

Yesterday, Rosi and Oliver Armstrong, along with Riley, had come over to Bryn's apartment, carrying enough food to last four people six days.

Bryn had rolled her eyes, earning herself a snack on the arm, but Bryn had just grinned, hugged Rosi tightly, passed her off to Rowan, and went to get enough plates and silverware for all of them. As they ate, with Rosi asking Rowan if she needed anything every two minutes—much to Rowan's amusement—Oliver had informed them he had called the current state attorney personally.

The state attorney had told Oliver he was appalled at what Rowan had suffered, could see absolutely no reason any charges would need to be brought, and he privately assured Oliver he would kick the ass of any "stupid fucktard publicity hounds" who might try to use the situation to make a name for themselves.

"And he will," remarked Oliver. "He's sharp, with a good head on his shoulders, and he's never had time for those kinds of wankers."

Before the Armstrongs left, Riley had pulled Bryn aside.

"*Mano*, there is definitely something going down with Kelly. The CIA has her information locked down tighter than ever, it seems." Riley growled in frustration. "There's no trace of her through conventional channels anymore."

Bryn thought for a moment. "I just talked to Kelly this morning, for quite a long time. She gave no indication that anything with her own situation had changed," she mused.

"Kelly was clearly stressed and worried about Rowan, although I did hear an echo underneath it all that points to something else that has her scared. I fucking want to know what it is. I know we've discussed a couple of interesting theories, but we don't have a whole lot of facts."

Riley blew out a big breath. "I swear to you, *mano*, I might lock her in a room when she gets here and shake it out of her. Something is scaring the fuck out of her and, from all indications, this is not a woman who scares easily."

Riley looked at Bryn determinedly. "Kelly is Rowan's little sister, which makes her family already, and you know how much the Seven and I love the fuck out of Rowan. If there is something that's threatening her sister, we'll find it and eliminate it. The question is, what the fuck is it?"

She clapped Bryn on the shoulder. "Go be with your woman, *mano*. Tomorrow is another day. If I happen to come across something tonight, I'll text you."

When the Armstrongs had left, Bryn had taken Rowan upstairs and proceeded to do all the things she had promised she was going to do when they were alone.

When Rowan was bare, Bryn had started to lick, kiss, gently bite, and caress every bit of naked skin on Rowan's body.

Bryn had growled ferociously when she saw the bruises that had formed on Rowan, caused by the restraints and the rough handling by Coravani. She reverently kissed each bruise, soothing each mark, descending down, down, down until she reached the juncture of Rowan's legs.

Bryn had captured Rowan's wrists, secretly testing Rowan's reaction to being restrained, but Rowan only cried and shuddered as Bryn licked her between her legs. Rowan squirmed in an effort to get away from the fierce sensations Bryn's tongue evoked, but displayed no evidence of trauma.

When Bryn had fucked her, holding her by the hips in a possessive, passionate grip, Rowan screamed and begged Bryn to make her come.

Bryn drew out Rowan's pleasure until they both finally went over the edge, Rowan crying and shaking from Bryn's whispered vows to make sure Rowan always knew to whom she belonged.

Now, Clementine held out a handful of mail for Rowan to sort through.

"I still don't know what shit is important and what shit can just be thrown away," Clem informed Rowan. "I'm going to go help the girls finish up in the classroom while you do that. Nia is going to send someone tomorrow to finish fixing the classroom door. I don't know which clumsy ass fuck hit the door hard enough to keep it from closing properly, but Nia says it's an easy fix."

"Okay. This shouldn't take me too long and then I'll be in myself." Rowan gave Clem a huge hug. "Go and I'll see you in a few."

Rowan sorted through the envelopes and immediately threw out a bunch of circulars and other junk mail. She frowned, however, when she saw a cream-colored envelope that simply had her name written on it, and tore it open.

She gasped and immediately turned pale when she pulled out a single sheet of paper and read what was on it.

Tell your sister the eyes of Percutio are everywhere and its "memory" is very long.

Rowan fumbled for her phone and immediately called her sister.

"Kelly. Thank the Goddess you answered," breathed Rowan, her voice shaky.

"What's wrong, Ro?" Kelly's voice was sharp. "I thought this clusterfuck with that asshole, Coravani, was all over with."

"It is, I promise. Although I have a few more details to tell you that I'd rather you knew now. Everyone was kind of the opinion we should wait to tell you the full story until you are down here, but I don't want to wait. This is about something else, though." Rowan blew out a huge breath.

"Okay. How about first things first, then?" Rowan heard her sister sit down. "Why don't you first tell me what you feel I need to know about Coravani and, I assume, give me more information on what actually happened that night?"

Rowan recounted the entire story for Kelly, starting from the time Coravani captured her in the bathroom of the WAC and ending with Rowan meeting with Vince Masterson, Bryn and Riley, and the Seven.

Kelly was quiet for a long time when Rowan had finished her story.

"Well." Kelly was matter of fact and her voice was even when she finally spoke. "It seems as though Armstrong left quite a few important details out of her version of events when we talked yesterday. I'm thinking she and I are going to have a small chat when I get down there about the omission of information in the future, especially when it comes to you. Thank you, big sis. I love you a fuckton and, even though I am absolutely furious you had to go through any of it at all, I couldn't be more proud of you and what you accomplished that night." Kelly's voice caught for just a moment. "How are you feeling, though? Seriously."

"I'm okay. I promise. I know I'm still going to have things I have to process and I'm going to have moments where things kind of catch me unaware, but I know I'll be able to work through it all with everyone's help here. I can't wait for you to meet them, Kelly. They are some of the most amazing people I have ever met in my life and I know you're going to love them as much as I do."

"Good." Kelly's voice was soft. "I'm looking forward to it. Now, what's the other thing you had to tell me?"

When Rowan explained to Kelly about the note she received, Kelly immediately started barking orders.

"Rowan. I want you to listen to me because this is critically important. You get Bryn or her twin or one of her people to come and cover you immediately."

There was a very short pause.

"Never mind, I just texted Armstrong myself. Are your doors locked and are you away from any windows?"

"Yes, to both. Kelly, what is going on? You're scaring me."

"I promise you, from the bottom of my heart, I will explain everything as soon as I see you, Ro. In the meantime, I need you to promise *me* you will stay where you are until Bryn or Riley or one of their Seven gets to you, okay?"

"Okay." Rowan was frightened by the fear she heard in her sister's voice. "Are you safe, little sis? I don't like any of this and I'm scared for you."

"I'm good, honey, I promise. I'm going to stay with you on the phone just until Bryn or Riley get there and then I'm going to go, because I have some things I need to take care of." Rowan heard steel in Kelly's voice.

"Rowan!" Bryn shouted from right outside and she swiftly unlocked the door.

"She's here, Kelly." As Rowan opened her mouth to say more, she realized Kelly had hung up.

"*Dulzura.*" Bryn held her in her arms as Riley and Teagan came in, guns drawn. "What the fuck is going on? All I know is Kelly texted me, told me you were fine, but I needed to get my ass to the WAC immediately."

"I got this strange note in the mail and I immediately called Kelly about it. It references something I've seen before with Kelly and I've always hated her reaction to it. Right away, she started barking orders, Bryn. She asked me if I was somewhere where the doors were locked and I was away from the windows. She told me she had texted you, and then she told me she was going to stay on the phone with me until you got here."

"The fuck?" Teagan muttered, looking back and forth between Bryn and Riley.

"Can I see the note, *dulzura*?" When Bryn read the note Rowan handed to her, she stiffened and her eyes grew hard.

"Does this mean anything to you, *mi cielo*?" Bryn asked her, kissing Rowan on her forehead, then passing the note to Riley and Teagan. They both read it, their expressions becoming just as hard as Bryn's.

"Not really. I know I used to be scared and freaked out at Kelly's reaction when she saw anything that referenced that word, but she always told me not to worry about it." Rowan looked anxiously at the three of them.

"We need the rest of the Seven here," Bryn said, pulling out her phone and sending a text. "It will take a little while because Drew and Trill are three hours out on an investigation. We'll all meet here."

"Clem and the girls are in the back." Rowan was still anxious.

Bryn sighed. "Until I understand exactly what the fuck is going on, *dulzura*, I really can't let them leave. It doesn't sound like this has anything to do with you or the girls personally, but I don't want to take any chances with any of you."

Rowan gnawed on the corner of her fingernail. "I think I might have screwed up, Bryn." Bryn raised an eyebrow.

"When I first got that note, I freaked out and called Kelly about it right away. But…umm… I was so happy to hear her voice, I kind of word-vomited everywhere and told her about *everything* that happened with Coravani. I told her we planned to tell her absolutely everything when she finally got down here, but she was a little less than happy that we didn't tell her right away." Rowan looked abashed.

Bryn sighed. "*Dulzura*. I would never in a million years ask you to hide anything from your sister. If she feels she needs to yell at me for being selective about what I chose to share with her, then she can do it when she gets down here. I'm grown, I can handle it."

"Okay," Rowan whispered. "When she found out about the note, though, Bryn… She was genuinely scared." Rowan looked worried. "Kelly can hide a lot from people, but I'm her sister. I knew."

"Let's wait for Drew and Trill to get back, then we'll talk about the situation more in depth and make some decisions then, okay?"

Bryn nuzzled Rowan's temple. "It's going to be all right, *mi cielo*. I'll make sure of it."

Several hours later, Trill and Drew had returned, and the entire APS management team was sitting at the tables in the Dream Creamery, discussing the possible meanings behind Rowan's mysterious note.

Rowan had filled the girls in on what was going on. Alyssa had wryly remarked that hanging around Rowan was more adrenaline-producing than anything else that had happened in Whimsy in years.

Clem had muttered that Alyssa might not feel that was a good thing if she ever caught Kelly in some of her moods.

Rowan's cell phone rang and she answered the phone. She had a quiet conversation until her voice raised and the heads of Bryn, Riley, and the Seven whipped around, immediately tense.

"You're *where*?" Rowan's tone was horrified, her body rigid. Her eyes shot to Clem. "Kel, seriously. You didn't have to…forty-five minutes? Are you freaking kidding me? … Okay… I said, *okay*… Fine, I'll see you then."

She ended the call, then tossed her phone on the counter. A moment later, her head followed suit as she banged it down on the counter right after it.

"Rowan?" Bryn's voice was sharp as she moved to Rowan's side. "What the fuck is it?"

Rowan raised her head and stared at Clementine in disbelief. "That was Kelly. She landed at MacDill Air Force Base a half hour ago and she'll be here in about forty-five minutes."

"Oh, shit, no," Clem yelped, leaping up from her seat, her eyes wide. "Christ on a crutch, Rowan. We are *so* fucked."

"Kelly? Seriously?" Bryn raised her brow at their panic and stroked a calming hand over Rowan's silky curls. "She was upset when I talked to her on the phone yesterday and she was even more upset after she talked to you today, so it shouldn't be a surprise that she would want to see with her own eyes that you were okay, *dulzura*. Plus, whatever the hell is going on with this note, which scared the shit out of you. But why would you be fucked?"

Clem groaned and dropped back down into her chair again. Nine pairs of probing eyes fixed on her unblinkingly, waiting for an explanation.

She looked at Rowan, ran her hands through her wild blonde curls in agitation, and sighed.

"First, let me explain something to you all about Kelly. People meet her for the first time, she's wearing a dress and looking all proper, she has her company manners on… They think she should have her gorgeous ass parked in an enchanted cottage somewhere in the middle of the forest, cooking for fucking dwarfs and talking to birds. Bitch looks just like a Disney princess. She looks more like that redheaded Little Mermaid than Snow White, though, except Kelly's got more fucking sense than to give up her legs for anyone." Clem rolled her eyes. "Who fucking does that? Except maybe some crack ho needs a fix and will do anything to get it."

"It was her voice, not her legs." Rowan closed her eyes and pinched the bridge of her nose in an effort to stay calm. "Ariel gave up her *voice* to have three days with the Prince, Clementine, she didn't have legs. She was a freaking mermaid."

"Voice, legs, what-fucking-ever." Clem waved a hand in impatient dismissal as she continued. "What I am saying to this crew here is that Kelly *looks* like a sweet little Disney princess, you catch her in proper attire and in the right company. You see her *not* in the right company, however, and in her usual gear, a sight to which I'd guess you are all about to be treated, what you got is a Disney princess gone badass. I mean... Bad. Ass. Emphasis on 'Bad.' My girl being a CIA operative and all, down with some pretty funky and scary-ass shit on a regular basis. Her showing up with no warning like this, someone fucking with her sister and sending that note, means Princess Spook is *pissed* and she is looking to wipe the floor with someone.

"And I am here to tell you that it might be us, collectively, that she wipes the floor with, seeing as none of us saw fit to tell her *everything* that jackass Coravani was doing until Rowan called her about the note. Add this note to all the bullshit been going down with Kelly over the past several months, whatever the fuck it is, and shit. Girlfriend is going to go totally nuclear on our asses. We. Are. *Fucked*."

"Shit," Nova echoed in a whisper, eyes rounded, as the rest of the girls froze in disbelief.

Rowan sighed and leaned against Bryn for support as Bryn wrapped her arms protectively around her. "Kelly is an information analyst for the CIA, not a spook, Clementine."

Clem snorted and rolled her eyes again.

"Yeah, right, the CIA constantly sends all their info geeks around the world at the drop of a hat. Guess most countries are still using a fucking abacus to count, they need an *information analyst* like Kelly to show them how to use a fucking calculator. Give me a break, Rowan. She has a MacDill Air Force Base pass, for the love of the Goddess. You trying to tell me, between that and her *other* huge-ass superpower..."

"Clementine." Rowan's voice cut her off sharply.

Clem clamped her lips shut and looked at the floor, avoiding some suddenly very interested gazes.

"What other superpower, *dulzura*?" Bryn asked quietly.

"Nothing." Rowan quickly dismissed it and frantically sought to change the subject. "I told her I was fine, Bryn, and we took care of that piece of crap, he's dead, crisis over. At least for me."

Rowan closed her eyes and pinched the bridge of her nose again.

"This other... I'm sorry, but I really don't know much detail. I just know that Kelly has always had a *very* adverse reaction to that name and it scares me when it comes up, simply because I remember the *look* that's always on her face when she hears it."

Riley looked at Clementine. "Her lover lets her run around alone like this?"

Clem shook her head no.

"Kelly had a fiancée, CIA like her. Couple of years ago she got killed in an operation, think it might have something to do with the shit going down right now. Although, you ask me, much as I liked Robyn the few times I met her and was real sorry when she was killed, she wasn't the right one for Kelly. Don't know there is *anyone* out there right for Kelly, since in my opinion, the Goddess has yet to create a butch with 20-pound balls, which is what she will need, she takes on Kelly and all the shit comes with her."

"What kind of shit?" Riley's voice was level.

Clem snorted again. "Kelly is always ass-deep in some kind of mayhem. She's not like Rowan, who's calm and sweet and everyone's oasis. Kelly's bold and badass and only hell knows the shit she's either in or causing half the time. She's one of the smartest women I know, she's fiercely fucking protective of those she considers hers, and she has a moral code that is absolutely uncompromising, even if the path she takes to get to the truth is often…uh…a bit circuitous."

Riley had a considering look on her face as she looked at her twin, then at everyone else.

"Bryn and I have both felt there has been something off with Kelly for some time now." Riley drummed her fingers on the table. "To be honest with you, I've been doing some digging recently and things just aren't adding up for us. Kelly is currently off the CIA books completely, whereas before she was listed in their internal directory as a low-level information analyst. Now there's no trace of her. I don't know much about how the CIA is structured, but I do know they don't make a still-active analyst just disappear from their books like that without a very good reason. I also found out recently they have a division called SAD, which stands for 'Special Activities Division.'" Riley looked at Rowan and Clementine. "Does that name mean anything to either of you?"

The two women shook their heads.

Riley steepled her fingers. "SAD is a special branch of operatives within the CIA. No one really knows anything about them, but they are apparently considered one of the most mysterious branches of operatives in the world. Think Navy SEALS or Delta Force." She nodded at the Seven, whose faces reflected dawning comprehension. "With SAD, however, one of the branches within the division is different from all the others in that it works more behind the scenes with covert operations, not with direct combat."

"This is purely speculation on our part," Bryn chimed in, "but it is conceivably possible the CIA has created a new covert mission within SAD to go after Percutio and cut off the heads of the Hydra once and for all. And Kelly is neck-deep in it."

The Seven looked at Bryn and Riley, and then at each other with hard, unhappy faces.

Bryn stroked a visibly upset Rowan's back soothingly. "I don't want you to worry, *dulzura*. When Kelly gets here, we'll get to the bottom of this and find out what it is that's had your sister so scared. And I promise you, we'll take care of it and we'll fix it."

Riley's smile was cold as she crossed her muscular arms across her chest. "Kelly doesn't know it yet, *mi corillo*, but she's now one of ours. And you know we *always* take care of what's ours."

Just then, a car door slammed out front. Clem peered out the front door, blanched, then turned to look at the assembled APS crew in trepidation before she whispered anxiously to the room.

"Shit. She's here."

WHIMSICAL DREAMS, BOOK TWO: WHIMSICAL PRINCESS

Kelly Holland is everything her sweet older sister, Rowan, is not: Kelly is bold, badass, and the best covert and clandestine operations analyst the CIA has ever had in their agency.

Kelly also has a secret. A very big, very *explosive* secret.

Riley Armstrong, Bryn Armstrong's twin, is intrigued by the flame-haired femme, but wonders why a simple information analyst like Kelly has attracted the attention of the head of Percutio—a malignant crime organization headquartered in Florida. Grigor Reizan is pulling out all the stops to get to Kelly, and Riley wants to know why.

Because Kelly Holland belongs to *her*.

When Riley, Bryn, and the Seven of Armstrong Protection Services learn Kelly's secret—and find out why Grigor Reizan has been so unyielding in his efforts to capture her—they are stunned. After Kelly loses her CIA agency status and protection because of a mole planted by Reizan, they vow they will do whatever it takes to keep Kelly safe.

But Reizan is just as determined to take Kelly for himself. He knows he can use her and her rare "superpower" to become the most powerful man in Florida—if not the world—and he's not about to let anyone stop him.

WHIMSICAL HAVEN

No matter who he has to kill to succeed.

COMING SPRING 2022!

ABOUT THE AUTHOR

Tiffany E. Taylor writes sensual lesbian romance fiction within the passionate butch-femme dynamic in a variety of genres: action/adventure, contemporary, and paranormal.

She lives with her spouse and their daughter in an idyllic queer-friendly little town on Florida's west-central coast. You can find out more about Tiffany at www.tiffanyetaylor.com, or you can follow her at:

Facebook: www.facebook.com/tiffanyetaylorqueerauthor
Instagram: www.instagram.com/tiffanyetaylor_lgbtqauthor
Twitter: www.twitter.com/LGBTQAuthor

And before you go…

REVIEWS are like rocket fuel for authors. You keep us going when you take some of your precious time and tell us what you think. I know you're busy, but I'm asking you to take just a few minutes to post a review on Amazon. It doesn't have to be long—just a few sentences would be lovely—but I will be immensely grateful.

Painted Hearts Publishing

Painted Hearts Publishing has an exclusive group of talented writers. We publish stories that range from historical to fantasy, sci-fi to contemporary, erotic to sweet. Our authors present high quality stories full of romance, desire, and sometimes graphic moments that are both entertaining and sensual. At the heart of all our stories is romance, and we are firm believers in a world where happily ever afters do exist.

We invite you to visit us at www.paintedheartspublishing.com.

Printed in Great Britain
by Amazon